HEARTS AND MOUNTAINS

LYNN ELDRIDGE

WOLFPACK
PUBLISHING
—— EST 2013 ——

Hearts and Mountains
Paperback Edition
Copyright © 2022 Lynn Eldridge

Wolfpack Publishing
5130 S. Fort Apache Rd. 215-380
Las Vegas, NV 89148

wolfpackpublishing.com

Paperback ISBN 978-1-63977-268-1
eBook ISBN 978-1-63977-269-8
LCCN 2022940577

From my Heart to our Mountains ~
Wild and Wonderful West Virginia

HEARTS AND MOUNTAINS

Tony ~

Feel the fireworks!

Lynn Eldridge

My bounty is as boundless as the sea, My love as deep. The more I give to thee,
The more I have, for both are infinite. – Juliet

Did my heart love till now? Forswear it, sight, For I ne'er saw true beauty till this night. –Romeo

~ William Shakespeare

CHAPTER 1

Tug Valley, West Virginia
Summer 1882

"PLANNING TO PAY FOR THOSE?"

On enemy ground, she instantly whirled around and looked up at the man towering over her. Humming her favorite tune as she picked blueberries, she hadn't heard his approach. With the sun shining in her eyes she couldn't see his face. But he was big. He was overwhelming. He was frightening.

He was a man to match the mountain behind him.

Murder always loomed as a threat for her or any of her kinfolk who ventured onto this West Virginia side of the Tug Fork River. As a foe, he was a dangerous force to be reckoned with especially since she was all alone. Her heart began slamming so loudly against her ribs— she could barely hear her brain shouting at her to run. But she couldn't run. He was blocking her path leading out of this berry patch to the river. Ice-cold panic washing through her veins, she stood her ground. Short of fainting, not an option, she had no choice.

What if the man before her was a gunnysacker like the two who had caught her and Lumpkin raiding this patch years ago? Those enemies had also snuck up from behind and tied gunnysacks over her and Lumpkin's heads. One of them had wrestled her into the nettles while the other one tackled her best friend. The sound of stone against bone had assaulted her senses. After the sickening strike of a second blow, Lumpkin had grunted and hit the ground.

Not having been confronted since that horrific day, she had foolishly let down her guard. She was an adult now and the punishment could be jail or, she swallowed hard, death. With that revelation came the onslaught of stinging and itching. In spinning around to face this latest threat she had mired herself into those same nettles which she'd expertly avoided for more than a decade. As covertly as possible she scratched her arm and dug at her collarbone.

"Don't scratch," the adversary said. "Letting the chemicals dry on the skin makes them easier to remove. Then wash with soap and water and you'll avoid a nettle rash."

She shaded her eyes trying to get a better look at him. No luck—the sun was blinding. In any case he obviously didn't know how to prevent or treat nettle rash. Inching her way out of the nettles, she lowered her gaze and spied both dock and jewelweed which often grew near nettles. Staying just out of reach of this possible gunnysacker/killer she grabbed leaves of the jewelweed. To properly avoid the nettle rash, she rubbed a leaf on her arm and followed an itch crawling up her neck.

"Who are you?" the mountain prodded, stepping closer.

Though he'd moved, the sun was still at his back glaring at her as she was sure he was. Stuffing the extra jewelweed leaves in her pocket, she squinted so hard trying to see his face, her eyes watered. "Maybe I'm the owner of this property."

"I own this property from the riverbank all the way up to that place on the hill." He jerked his thumb over his shoulder toward the beautiful, big house which had set vacant forever. "And beyond it, north, south, and east, Miss—?"

He moved again and she scratched harder. This time her path was blocked, years prior it had been her view. For all intents and purposes, her view was blocked again. But back then she had clawed her way out of the stinging nettles, untied the gunnysack and yanked it off her head. Ready to fight the cowardly assailants if need be, they'd been long gone. Unable to rouse Lumpkin, as his blood turned the riverbank red, she'd feared if she left him alone as long as it would take to get help he'd bleed to death. Holding his head in her lap she had wished for yarrow, a plant known to stop blood loss. But she'd had none and pressed her hands to two savage head injuries and prayed for his life. Only when the bleeding subsided had she poled across the river in search of help. During the week he lay unconscious she'd vowed to learn how to do more than just keep a bedside vigil. To her sorrow, Lumpkin had never fully recovered. To this day never again had she brought him across the river to pick berries with her.

"I may not know where your property begins and ends," she turned her head left and right as though she might be a tad confused, "but I'm your neighbor."

Not only a trifle true but brilliant. Maybe he wouldn't kill a neighbor. As fluffy white clouds passed over the sun she got her first real glimpse of the interloper. Starting at his head, she saw thick hair as black as the coal hidden in the mountains. He had a high forehead and rakish, black eyebrows set over eyes narrowed with a savvy glint. He was clean-shaven. Odd, since most men in this valley were bearded. The nostrils of his straight nose flared and when his square jaw clenched she noticed his chin had a masculine cleft. One thing for sure he owned a rich, melodious voice. This man could tell her the world was ending, and coming from his lips it wouldn't seem so bad. Then again, her world might be about to end.

"Has that spreading rash given you amnesia?" he asked.

"Certainly not." She furiously rubbed the leaf up and

down her arm and around her neck. "But you don't need to know my name or where my property is."

Brushing the tops of his ears, his hair appeared cut by a barber. Did black hair also grow on his broad chest? The dove-gray shirt was open at his throat and she followed the buttons down his muscular torso. Sleeves rolled up to his elbows showed thick wrists as he folded sinewy arms above a flat stomach. She was accustomed to men in baggy overalls. But not this man. With his trousers tucked into knee high boots, he wore black suspenders. The suspenders must be for fashion as his pants were nearly as snug against his thighs as bark to trees. When he cocked his left hip to one side, she noticed the male bulge in the crotch of his pants. Fists moving to his waist, he tapped the toe of his expensive-looking black boot.

This was the stance of a mountain ready to blow its top.

CHAPTER 2

"I've been looked up and down before, but never quite so blatantly," he growled.

She jerked her gaze back up to his. Red-hot embarrassment heated her itching neck and cheeks which she scratched, while freezing ghost fingers swept down her spine making her shiver. In addition to this man's intimidating stance in the middle of her escape route, his piercing stare rooted her to the spot. The gleam and color of his eyes reminded her of quicksilver, the fascinating liquid gray of mercury. Mercury—a shimmering, deadly poison!

"If I was taking your measure it's because you're so different looking," she said.

"You're different sounding. You don't speak with an Appalachian twang. How come?"

He held out a remarkably uncalloused hand toward her. His fingers were long, with blunt ends, his palm big and square and his nails short and clean. The perfect hand for a man, but she didn't take it.

"I don't answer personal questions from strangers."

"If we're neighbors," he lowered his hand, "we aren't strangers." But she was his foe he just didn't realize it, yet. "I take it blueberries don't grow in your garden."

"Correct." Pride wouldn't allow her to stay backed into

the bushes trembling like a berry about to fall off the vine. Dropping her jewelweed leaf, she took two steps toward her getaway path to the river and said, "I can only grow raspberries and blackberries."

"Blueberries have always grown wild down here by the water. I like them, too." Casually gesturing to the river he'd mirrored her steps, keeping her path obstructed. "That's why my brother and I dug up a couple of bushes and replanted them by the house years ago."

"Years ago?" He and his brother were the gunnysackers. Flashes of the attack seemed like yesterday, simultaneously draining her and giving her strength. She squared her shoulders and lifted her chin. "I'm not a scared little girl today. I help people hurt by other people. I'm the closest thing there is to a doctor in my holler."

"Actually you do look a little scared," he said, dead-on accurate. Then he frowned as if puzzled. "What does acting as a doctor have to do with this?"

"I borrow your berries to make herbal teas, tonics, and remedies."

He glanced to her bumpy apron pocket. "Borrow?"

Her skin prickled from head to toe. It was escape or die. Preparing to run, she untied her apron full of berries and flung it at his feet. "Steal."

Knowingly or unknowingly, it was hard to say for sure, but in moving his feet out from under her apron he further prevented her flight. "You can have the blueberries."

"For a price." She knew that only too well and raised her left hand to scratch her cheek.

She gasped as he snared her wrist and stopped her from scratching. She raised her right fist, but he seized that wrist in an iron-like grip. He hauled her up against his rock-hard chest until only her tiptoes touched the ground between his black boots. He had a fresh, pine scent. He must endorse regular bathing, as did she. A lock of shining hair had fallen across his forehead and she pictured brushing it into place.

If her hands had been free she might have trailed her fingers down his neck and over his broad shoulders. *What? No!*

Her unexpected reactions to this man were as perplexing as they were riveting, as exciting as they were terrifying. Now of all things her breasts itched. She rubbed her breasts against her forearms until her bosom collided with his chest. Her nipples immediately beaded beneath her thread-bare summer shift. She glanced up to see if he had noticed. The smoldering in his dark silver eyes said yes. Keeping her wrists captured, he lowered her heels to the ground.

"Stop scratching or that rash will become lesions."

Talking as fast as possible she said, "You probably think I didn't learn my lesson the first time. But if you let me go—"

"The first time?" His whisper was intimate. When a cocky grin spread his lips, straight teeth were a pearly white slash in his face. "Did we have a first time, little girl?"

"You *do* remember that little girl." Terror pulsed in heated waves, making her fear her bones might melt inside her skin. "We certainly did have a first time and you know it." But the furrowing of his brow indicated he didn't know it. Had he gunnysacked so many people he'd forgotten about her and Lumpkin? "If you let me go I promise you'll never see me again."

"No," the black-haired brute replied. He scowled as if in thought and then bargained, "But I will let you go for now on two small conditions."

"State your pig-piffle conditions and I'll be on my way."

"Pig piffle? What's that?"

A chuckle deep in his throat contradicted his fierce manner and the unbreakable hold he had on her. But maybe he was laughing at her. Her angst turning to anger, she knew just how to wipe that smug grin off his handsome face.

"A person who is pigheaded ought to know pig piffle means trivial." When his lips tightened as if riled, she quickly added, "Trivial means insignificant."

"I know what trivial means. My first condition is that you tell me your name."

Find out his. Maybe her fears were for naught. She braced herself. "What's yours?"

"Stone—"

"Stone!" Trauma bashed her from all sides. In her mind's eye she saw the bloody stone that had laid Lumpkin's head open to the bone in two places. Her first thought was the gunnysackers had killed him and she occasionally still woke screaming from that recurring nightmare. Pressing her fists against the intruder's muscular chest, she tried to break free. But she might as well be shoving at the mountain. Trapped and doomed, she ducked her head beneath his chin and whispered, "Please have mercy this time."

"Calm down. The last thing I'd do is hurt you. I'm a doctor."

He was trying to lull her into letting down her guard. She'd already made that mistake and look where it got her. "Let me go and I'll be calm," she said. Slowly he unlocked his hands from around her wrists. Instead of liberated, she felt abandoned. She scratched her head from wonder as much as from the nettle rash. He grasped her right hand and goose bumps raced up her arm. "You said you'd let me go."

"You're still scratching and you don't look any too calm, yet."

She yanked on her hand with all her might. Stumbling backward onto the hem of her dress, she teetered precariously. Taking a step, he kept her from falling but trod on her toes.

"Ouch!" she cried. "Get off my foot, you pigheaded bully." Releasing her, he moved his booted foot, but it felt like all five toes had been scraped through her thin slipper-like shoe.

"I'm really sorry." He sounded amazingly sincere and appeared concerned as he plowed a hand through his hair. "Come up to my house and I'll put some salve on your toes."

"I use honey." If he killed her up at his house what would happen to Lumpkin?

"Spicy!" came a distant bellow.

Inadvertently giving herself away as to her name, Spicy scanned the opposite shore of the Tug Fork which was a tributary to the much larger river known as the Big Sandy. She couldn't see Lumpkin through the Kentucky trees, but that was his voice.

"Your name is Spicy." It was a statement, not a question. "As I said, mine's Stone."

"Have me arrested. Kill me if you must, but please don't hurt Lumpkin. He's so sweet and harmless."

"I'm not out to hurt you." His consistent sincerity almost seemed real. "My second condition to letting you leave is that you bring me some of your blackberries and raspberries."

Making this foe no promises and to sidetrack him from grabbing her again, she whacked his booted shin with her good foot. The second he took a step back clearing her path, she ran for her sake and possibly his.

CHAPTER 3

"OUCH!" STONE CALLED AT HER BACK.

Following in her footsteps, without trying to catch her, he watched the dazzling woman leap onto a raft. Grabbing a pole, at least twelve feet long, she expertly set herself adrift across the Tug Fork River.

Spicy. He liked the name and boy, did it fit her.

Earlier, from the porch of his hilltop view, he'd spied someone in his blueberry patch. With nothing better to do at the moment, he figured he'd confirm the date of the upcoming election. Though no longer eligible to vote in Tug Valley, he would escort his mother and aunt to the Magnolia Precinct where they'd join the festivities and visit with friends. He'd crossed the clearing in front of his house and lost sight of the person as he descended the mountain into the forest. The woods had grown so thick in his absence it had narrowed his road to the river. Not wanting to alarm the trespasser he'd quietly walked out of the trees again near the berry patch along the riverbank.

Laying eyes close up on the back of the feminine form as she picked berries, he became more interested in finding out about her than the election. As she hummed a favorite tune of his he'd admired her from behind. Her glossy, brown hair with a hint of ginger reminded him of the color of syrup from a sugar maple tree. He'd gotten a good look because her tresses weren't confined in a bun, like the coiffures of most women. Her sugar-maple locks bounced loose halfway down her back. Speaking in jest about paying for the berries, when she'd spun around her manner of dress had surprised him. Instead of the typical high-necked décolletage, Spicy's simple frock with its scooped neckline tantalized him with mouthwatering cleavage. Instead of a formless skirt, Spicy's forest-green dress clung to her flat tummy and shapely hips.

Noting the sun in her eyes, he'd moved but that seemed to worsen her scratching. Luckily a group of clouds had resolved the problem. When he'd pulled her close, her cheeks had blushed the color of raspberries, she'd smelled of cinnamon and her breath was blackberry sweet. From her pink lips to the toes he'd trod, she'd whet his appetite more than any spice ever had. The tips of her breasts puckering against his chest brought him within an inch of kissing her. The excitement of holding her body to his had been as contagious as all get-out, making him want a bigger dose. Yet her desire to flee, the cry in her voice and fear in her eyes said she was terrified of him.

Damn these mountains. Stone knew why.

Back to the eyes of the beguiling creature. Deep purplish blue, they rivaled the color of the blueberries she'd picked. Big and bright they were so inquisitive and totally intoxicating he had become fascinated almost to the point of lost. When she'd looked him up and down, hot blood pulsed through his veins and surged into his loins. He'd growled at her to get those unforgettable eyes off his crotch before his lower body succumbed to her invisible touch and betrayed his thoughts. He had hurt her toes and for that he wanted to kick himself. While he felt like the pigheaded bully she'd accused him of being, only an angel would risk raiding his blueberry patch to make teas, tonics, and remedies to help people.

She was a woman with a heart full of heaven.

On the Kentucky side of the river now with her back to

him, Stone noted Spicy's saucily rounded fanny was speckled in purple, evidence of backing into his berry patch. Securing her raft to the opposite bank, she yanked up her dress and pranced out of the water onto dry land.

Whoever she was, this sensational siren had instantly ignited Stone's carnal appetite for intimacy. Since his bargain with Victor Vanderveer, to marry his daughter, only a few women had distracted him away from the hospital long enough for sex. Why did he think of the word intimacy instead of sex when it came to Spicy?

Was Spicy the proverbial needle in a haystack?

She suddenly twirled and looked directly across the Tug Fork River at him. Staring back, he raised his hand. She took a step forward and he thought she was about to wave. Instead she dropped her pole onto the raft and sashayed away from the riverbank. In the next heartbeat, the enchantress in emerald was swallowed up by the thick, green woods. Stone gradually lowered his hand to his side.

Animal magnetism. Like a buck to a doe. He stood mesmerized.

He had never believed in fellow physician Franz Mesmer's claim of hypnosis-induced animal magnetism. Attraction to a member of the opposite sex so compelling, so fascinating that it mesmerized? No, Stone hadn't thought so. Until today. On the West Virginia side of the river, in spellbound silence, Stone remained fixated on the spot where the alluring wood nymph had vanished into the Kentucky forest.

Please have mercy this time.

What time? Too late to ask her now. She had literally slipped through his fingers.

Kill me if you must, but please don't hurt Lumpkin.

Who was Lumpkin? The man who called to her? Why hadn't he asked? Was the man her husband? If that were the case, surely she'd have threatened Stone with her spouse's wrath.

Short of swimming, he had no way across the river.

Cross it? Why would he do that? To be friends, not foes. He hadn't voted at the election here in Tug Valley two years earlier. But he'd sure heard about the chaos.

Election Day, June 18, 1880, a fight had broken out involving a man named Bill Staton against Sam and Paris McCoy. Staton was related to the McCoys by marriage, but he'd made a fatal mistake back in 1878, by testifying in court on behalf of Floyd Hatfield against patriarch Randolph McCoy. The dispute had erupted over who owned a hog—Hatfield or McCoy. A jury of six Hatfields and six McCoys was convened. Staton's testimony convinced Selkirk McCoy to vote in Floyd Hatfield's favor. Randolph McCoy accepted the verdict and loss of the hog. His nephews, Paris and Sam, did not. There were no witnesses to the shooting but when Staton's body was found in the woods, most folks figured Squirrel Huntin' Sam had pulled the trigger. Recently, an acquittal on grounds of self-defense had been ruled and it was rumored this was due to patriarch, William Anderson Hatfield's influence with the judicial system. The judge had been Valentine 'Wall' Hatfield, older brother of William Anderson known as Devil Anse. Evidently, Devil Anse was too busy running his timber business to become immersed in a feud.

Maybe the man who'd bellowed Spicy's name was her father, brother, or cousin. Maybe Stone could find out at the election site, but that day was still a ways off. Tug Valley consisted of three districts on the Kentucky side—Blackberry Creek, Peter Creek, and Pond Creek. On the West Virginia side there was just one district—Magnolia. During an election it was customary to visit your precinct and the others to catch up on the news, share hunting stories, eat delicious baked goods, and sample your neighbor's moonshine.

On the other hand, he was betrothed.

"Damn hog," Stone muttered.

CHAPTER 4

"TARNATION."

Hidden among the sweetgum, white pine, silver birch, and elderberry trees Spicy sank to the ground and leaned against a sugar maple tree in relief. Pulling a jewelweed leaf from her pocket, she rubbed it over her skin but kept her eyes fastened on the most alarming man she'd ever met. Stone's every move captivated her as he swaggered toward the path leading up the wooded mountain. One could see that house, high on the hill, from her side of the river and she had investigated it once long ago. While massaging the toes Stone had indeed scraped and the ones she'd whacked against his shin, he disappeared into the dense West Virginia forest. Their meeting had been so thrilling the pounding of her heart still echoed in her ears.

Thrills could result in heartbreak. Just ask Roseanna McCoy. At the June election of 1880, Roseanna met Johnson Hatfield. Realizing her brother, Tolbert, had gone home without her and totally enamored of Johnse, as Johnson was called, Roseanna crossed the Tug Fork into West Virginia where Johnse lived with his father, Devil Anse. She must have reckoned that was safer than Johnse escorting her home where her own father, Randolph McCoy, known as Ol'Ranel, had a reputation of being as cantankerous as he was gossipy. Eighteen-year-old Johnse was virile and handsome. He had wild oats to sow and due to Hatfield timbering he had money. Roseanna, like many McCoys, struggled against poverty. At twenty-one she was ready to marry and grew jealous over Johnse's dalliances. Neither Devil Anse nor Ol'Ranel favored a union. When she and Johnse parted six months later she was pregnant. The spring of 1881, Roseanna gave birth to a girl and Johnse married her cousin, Nancy McCoy. The baby died of measles later that year and Roseanna was miserable. Grudges, envy, and bitterness could yet explode in a feud.

"Pigheaded folk," Spicy said just as shuffling sounded behind her.

"Spicy?"

"What?" Quickly, she scooted around to see the man who'd spoken walking toward her alongside his younger brother, Lumpkin. "Clayphus McCoy, you scared me."

"You wasn't tendin' yer gardens and I's frettin' you poled acrost the river."

"We's frettin'," Lumpkin repeated.

Spicy studied the homespun shirt and overall-clad brothers in a new light. Slouch hats were yanked low on their heads and worn-out brogans covered their feet. The heavy, coarse work shoes which reached their ankles were a far cry from polished black boots. Stone's clothing, store-bought she decided, wasn't the only thing different about him. Besides his striking good looks and soothing deep voice, there was his unsolicited medical advice.

"He must have come from a world away," Spicy whispered.

"What?" the shorter man asked. "Who?"

Answering Clay, Spicy improvised saying, "It sounded like Lumpkin called from a world away."

She had protected Stone. Why? Because he hadn't hurt her. Except for her toes and she believed that was an accident. Shifting a rifle to his left shoulder, Clay extended his right hand. When Spicy took hold he yanked her to her feet.

Opposed to eyes shimmering like quicksilver, Clay's eyes were as flat as dried mud. Instead of a straight nose and kissable lips tightened into a smug grin, Clay's nose bore a curve and he snorted into his bushy orange mustache and beard when riled which was most of the time. Being called carrot-top as a kid had enraged him and he'd always thrown the first punch. After a dozen fights, Clay had lost a front tooth, been kicked out of the one-room schoolhouse, and been left with only two friends. At six feet, Clay was half a foot taller than Spicy, but he wasn't the six foot four she guessed the handsome stranger with the coal-black hair to be.

"I'm going home," Spicy said.

She had to get away from the river's edge before Clay spied Stone and took him for a revenuer. Because however plain Clay was, he had muscles, a rifle, and a moonshine still.

"We's walkin' ya home," Clay told her.

Flanked by the brothers, Spicy followed her well-worn path into Raccoon Hollow and was soon trailing alongside Blackberry Creek. Her heart had yet to settle into a normal beat and Stone's iron-like grip lingered around her wrists. The fact her breasts had touched his muscular chest excited her now as it had then. While trapped in his sinewy grip she'd sensed he'd almost kissed her. Could she have survived his kiss without swooning?

She'd never know.

Spicy was promised to Clay all because of some bad pork. When her parents lay dying after ingesting the spoiled meat, her father thinking to protect and provide for his only child had asked Clay to marry her. Such arrangements were not uncommon, but Spicy was appalled and protested. He was her cousin. She wanted to marry the man of her choice. Mama had soothed her in a death rattle. Spicy's relation to Clay was distant and insignificant. Lumpkin had no way to make a living and so Clay was it. Clay had remained throughout the discussion and not wanting her already-suffering parents to die during an argument, she'd said no more.

Clay had pushed to move in the day after her folks passed. And why wouldn't he? Her log cabin was clean and cozy. The front room was furnished with a table and chairs near the hearth. At the table Mama had cut cloth made with their loom and, unlike Spicy, she had enjoyed sewing. There were easy chairs on either side of a sofa near a window where Papa had often buried his nose in Grandpa's books about the Dutch East Indies. His favorite was the one on smuggling nutmeg, pepper, cinnamon, ginger, cloves, and sage out of the Spice Islands. Spicy liked that book, too, as well as Shakespeare's story of *Romeo and Juliet* which she had read countless times. But she longed for a book on medicine.

"Where ya been?" Clay asked. "Why's yer dress stained?"

Ignoring his first question she said, "I was picking berries, but I met up with a big buck and he looked mad to find me stealing from him." Spicy desperately needed to scratch, but refrained so as not to give away having tangled with the nettles across the river.

"Facin' down a buck's safer'n meetin' up with a cussed Hatfield. If'n any of them land greedy, hog stealin' varmints crosses the Tug Fork and trespasses on my property," Clay glared meaningfully at Spicy, "I's shoot 'em dead. You berry hunt on the Kentucky side."

Spicy bristled at his bossiness, possessiveness, and threats of killing. "Just because you're one of the few McCoys who doesn't timber Hatfield trees or farm on Hatfield land, doesn't mean you can kill one of them for a harmless trespassing. If everyone felt that way I'd—" she stopped herself just in time. "Try to get along, Clay."

"Get along, Clay," Lumpkin agreed with effort.

Spicy smiled at Lumpkin whose face was as round as a pie. With light blue eyes, his hair and chest-length beard were the color of wheat. His vulnerable, gap-toothed grin made Spicy want to protect him always. Weighing twelve pounds at birth, everybody called him Big Lump except for Spicy and his mama before she'd passed. Taking his arm she hugged it to her.

Lumpkin beamed. "Love Spicy."

"I love you, too, Lumpkin."

Clay sneered, "I wanna hear you say that to me, Spicy." Then correcting himself he said, "No, what I wanna hear in my damn bed is yer in love with me."

Spicy swung her head sideways and assured him, "You are my distant cousin, Clay, and I will never be in love with you."

Despite Lumpkin's presence, Clay persisted, "I'm thirty and yer an old maid. How long I gotta sleep alone?"

"I'm not an old mail and you don't sleep alone," Spicy said. "You sleep with half the girls this side of the Tug Fork."

"I wouldn't if'n you was sleepin' with me."

Fearing what he would do to her if she outright refused to marry him, Spicy didn't reply. The sun had glowed vibrantly with Stone but a gloomy sky settled overhead with Clay. Their ongoing tension made the trek through the hollow feel like forever before her cabin came into view. She wanted to enjoy a cup of elderberry tea, rub some honey on her toes and think about all that had happened across the river. The brothers lived on the Peter Creek branch of the Tug Fork River which gave her some breathing room. But lingering near her porch, Clay didn't look ready to go there just yet. She had put Clay off for a year and he was becoming harder to get rid of every day. Spicy walked up the three steps to her porch as she heard Pepper crow. The strutting rooster, she'd raised from a baby chick, had a big red comb on his head, red wattles on his beak, an orange, burgundy, and black body and high-arched black tail feathers. Keeping his distance by the chicken coop, Pepper squawked again giving her an idea.

"Tomorrow will dawn and you'll be behind in your work

because of the time you wasted looking for me, Clay." He maintained a cornfield for his illegal whiskey. His moonshine was probably the highest proof in all of Tug Valley and always in demand. "Now that you've found me, mosey on home and tend your business."

"No." Clay tromped up the porch steps and grabbed Spicy's hand. He squeezed it way too hard. "When we getting hitched?"

"Lots of girls between Raccoon Hollow and Peter Creek would marry you tomorrow, Polly in particular who you *should* marry tomorrow. I told you last summer I wouldn't hold you to the agreement you made with Papa."

"I's holding you to it."

She knew the agreement was the only thing keeping Clay from forcing himself on her. That being her worst fear, she'd told him there would be no relations before marriage. In the meantime she'd hoped and prayed he'd lose interest. She cautioned herself to tread lightly.

"We'll see about that, Clay," she replied, pulling her hand from him.

Clay gaped, obviously as stunned as Spicy herself at her reckless choice of words. Lumpkin sucked his lips between his teeth, rolled his eyes skyward and clasped beefy hands over his rounded belly. Pepper continued to pace and protest Clay's presence.

"We *will* be hitched and I *will* bed you," Clay said.

If the stranger across the river asked to take her to bed would she tell him no? He'd almost stolen a kiss today. Given the chance what else would Stone try to steal? What else might she freely offer? Unfamiliar shivers coursed through Spicy. The fact that she was the same age as Roseanna McCoy had been when she met Johnse Hatfield didn't escape her. She surely didn't want to experience a similar outcome.

"Spicy," Clay snorted. "Yer not actin' yerself. What's afoot with you?"

She wasn't sure. "We'll discuss it some other time."

"We's gonna talk 'bout it richeer'n now."

Spicy stamped her foot and pointed. "To your farm with him, Lumpkin."

"Yes'm," Lumpkin said. He grabbed Clay by the back of his overalls and easily hauled his sputtering, flailing older brother off the porch. "Ta farm."

"Stay in Kentucky, Spicy," Clay said over his shoulder.

"I'll go wherever I want to, Clayphus McCoy."

Shocked at herself once again, Spicy watched Lumpkin drag Clay across the grassy front yard. When they had disappeared into the woods she called out to Pepper assuring the rooster everything was all right. Hinting to Clay she might not marry him somewhat eased the ever increasing burden weighing her down. What *had* come over her? In her head played the sights of quicksilver eyes and rippling muscles, the sounds of a deep voice and low chuckle. Still overwhelmed by the mystery man even when he was clear across the river, Spicy trembled. Plopping down into one of the two rocking chairs on the porch, the dusty loom set off to her right. With Clay gone, Pepper had quieted and her raccoon scampered up on her left.

"Nutmeg," she scooped up the gray and black furball and tucked her beloved pet onto her lap, "that big house on the mountain is no longer vacant." Who was the heart-stopping stranger she'd met across the river? As far back as she could recall the two-story house, not log cabin, had set empty. Years ago, when peeking through the ground floor windows she had seen large rooms with furniture covered with sheets and quilts. Did he really own the property? Had he once lived there with a brother? If he were a real doctor, with book learning, he did come from far away. If he were from far away then maybe…"Stone, please don't be a Hatfield."

CHAPTER 5

"Stone Hatfield. Thank God you're finally here."

He'd sent a telegram of his impending visit. Having hiked the backwoods this morning from his house to Mate Creek, he'd crossed the stream at a shallow point which put him near the frame house where his mother lived with his aunt. Reaching the property, Stone had paused among the magnolia trees and realized the blooms of the mountain laurels had a spicy scent. Spicy. During his trek to Warm Hollow, Stone wondered where Spicy lived. Hoping she would return for her apron, he had watched for her long after the sun had set. Cursing the fact it had grown dark early without a full moon and exhausted from his trip into Tug Valley, he'd finally stretched out in bed. Once there, he'd wished Spicy was next to him.

Under him. On top of him. One with him.

Those images tossed and turned Stone until he had fallen into a fitful sleep. In vivid bits and stingy pieces he'd dreamed of a beautiful siren with sugar-maple curls and blueberry eyes. From across the river she had beckoned him with outstretched arms. When he had reached out, her forest-green dress blended into the misty Kentucky woods.

He'd poled across the water and chased her. Just as he'd caught her, he'd been awakened by chirping birds.

And with a long-absent primitive urge to mate.

Stone chuckled now as he stood on his aunt's porch. "Hello to you, too, Hilda Hatfield."

"Come on in, honey," Aunt Hilda invited.

Honey. Had Spicy rubbed some on the toes he'd scraped? Stone decided as soon as it was polite, he'd ask his aunt and mother about the gorgeous woman who'd robbed him of an apronful of berries and a good night's sleep.

Aunt Hilda ushered him inside her familiar, single-story home. He'd barely stepped onto a braided rug in the front room, when she hugged him. Almost as pretty as his mother, Hazel, the Vance sisters had grown up at the base of a summit in the Eastern Panhandle of West Virginia, called Stony Mountain. As children the girls had moved with their parents to Tug Valley in order to help care for ailing grandparents. Later on, the Vance sisters had met and married Hatfield brothers. Stone's uncle had died of natural causes leaving Aunt Hilda all alone. The following year Stone's father had been killed. At Aunt Hilda's urging, his fragile mother had packed up his younger brother, Jet, and moved in with her.

By that time, Stone was sixteen and living in Philadelphia. With a mother in poor health and then losing his uncle and father much too early, he had become interested in medicine. At eighteen he enrolled in the University of Pennsylvania's School of Medicine. In addition to classes in chemistry and anatomy, to earn his bachelor of medicine degree, he'd served as an apprentice to a practitioner in physic. He'd studied Latin and mathematics and passed a public examination in 1875, when he was twenty-one. For his doctorate of medicine degree, Stone had attended lectures and practiced medicine for the mandatory three years. He also wrote and publicly defended a thesis on surgery published at his own expense. In 1878, at the minimum required age of twenty-four, he had graduated from the university with honors.

Since graduation he had divided his time between the University of Pennsylvania's teaching hospital built by the university for its medical school and the original Pennsylvania Hospital established in 1751. Dr. Victor Vanderveer wanted to retire and was grooming Stone to take over the surgical department in the teaching hospital. Stone wanted that more than anything, but the fly in the ointment was the daughter. In 1880, Vanderveer had said his daughter, Eunice, was a spinster. He felt it was high time she married and Stone was the perfect man for her. Stone had been stalling the Vanderveers for two years. He was twenty-eight now and Eunice was thirty-five. Stalling wouldn't last much longer.

His aunt's *Thank God* echoed in Stone's mind.

Not seeing his mother, Stone asked, "Aunt Hilda, is something wrong?"

Gazing past him, through the open door to the porch, she questioned, "Where's that lawyer, little brother of yours?"

"Jet's stuck in Philadelphia on a murder trial," he replied. "I stopped by yesterday, but you weren't home. So I went to my house for a look around."

"You spent the night in that big old dusty place?" Aunt Hilda asked as she closed the front door. When he nodded, she shook her head. "You could have stayed here even though nobody was home."

"Thanks." But if someone had been here he wouldn't have returned to his house and run into Spicy. "I decided to stay the night there." His plan to stay with his mother and aunt had changed after meeting Spicy. "For old time's sake." And new time's sake.

"You're here now and that's what matters."

Making him feel welcome, Aunt Hilda took his arm and tugged him toward the kitchen. She would have been a great mother had nature cooperated. If she'd said it once, she had said a hundred times that Stone and Jet were almost like having her own sons. She pulled out a chair at the head of the kitchen table. Stone took his cue and sat. Many Tug Valley homes were log cabins consisting of one structure for eating and one for sleeping with a walkway referred to as a dogtrot between them. Aunt Hilda's house and his were built in the fashion of many homes found in the Eastern Panhandle.

"Everything looks about the way I left it," Stone said.

"Except my hair has more gray than black hair nowadays," Aunt Hilda said, pouring him a glass of milk.

Stone hadn't asked for milk and if she brought out rhubarb pie, he'd tense. Most mountain folks considered rhubarb to be a stomach soother. Thus it was often eaten during times of crisis or bad news. A disturbing thought rapped on Stone's heart.

"Where's my mother?"

Picking up a pie tin, Aunt Hilda asked, "Didn't you get my telegram she was ailing?"

Stone's stomach clenched. "No, I must have left Philadelphia before it arrived. Is she in the hospital in Wheeling?" Wheeling Hospital was the first hospital to be chartered in western Virginia in 1850, before West Virginia became a state in 1863. During the Civil War it had been used by the military. Wheeling Hospital was well-thought-of although it lacked the innovation, prestige, and financial backing of the Pennsylvania hospitals where Stone practiced.

"No, she's not in Wheeling."

Stone felt like a little boy instead of a grown man. "Will she be back soon?"

Aunt Hilda placed rhubarb pie on the table, pulled up a chair, and sat down next to him. Stone sensed a sheen of cold sweat dampen his brow.

"I wasn't here yesterday to greet you because I'd traveled to Logan to send you a second telegram, telling you she's gone. A good friend of mine dropped me off at home today shortly before you arrived."

Stone went rigid as Aunt Hilda's eyes teared. "When did my mother die?"

"Last week. She tried to hold out until you arrived, so she could say goodbye. But she was so tired she drifted away in her sleep." Aunt Hilda reached across the table and placed her hand over his. "I had to see her buried before I could go to Logan."

"Was she able to be examined by a doctor?" Stone asked and thought of Spicy.

"Dr. Rutherford, who treats a lot of us Hatfields, saw Hazel but he said there wasn't anything he could do."

"She was only sixty," Stone said. "She should still be here."

His mother had been thirty-two, four years older than he was now when he was born. It took more than three years to conceive Jet who had just turned twenty-four. His mother had always said she and her sister, who was older by five years, just weren't meant to have a dozen children like most folks in these hills.

"Suffering scarlet fever as a child weakened her, Stony," his aunt reminded him.

Only family and old friends called him Stony. While his house was situated a little ways up on one mountain, his aunt's house set on a second one. With a lush valley in between, his and Jet's paternal great-grandparents had owned all of it. After the Hatfield brothers had married the Vance sisters they inherited the double mountains and named them Stony Mountains after the West Virginia summit where the sisters had been born. Stone had been named for the mountains themselves while Jet, whose hair was as black as Stone's, had been named for the jet-black coal locked inside them. No one in Philadelphia called him Stony except for Jet sometimes and no one had said it like his mother. Now, he'd never hear her voice again.

"I waited too long to come home." Stone saw the same love and understanding in his aunt's eyes he'd always seen in his mother's. He whispered aloud what Aunt Hilda already knew, "If I hadn't been offered my job at Pennsylvania Hospital the day I graduated from medical school I'd have come home years ago."

"If you would have turned down Pennsylvania Hospital, your mother would have been mighty disappointed."

He smacked his fist down on the table and suddenly decided, "I wish I'd never heard of Pennsylvania Hospital."

"You don't mean that," Aunt Hilda insisted. "You did exactly what you and your folks wanted—to get an education and establish yourself in Philadelphia." His aunt patted his closed fist. "Don't have any regrets, because your mother had none. She was so proud of you and Jet."

Stone pulled his hand from under hers and ran it through his hair. His eyes burned and his heart ached. "Proud of me for not coming to see her since I left home at sixteen? Proud of me for taking Jet out of these hills, too? I doubt it."

"Stony, your mother could have visited you. She chose not to for the same reason she didn't press you to visit us. She wanted nothing to interfere with you being a doctor." Tilting her head and smiling, Aunt Hilda said, "When you sent for Jet, she lectured that boy for a week on how he was to do exactly what you told him and not get in your way." She sat back and clasped her hands in her lap. "She was proud as a peacock of the doctor and lawyer she and your father raised."

Stone rested his elbows on the table and pressed his fingers to his forehead. "I'd hoped I could talk the two of you into going back to Philadelphia with me and living there."

With her usual candidness, Aunt Hilda said, "She wouldn't have moved. As for me, I'll live and die in these Appalachian Mountains."

Stone raised his head in wonder. "Why?"

"Because it's home."

"Maybe I could have saved her if I'd been here."

"No, it was just her time, Stone." Aunt Hilda sliced a

piece of pie and put it on a plate. "Now eat your pie, drink that milk, and then we'll go for a walk over yonder to the Hatfield Cemetery. She's next to your father."

So as not to hurt his aunt's feelings, Stone ate a couple of bites of pie and washed it down with the milk. Numbly, he stood and walked to the door. Outside the sunshine mocked him. The clouds should be crying for his mother. Stone blinked back tears. On their way to the cemetery, he and his aunt neared a homestead not far from Mate Creek. The property belonged to Ellison Hatfield, Devil Anse's younger brother. Ellison at six foot four was the same height as Stone. Handsome and popular, Ellison was beloved by the Hatfields. Hilda said Ellison had been at Hazel's graveside service. Just exiting his house, Ellison, a hale and hearty Confederate veteran and hero at the Battle of Gettysburg, spotted them and shook hands with Stone. Stone vaguely wondered if Spicy was a Confederate sympathizer or a Yankee like himself.

"Never doubted you'd come marching back home as a doctor, Stone." Loyalty rang in Ellison's voice. "I want you to tend me next time I'm poorly."

"Thank you." Stone didn't say he wasn't planning on staying. Ellison expressed his sympathies about Stone's mother. "I appreciate you attending her service, Ellison."

"Let's go huntin' soon," Ellison suggested cheerfully. "And if you need a horse, I got a big chestnut stallion, named Logan, you're welcome to."

Stone thanked him, they bid him farewell, and continued along fairly smooth terrain to a gently rolling hill where his ancestors were buried. Finding his father's lovingly tended grave, Stone lay his hand atop the headstone. Then he knelt at his mother's fresh grave. Having been recently unearthed, the ground had a pungent smell. Stone picked up a handful of the dirt and squeezed it. Barely moving his lips, he said goodbye to the mother he loved.

Staring at her grave, Stone said to his aunt, "Jet will be given the telegram you sent."

"He still lives in the same boardinghouse as you?" she asked and Stone nodded. "I want you to know I didn't let Vorticia Hatfield near your mother."

Stone patted the fistful of dirt in place and stood. "Does that old crone still live in the cave on the back side of my mountain?"

Aunt Hilda shivered. "Yes, along with the bats, rats, and snakes she uses in the practice of her medicine."

"Vorticia doesn't practice medicine," Stone said. "She's a self-proclaimed witch. Her cures are dangerous concoctions and ancient spells based on superstitions."

His aunt agreed. "The way she claims her powers come from the coal would lead one to think Vorticia owns the Stony Mountains. Truth is she's a squatter."

"If she doesn't outright kill people, they're worse off after she gets her hands on them." In Stone's ear, Spicy's words echoed with sincerity, *I'm the closest thing there is to a doctor in my holler*. He wanted to ask his aunt about Spicy, but his mother's grave wasn't the place.

"If I'd thought she could've helped your mama," Aunt Hilda began and took his arm, "I'd have risked sending for a young woman across the Tug Fork River named Spicy McCoy."

CHAPTER 6

Spicy's fingers were bloodless from clutching the basket handle. It had taken her two days to work up the nerve to cross the river and trek up this hill. As she had recalled, where the woods left off was a clearing. There, she had paused at a fork in the narrow road to get her bearings. The front of the home had a river view, but far enough away from the Kentucky side to render anyone on this West Virginia property unrecognizable. The left fork of the road was shorter and veered to the house while the right fork, maybe three times as long, led to a barn in the distance. Skirting the overgrown yard, in nearing the house, she passed the blueberry patch Stone claimed he and his brother had planted. A wide front porch boasted two rocking chairs much like hers. Venturing forth, she'd walked up the steps, took a steadying breath, and knocked on the front door. When no one had answered, she'd considered leaving, but with determination she perched in a rocker praying Stone hadn't left for good. Despite her fears, she needed his advice about a patient. As she'd waited, sunshine gave way to rainclouds before she heard horse hooves.

From out of the woods, Stone emerged atop a shining chestnut horse, a stallion by the size. Not seeing her, he took the right fork toward the barn. Sitting tall in the saddle, he had the aura of a man accustomed to being in command. Mountain men were often stooped from back-breaking labor. Not Stone. Further evidence he had come from far away. Vanishing into the barn, he came back out leading the unsaddled horse to a water trough. Spicy didn't interrupt him as she figured he would head to the house any moment. But instead he strode around the side of the barn and spread the branches of a thick copse of bushes as if looking for something. Feeling intrusive at this point, Spicy stood and eased a crick out of her back.

Braced for whatever Stone's reaction might be at finding her on his property again, she called out, "Hello?"

Stone pivoted with a look of complete surprise. His eyes mirrored the dark gray of the clouds hanging low over the mountain. Spicy wondered if his mood was about to turn as stormy as the threatening weather. Then a benign mask fell over his face eliminating his astonishment. Grabbing the reins to the horse, he sauntered toward her.

Seeing Stone at a distance allowed Spicy to take him in all at once. His coal-black hair was windblown, adding reck-lessness to the danger he represented. His white shirt stretched across his broad shoulders and the sleeves were again rolled up his forearms. The coming storm made the evening humid and perhaps because of the cloying heat, he'd undone a few shirt buttons. Spicy swallowed. His half-open shirt revealed the very thing she dreamed of in a man —a rock-hard chest lightly furred with masculine, black hair. She'd seen Clay McCoy working shirtless in his cornfield, and though he wasn't stooped, his chest was smaller and hairless.

How exciting it would be to trail her fingers through those black curls and feel the muscles ripple under his skin. As Stone neared, Spicy followed the buttons of his shirt down to the buttons on his gray breeches. These pants, like his black ones, were snug enough to remind her that he was male. A magnificent one.

A full-grown and no doubt fully experienced male.

"I see you're up to your usual tricks."

He stopped at the bottom of the porch steps and wrapped the horse's reins around a hitching post. She'd looked him up and down again. Is that what he meant by her usual tricks?

"What tricks?"

"Your trespassing tricks, Miss," he paused, "McCoy."

Spicy cleared her throat. "I am a McCoy and I know I'm trespassing, Mister—"

"Doctor," he reminded her. "Hatfield."

"Dr. Hatfield." Spicy had known in her heart of hearts the man who lived up on this mountain had to be a Hatfield. Now, didn't she? Yes. But she'd come this far, no turning back.

"How are your toes?"

"Fine. How's your shin?"

"Fine. What's in the basket?"

"I baked you a blackberry pie with real hard-to-come-by sugar."

Stone walked up the porch steps and stopped unnervingly close. He jammed his fists on his hips. Why was she taking this crazy risk? For her patient or for Stone?

"Just one pie won't do it, sugar'n *spice*," he said.

Sugar'n spice? Her heart fluttered and her pulse raced. Clay referred to her as his pet, having gone so far as to say he'd own her as his wife. She had assured him he would not. But sugar'n spice felt like an off the cuff clever compliment. Stone tilted his dark head waiting for her reply. He was right, after all the berries she'd stolen, of course one pie wouldn't do it.

"How many pies will it take?" Spicy asked.

"It's about to rain. Let's negotiate inside."

Stone opened the door and she stepped into the house. Although she had spied through the ground floor windows of this house she had never been inside such a residence, only log cabins. She found herself in a large entryway boasting a tall, straight staircase. On either side of the foyer and hallway were the lovely, airy rooms she remembered full of furniture still covered with sheets and quilts. After closing the door, he led her down a wide hallway to a kitchen with a big cooking hearth. Pulling a ladder-back chair away from a table, he splayed a hand.

"Please sit."

"First, take the pie as a gesture of my good will," Spicy bargained.

"Only if you promise to make a raspberry pie for me, too."

Still holding the basket with both hands, from stress as well as to keep the pie from spilling over one side of the tin or the other, she nodded. "I will."

With their negotiation completed he grasped the basket handle. Spicy tried to let go, but her fingers were frozen. Stone tilted his head and cocked a brow in question. Spicy glared at her stiffened fingers until she forced them off the handle. Smothering a grin, he took the basket and she dropped her arms to her sides sitting as invited.

Stone took the blackberry pie out of the basket and without preamble asked, "Who was the man who called for you the other day?"

"A relative."

"Husband?"

She shook her head. "I'm not married."

Still standing, Stone narrowed his eyes. "How's the rash?"

"Better." Tingles ran rampant. Please don't let the nettle rash act up due to the nerve-racking prickles raging across her skin from head to toe. "It's almost gone."

"You get ten points for being brave enough to bring a pie to my house. Thank you."

"You're welcome." Ten points? "I promise I won't take up much more of your time."

"My time is yours." He placed a hand on her shoulder and Spicy might as well have been glued to the chair. "You're as skittish as a doe," Stone observed. "Why?"

Scratching at her throat, she said, "You're a Hatfield and I'm a McCoy!"

"Right. My aunt, Hilda Hatfield, told me about you."

"She did?" Rubbing her collarbone, she brushed his hand where it rested on her shoulder. He moved his hand and she reckoned she'd float to the ceiling because now she couldn't feel the floor under her feet. "You know we're enemies by blood." She dug at her neck.

"I don't believe in blood enemies," Stone said and frowned. "Do you scratch all the time or just when you're with me?"

"You're making my nettle rash act up," she admitted. "It would help if you'd sit down." Easing her anxiety a trifle, he took a seat across the table from her.

"Nettle rash is an allergic reaction to a plant or an herb, not to fright or nerves. If your nettle rash is all but gone, what you're experiencing is a psychosomatic reaction."

"A psycho," she tilted her head, "what kind of reaction?"

"Psychosomatic. A reaction caused by your head," he explained. "Do I frighten you or make you nervous?"

Spicy filed the big-city word away. "Both."

"Why are you in my house if I scare you?"

"I need your advice. Why are *you* here?"

With a glance around the kitchen, he said, "I grew up in this house and inherited it after my father died. I came home for a long overdue visit with my mother and aunt and to escort them to the August election next month."

When he met her gaze again, Spicy could have sworn she saw a tear glistening in his eyes. Stone blinked and the moisture was gone. She must have been mistaken.

"Where have you been?" she asked.

"Philadelphia, Pennsylvania."

"What's in Philadelphia?"

"The University of Pennsylvania. I went there to become a doctor." With a shrug he added, "A body can't stay in these hills and do that."

Spicy shot to her feet. "In a pig's eye, they can't. I doctor folks," with a sharp bob of her head she tapped her fingers to her chest, "and I have never left this valley."

"I meant no disrespect. Please sit back down," Stone said. "I define the region as hills, but you see it as a valley. Our definitions of doctor are different." After she was seated again, he raised his palms in surrender and asked, "May I call you Spicy?" She nodded. "Well, Spicy, I wanted to be a surgeon. I had to go to medical school to learn how to operate on people."

"Operate means you cut people open." She chewed her lower lip and said, "You remove something or fix something inside, then sew them up and they get better?"

"Usually they get better and sometimes it's to deliver a baby."

"I guess being a surgeon-kind-of-doctor," Spicy stared across the table at him, "is the closest thing there is to being God."

CHAPTER 7

For a moment, Stone couldn't speak. Was Spicy mocking his definition of doctor or was she being sincere? When she tilted her head, he saw such genuine longing on her face his heart constricted with tenderness. He'd like to get up and pull her into his arms, but she'd stopped scratching for the moment and he didn't want to set off her itching again.

"That's a profound compliment. Thank you," he said, humbled to his core. "But I'm just a man."

"Yes, I've noticed."

Spicy smiled at him for the very first time. Her teeth were white and straight between perfectly plump lips and two sensual dimples dotted her pretty cheeks. Shrugging bashfully, she tossed sugar-maple curls over the gorgeous curve of her full breasts. Not only did the burnt orange color of her dress remind Stone of cinnamon, she had a hint of cinnamon about her that enveloped him. Dainty elbows rested near her tiny waist as her hands sat clasped in her lap. Spicy McCoy was femininity at its intoxicating best.

Desire coiled in Stone's belly and his blood heated. No. His mother wasn't cold in her grave. He had no right to feel anything but grief. But talk about the needle in a haystack. Spicy was unique from all other women he'd ever met, especially the Vanderveer woman. Women he knew didn't discuss medicine and surgery nor had they been born in these familiar hills.

"You wear your heart on your sleeve, don't you?" he asked. When she lifted one shoulder toward her ear and didn't reply, he clarified, "You say what you think."

Her expression changed to one of a challenge as she raised an arched brow and replied, "Be careful or I'll say what I think of you."

This lively banter was the complete opposite of the tedious discourses with his betrothed about her collection of antique crucifixes. Severely plain with layers of high-necked clothing covering an emaciated frame, the woman, whose name had momentarily slipped his mind, rarely spoke above a prim whisper. In a letter she'd written to him, as she couldn't speak aloud on the subject, she had informed him as to intimacy he must satisfy his male needs elsewhere. No problem. Sex never entered his mind in her presence. He had his share of city women. Yet marriage, like the good one his parents had, should mean something. Fidelity. But hell, he couldn't become a monk. And he wanted a couple of kids.

"By all means, say what you think of me," Stone dared the exhilarating woman.

"Long shot," Spicy said from across the kitchen table.

"Which could be taken a couple ways." Stone watched the blueberry eyes sparkle.

"You being here just when I need you is a long shot."

Stone needed her, too. An image of making love to Spicy, with an evening storm cooling off the day while they heated up his bed, rumbled like thunder in his lower body. Making love to Spicy had been on his mind since the moment he had laid eyes on her. But this was Tug Valley and his code of honor warned him against bedding her and disappearing. In his wake, she could become an outcast with the McCoys. To that end, he had to get her out of his house before he tossed her over his shoulder and carried her up the stairs.

"Tell me what you need. I'll help any way I can and then you can head on back across the river before the storm hits."

"A patient of mine returned to me. Her quinsy is worse."

"Tonsillitis."

Spicy's eyes widened as if she didn't want to miss a single word he said. "Tonsillitis," she solemnly repeated. "Is that what they call quinsy in Philadelphia, Pennsylvania?"

"Yes." Stone stood up from the table and motioned to her.

Spicy was endearing. She was sexy. She was irresistible. How old was she? He forced himself to walk away from her and down the hall. She followed him to the front door. He opened the door to raindrops splattering the roof of the porch. Facing Spicy he tried to ignore the memory of how good she'd felt in his arms the other day.

"So, do you know how to cure qui—tonsillitis?" she asked as the raindrops quickly grew heavier and fell faster. "Her throat still hurts in spite of my—your blueberry tea."

"What do I get for giving you my medical advice?" he asked. She scratched her wrist, scrubbed at her slender hip and stepped past him onto the porch. "Spicy, stop scratching and talk to me as you would to somebody on your side of the river."

"You're not like anybody on my side of the river."

Joining her on the porch, Stone replied, "You're not like anybody I know anywhere, but you don't see me scratching." No, he was just fighting like hell to keep an arousal from stretching the front of his pants. "Talk to me."

Spicy clasped her hands at her waist and said, "In exchange for your medical opinion, Dr. Hatfield, I'd be willing to show you some honest-to-goodness mountain magic."

"Please call me Stone." He was happy to see her nod instead of scratch. "But not Vorticia Hatfield's magic I hope."

"Never. This valley is full of magic, both good and bad. My

magic is good. Vorticia's magic is worse than bad," Spicy whispered as though afraid the witch could hear her. "She uses truly evil magic. If she's your blood kin, I mean no offense."

"None taken. I agree with you about Vorticia." Spicy was working her magic without even touching him. But he wanted her to touch him and it was taking a will of iron to keep his hands off her. "What kind of mountain magic would you show me?"

"Spicy!" came a distant and vaguely familiar bellow.

"Tarnation!" With the mild swear, Spicy hurried down the porch steps.

"Wait." Amused by her euphemism for damnation, Stone chuckled as he followed her into the front yard. He seized her upper arm and said, "Don't you dare run from me again today, Spicy McCoy."

"I go where I please when I please, Stone Hatfield." She yanked her arm from him and looked up through splashing raindrops to say, "If he finds me here, he'll hurt you."

"He? Who?" Stone figured she meant a McCoy. She just shrugged. "I thought you were worried about me hurting you. Which I've never done. You and I never had a *first time*."

That gave her pause as she blinked away raindrops. "When did you leave Tug Valley?"

"Twelve years ago when I was sixteen. And I haven't been back here since."

"Twelve years ago I was nine." Her eyes darted as though she was doing some figuring.

"The gunnysackers attacked Lumpkin and me when we were ten, so you were gone by then."

"Gunnysackers?" She was twenty-one now. "Who in the hell would attack a ten-year-old? What are gunnysackers? Who's Lumpkin?"

"Spicy!" came a slightly less powerful roar.

"That's Clay McCoy, Lumpkin's older brother. They're on this side of the river."

"No." Stone shook his head and swiped the rain off his

face. "Voices and noises echo up this mountain sounding closer than they are." The sky opened with full force then, soaking them to the bone. Feeling protective, he said, "You shouldn't go, Spicy. By the time you make it to the river it will be moving too fast to safely cross," he reasoned as the worsening storm made him blink. Reason? He'd lost all reason when it came to this woman.

"I'll be all right," she assured him, swiping rivulets of water out of her eyes. "I've crossed the Tug Fork River during squalls."

"Stay with me tonight and you can show me where you live tomorrow."

"No!" Spicy all but shrieked and flattened her right hand in the opening of his shirt. "You'd be shot. Only on voting day can West Virginia Hatfields venture into the McCoy woods on Blackberry Creek. And then it's just to see how the handful of Kentucky Hatfields is faring in the election. You've been away too long to realize just how much some Hatfields and McCoys dislike each other."

"I realized it the day a McCoy killed my father."

Spicy moved her hand and cupped it over her eyes. "Are you sure it was a McCoy?"

"A shot was fired and a man, who was never identified, was seen crossing the Tug Fork back into Kentucky," he replied, still feeling her warm touch on his skin. "Regardless, I don't despise the McCoys."

"Maybe you have reason to despise us."

"Does that mean you hate all Hatfields?"

"My patient with tonsillitis is a Hatfield."

"Spicy!" came the bellowing voice again.

"I have to go," Spicy said earnestly.

"I don't want you to go," Stone heard himself admit. The blowing rain beaded her nipples against her thin bodice taunting him with the image of molding her breasts to his chest and kissing her. "But if you're determined to go, at least," he nodded at the horse, "Logan and I can get you to the bottom of the hill. I want to see you make it across the river safely."

Stone untethered the horse, grabbed his mane, mounted and tugged Spicy up behind him. Her skirt slid past her knees and her arms wrapped around his waist. With her soft breasts pressed to his back and her nearly naked legs molded to his thighs, Stone choked off a groan.

"They can't recognize me from this distance. Anybody could be riding across this mountain or through the woods," Spicy said as if reassuring herself. The horse galloped past the clearing and upon entering the forest, she added, "Only take me down the hill to the edge of the trees. They won't know I've been up here if I come out by your blueberry patch."

"Are the men looking for you going to hurt you?" Stone asked with concern as the thick woods provided some shelter from the storm.

They were halfway down the hill before Spicy answered him with, "Stay out of sight for your sake and don't cross the river."

"If I don't cross the river how will you show me your magic?"

"Spicy!" It was two voices together this time.

They'd reached the edge of the forest. Spicy released her hold on Stone and slid off the horse before he could help her dismount. She lifted her skirt, darted into the blueberry patch and then followed the path to the riverbank. The rain was relentless and the river raging. But she grabbed her pole and pushed off across the water on her raft. Just as he realized he'd not said what her patient needed, the Kentucky trees parted.

Staring, Stone breathed, "My God."

CHAPTER 8

He's a giant.

That was Stone's first thought about the blond man across the river. He had to be almost seven feet tall, at least three hundred pounds. In sheer fascination Stone watched him wade into the rushing water. Then a second man with a bushy orange beard emerged from the woods and glowered across the river. But at Spicy's request, Stone remained out of sight.

"Stay there!" Spicy's voice drifted to Stone.

She wasn't addressing him, she was waving back the blond man. She'd poled three-quarters of the way across the churning water when floating debris crashed into her raft. As the raft spun, she floundered desperately trying to regain her footing. Her pole snapped dropping her halfway over the side of the raft and slamming her headfirst against the debris. Spicy tumbled into the river and vanished under the surface of the river. Riding out of the woods, Stone didn't care who saw him.

"Spicy!" the giant shouted, waist deep in the river.

Stone leaped from Logan to the riverbank. When he yanked off his boots, his Bowie knife stayed in the right one. Stone strode into the water as the smaller man across the river jerked a rifle out of a sling on his back. He seemed oblivious to the woman who had disappeared in the river as he walked to the water's edge and raised his gun. The giant fished a limp Spicy from the treacherous undertows known to have taken many strong swimmers to a watery grave. Knee-deep in the Tug Fork, in the onslaught of rain and wind, Stone swiped rain out of his eyes with his forearm as Spicy's head hung backward against the giant's shoulder.

Cupping his hands around his mouth, Stone yelled, "Is she alive?"

No one answered. The man toting the rifle aimed it at him as the blond man carried an unresponsive Spicy onto the Kentucky riverbank. With the fury of the tempest, Stone figured a bullet wouldn't find its mark. A shot sounded and a sapling behind him split in two. Damn feud, Stone thought standing his ground as it were in the river. He had purposely not called out Spicy's name. That way, she could deny knowing him if she needed or wanted to. As far as those men on the opposite bank knew, he was just a passerby who witnessed a woman falling into the river. With his next breath, relief charged through Stone's anger to touch his lips as Spicy wrapped an arm around the giant's neck.

Thank God. She was alive.

The smaller man rubbed his forehead as though baffled by Stone's smile in the face of a rifle. Stone raised his chin as if to say, until next time. As the giant carried Spicy into the woods the man with the orange beard turned, smacked some branches aside, and followed. Only then did Stone wade out of the turbulent water. Riding the stallion back up the sloping hill and across the clearing in front of his house, Stone headed to the copse of trees where he'd been when Spicy had called hello. According to Aunt Hilda, Jet had left their boyhood canoe there.

≈

"Hush up, Pepper," Spicy moaned, wishing the rooster would crow only at daybreak. But this fellow crowed when he hunted for food— particularly berries—defended his territory against predators or was bored and wanted attention. "It's still dark."

Yesterday, her head had smacked that pile of debris so hard, she had blacked out before hitting the water. She barely registered Lumpkin carrying her home. On her porch, she recalled him wading into the river and thanked him for saving her life. Clay was nowhere to be seen. Lumpkin had said Clay had taken off to Ol' Ranel McCoy's place after shooting at a stranger across the river. Imagining Stone dead, Spicy had stiffened with terror. But Lumpkin assured her Clay's bullet had missed. Spicy had hugged Lumpkin and sent him on his way. In a woozy fog, she had managed to heat some water, sink into her tin tub and bathe away the blood and gritty river remains from her hair and skin. Donning an age-soft nightgown, she'd crawled into her bed where a nightmare of drowning washed over her. She had awakened gasping for air. Now the pounding on her front door matched the pounding in her head.

"Spicy!" came a voice through the latched door.

"Pignuts," Spicy whimpered as Pepper continued to caution her from a distance.

Clay. Nauseous from her headache or because of Clay's arrival was a toss-up. To Spicy, Clay was as useless as the bitter hickory nut or pignut as Papa had called them. Managing to roll out of bed she lit a lamp. Then slowly pulling on a robe over her gown she padded out of her bedroom to the front room. She spied little Nutmeg, having been kicked once too often by Clay, peeking out from behind the sofa. Setting the lamp on the table, as soon as Spicy unlatched the door Clay barged in shoving her out of his way. She stumbled sideways and glared at Clay's back as he craned his head this way and that. Had he expected to find someone with her? Stone Hatfield, maybe?

"What are you doing here before the sun is up, Clay?"

"I come to see what's afoot with you," he said and pivoted.

Spicy stared. "You shaved off your beard." Only a bushy orange mustache had survived his razor, which she figured he'd left to mask his missing front tooth. The beard being gone revealed a receding chin and pasty skin instead of a strong jaw and a chin with a cleft like Stone's. "Why did you suddenly shave?"

"Ain't sudden!" Clay snorted and frowned. "Been fixin' to shave fer a spell."

Spicy wondered if that spell was since Clay had spied a clean-shaven Stone Hatfield. She knew better than to suggest that reason as she eased into a spindle-back chair at the table.

"If you came to see how I'm feeling, I'm alive. You can go." Spicy knew as she said the words, he'd be harder to get rid of than that. Sure enough he shook his head. "Clay, I need to rest and you need to be with Polly."

"Polly ain't my concern richeer'n now."

"She should be. Don't let me keep you from tending her or your moonshine still."

He kicked the door shut and grinned. "I's gonna tend you."

Clay yanked her off the chair and into his arms. Compared to Stone Hatfield, Clay lacked not only height but at least twenty-five pounds of hard muscle. However Spicy was no match for him, especially in her weakened state. She pushed at his chest with her fists, but his mouth clamped over hers. He tasted of chewing tobacco and dirty mustache. She bit his lip.

Clay yelped. "Damn you, woman!" He swiped at the blood on his mouth, released her and staggered back. "You said we had to wait 'til we's hitched. I's tired of waitin'."

Pointing at the door, she spat, "Get out, Clay."

"Didje let Hatfield kiss you acrost the river?"

Spicy instantly masked her surprise, but didn't deny

having met Stone. Cautiously she asked, "What makes you think he's a Hatfield?"

"Ol'Ranel knows ever'thing." The sneer spreading Clay's lips revealed his yellowed bottom teeth, chilling her despite the warm morning. "I got me a hankerin' to go huntin' fer a great big Hatfield. After I bag him I'll skin him fer ya."

Fear and anger surfaced quickly and Spicy said, "That man is a newcomer. He's done nothing to you. He's a doctor from Philadelphia. Leave him be."

Clay grabbed the back of her neck and jerked her nose to nose. "If'n he's in West Virginny, he'll side with them cussed Hatfields in a feud. And if'n Dr. High and Mighty crosses the Tug Fork," his grip tightened, "or me and *my* pet, I's gonna kill him."

"I said—" Spicy's hiss broke with fury. "Get out!" Instead, Clay crushed his mouth over hers again. Tasting the blood she'd drawn she almost retched. Savagely he grabbed her left breast. Spicy forced her head to the right, slapped his clean shaven jaw and called, "Lumpkin, are you out there?"

"Yes'm." The door burst open. Lumpkin ducked and entered the cabin. With a blank expression, he sized up the picture of her struggling in Clay's arms. "Ta farm?"

"Yes, to your farm with him," Spicy said.

"Yes'm." Lumpkin put his hand on Clay's shoulder to drag him out.

"Get yer hand off me." Clay shoved at his brother's hand which didn't budge. Swiping at his bloody lip, he said, "You crossed the Tug Fork to see that uppity-dressed Philadelphy, didn'tje?"

Spicy squared her shoulders. "For the third time, get out!"

Clay's mouth turned down at the corners. "Just figure on my next shot not missin'," he threatened as Lumpkin dragged him out of the cabin.

What about the magic she'd promised to show Stone?

The magic would be so much better on her side, but she could take it to him.

"G'bye, Spicy," Lumpkin managed over his shoulder.

Exhausted and her head still aching, Spicy whispered, "Goodbye, Lumpkin."

∾

THE NEXT TIME Spicy'd had to deal with Clay was far worse. That day had turned as tragic as the attack on Lumpkin in the blueberry patch, as sad as the afternoon her parents passed, and as terrifying as the evening she nearly drowned. With an unrelenting combination of these nightmares plaguing her, restful sleep had been elusive. Each night, from the moment her head touched the pillow until Pepper crowed, she tossed and turned with guilt and grief.

That was until the night Spicy found herself twining coal-black hair around her fingers as quicksilver eyes narrowed in approval. A cocky smile played on lips scant inches from hers. A deep voice soothed her. Rippling muscles held her against a rock-hard chest. Enticed by his irresistible masculinity she wound her arms around his neck. Flesh heated. Desire danced.

Pepper cock-a-doodle-dooed.

Spicy opened her eyes expecting to find Stone in bed with her. Had that only been a dream? It seemed so real. In reality Stone probably had a wife and ten children in Philadelphia. Even if he didn't, so what? Well, he was gorgeous. A real doctor. But he was a Hatfield. A blood enemy. No, he didn't believe in blood enemies. And neither did she.

Spicy sighed in relief when no pounding met with her front door after Pepper's warning. The rooster must have realized it was not daybreak and everything was fine because he quieted. Wishing she could pick up her dream where she'd left off, Spicy took hold of the damp cloth she'd placed on her forehead before falling asleep. Turning the cloth to the cool side she smoothed it over her forehead and tucked her hands under her cheek. The cornhusk mattress cradled her body and a pillow stuffed with chicken feathers cushioned her head. A warm breeze fluttered the chintz curtains, scenting her bedroom with roses. She closed her eyes.

"Stop being a ninny over Stone Hatfield."

CHAPTER 9

STONE HAD HEARD A ROOSTER COCK-A-DOODLE-doo and stopped in his tracks, hoping the next sound wasn't the cocking of a gun. All was quiet until the flapping of wings came his way. Roosters were protective and could be aggressive. This one halted directly in front of him, clucked, and waited. Taking his chances at getting pecked or spurred or both, Stone leaned over and patted his neck. Satisfied, the rooster clucked and strutted away into the darkness.

Standing up again, Stone paused for a good five minutes and just listened. He knew it was dangerous and dumber than hell for him to be in McCoy territory. But then, wasn't that why he'd ventured across the Tug Fork River at night? Partly, yes. But mostly he didn't want to bring the feud to Spicy's door. Silently, he eased around the side of a log cabin which lay nestled in a pocket of this dense Kentucky forest. All around him, shade trees blocked the pale light of the moon and stars, rendering the woods almost pitch-black. Reaching the front of the cabin, a lantern flickered on a windowsill.

The boyhood canoe had been so riddled with decay and holes he'd had to chop down a tree for the wood needed to basically rebuild it. He'd cursed the days lost but finally the canoe was water tight. With no oars to be found, not that they'd been usable anyway, he'd fashioned a couple and paddled across the river. According to Ellison Hatfield's directions he'd found Raccoon Hollow and trailed a well-worn path along Blackberry Creek until he'd spotted this cabin. But was it Spicy's cabin? If not, he'd apologize and leave. If so, would she be alone? The possibility she could be in bed with one of the two men he'd seen her with the other day tied a knot in Stone's stomach. If a giant with blond hair or a man sporting a bushy orange beard answered the door he'd say he had the wrong cabin and, in every way that mattered, the statement would be true. He hoped he'd find Spicy all alone. Wouldn't know until he knocked.

The yellow lantern light beckoned him.

Crossing a grassy yard to the porch, Stone noted weathered shutters were the cabin's only defense against the elements. During the winter people sometimes placed greased paper over glassless windows to help deflect the cold and snow. The scent of roses came from underneath some of the small, high windows and he wondered if rosebush thorns discouraged unwanted visitors. Focused on the gaping holes, where glass panes should be, Stone walked up the porch steps and almost stepped on someone sprawled across the wooden planks.

"Spicy?" came a groggy grumble.

Stone stopped short once again. At least he had found Spicy's home. In answer to the question he said, "No," and stepped back. It was the blond giant. "Hell."

"Hell-o." The man rubbed his eyes and asked slowly, "Who're you?"

"Who are you?" Stone countered.

The elephantine man got to his feet. In the lantern light, he held out a hand the size of a ham hock. Stone took it, figuring the man outweighed him by nearly a hundred pounds.

"Big Lump McCoy," he said with effort and let go of Stone's hand.

"Nice to meet you." So this was sweet and harmless

Lumpkin, the man Spicy didn't want him to hurt. "I'm a friend of Spicy's. Stone Hat— just Stone."

"Just Stone." The man's frown seemed to be from concentration, not anger.

Stone realized Big Lump was slow. "Is Spicy home?"

"Yes, sir."

"Will you tell her I'm here?"

Big Lump said, "Cain't."

"How come?"

"She's ta sleep."

Stone said, "I want to make sure she's all right." Big Lump squinted, perhaps trying to decide if Stone looked familiar. To ease Big Lump's worry and give them common ground, he said, "Thank you for fishing Spicy out of the river the other day, Big Lump."

Big Lump beamed. "Love Spicy."

Did the rifle-toting man, who'd been with Big Lump that day, also love Spicy? If the man before him was Lumpkin, did that mean the man who'd shot at him was Clay? Was Clay McCoy in love and in bed with Spicy at this very moment?

Stone steeled himself. "Is Spicy alone, Big Lump?"

"No, Just Stone." Big Lump plopped a hand on Stone's shoulder. "We's here."

Stone didn't know if 'we' was himself and Big Lump or Clay and Big Lump or someone else altogether. He was back to finding out for himself. He wondered if knocking on the cabin door would bring that rifle in his face.

"I come in peace, Big Lump. You can go back to sleep now."

"Yes, sir." Big Lump stretched out on the porch floor again.

"Want me to put out the lantern on the window sill for you?" Stone asked.

"Skeered of dark."

Stone couldn't imagine the big man being afraid of anything. But he left the lantern burning. When Big Lump pointed at the door instead of knocking, Stone opened it. A second lantern softly illuminated an immaculate cabin with a cloth covered table and four spindle-back chairs directly in front of him. To his left was a hearth. In Philadelphia, they had cast-iron stoves but in Tug Valley many people still cooked over open fires. Scanning to the right was a sofa, a couple of overstuffed chairs and a small bookcase. He shut the cabin door and stepping up to the table he placed the items he'd brought with him on it. Picking up the lantern he saw two open doors along the back wall. Walking to the one on the left, he peered into a bedroom with two empty beds. He made his way to the room on the right and sucked in his breath.

In a far corner, on a bed was an unforgettable woodland nymph. All alone. Facing him, Spicy lay on her side, a cloth on her forehead and hands under her cheek. A warm night, no blanket covered her. A breeze fluttered a curtain at the window and wafted the scent of roses into the bedroom. Spicy's sugar-maple curls fanned out over her pillow and around her white nightgown. The curve of her breast showed temptingly in the lantern's flickering light. As if his bold curiosity had penetrated her sleep, Spicy rolled over and faced the wall. She'd hidden her breasts from Stone's rapt gaze but never had a gauzy gown hugged a sexier bottom.

Only Spicy possessed the power to hypnotize him like this and was doing so even in her sleep. He remembered how this stunning beauty's voice had bewitched him the moment she'd first spoken. Her accent was flavored with the East Coast. How could that be since she lived in Tug Valley? Stone rubbed his temple and smiled. Spicy's scratching had been endearing and her explanation of pig piffle had made him laugh for the first time in ages.

Spicy herself was honest-to-goodness mountain magic. Admiring her fanny, Stone imagined how good it would feel to flatten his hands to her rounded, feminine flesh. Hearing her whimper, he made sure they wouldn't be interrupted and then strode back into her room. He set the lantern on her bedside table. Was she crying? He picked up a cloth that had fallen on her pillow and placed it on the table. Another sob brought Stone to sit down on her bed.

"Spicy?" he whispered.

She stirred, but didn't open her eyes. Stone saw a healing bruise on her forehead. She lay so vulnerable and virginal in her white gown. Was she a virgin? Why did he suddenly consider shooting any man who tried to bed her?

"Don't shoot him," Spicy whispered ironically, eyes closed.

Stone cocked his head. "Don't shoot who?"

Spicy grimaced and swiped at her mouth. "Get out."

"Spicy," Stone said more forcefully. "You're having a nightmare."

"Stone?" Her murmur had a faraway, dream-like quality.

"Yes."

Stone knew she wasn't fully awake but the sensuous rasp of his name in her bed fueled the desire already pumping through his veins. He gently rolled Spicy to her back. Her full breasts strained against the thin fabric of her gown. In the glow of the lantern, Stone could see the tips of her breasts were the same sugar-maple hue as her long curls. Tears had made wet spikes of her dark lashes and Stone knew she was still in the clutches of a bad dream.

"Help me," she whimpered.

Without hesitation, Stone tugged Spicy's sleep-pliable body off the bed and across his lap. Her head rested against his and warm tears slid into the open collar of his shirt. Her bottom pressed against his manhood and he pictured cupping her breast. But not like this. What was he doing here anyway? He didn't want Spicy. Like hell he didn't.

"Spicy, wake up." Stone felt her tense as she came around. "Don't be afraid," he soothed, loosening his grip to accommodate her waking up and letting her know she could crawl off his lap. "Tell me how I can help you."

"Stone!" She was fully awake now. Curls framed her face

in sexy disarray, but the tear stains on her cheeks were not the dimples he'd rather see. She indeed crawled off his lap and sat on her bed facing him. "How'd you get past Lumpkin?" she asked, swiping at the stray curls and tears on her cheeks.

"I'm a good negotiator."

"What are you doing here, Stone?"

"I saw you hit your head and lose consciousness the other day. I came to check on you."

"But you know it's not safe."

"I can take care of myself," he said. "Have you had headaches and nausea?"

"Yes, every day. I've been drinking ginger tea for the nausea." She lowered her head to her hands. "The headaches are lessening."

"You have a concussion. I told you not to cross that river."

She looked up, placing her hands in her lap. "I have a what?"

"Concussion. When someone hits their head like you did, it jostles the brain."

"That can make a person ill?"

"Yes."

"How? I want to know."

"The first brain surgeon in America, Dr. William Keen, lectured at the Philadelphia School of Anatomy and taught us that injured brains swell and press against the skull causing headaches, nausea, fatigue, and wooziness," Stone explained and in the lantern's glow Spicy stared at him as if making note of every single word he'd said. "Among other symptoms."

"I've had all of those symptoms."

"The effects are usually temporary. As the swelling subsides, the condition improves and symptoms disappear. Since your headaches are lessening, we won't have to drill a hole in your skull like the ancient Peruvians were known to do."

Spicy gave him a weak smile. "Lumpkin's injured brain never improved."

"What do you mean?"

"The gunnysackers I told you about were two people who pulled burlap bags over my head and Lumpkin's when we were in your blueberry patch," she whispered.

Stone asked, "Who were those people?"

"I don't know. They were never caught. But one held me back while the other one slammed a huge rock against Lumpkin's head. Twice. Luckily, Lumpkin doesn't remember it happening."

"Sometimes brain injuries are so traumatic the damage is irreversible. Another symptom is amnesia which often involves forgetting the event which caused the injury," Stone said as Spicy nodded her understanding. Hating the vicious and cowardly attack on a couple of ten-year-old kids, it explained Big Lump's mental deficiency. "But at least Big Lump didn't die." He paused and asked, "Spicy, why were you calling my name just now?"

"I had a nightmare Clay McCoy shot you," Spicy whispered and then looked away as if she wished she hadn't answered so quickly. "Just like he's threatened to do."

Sitting on her bed in the quiet of the night, this was his opening. "Exactly who is this Clay McCoy to you?"

CHAPTER 10

"CLAY AND LUMPKIN ARE DISTANT COUSINS." SPICY looked past the handsome man toward the porch and then turning her attention back to Stone she said, "I don't know how you crossed the river or found my cabin, but you can't be here."

"I wanted to see you." Stone's expression briefly hinted that he'd spoken before he could stop himself. "To make sure you were all right."

"I'm not all right." Spicy trembled from a horrific memory. "Since I saw you last, I lost two patients. I couldn't get a baby turned and the mother's stomach should have been cut open. But I can't do that."

"You know I can," Stone said. "Why didn't you send for me?"

"I did," Spicy cried, fresh tears welling in her eyes. "For the first time since Lumpkin was hurt I asked him to pole across the river into enemy territory to get you. Clay said he was afraid Lumpkin would get shot and offered to go in his place."

Stone splayed his hands. "So why didn't Clay go in his place?"

"He did!" Spicy balled both fists and smacked the mattress on either side of her hips. "You know he did."

"I know he did not. I've been home every day rebuilding an old canoe which brought me across the river tonight. I've had no visitors."

"Liar," Spicy accused, but without much conviction. "Clay said he begged you to come. But you refused to help us because Polly and her unborn baby were McCoys."

"My God," Stone growled under his breath.

"Clay said he offered you money and moonshine." Even as Spicy said the words, she wasn't at all convinced of the story she'd been told. "Clay took so long trying to persuade you to help by the time he returned, Polly and the baby were dead."

"None of what McCoy told you is true," Stone said. "He is the liar here, Spicy. Clay McCoy is dangerous. After you fell into the river, his priority was in shooting at me rather than saving you. Now he's let an innocent woman and baby die."

Spicy shook her head. "I don't think Clay wouldn't let Polly die because she claimed the baby was his." Her shoulders slumped as she confided, "Clay says it's my fault they died because I didn't know what to do."

"Maybe it was more important for McCoy to get rid of me than to help you save them."

Wiping a tear, Spicy felt confused and asked, "What do you mean?"

"An unprovoked killing of a man, even a Hatfield, could make Clay McCoy look bad in your eyes, right?" Stone waited and when she nodded, he said, "But telling you he begged me for help and I refused makes me look like the villain."

"All I know for certain is Polly and her baby are dead."

Stone reached for her and Spicy pictured crawling into his arms. But keeping her guard up, she shrank into the corner of her bed against the log wall and locked her arms around her legs. Stone clenched his fists atop his thighs as Spicy rested her cheek on her knees and sobbed.

"Aww, Spicy, please don't cry. I've lost patients, too," he

soothed. Taking her hand and unwinding her arm from around her legs, he lightly tugged. "C'mere."

"No." She yanked free. "You're a blood enemy, Stone Hatfield."

For a moment, as they faced each other on her bed, silence reigned. But Spicy inwardly rebuked herself because neither she nor Stone believed in blood enemies. She didn't despise the Hatfields and yet she'd singled him out as the villain in this situation. That wasn't fair. What she despised was the stupid feud.

"When my father was shot I was living in Philadelphia," Stone swallowed hard and continued with empathy, "I was mad at the whole world for a while. But my mother wrote to me saying we had to assume it was an honest hunting accident. She said it might help me to move forward by helping others heal. That sealed my decision to study medicine."

Contritely, Spicy said, "Tell your mother she is a smart lady."

His gray eyes misted. "I can't."

Spicy had seen this same mist the last time his mother was mentioned. "What do you mean you can't?"

"I mean she's gone."

"Will she be back soon?"

"No." Stone's crooked smile seemed to say he had wondered the same thing. "Of all people I should have helped I was too late to save my own mother. She died shortly before I returned to Tug Valley."

"Oh no." Regret nailed Spicy to the wall. Despair burned her throat. Sympathy seized her heart. Compassion pulled her out of the corner. When she spoke her voice shook. "I am truly sorry. I would have done what I could for your mother had the Hatfields sent for me."

"Thanks." Stone nodded as though he believed her. Then he stared down at his hands as if plagued with guilt and grief, similar to hers, at not having prevented death.

"I couldn't save my folks from dying of food poisoning.

So I understand how you feel not only as the offspring but as someone whose desire is to heal."

"Losing them both at once must have been very difficult. You have my condolences."

"Thank you," Spicy said. She thought he'd look up. He didn't. Maybe he was clearing the mist from his eyes. When Stone remained quiet, she impulsively took his hands and ran her thumbs over his knuckles. His hands were so much larger than hers. Clay's hands were big, too, and he'd been rough with her on numerous occasions especially when she'd refused his attentions. But Stone's were the hands of a man who healed people, not hurt women and children. "Stone, some things are in God's hands, not ours."

Stone's head raised and his shoulders squared. "I hope you told McCoy that when he blamed you for those deaths." Spicy shrugged and pulled on her hands, but Stone held tight. "Despite the hatred you feel for me as a Hatfield, I certainly don't hate you, Spicy."

When Clay had come back from West Virginia empty-handed Spicy, distraught by the loss of lives, had initially been furious with Stone. But even before Stone had presented his side she had known in her heart of hearts this man before her, this surgeon, would never let a mother and baby die because of their last name.

"I don't hate you, Stone."

"I promise you if Clay McCoy had come to me for help, I would have been here in a heartbeat." Stone had stated that firmly, eyes unblinking. After a moment he asked, "Despite Polly saying McCoy was the baby's father, did she have a husband?"

"No, Polly wanted Clay to marry her."

"Why didn't he?"

"Because my father betrothed me to Clay before he and my mother died after eating some bad pork. Clay's determined to hold me to that bargain." Spicy hung her head. "That makes me doubly responsible for Polly's misery and her and her baby's deaths."

"Spicy, that's just not true. You tried your very best to save them, didn't you?" He paused as she nodded, her head still bowed. "Do you believe Clay fathered Polly's baby?"

"Yes."

"Then if I were you," Stone put a finger under Spicy's chin and lifted her head until their eyes met, "I'd give a great deal of thought as to why Clay McCoy didn't get me here. If McCoy had any intention of saving Polly he would have dragged me here hogtied or walked me at the end of his rifle if I'd refused to come."

That statement was so true, Spicy winced. Her throat closed with emotion. As if to reinforce his words, Stone gently squeezed her hands before letting go. The warm breeze fluttered the curtains again and a loud snore said Lumpkin wasn't innocently eavesdropping.

"I believe you would have saved Polly and her baby, but you're confusing me with doubts about Clay."

"I'm clarifying the truth for you about Clay McCoy."

"Stop it."

"When hell freezes over."

Heaven, to Spicy, had been holding Stone's hands. Every nerve in her body was acutely aware of the close proximity of the gorgeous rogue in the snug confines of her cabin. As Stone raked his fingers through his hair, lantern light played with the coal-black waves. Was his hair soft? She wanted to find out. Spicy wondered what his caress would feel like. He clenched his jaw and she studied his lips. How many women had been lucky enough to kiss him? An odd pang pinched her heart at that image. He sighed and she detected the sweet scent of apple. Like Eve in the Garden of Eden, a rush of the forbidden swept over Spicy. When Stone rubbed his temple, a lock of hair fell across his forehead. Spicy lifted her hand to brush it into place.

The movement made Spicy aware Stone could see way too much through her age-thin gown. She'd certainly remembered her robe before Clay had barged in. She lowered her hand and folded her arms under her breasts.

That pushed her cleavage into view and Stone's smoldering gaze lingered on her scantily clad bosom. She quickly criss-crossed her arms over her bosom and Stone cocked a brow as he stifled a grin.

"If you're here just to see what you can see you can get out you big, randy billy goat."

Stone chuckled. "Randy billy goat?"

"Randy means without sexual restraint."

"I am the most sexually restrained man you'll ever meet, you backward little hillbilly."

Spicy's breath caught in her throat. This book-learned, city doctor knew how ignorant she was. This time she crossed her hands over her heart to cover the sound of it breaking.

"Hey, I'm sorry." Stone placed a hand over his own heart. "I'm from the hills across the river. If you're a hillbilly, so am I. It's not easy being restrained around you but that's no excuse for looking. I apologize. Forget about me. You're the one with the concussion."

Forget about him? Spicy knew she would never forget Stone Hatfield. Truth be told, she had looked him up and down more than once. She needed to start playing fairly. Right now.

"My concussion has improved like you said and I appreciate you checking on me." Spicy raised her chin and sat up straight. "I live in Tug Valley, so I am a hillbilly. Polly and her baby would be alive if I weren't backward."

"Surgeons lose patients every day," he reminded her. "How's the Hatfield with tonsillitis?"

"Abigail is better, but I'd like to hear your medical opinion."

"Is Abigail's father, Otis Hatfield?"

"Yes, he is."

"I know those Hatfields," Stone replied. "They live here on the Kentucky side, right?" When she nodded, he asked, "Does your offer to show me the mountain magic still stand?"

"Yes, it does." Spicy bobbed her head. "My word is good."

"So is mine. If Abigail continues to have trouble she should have a tonsillectomy which means her tonsils should be taken out."

Spicy flinched. "I wouldn't know how to do that." Gathering all her courage and fearing his complete rejection, she urged, "Help me move forward. Like you did, Stone."

Stone's voice harbored a ragged edge. "How can I help you move forward?"

Encouraged, she asked, "Do you plan to live here?"

"No, I just came for a long overdue visit with my mother and aunt. I'll escort my Aunt Hilda to the upcoming election and head back to Pennsylvania."

Spicy didn't take time to let that hurt. "Folks can't change these hills and valleys for the better with just one election."

"Gotta start somewhere." He shrugged. "Or a better tomorrow will never come."

"For better tomorrows," Spicy began, "until you leave, could you help me move forward by teaching me about cutting into folks?" Stone didn't answer. Pepper crowed. "Never mind." She waved her ridiculous request away. "It will be daybreak soon. You'd better go, before Clay steps over Lumpkin and shows up in my front room."

"McCoy won't show up in your front room."

"You need to slip out the back door here in my bedroom."

"I'm not afraid of McCoy." Stone stood up and tilted his head. "Are you afraid of him?"

"I'm afraid of him only for your sake," she replied, but couldn't meet his eyes.

"I'm not sure I believe that, but I don't want to cause you any trouble. Before I go, come into the other room with me. I brought you something."

Stone held out his hand and when she took it he tugged her off the bed. Toe-to-toe the attraction between them sizzled. With a knowing grin he turned away and she followed him on wobbly legs. Her basket set on the table. In it were her apron, pie tin, and a book on surgery. Spicy glanced up at Stone. The break in her heart turned into a smile on her lips. He'd planned to help her move forward even before she'd asked. Pepper squawked frantically.

"Mornin'," came Lumpkin's cheery voice from the front porch.

"She still sleepin', halfwit?" Heavy brogans clomped up the porch steps.

"Clay," Spicy mouthed, eyes wild. She grabbed Stone's hand and led him through the cabin to her room. Opening the back door, she whispered desperately, "Go."

"Are you well enough to pole across the river to come see me later?"

Clay called from the porch, "Mangled-mind's ou'chere. So, why's yer door latched?"

"Did you latch my front door?" Spicy asked Stone.

"Yes, I didn't want to be interrupted. Come join me for a noon meal."

"I'll try to smuggle myself out of here at dusk," she bargained. As she nudged him out of the door she whispered, "You get ten points for being brave enough to check on me."

CHAPTER 11

Sitting atop Logan, Stone peered through the trees near the Tug Fork River. It galled him to hide while he waited for Spicy to slip away. But just as she feared for his safety, he did for hers as well. This feud had been the furthest thing from his mind in Pennsylvania. But here, he was in the thick of it. Maybe he just needed to get out of these West Virginia hills and go home. He *was* home and here she came.

Sashaying out of her Kentucky valley, Spicy darted toward the river. Stone nudged Logan to the very edge of the cover of trees, stopping just short of the blueberry patch. He smiled in anticipation as she spotted him and waved. Watching her pick up one of several long poles off the ground and board the raft, Stone tensed even though the river was calm today. She was soon halfway across and Stone relaxed when her raft touched West Virginia soil. With a glance toward Kentucky, he dismounted the horse. Spicy stepped onto the riverbank and immediately started dragging the raft behind the blueberry patch.

"Spicy, what are you doing?"

"Clay can think the raft floated down the Tug Fork and I drowned for all I care."

Wishing it wasn't necessary, Stone took hold of the raft

and together they hid it. Back in the saddle, he took his foot out of the stirrup for Spicy and tugged her up behind him. Her slender arms curled naturally around his waist, but something hard lay between her chest and his back. Logan easily trotted up the gently sloping hill through the woods. Veering left they crossed the clearing to Stone's house. Reaching the hitching post, Spicy slid off the horse to the ground. As Stone joined her, he realized she wore a small pink apron made of the same pink fabric of her dress. From the apron pocket Spicy retrieved the medical book he had taken to her.

"So that's what was between us on the ride up the hill," he said, tethering Logan.

Hugging the book to her heart she said, "It's a magical book. I want to talk about all the fascinating sketches. The diseases, causes, cures, cases, and operations."

"We will," Stone said as they walked up the porch steps. Only she could mix sexy with studious. They crossed the porch and he welcomed her into his house. Having removed the coverings from the furniture it already felt more like the home he remembered. In the library above the fireplace, a black mantel clock with an ivory face, black numbers, and gold hands hadn't been touched in years. Finding the key behind the fancy gold left foot, he'd wound the clock, but sadly it had stopped again. "I made ham and beans for supper. It'll be ready soon."

"Smells wonderful," Spicy said in the foyer as the aroma wafted from the kitchen. "The first time I was in a house with a real kitchen or an upstairs was when I visited you here." She looked right into the parlor and left into the library. "Your home is beautiful."

"Thank you." Stone led her into the library where built-in bookshelves lined the wall behind an oak desk. Noticing Spicy taking in the mostly empty shelves he said, "When I moved out, I took the classics I liked which are in Pennsylvania. When my mother and brother, Jet, moved in with my Aunt Hilda over on Mate Creek, they didn't need to take much except for the books they wanted and their clothes. I'm surprised my mother didn't take the mantel clock. It was always my favorite thing in this house. But I didn't feel it was mine to take."

"Maybe your mother left it for you, Stone."

"Maybe so." He hadn't thought of that. With a chuckle and a shrug, he said, "Then again she may have left it because it only runs for an hour at a time."

"My father tinkered with clocks and taught me how they work. If I clean and oil it for you, it should run for a week at a time."

"Thank you. I'll take it with me when I leave." He swept a hand toward one of the two sofas. "Please sit."

"Do you have many books on medicine in Philadelphia?" Spicy asked, taking a seat on the comfortable sofa and holding the book in her lap.

"Yes. I was reading the newly published one I gave you on the way here," he replied. With an oval table between the matching sofas, he sat on the sofa opposite her. "I read as far as I could travel by train anyway. After that, it takes more effort to get into Tug Valley."

"I've never been on a train, but we need them as much as we need a hospital."

"True."

"I read in this book," Spicy tapped the cover, "that Benjamin Franklin was the primary founder of the school which became the University of Pennsylvania."

"Right. Franklin was a huge advocate of higher learning and wrote *Proposals Relating to the Education of Youth in Pensilvania* back in 1749."

"I didn't know that until I read the prologue about Franklin's aims of education," she said and noted, "Ironically, he spelled Pennsylvania incorrectly."

Stone chuckled. "He did. But all things considered, Ben Franklin was ahead of his time."

"Yes, he was. Please tell me about your hospital."

Wondering where to start, Stone splayed his hands and

then brought them together again in his lap. "Pennsylvania Hospital was founded in 1751, making it our nation's first hospital. In 1765, the University of Pennsylvania opened the nation's first school of medicine. When the University of Pennsylvania moved to its campus west of the Schuylkill River, the medical faculty convinced the trustees to build a teaching hospital. By eighteen 1874, the Hospital of the University of Pennsylvania became the nation's first teaching hospital built for a medical school."

Spicy shook her head in wonder. "How long have you been working there?"

"I started at seventeen in the medical library at Pennsylvania Hospital."

"If you moved there twelve years ago when you were sixteen, you're twenty-eight now," she said and he nodded. "How did you become a surgeon so young?"

He tilted his head and chuckled. "No one has ever asked me these questions."

"I'm so impressed and truly interested, please tell me."

Stone smiled, touched by the rapt look of awe on Spicy's face. "I went as far as I could go in school here and finished up the higher branch in Philadelphia at seventeen. I applied to the university's medical school and was accepted at eighteen. Being in the right place at the right time, at twenty, I transferred to a job in the new teaching hospital's surgical amphitheater."

"I read all about surgical amphitheaters in your book." Spicy gave the book a pat. "Pennsylvania Hospital's first one was built in 1804, establishing surgery as a recognized discipline. They are circular, at least thirty feet high and centered under a skylight. Do you often operate with more than a hundred people watching?"

Stone nodded. "Yes. Usually starting in the morning at eleven and finishing around two. That's when a surgeon has the best light. Working there proved invaluable. I got to know the surgeons and was allowed to observe any operation that interested me down on the floor as opposed to up in the gallery. One day I was fortunate enough to observe the chief of surgery, Dr. Victor Vanderveer. He asked questions, as teaching physicians do. I was able to answer correctly when students more advanced than I was couldn't. He took me under his wing and the next few years flew by." He chuckled and shrugged. "No pun intended."

Spicy sighed as if in wonder. "When did you perform your first surgery?"

"I assisted when I was your age. Twenty-one." The arching of her brow acknowledged that he'd bothered to figure her age as she had his. "Typically in a teaching hospital first you observe the procedures in the book I gave you. When you're qualified you assist the surgeon before performing any on your own. Since Vanderveer was the head of the department he allowed me to assist him and then operate early on. I graduated from the school of medicine in 1878 and have been practicing and teaching medicine the past four years."

"Besides saving lives of course, what's your favorite part?"

"Anesthesia," Stone replied seriously then chuckled. "Prior to 1840, patients were limited to opium, liquor, or a knock on the head with a mallet to render them unconscious."

"Yes." Spicy appreciated the very real horror blended with his sense of humor and smiled. "Mama said chloroform was available and used on Papa when they set his broken leg."

"Must have been a bad break. Tell me more. I want to hear about you now."

"When I can't sleep I drink cinnamon tea with a tincture of magnolia bark." She held up her thumb and index finger close together to indicate how small a tincture was. "Then I slide rose petals and mint leaves under my pillow." A self-effacing laugh escaped her and she said, "I admit it's somewhat unreliable and not suitable for surgery."

Stone chuckled again. "Where on earth did you come from?"

"Kentucky," Spicy replied as Stone narrowed his eyes as if he wasn't sure about that. She shrugged her left shoulder and added, "If I am to believe anesthesia is your favorite part of surgery, surely you can believe I'm mostly from Kentucky."

"Mostly?" Stone smacked his knee and laughed. "I knew it. Your accent, or lack of one, gives you away. Explain what mostly means or I'll accent my lack of sexual restraint." In teasing Spicy, did he detect excitement along with a touch of trepidation on her face? Yes, because her blueberry eyes sparkled as she scratched her neck. Placing his book on the oval table, she eyed the front door. He cocked a brow and said, "You don't need to run from me."

"Says you. Pretty sure I can make it to the door first," she challenged.

"I doubt it." Stone grinned. They'd gone from serious to playful in a blink of an eye. Enjoying every minute, he stood, rounded the table and sat beside her on the sofa. "But I've only got a tincture of restraint left," he joked, "so you better talk fast about where you're from."

With a saucy tone in her voice, Spicy said, "Try to keep up." Though sounding brave, she rubbed her arm and then her elbow. When Stone tilted his head, she rattled off facts in rapid fire, "My accent came from my mother, Rosalind Hayden. Mama was a gracious and beautiful belle who grew up in Norfolk, Virginia, a pretty seaport on the southern tip of the Chesapeake Bay. Grandpa Hayden was a sailor. In his youth, he sailed to the Spice Islands and lived there for a few years. When he returned to the colonies it was with a whole passel of plants and spices he'd smuggled out of the Dutch East Indies."

"I've never known anyone who could talk as fast as you. Slow down." Something occurred to him and he asked, "When did your itching first occur?"

"Just now."

"I mean did it start before you met me?"

"Yes." She thought a moment. "Right after Lumpkin was hurt."

"I will never hurt you, so don't be nervous."

"But there's Clay."

"Who keeps you on edge. Did he hurt you after I left this morning?"

"I handled it."

"That means yes." Stone frowned and with concerted effort changed the subject. "Come on, before we look at the book and have supper I'll give you your first upstairs tour while you tell me how your mother came to live in Kentucky." When Spicy dug at her collarbone, Stone snared her hand. He tugged her off the sofa and led the way to the foyer. Never letting go of her hand, they started up the wide staircase. "Talk to me, I like the sound of your voice."

Those sensual dimples appeared on her blushing cheeks. "My father, Calvert McCoy, opposed slavery even before the Civil War was declared. To honor his beliefs he joined the Union Navy, which as you may know was founded in Philadelphia."

"I did know that," Stone replied. "What was your father's job in the Navy?"

"He was a barber."

"A barber?"

"And a sailor," she laughed. Stone grinned, much preferring Spicy's smiles and laughter to her fright and tears. "Someone has to cut the crew's hair. Papa told me stories about the USS Monitor. It was the first ironclad warship built for the Union Navy in early 1862 and he was fascinated by it," Spicy said as they climbed the stairs holding hands. "But you're right about my father's leg. It was broken both above and below the knee while he was serving. He was taken off his ship to a hospital where my mother read to patients and fed those who needed such help. Papa was alone in Norfolk and Mama spent extra time with him while he recuperated in the hospital."

"No wonder they put him to sleep. Did such a badly broken leg lead to the end of his Navy career?"

"Yes. Grandpa Hayden was the originator of our family tonics, teas, and remedies using spices. He took them to the hospital and those remedies helped Papa regain his strength. My father and grandfather had sailing in common and became great friends." They reached the top of the staircase as she said, "When Papa was released from the hospital and honorably discharged from the Navy, he was welcomed as a fellow Yankee into the Hayden household." She looked up at Stone and said, "I was soon conceived."

"So you were born in Norfolk, Virginia?" he asked stopping in the middle of the second-floor landing.

"Yes, two months after the Civil War was declared in April of '61. Grandma Hayden passed away the day after I was born, but she and Grandpa both hoped I would be named Spicy. Norfolk fell to Union forces in May of '62 and then Grandpa passed away. With nothing holding us back East, we moved to Kentucky where Papa had inherited land from his folks. They're gone now, but I have a few cousins like Lumpkin and Cl—"

"Yeah," Stone cut her off before she completed the last word. He slid his hands under her arms and, muscles flexing, lifted her up against him. "Slow down."

"I explained what *mostly* meant," Spicy reminded him.

"Only after I coerced you to confide in me. But don't talk so fast you'll faint."

"I'll do my best not to swoon."

Stone detected a sassy twinkle in her blueberry eyes as he lowered her feet to the floor. Placing gentle hands to her soft cheeks, he lowered his head. Spicy touched her dainty hands to his chest but didn't push him away. When his lips brushed hers only a whisper of her warmth teased his mouth but liquid lightening raced through his veins. As Stone sealed his mouth to hers, Spicy slid her fingers under his suspenders and tugged herself closer.

"Mmm," he groaned.

CHAPTER 12

CURIOUS DESIRE AND BLOSSOMING HUNGER RACED
through Spicy from head to toe.

Stone's kiss was so devastatingly delicious, Spicy feared
she was asleep. It wouldn't be the first time she'd awakened
and nearly cried out at finding she'd only dreamed of
Stone's kiss. Clay's mouth had crushed hers painfully.
Stone's supple lips coaxed hers to respond. Releasing her
grip on his suspenders, Spicy trailed her hands up his chest
to his broad shoulders. She had imagined this a hundred
times. In turn, Stone flattened his hands to her back,
burying them in her hair and molding her breasts to his
chest. Shoulder muscles rippled under Spicy's palms. As
their kiss deepened, she caressed his neck before threading
her fingers up through the coal-black hair at the back of his
head. It was soft and thick. She felt Stone shiver just before
his arms circled her in a sinewy hug. Stone's embrace was
commanding. Clay's grip had been punishing. Spicy trembled with breathless anticipation as Stone's hands slid up
her ribs. When his thumbs brushed the sides of her breasts,
she moaned.

Survive his kiss. Don't succumb to it.

Spicy heard her inner voice and decided she was

surviving to the fullest. But when he palmed her breasts, she pushed against him and broke the spellbinding kiss.

"Stone Hatfield, have you lost your restraint?"

Hadn't she?

"If I had," his eyes were hooded, his voice husky, "we'd be doing this naked in my bed."

Spicy's nipples beaded and Stone must have felt it because his smile was a wicked one. Moving his hands to her wrists he wound her arms around his neck. Wrapping her in a band of steel, he closed his eyes and seared her lips with another sensational kiss. Somehow Spicy's fingers returned to Stone's hair. Somehow Stone's hands recaptured her breasts and a second moan escaped her. Stone broke the kiss this time and gave himself a shake. Feeling bold, Spicy swept a lock of hair away from his forehead and smiled.

Stone smiled back, grasped her hand and started the tour of the second floor. The first bedroom was large and sunny and the one his parents had shared. Stone said the next room belonged to Jet, who was younger than he by four years. The third and last bedroom was Stone's. With a high ceiling and tall windows it also had built-in bookshelves. Entering his room, Spicy gazed at the bed and her body heated with anticipation.

Anticipation of what exactly?

"It's a wonderful room." Letting go of Stone's hand, she picked up a fluffy pillow off the bed and hugged it to her. What would it be like to share this bed with Stone? "I mean it's a wonderful house for a boy to have grown up in."

"It was," Stone said. "Jet and I had a lot of adventures here on our mountains. We never ran out of places to explore and go hunting."

"I never met your brother but then, I went to school in Kentucky."

"By the time you poled across the river, Jet and my mother were living with my Aunt Hilda. Jet attended school in West Virginia just south of her place."

"I know the schoolhouse you mean. It's abandoned

now." A bit giddy as Stone walked toward her, Spicy said, "This doesn't feel like chicken feathers in this pillow."

"Goose down." Stone took her and the pillow in his arms. His head lowered and as he kissed her, she knew she was in danger of saying yes to whatever else he wanted to do. But she needed to say no, didn't she? Yes. But Clay always reacted badly to her refusals.

"Stone, no," she murmured against his warm coaxing lips.

Instantly, Stone's mouth left hers. His hands dropped to her waist. With a smile on his handsome face, he released her and winked. To show she wasn't upset she playfully thumped him with the pillow. Goose down flew. She gasped. Stone laughed and pulled her to him. When she tilted her chin up, he took the invitation to kiss her again. His low chuckle vibrated her lips. Spicy giggled against his mouth. He stepped back and tossed the pillow onto his bed.

Aflame from his kiss and touch, Spicy's trust soared. He would bring things to a halt if told. She barely stopped a pout from rising to her lips from not having his mouth on hers. He plowed his hands through his hair and took a deep breath. His stomach bowed inward and below his waist she saw male hardness distending his button fly. Heat surged in a secret place between Spicy's thighs. Her heart raced and her body tingled.

"Let's head downstairs," Stone suggested. "I'll scoop us up some of the ham and beans and we can have the last two slices of that pie you made. Then we'll look at the medical book."

It was all way too good to resist. Her own self-control definitely weakened from his kisses and caresses, Spicy eagerly accompanied him. In the kitchen, she tried without success to distract herself from her swirling thoughts about Stone by setting the table and putting the pie on plates. Stone ladled ham and beans into bowls and Spicy's mouth watered. Self-conscious, she found it a bit hard to eat in front of him. She finished all of her soup but only half of her piece of pie. He helped her out with the other half. Then returning to the library with cups of coffee, Stone lit lamps and they settled onto the sofa to study the medical book. Stone pointed out the latest findings on diseases and the newest treatments as well as the surgeries he had performed. Spicy asked a million questions to which he had the answers. Two hours flew by.

"I'd better go," Spicy said as moonlight glimmered through the window.

"Are you sure you're feeling strong enough to pole back across the river?"

"Yes. You've been quite the medicinal remedy I needed, Dr. Hatfield."

"Good." Stone grinned at the compliment, pulled her close and whispered, "It's dark. Stay with me tonight."

"In a separate bedroom?"

He stretched his arm out behind her along the top of the sofa. "Sure."

"Lumpkin would worry about me and tell Clay."

"If you can't stay, I hope you'll come back for supper again tomorrow."

"Abigail Hatfield's family invited me to supper tomorrow." She thought for a moment and suggested, "You should go and take a look at her throat. Since they know you they would be thrilled if you joined us, Stone."

"Whether or not I have supper, I'll walk you there and take a look at her tonsils."

"Because of Clay, it's too risky to walk with me in the afternoon," Spicy warned and gave him directions. "I'll meet you there at five."

Stone reluctantly agreed to that. He handed her the medical book and she carefully tucked it back into her apron pocket. Logan gave them a ride down through the woods and Spicy poled across the Tug Fork. It was so dark she couldn't see Stone by the time she called out she was safe on the Kentucky side. He called back. Then only the chirping of crickets could be heard. She sighed, wishing she'd stayed with him in West Virginia.

~

THE NEXT MORNING, feeling like her old self again, Spicy hopped out of bed and picked enough raspberries for two pies. One for Abigail's family and one for Stone, as promised. She baked the pies, saw a couple of patients, fed Pepper and the chickens, gave Nutmeg some honey from her beehives, and counted the hours until she would see Stone. Finally, packing up a warm pie, blueberry tea, and a jar of honey in her basket, it was time to leave for Abigail's.

When her friends' cabin came into view she saw Stone already on the Hatfields' porch. Wearing a summer jacket, white shirt, and dark britches, Stone was as dashing as ever. Otis and Martha, Abigail's parents, were indeed so thrilled their longtime friend and surgeon from Pennsylvania Hospital was paying them a surprise house call, they were literally fawning over him. It was to such an extent when Stone saw Spicy, he covertly rolled his eyes. Spicy laughed under her breath, unable to hide her happiness.

Surprisingly Lumpkin was also there. Hmm. If Spicy didn't know better she would have thought Abigail had a notion to spark with Lumpkin. Abigail was plump and plain and as sweet as could be. Lumpkin was smiling ear-to-ear as Abigail stood talking to him, with her hand on his arm. How perfect a union would be between two of the kindest people she knew.

"Hello Spicy," Martha Hatfield called. An older version of Abigail, Martha addressed Stone saying, "I believe I heard you say you and Spicy have already met."

"Yes, ma'am, that's right," Stone replied with a smile at Spicy.

The sunlight being brighter than lamplight, Stone examined Abigail's throat on the porch. He said it didn't look serious at the moment, but gave them the same advice about a tonsillectomy if the tonsillitis persisted.

"I brought blueberry tea and honey for your throat," Spicy told Abigail.

Otis, a chubby, good-natured fellow, ushered everyone inside, starting with Stone. Having accepted the supper invitation Stone pulled out a chair for Spicy. Watching him, Lumpkin managed to do the same for Abigail whom he called Abby. Everyone was soon discussing the upcoming election over smoked venison, succotash, boiled potatoes, and freshly baked corn pone.

"Our polling place is Jeremiah Hatfield's house," Otis said, between bites. "Like us, Jeremiah is one of the few Hatfields who lives in Kentucky."

"In West Virginia there is a school tax on the ballot I hope passes. I've been away too long to be eligible to vote for it or I would." Stone spread some of Spicy's honey on a slice of the bread-like corn pone and said to her, "I've heard honey is good for scraped toes."

"It is," she said, enjoying every minute.

"I hope the school tax passes, too," Abigail said. "I have the qualifications to teach."

Lumpkin, along with the others all smiled at her. Abigail had the perfect combination of compassion and patience to be a great teacher.

"I pray this election is a quiet one," Martha commented. "Last time, Tolbert McCoy and his sister Roseanna rode in on horseback. It wasn't long before Devil Anse's oldest son, Johnse Hatfield, and Roseanna McCoy were sparking. Next thing I knew they had left the polling place together. Ol' Ranel was against them being together as much as Devil Anse."

"Yes, I remember that very well," Spicy said. "When I heard Roseanna was expecting Johnse's baby I feared she was in for a bad time of it from the McCoy side of the family."

"A shame Johnse Hatfield wasn't allowed to marry her,"

Martha said with sympathy in her voice. "Then their baby died of measles."

"Ol' Ranel is still so angry, Roseanna has since become somewhat of an outcast and lives with different family members who need her help," Spicy summed up sadly.

"I don't remember Roseanna," Stone said. "But as a kid I saw Ol' Ranel a time or two."

"Ol' Ranel and Devil Anse fought for the same side during the Civil War." Otis shook his head and continued. "I always reckoned it was unlikely the feud started when Asa Harmon McCoy was shot and killed after fighting for the Union Army because he was considered a traitor by both Devil Anse and Ol'Ranel who were Confederates."

"Makes sense," Stone agreed. "I know Asa McCoy was killed by a Confederate guerilla unit called the Logan Wildcats. Devil Anse led that unit and Ol'Ranel also served with the Logan Wildcats."

"Right." Otis added, "There was never any retaliation by Asa's family because they couldn't defend him choosing to be a Yankee."

"That's the consensus," Stone said. "It's more likely the feud started over that hog."

"That hog was the straw that broke the camel's back because Ol' Ranel's real anger is not being a timber baron like Devil Anse," Otis offered this common, though somewhat controversial opinion. "Most of the Hatfields just plain got more money."

Spicy told herself Otis hadn't intended any harm, but just the same her shoulders sagged along with her spirits.

"Spicy?"

CHAPTER 13

"Yes?" So pretty in a plum-colored dress, Spicy looked at Stone with a smile.

"Didn't you bring a raspberry pie?" he asked to change the subject.

Stone winked at her and Spicy gave him an appreciative nod. Ever so graciously, she helped Martha serve the pie and received well-deserved accolades all around for her delicious dessert. Afterwards, he and Spicy thanked their hosts for the fine meal and were heartily encouraged to come back again soon. He heard Spicy quietly remind Big Lump not to mention him and they left the gentle giant beaming at Abigail. Stone snared Spicy's hand and asked to walk her home. Since the sun had set, she said she thought twilight would make it safe.

"Did you see Lumpkin and Abigail sparking?" Spicy asked.

"If by sparking you mean flirting, yes. Good for Big Lump."

"Those Hatfields have lived in Kentucky forever so even though Lumpkin is a McCoy, it's not dangerous for him to be sweet on Abigail," Spicy said as they strolled along Blackberry Creek. "But a West Virginia Hatfield always puts his life at risk in Raccoon Hollow."

"I have a gun."

"You do?" Her expression registered surprise as she looked up at him.

"Yes, a Colt .45. Day after tomorrow I'll have a second gun because I promised some other West Virginia Hatfields I'd go bear hunting with them."

"What Hatfields?"

"Devil Anse, Johnse, and Anse's younger brother, Ellison."

"They say Anse is short for Anderson and Devil was tacked on to Mr. Hatfield's name because of his devilish sense of humor. As you know, the McCoys don't think he's funny."

"I'm sure they don't."

Trekking through the thick trees of the hollow, after a few minutes Spicy said, "Johnse is married to Nancy McCoy now."

"See there?" Stone's smile was an encouraging one as he said lightheartedly, "Hatfields live and mingle on the Kentucky side and McCoys eat supper with a West Virginia Hatfield. Hatfields and McCoys even get married. We *can* get along."

Spicy replied, "I'd be interested in hearing Johnse's side of the story with Roseanna."

"I'll see what I can do."

They continued on, each lost in thought. Stone listened to owls hoot, frogs croak, and crickets chirp along the creek. He'd lost touch with these sounds in Philadelphia and realized how familiar they felt. Nearing Spicy's cabin, from a safe distance, they stopped to assess. The rooster pecked around a henhouse and a raccoon raced by. McCoy was nowhere in sight.

"Thank you for walking me home," Spicy said as they reached the porch steps. "Would you like to come in?"

"I'd better stay outside or I might not leave."

"Just for a minute? I made a raspberry pie just for you."

Stone fully expected her to open the door and half

expected to be met by Clay McCoy. Instead of opening the door, Spicy set her basket on a wooden bench underneath a small window next to her front door. A pillow and blanket also lay on the bench, which she said belonged to Lumpkin. Stepping onto the bench, she swept aside the curtains. Leaning head and shoulders into the window, her fanny draped over the sill.

"Now what are you up to?" It was all Stone could do to keep his hands off her.

"Unlatching my door." Her voice came from inside the cabin as her sexy derrière wiggled provocatively. "Clay can't fit in the window to unlatch the door."

"Are you ticklish?" Stone teased, putting his fingers to her ribcage.

"Don't you dare."

"I'll take that dare." Stone tickled her and Spicy laughed. He howled as she slipped further over the sill. "Falling on your head won't do your recent concussion any good."

"Then you'd better not let me fall."

Chuckling, he grasped her hips and asked, "Are you sparking with me?"

Halfway inside the cabin, she assured him, "I'll run to the river and drown myself before I spark with a big pig in a poke like you, Stone Hatfield."

"Is that right Spicy McCoy, my puddle of passion?"

As Spicy as her name, she shot back, "I'll be your puddle of passion when pigs fly."

Stone pulled her safely back through the window. As her toes touched the bench she whirled around so fast she fell into his arms. Stone gave the door a light kick and it swung open. Just inside, Stone's lips slashed across hers and her arms twined around his neck. When she returned his kiss, he seriously considered dipping his tongue into her sweet mouth. He wanted nothing more than to carry her straight ahead to the bedroom. Instead, with a will of iron, he broke the kiss. He planted her feet on the floor, but her arms stayed draped around his neck.

"I have to get outa here while I still can," Stone said, her breasts pressed to his chest.

"Because of the hostility," Spicy surmised. "I hope you never have to use it but at least you have your gun. I can feel it pressing into my tummy."

"That's not my Colt." Stone grinned at the naiveté on Spicy's beautiful face.

As his meaning dawned on her, Spicy slowly backed away. "I'll get your pie."

He lit a lantern on the kitchen table for her as she retrieved her basket from the porch and put his raspberry pie in it.

"Don't leave lanterns burning when you go to bed," Stone said feeling protective.

"I haven't gotten used to being alone at night."

So, it was Spicy and not Big Lump who was scared. "Do you mean alone since your folks died?" She nodded. "Doesn't Big Lump sleep on the porch every night?"

"I've told Lumpkin he could come inside and sleep in my folks' bedroom, but I guess he thinks that would be improper." Spicy shrugged. "And no, he only sleeps on the porch when there's been trouble with—"

"With what?" Stone thought a minute. "Clay?"

"You'll coerce no more confidences out of me, Dr. Hatfield," she said playfully and handed him the basket. Her enchanting dimples dotted her cheeks while her blueberry eyes glittered with mischief. "I can be as restrained as you."

"Tarnation." He teased her with her word, wanting to experience her magic all night long. "Latch the door," he grumbled then, knowing she latched it because of McCoy.

"Since you have a canoe now and are determined to cross the river whenever you feel like it," she rolled her eyes and then grew serious, "come back for the magic, Stone."

"When?"

"Day after tomorrow there will be a nearly full moon and the next night is the blue moon. You can only see the mountain magic on a night so deep the blue moon covers the forest in purple," she whispered. "When the mist hovers over the ground," Spicy slowly moved her hands across thin air, "the magic hides in the laurel thicket."

Stone was totally intrigued. "Does this magic have a name?"

CHAPTER 14

"Maybe." Spicy raised her brow in an unspoken challenge, hoping he'd want to find out.

Stone grinned. "I'll be back on the night of the blue moon if not sooner."

Wishing she didn't have to be concerned about his safety but knowing he'd be at risk, she added, "Come after sundown and don't let Clay catch you."

"To hell with McCoy," Stone growled.

Almost as if Pepper knew Clay's name and was agreeing with Stone, he flapped his way up the steps and strutted into the cabin. Pepper stopped next to Stone, clucked and waited.

"This is Pepper," Spicy said, amazed at Pepper's tame reaction to Stone.

"We've met."

A giggle escaped Spicy at Stone's deadpan delivery. "You have?"

"Yes. That morning I came to check on you." When Stone gave the rooster a couple of strokes on the neck Pepper strutted back outside and flapped his way down the porch steps. "You should be honored," Spicy said only half teasing. "Pepper obviously likes you."

"Uh-huh." Stone rolled his eyes. "By the way, are you the only one who uses that raft?"

"No, why?"

"Because if you were the only one, even if you hide it in the blueberry bushes, McCoy will suspect you're with me."

"To hell with Clay McCoy."

Stone was the one who chuckled then, evidently surprised at her echo of his sentiment. Then a frown crossed his face. "Have you shown McCoy the magic?"

"No." She shook her head. "I've only shown Lumpkin."

"Why not McCoy?"

"I haven't wanted to and besides he's afraid of the fairies."

"Who?"

"The forest fairies." Widening her eyes and lowering her voice, she whispered, "It's well known the fairies detect good from bad. For the good, they bestow riches in countless varieties. Upon the bad, they cast dire financial woes."

"Surely you don't believe that. Nope, don't answer." Stone raised a hand, walked to the door, and turned to her to say, "If I stay any longer my restraint will fly out the window."

A gilded frame could not have graced a more magnificent portrait than the log doorway bordering Stone Hatfield. The silvery light of twinkling stars silhouetted the silver-eyed rogue. His dark head held high and broad shoulders squared, one hand pulled a big gun from under his jacket while his other hand held a pie in a basket. Behind the button-fly pants, she had felt his desire for her. As if Stone knew her resistance was waning, he leaned his muscular body into the cabin. Like a summer storm he rained on Spicy, his masculinity and intelligence flooding her with yearning and curiosity. His cocky smile, put there by a maddening drop of arrogance, made him all the more irresistible. This man was so visually attractive and sensually stimulating, a swooping pull of his sheer magnetism pulled her forward a step.

"Will you be safe tonight without Big Lump on your porch?"

"Stone—" Her heart pounded from her almost tangible attachment to him. It was on the tip of her tongue to beg him to stay. "Yes, I'll be safe."

"Latch the door," he repeated, shut it, and was gone.

STONE GLARED through the window toward Kentucky. Hiking out of Raccoon Hollow the previous night, he had swiped cold sweat off his temple. It had been nearly impossible to turn his back on Spicy's hot response to him. Clad in the plum-hued dress, it occurred to him her lips were just a shade lighter than the fruit and every bit as tasty. He'd dragged himself away from her before drowning in her passion.

"Damn her."

Washing dishes across the room, Aunt Hilda asked, "Who?"

First, sparking with Spicy, now breakfast with his aunt, and next hunting with Devil Anse and his crew. If he didn't get out of here soon, he'd never leave. Stone drummed his fingers on the kitchen table. He'd go see Spicy's magic and be done with her. She could learn about surgery from his book. He'd donate the book to the need for modern medicine in Tug Valley. He grinned remembering the fun he'd had tickling Spicy as her fanny wiggled. What was she doing right now? He looked at his aunt as she took a seat across the table from him.

"Sorry," Stone said. "Did you say something?"

"Were you just referring to the fiancée you told me about?"

"No." He blew out a sigh. "But Eunice is a problem. Her father's a good man and I owe it to him to marry his daughter."

"No, you do not." His aunt frowned and shook her head.

"You are the best surgeon at that teaching hospital—so much so that he not only wants to snag you as the chief but as the husband for his daughter."

Stone's head pounded and he rubbed his temple to no avail. "I've stalled him and Eunice for two years. I'm stuck."

"Malarkey. Get unstuck." Aunt Hilda smacked the tabletop with her open hand. "You're a surgeon. Cut yourself loose, boy."

Cut himself loose. An appropriate suggestion. What repercussions, if any, would he face in freeing himself from Eunice? Dr. Vanderveer had final say about the man who would replace him. There were other hospitals but damn, he wouldn't be chief of surgery come September anyplace but the Hospital of the University of Pennsylvania.

Aunt Hilda continued cryptically, "Logan is only twenty miles away. You can send telegrams, shop, and have a bite to eat there."

Was she suggesting breaking off with Eunice by telegraphing her from Logan? Or were his thoughts just running amuck? In any case, it was time to head out to Devil Anse's cabin where he would meet up with him, Ellison, and Johnse.

"Hello, Stony," Devil Anse called from the porch while petting his coon dog, Watch.

Stone greeted him. Being a Confederate ex-captain, Devil Anse's ability with his Winchester was legendary. He was considered the best marksman as well as the best horseman in Tug Valley. Despite rounded shoulders and a slight stoop he was about six feet tall. He had dark hair, a broad forehead, piercing eyes. His nose was hooked liked a scimitar, and below a bushy mustache he wore a long beard. A family resemblance shone around his brother's eyes but Ellison was a better looking and much bigger man.

In Aunt Hilda's frank opinion, everybody in Tug Valley

had their own version, Devil Anse was an agitator in terms of the feud and Ellison tended to be a peacemaker.

"Levicy says to bring her 'nough opossum tails to make soup for the whole valley, less the McCoys o'course," Devil Anse said to Stone, Ellison, and Johnse in regard to his wife.

Levicy, as Stone recalled, wore her hair in a tight bun and her mouth turned down at the corners, giving her a severe expression. But she, like her husband, had always been kind to Stone and his family. Picking up their guns, it was off to the woods along Mate Creek. Stone enjoyed the time spent in the hills and the activity took him far away from the hospital and the Vanderveers. Spicy however stayed in his thoughts. Opossums, not just their tails of course, squirrels, grouse, muskrats, and a turkey were bagged before calling it a day.

"No bears," Devil Anse grumbled, traipsing through the woods.

"You still like to trap and train the cubs?" Stone asked Devil Anse.

"Until they's growed and then we eat 'em."

They crossed Mate Creek and once they arrived at Devil's Anse's cabin, he insisted Stone, along with Ellison and Johnse, stay for supper. Stone was surrounded not only by his hunting partners, but Levicy and eight children, the youngest being one-year-old Troy.

As several conversations took place around the table, Stone quietly asked Ellison, "Did you get the feeling today, a time or two, that we were being tracked?"

"Yeah." Ellison looked at Stone and nodded. "At least twice."

"Ellison's wife won't never forget how them murderin' McCoys kilt her brother, Bill Staton, after the hog trial," Devil Anse said as if the feud nowadays was never too far from his mind. "Will she, Ellison?"

That damn hog again, Stone thought.

Ellison's resigned reply was directed to Stone, "You

mighta heard Paris and Sam McCoy were acquitted on the grounds of self-defense this spring."

"Yeah. Evidently, the McCoys have their side of things," Stone pointed out. He suggested in an easygoing tone of voice, "Devil Anse, if you and Ol' Ranel didn't oppose Hatfield and McCoy relationships in the younger generation maybe the feud would fade."

Silence permeated. Ellison sat poker-faced. Johnse nodded. Levicy tended the children.

Devil Anse's deep-set eyes narrowed to slits. "Am I right in suspicionin' your Aunt Hilda tol' you 'bout Johnse and Roseanna, Stony?"

"Everybody knows," Johnse said between bites of hog and hominy.

"That whole goldurn mess festers me terrible!" Devil Anse barked.

"Simmer down, Anse," Ellison said and then looked from his brother to his sister-in-law. "Levicy, is there any more cracklin' bread?"

Maybe the feud was as bad as Spicy claimed. All the more reason for getting out of these hills. Chief of surgery or not, he couldn't operate on anybody if he was dead.

"I ain't gonna settle down, Ellison. Them McCoy girls chase our men on accounta we got so much more land an' money than their men got," Devil Anse complained. "Them poor McCoy men is jealous of us."

So this opinion was popular on both sides of the Tug Fork. As for the other side of the river, he missed Spicy. When supper was over, he thanked Levicy and waved goodbye to the kids. Devil Anse, Ellison, and Johnse walked him onto the porch where a nearly full moon was making its appearance in the deep blue sky.

"Goin' to see a woman, I reckon?" Devil Anse asked.

"Maybe after I clean up from hunting," Stone replied.

Devil Anse prodded, "Is it a Staton or Mahon girl?"

"Neither," Stone said of other families in Tug Valley.

"A Weddington or a Mounts? Maybe a Chafin like Levicy?" Devil Anse tried.

"No," Stone replied knowing these families were all acceptable in Hatfield eyes.

Devil Anse frowned. "I guess it don't matter long as she ain't no blamed McCoy girl."

"Johnse married a McCoy girl last year," Ellison said.

Stone was all ears.

"Nancy McCoy," Johnse said to Stone.

"Nancy's one tale-tellin' McCoy girl," Devil Anse waved his fist in the air, "what needs to have her flappin' trap shut. Roseanna weren't no better."

"Leave Roseanna be," Johnse said. "We just wasn't right for each other. Roseanna don't even have the baby, Sarah Elizabeth, to love no more. At least I got Nancy."

"Johnse, you got any moonshine here or is it all at Grapevine Creek?" Ellison asked, as to where Johnse lived and changing the subject to diffuse an old argument.

"Got several of my three-cup-sized jugs here," Johnse said.

"Fetch Stony a jug afore he leaves," Ellison said pleasantly and patted Stone's shoulder. "Whoever your girl is, she ain't going nowhere without you. Right?"

Stone didn't breathe. *Ain't going nowhere without you.* Medically speaking, anyway. Stamped on his conscience was her soft voice as she beseeched him to help her move forward. Could he just leave that book with her and disappear? Hell, he wanted to teach her more than medicine. He wanted to teach her how to make love. Maybe Spicy's passionate responses had already been taught to her by Clay McCoy. Or by some other man. Men? Stone's jaw clenched as possessiveness curled his fists. He wanted to be first. He had no right to want that. He rolled his shoulders to throw off his tension. He was accustomed to being in control of his emotions. His head ruled his heart. Yeah, but who was ruling his lower body? Spicy McCoy. And she was making him a little crazy.

"Right, Ellison, she likely won't go far," Stone said.

~

"TOMORROW NIGHT WILL BRING us the blue moon," Spicy told Nutmeg.

The rosy pink and ginger-orange sun had slipped behind the trees leaving twilight in its place. Spicy rocked on her porch and petted the raccoon dozing off in her lap. As usual, a lantern glowed in the window of her cozy cabin. Spicy wondered what Stone was doing. He wasn't due to show up until the following evening, however it would be thrilling if he were sitting beside her right now. A man as good-looking as Stone could be sparking this very minute with any woman he chose. Maybe that's exactly what he was doing after a day of hunting with the Hatfields he'd mentioned. Spicy rapped her fingers on the arms of the rocking chair wishing she had a home remedy to cure the hold Stone Hatfield had over her.

"Where are you tonight, Stone?"

She hadn't seen Clay since before the supper at Otis and Martha Hatfield's house. But what she'd heard from patients was the tragedy with Polly and the baby hadn't slowed Clay down one iota. Thus, he was no doubt bedding some other woman on this side of the Tug Fork. Spicy fervently hoped that was the case. She prayed Lumpkin hadn't slipped about the supper they'd enjoyed with Stone and their Hatfield friends.

A distant gunshot blasted the silence.

Spicy instantly stopped rocking and stiffened. Startled, Nutmeg sniffed the air and twitched his furry ears. Pepper crowed near the chicken coop. Gunfire after dark was almost always a sign of trouble since hunting was done during the day.

"Ee-oo-ee!" came the frightening, forlorn call from the direction of the Tug Fork, signaling a stranger was trespassing in the valley.

Both McCoys and Hatfields used this same warning. Thus, Spicy had no idea who had spotted whom. Her heart thudded as she gripped the arms of the rocking chair. What if Clay had gone hunting for a certain Hatfield? Spicy sat unmoving, listening intently. Crickets chirped at the edge of her porch. Owls hooted in the nearby trees. Frogs croaked on Blackberry Creek. Several peaceful minutes passed. Spicy slowly began to relax. Perhaps all was well.

"Eee-ooo-eeeee!" rang out eerily from somewhere in Raccoon Hollow.

A second shot exploded much closer this time.

Nutmeg bailed off her lap. Spicy sprang out of the rocker. Pepper flew behind the henhouse. As Papa had taught her to do in a feud outbreak, Spicy closed all but one set of shutters and raced into the cabin. She called Nutmeg and when the raccoon scampered past her, she shut and latched the door. Grabbing the lantern off the window sill, Spicy set it on the table and closed those shutters as well. Hearing the sound of someone running, she held her breath.

Thud! Thud! Someone was on the porch steps. Clomp! Clomp! They crossed the porch. Bam! Bam! The knocks on the door shook Spicy's quaking soul.

CHAPTER 15

"Open up!"

"Is that you, Clay McCoy?"

"O'course it's me! Dumbass got hisself shot."

"Oh, no!" Spicy quickly unlatched the door and Clay barged into her cabin alone. "Don't call Lumpkin names. What happened?"

Rifle in hand, Clay scanned the front room and then glowered at her. "Why're you all gussied up, Spicy?"

"Where's Lumpkin?" Spicy, as usual, had washed her hair while bathing in the tin tub next to the small wardrobe in her bedroom. This evening, in hopes Stone might stop by early as he'd hinted, she'd curled her hair by wrapping it around strips of cloth laundered in rose-scented water. Though all of her few dresses were plain, this one was a favorite because it was almost as red as her roses. She'd even pressed it after it had dried on the line. As a finishing touch, she'd sprinkled rose-scented water on the bodice. "Clay, answer me."

"You smell extry good, too," Clay growled. "What's afoot?"

Ignoring him, Spicy said, "I asked you where Lumpkin is."

"He's acomin'."

"You shouldn't have left him," Spicy scolded. "Who shouted the warning of strangers?"

"Josiah. Or I reckon it coulda been Uriah," Clay said of Josiah Cline's brother.

As kids, Clay and the Cline brothers were known as 'that gang up the branch' referring to the Peter Creek branch of the Tug Fork River where they all still lived. Over the years, the trio had been suspected of cutting Hatfield timber and burning Hatfield property. Clay justified these actions saying if he didn't have something, *them Hatfields don't need it, neither.*

After Clayphus McCoy, Sr. died, Clay had boasted how he, not he and Lumpkin, had inherited the two-room cabin, moonshine still, and small cornfield. He bragged about not paying taxes and would kill any revenuer who came to collect. With a plot of land and the still for making money, why hadn't he married Polly and been a father to their child? Because Polly had no dowry? No land? No cabin of her own? On the other hand, Spicy did have five acres of land, the cabin, and a well.

"For your information, Clay, I'm certain the doctor from Philadelphia would have come to deliver Polly's baby whether her name was McCoy or not. Where did you go that day?"

Perhaps taken by surprise at her change of subject, Clay went slack-jawed for a moment. His flat-brown eyes darting, he sneered, "None of yer damn business where I go, woman." Shifting the rifle to his shoulder, he folded orange-haired arms across his chest as if barring her questions. "Fer *yer* information, that Philadelphy doctor done shot Big Lump tonight."

"You're telling me you saw Stone Hatfield shoot Lumpkin?"

"Yeah. Then he done hid in the woods with some other Hatfields."

"I don't believe you." Spicy snatched up the lantern and stalked past Clay onto the porch. He followed her as far as the door. Holding the light aloft, she called into the darkness, "Lumpkin!" When he didn't answer, she shifted the light to better see Clay. "What kind of trouble were you stirring up this time, Clay?"

"None." Furrowing his brows into what he must have considered an earnest expression, Clay said, "Me and the Clines been tryin' to catch that big razorback hog what's runnin' wild in yer holler so it don't hurt nobody."

"You mean so you could mark its ear and claim it."

She smelled the Clines even before they rounded the corner of her cabin. No matter how handy the creeks were they apparently had an aversion to bathing. Raising their rifles, as if in salute to Clay, the Clines rutted their way through the trees as Lumpkin lumbered into view.

"Lumpkin, were you shot?" she asked, darting down the porch steps to him.

"Yes'm." Wide-eyed, he pointed to his bloody left arm. "I's awful skeered."

"Told you dumbass got hisself shot." Clay shrugged.

"I'm so sorry you were hurt, Lumpkin," Spicy said and took his other arm. "Did you see who shot you?" When he shook his head, she guided the giant up the steps, past Clay and into the cabin. Setting the lantern on the table, she lit a couple of lamps. She grabbed her medical supplies and placed them on the table. After inspecting Lumpkin's wound she assured him, "Looks like a single-rifle bullet grazed you. A shotgun would have likely caused more than one wound. I'll clean and dress it." While she worked Lumpkin sat as still as a statue. "You're lucky you don't need stitches. Leave this linen strip around your arm until tomorrow, then let the air get to it and it will scab over."

"Philadelphy and them other Hatfields was trespassing on our side of the river tryin' to steal our hog," Clay insisted, lurking near the door. "Since they couldn't catch the razorback, Philadelphy shot Big Lump."

"No," Lumpkin paused in thought before finishing, "comes in peace."

Spicy figured Stone must have said something to the effect of coming in peace to Lumpkin the night he found him asleep on her porch. At the sudden raising of Lumpkin's brows, Spicy knew he had just remembered he wasn't supposed to mention Stone around Clay. But it was too late. Clay's temper ignited and he charged his brother.

"What?" Clay shouted at Lumpkin as he gripped his injured arm, "What do you mean comes in peace, you big, stupid lummox?"

"Stop it!" Spicy snapped. "Lumpkin is very smart. Don't hurt him."

"Shut up!" Clay pushed Spicy aside and snarled so viciously at his brother, both spit and words flew in Lumpkin's round face. "Do you know something 'bout Philadelphy and Spicy, you brainless baggage?"

Obviously, Lumpkin had not mentioned the Hatfield supper. But his lips quivered and his eyes teared.

"Clay!" Spicy's voice was sharp. "Do not ridicule Lumpkin. Leave! Now!"

"Don't go gettin' yer back up with me, pet." Clay released Lumpkin, turned to Spicy and ran his hand over her freshly washed curls in a petting motion.

"Don't touch me." Standing her ground, Spicy slapped his hand away. Though Clay withdrew his hand, the surly scowl on his face made her inwardly cringe. "And stop calling me pet. You hate all animals."

"Philadelphy sure ain't gonna be touchin' you."

"What are you talking about, Clay?" Spicy asked.

Clay grasped her wrist, hauled her up against his chest and said, "After Philadelphy shot Big Lump, I heared Devil Anse yell to Ellison and Johnse their second shot hit Stony instead of me'r the Clines."

She had heard two shots. Did old friends refer to Stone as Stony? Clay might be telling the truth. Spicy couldn't breathe. "You said they were hiding in the woods. How do you know who was with Stone?"

Clay's eyes shifted and he shrugged. "Don't matter which Hatfields. They's all killers."

"Is Stone dead?"

"As dead as Polly, you mean at the hands of their own kind?" Clay's face took on a hangdog look and ignoring the fact he had a brother, he said, "Yer all I got left since you let Polly and my baby die."

"*You* let Polly and your baby die." He'd touched Spicy where she was most vulnerable, but due to her conversation with Stone she held her head high. "You would never have let Stone refuse to come. You'd have gotten him here hogtied or at the end of your rifle if need be."

Clay's face contorted with rage. "If'n that Philadelphy dandy shooting Big Lump ain't proof he refused to come with me, then I don't know what it's gonna take."

Clay released Spicy with a shove. Bellowing like a madman, he smacked the medical supplies, which Spicy had used on Lumpkin, off the table and onto the floor. Moving in front of Lumpkin, and facing Clay, Spicy splayed her arms to shield him from Clay's fury.

"Stop it and get out!" Spicy ordered again.

Clay sneered, "Since the day you said 'we'll see' 'bout gettin' hitched, I suspicioned another man was behind it. I's got the right to kill Hatfield fer shootin' Big Lump."

"Kill Stone and I will never marry you. No matter what bargain you made with my folks," Spicy said.

Clay's hatred smeared his mouth into a snarl of yellow teeth. When he took a step closer to Spicy, Lumpkin rose to his feet behind her. Clay flinched and retreated.

"If Philadelphy ain't dead already he can live as long as you agree our gettin' hitched deal is back on track." Clay didn't wait for her answer before heading out the door. "See you in a few days when I get home from selling my moonshine in Williamson, West Virginny." Then to Lumpkin he hollered, "Get yer lick-spittle, Hatfield-siding ass out here, Big Lump."

"Ta home." Lumpkin's eyes and slump of his shoulders

said he was sorry for the trouble with Clay. "Love Spicy."
His voice quivered with a fear of rejection. "Love Lump?"

"Oh, yes, Lumpkin," Spicy said instantly and hugged
him. "Always."

With a sigh, Lumpkin followed Clay across the porch
and down the steps. From her doorway Spicy watched them
go. Pepper squawked in the yard and flapped toward Clay
who aimed his rifle. Lumpkin grabbed Clay's arm as he
pulled the trigger and the bullet missed the rooster. Spicy
shook with rage. Where the trees thickened, Clay did an
about-face.

"I'd say we got us a *dandy* new deal, pet!" Clay bellowed
and fired his rifle into the air as if to emphasize his words.
"You stay in Kentucky!"

Spicy was already planning to pole across the river to
find out if Stone had been shot. After Lumpkin and Clay
vanished into the woods, she whirled around at hearing a
noise toward the far end of her porch.

"Stone?"

"Sorry to be dropping by so late. Is everything all right?"

Zeke McCoy appeared to be tying something to a corner
porch post. He was joined by his daughter and son. Cousin
Zeke was a stocky man with light brown hair. Daughter,
Sunshine, and son, Shadow, were both blond like their
mother, Goldie. Sunshine at eighteen was already a beautiful
young woman. Twelve-year-old Shadow, as cute as could be,
had been named such due to a small, tan birthmark along
his chin which resembled a shadow of a beard. Zeke, Goldie,
and their children didn't have a plug nickel. Yet they had
cheerful attitudes, made a point to help others, and were a
happy family. Spicy loved and envied them.

"I'm fine, Zeke," Spicy said, disappointed it wasn't
Stone. "What's wrong?"

Zeke said, "Shadow's earache is so bad this time, he
cain't sleep."

Placing a trembling hand over his left ear, Shadow
nodded. Spicy stared hard toward West Virginia. Stone

might need her, too. She could just run off and forget about Shadow.

"Come on, Shadow." Spicy ushered them inside and sat the boy in the chair where Lumpkin had been. She apologized for the medical supplies being on the floor.

"Clay McCoy?" Zeke asked knowingly as to the scattered medical supplies. Like Spicy, Clay and Lumpkin were his distant cousins, too. "We thought that was him yelling."

"Yes." Spicy lit a third lamp and brought it close to Shadow's ear.

"I don't mean to speak out of turn," Sunshine began as she transferred the supplies from the floor to the table, "but Clay is a horrible bully. It's awful the way he treats Big Lump."

"It's awful the way Clay treats everybody," Zeke said and gave his children a meaningfully glance. "Sunshine and Shadow understand they are to keep their distance from Clay," Then looking back at Spicy, he added, "We'll give you a safe place to stay if you ever need it for as long as you need it, Spicy."

"Thank you, Zeke." Spicy examined Shadow's ear. She gathered up some tiny, aromatic leaves with violet flowers and put them in a small pan. "Shadow, I'm going to make some medicine for your ear. Nothing came out last time, but let's try again and see if we can fix it."

"I wish I knew more about medicine, especially midwifery," Sunshine said. So caring and capable, she would make a wonderful midwife. "How will you fix Shadow's ear?"

Adding water and holding the pan over three candle flames, Spicy explained, "I'll boil this pennyroyal and pour it in a glass. Then I'll drape a cloth over the glass and Shadow can hold his ear to the mint steam. I hope it will loosen the recurring infection that hardens like wax. If so, maybe his ear can finally heal and drain normally again." They followed the treatment as Spicy instructed. Soon, with tweezers, she was able to remove a brownish kernel, about the size of her pinky fingernail, from Shadow's ear. "How's that feel, Shadow?"

"It don't hurt no more," the boy said with relief. "I can hear better."

"We're much obliged to you for always taking care of whatever ails us," Zeke said.

"It's my pleasure," Spicy replied honestly. She desperately wanted to cross the river to make sure Stone was alive, so politely said, "I'll see you out before it gets any darker." She led the way carrying a lantern, which she placed back on the window sill.

"Since you told Goldie opossum don't agree with you, we didn't bring none for payment," Zeke told her on the porch.

"You're family." Her smile included all of them. "No payment is ever needed."

Shadow chimed in, "I told Pa since you're always talking 'bout pig piffle and pignuts, I reckoned you'd like a piglet. It's a shoat, meaning it's just been weaned."

"The only pen I have is my chicken coop. I fear Pepper and my chickens would peck the piglet especially if it managed to get into the henhouse."

Shadow was quick to reply and made a pecking motion with his hand. "They cain't peck your pig if'n cousin Lump and me was to build you a pigpen."

"Well," Spicy hesitated, but she had plenty of acreage. Lumpkin and Shadow were great friends and Lumpkin had a knack for building things. She knew Lumpkin would thoroughly enjoy making the pen with Shadow. Plus, it would give him a reason to be away from Clay. Shadow was grinning at her and Zeke was smiling down at his son. To refuse Shadow's offer and the piglet would be an insult. "That would be wonderful, Shadow."

"Oh, boy!" Shadow whooped. "It'll be a fine pen, for sure."

Zeke nodded and Sunshine smiled as Shadow untied the piglet from the porch post. Small and pink, with a curled tail, it was sort of cute. Shadow nuzzled the animal before handing it over to Spicy. She held tightly so as not to drop the wiggling little shoat.

"Thank you," Spicy said. With goodbyes and waves Zeke and his children headed home. The moment they were out of sight, she told the little pig, "I'll be back later."

Planning to tether the piglet to the porch post, Spicy spun on her heel and smacked into a wall. A wall of rock-hard muscle. Spicy gasped and jumped back. The little pig squealed and bailed out of her arms. The man before her easily caught the piglet.

"So," he drawled, "pigs can fly."

CHAPTER 16

"STONE!" SPICY GASPED.

"Did you or did you not say you'd be my puddle of passion when pigs could fly?" Stone asked, cradling the piglet in the crook of his left arm and holding a shotgun in his right hand.

"I said I'd drown myself, you big pig in a poke." Spicy was so relieved he was alive, had Stone's hands not been full she might have thrown herself into his arms. "How'd you get inside my cabin?"

"The back door was open. I latched it when I came in."

In the chaos, she'd forgotten to latch it. "Are you all right?"

"Where'd the pig come from?"

She took the piglet and Stone joined her on the porch. While tying the squirming shoat to the porch post she explained about treating Shadow McCoy's earache with the piglet as payment. With a quick glance around for Clay, and not seeing him, she motioned Stone to follow her into the cabin. In the front room, she turned and confronted him.

"Why do you have that shotgun, Stone?"

"I went bear hunting today. Remember?"

"Bear hunting or McCoy hunting?"

"Bear hunting." Stone visibly tensed.

She raised a brow. "In a clean white shirt and nice black britches?"

"I took a bath before crossing the river. Why?"

"Clay was here. He says you were trespassing in Kentucky and shot Lumpkin tonight."

"I did not shoot Big Lump. Is he all right?"

"Just a graze to his arm."

Stone glared over Spicy's head through the front door. "I swear babies in Tug Valley are born with their fingers bent to pull a trigger. Most have murder in their hearts before they're ten." Lowering his eyes to Spicy's, he said, "That goes for Hatfields *and* McCoys."

Spicy bristled. "Shadow, the boy I treated tonight, is as peaceful as Lumpkin." She paused and then said, "Stone, I want to believe you come in peace."

His brow furrowed. "Believe it."

"Then who shot Lumpkin?"

"I don't know." Stone ran a hand through his hair. "Devil Anse, Ellison, Johnse, and I hunted in West Virginia all day. I left them at Anse's house after supper and rode home. I watered and fed Logan, cleaned up and was on the riverbank by the blueberry bushes when I heard the first shot. I felt something sting me and barely caught a glimpse of a man before he disappeared into the Kentucky woods. I heard the trespass warnings, another shot and a roar of pain. I assume the roar came from Big Lump."

"Where were you wounded?"

"Deeper and I would have lost a kidney," Stone said and cocked a brow.

Spicy arched a brow and said, "Having studied your medical book I know you mean just below your ribs in your back. I'll clean and dress it for you like I did for Lumpkin."

"Where'd McCoy go after he left here?"

"Home. Clay won't be a threat for a few days. He's heading to Williamson to sell his moonshine." After closing and latching the front door she gasped. Stone had turned his back to her as he leaned his shotgun against the sofa.

"Stone, the back of your shirt is ripped and soaked in blood."

"A bullet and paddling a canoe across the river will do that," he grumbled.

"Yes, of course." Collecting herself she said, "I admire how calmly you're taking it. And I'm sorry you had to paddle the river. There needs to be a bridge built in this area."

"Aunt Hilda says they're working on one up north near the abandoned schoolhouse we talked about."

"Right, that bridge is nearly finished." Spicy quickly fetched a handful of freshly washed linen strips and set them next to her medical supplies. "Before I have you sit down backward on a chair, let's take your shirt off."

"At least."

Despite being shot, slowly and seductively Stone's gaze flowed like mercury over her curled hair to the bodice of her dress before returning to her eyes. A lurch of insecurity made Spicy realize how much she wanted to meet with this sophisticated physician's approval. Especially now when he needed her medical attention.

Taut nerves snapped in her voice, "Shall I toot a flute while you look your fill?"

Stone's bold gaze lingered lazily on her mouth. "Sure."

Was he imagining her playing a flute? "Oh, for pity's sake, I don't have a flute." Self-consciously, Spicy licked her lips.

In a husky voice, he said, "If you did, it wouldn't take a Philadelphia lawyer to know you'd play second chair to no one."

"Are you sparking with me, gunshot wound and all?"

"Trying my best to."

"Take your shirt off."

"I see it's working."

Spicy raised a brow and Stone began unfastening his shirt. Button by button a chest with masculine black hair and bulging muscle rippled into view. He slipped the suspenders off his broad shoulders and pulled the shirttails out of his snug britches. His flat stomach resembled her washboard and black hair swirled his indented navel. When he tried to shrug out of the bloody shirt, a groan escaped him.

"Let me help." Spicy could almost feel the pain she knew he was masking. She moved in back of him and said, "Place your arms slightly behind you."

Stone did so. As she carefully eased the shirt off his shoulders and his arms out of the sleeves, he told her about a patient in Pennsylvania Hospital, who'd had a bullet lodged near his spine about kidney level. Spicy placed his shirt aside and marveled that he had removed the slug without paralyzing the man. Now it was she who looked her fill. Despite the torn flesh, Stone's muscular back was as gorgeous as his lightly furred chest. His shoulders were broad, his torso tapered and his muscles corded underneath his skin.

"How's it look?" he asked.

"Even better than I imagined."

"What's that mean?" he asked trying to look over his shoulder at her.

Spicy improvised with, "It means your injury could have been worse."

"How long is the gash?"

"About an inch. It'll take four or five stitches to close it." Holding a lamp closer, she said, "Your rifle graze looks a lot like Lumpkin's only deeper." She pulled out a chair for him and turned it toward the light. "Sit down."

"I'm packing a shotgun." Stone pointed to the gun then sat down and rested his forearms on the spindle back of the chair.

Spicy followed his train of thought. "So, you couldn't have shot Lumpkin." She moved around him enough to make eye contact. "I'm sorry for questioning your innocence. For what it's worth, I told Clay I didn't believe him and Lumpkin said you came in peace."

Quietly, Stone said, "Thank you, Spicy."

"I spoke the truth. Now, let me sponge away the dried blood."

"Do you have any boiled water?"

"You mean like I boil for tea or a tonic?"

"Exactly."

"Yes, I have an almost full teapot. But the water's cool now. You want tea?"

"No. Use that water to clean the wound."

Spicy did so without further question. When she had gently cleansed the skin around the injury, she asked, "Ready for the stitches?"

"Do you have catgut for suturing?"

"Cats? No. I use thread to stitch."

"Suture. It's called catgut but it's made from sheep or bovine intestines. Boil the thread and needle first."

"Why would I do that? Why did I have to use boiled water on your wound?"

"Boiling water kills germs. In Philadelphia, I require an antiseptic known as carbolic spray to be used to disinfect the operating rooms before every surgery. Eliminating bacteria reduces cases of septicemia."

"Septicemia?"

"Blood poisoning."

"There is so much I could learn from you, Stone."

With a wicked grin, he said, "You have no idea."

It was her turn to ask, "What does that mean?"

"It means boil the needle and thread and hand me that anesthesia, please."

He pointed to the stoneware jug on the floor next to his shotgun and said Johnse had given him the moonshine before he'd left Devil Anse's place. She handed it to him and he pulled out the corncob stopper. Stone asked her to pour a little over the wound. When she did so he barked a curse and reached for the jug. She handed the moonshine back to him and he tossed back a few swallows. Stone's yelp had awakened her little raccoon and he crawled out from under the sofa.

"Have you met Nutmeg?"

Stone swiped at his mouth with the back of his hand and said, "Can't say that I have."

"Nutmeg, this is Dr. Hatfield."

"Nutmeg," Stone said and tipped the moonshine jug in the raccoon's direction.

Spicy laughed. Instead of growling, as Nutmeg always did at Clay, he sniffed Stone who petted his head. Spicy let the nocturnal creature out for a night of prowling and gathered her poultice ingredients. After the water came to a boil she knelt behind Stone with her needle and thread. He sat stoically, taking an occasional swig as she stitched. To distract him from the pain, Spicy described Lumpkin's wound saying it hadn't required stitches or a poultice.

"But you need a poultice to draw out any poisons between the stitches."

"I have salves and alcohol to limit pain and infection." He rolled his shoulders. "But since I was down by the Tug Fork when this happened my medical bag is up at my house."

"For now you'll just have to make do with my mountain-medicine poultice. But I'd like to see your medical supplies sometime."

"I'll see what I can do."

"I'm knotting the fifth stitch," she said and clipped the thread. "Now for the poultice."

Stone swiveled at the waist, grimaced and said, "I just realized the man I glimpsed running into the woods looked like McCoy but without the long orange beard."

Thoughts swirling, Spicy moved to the opposite side of the table. Placing the ingredients for the poultice into a bowl, she tried her best to focus on mixing the medicament. But all she could see was the guilty shooting the innocent. She stopped and looked across the table.

"Stone, I know who shot you."

"We both know it was Clay McCoy."

Spicy blurted out, "Yes, because Clay shaved his beard and said his next shot wouldn't miss." Her voice cracked and she swallowed. Splaying one hand toward Stone, she scratched her neck with the other hand and said, "But I thought he shaved to look more like you, not to disguise himself so he could shoot you."

"Ellison and I sensed we were being tracked today." With a frown of anger turning to concern, he said, "Calm down. Don't scratch."

"Clay said he heard Devil Anse yell to Ellison and Johnse that Stony was shot."

"Which is another one of McCoy's lies."

"Clay and the Clines were tracking you and that's how he knew they call you Stony."

"Yeah, only old friends or family call me Stony. Tracking us is how McCoy knew who was with me." Stone took a deep breath and let it out. "Let's change the subject."

"But I'm furious you were shot!" Spicy clasped her hands to keep from scratching.

"Take a deep breath and let it out slowly. Do you know why they call me Stony?"

CHAPTER 17

FOR STONE'S SAKE SPICY TOOK A BREATH AS HE'D asked, let it out, and went back to mixing the poultice ingredients. "Because you own the Stony Mountains?" She waved a hand to erase her question. "That's none of my business."

"It's not a secret," Stone said from across the table. "My family has owned the double mountains for generations." As he told her how the Stony Mountains came by their name, she figured he was hoping the story would distract them both for a few minutes. "My folks almost sold off some of the property before finding out what the coal was worth. Our family agreed before my father's passing, the house and mountain to the south would go to me and Jet would inherit the north peak when our uncle passed. Aunt Hilda willed her house to Jet years ago."

With his furry chest and bulging muscles Stone was all man. Calm like he was now, she could easily envision him in a surgical amphitheater remaining cool and collected under life-and-death circumstances. So virile and rugged, his presence seemed to shrink her roomy cabin. Spicy was more than intrigued by this half-naked man and his half of a double mountain range.

Striving to remain composed, she asked, "Why did your folks almost sell?"

"To send my brother, Jet, and me to college," he replied. "I told them I'd work my way through which as you know, I did at the hospital. I sent for Jet and he passed his final law exams a couple of years ago, so their dream came true. And we still own the mountains."

"Good for you," Spicy said. "Obviously, your family was a happy one. There's nothing better than a loving family." Still inwardly furious he'd been shot, she continued taking a deep breath here and there to keep from screaming, scratching, or crying. She plucked several clean linen strips from the basket to use with the poultice. "Clay has obviously figured out who you are. Now that he knows you're a Hatfield landowner and not a Philadelphy dandy—"

"Dandy?" His bark made her jump. "Sorry." He chuckled. "I like randy better."

Stone Hatfield was a man confident in his masculinity. Watching him rein in his temper and appreciate the humor of Clay's ludicrous accusation, Spicy was increasingly impressed by Stone. She picked up where she'd left off, "You have to be even more cautious of Clay now."

Back to that subject, Stone frowned. "I don't underestimate any man who'd shoot his own brother."

"It's hard to believe Clay is capable of shooting Lumpkin."

"I can vouch for Devil Anse, Ellison, and Johnse." Stone cocked a brow. "But McCoy let Polly and her baby die. He turned the blame on you and me so successfully I found you crying in your bed. Didn't I?"

Spicy winced. "Yes."

"Then don't be blind as to what McCoy is capable of," Stone said. "Where was he the day Polly died trying to give birth to his child? Because he sure as hell wasn't looking for me."

"I asked him that and he said it wasn't any of my business."

"Did he hurt you?"

"No, but—" she shrugged.

"But he has in the past and you thought he might again."

"He has been rough with Lumpkin and me," Spicy confided and hugged herself. "But that doesn't mean Clay would shoot Lumpkin. Josiah and Uriah Cline were with them. Maybe they shot Lumpkin. And if they did it could have been accidental."

"Yeah, as accidental as my father's death," Stone grumbled, massaging a spot near his wound. "When I rode Logan home from Anse's house, McCoy and the Clines couldn't have tracked me on foot. But while I was at my house they had time to catch up and cross the Tug Fork ahead of me. After McCoy took a shot at me like he did the day you fell in the river, he also shot Big Lump to throw you off his trail."

Spicy not only recalled Lumpkin telling her Clay shot at Stone the day she fell in the river, but the Clines running past her house earlier and lifting their rifles as if they had been on a mission with Clay. With the linen strips in hand she walked around in back of Stone.

"This poultice may ease your pain, so I need you to—"

"I need you to ease my mind." When she didn't respond, Stone snared her right wrist and pulled her to his side. "Come back to me, Spicy."

"What do you mean? I'm right here."

"Come back to me mentally." His baritone voice was urgent and then a slow smile indicated patience. "A few minutes ago we were of like minds about McCoy."

"I fully believe he shot you. But it's hard for me to see a man I've known all my life appearing evil enough to shoot his own brother."

"Not appear. Is. McCoy *is* that evil."

"You're going to have to lie flat on your stomach in order for me to apply this poultice."

Sliding off the chair Stone picked up a lamp and headed for her bedroom. "Let's go."

"I meant my folks' room."

"Does it have a back door?"

"No."

"Then I'll be in your room." He sauntered into her room, tugged off his britches, and lay down on his stomach. "Did you hear what I just said about McCoy?"

"Loud and clear," she replied. Never had she seen a man clad only in his drawers. Not only that, this one was in her bed. Struggling to keep her senses about her, Spicy took another deep breath and summed up," Clay always throws the first punch. He did nothing to help Polly and the baby. He calls Lumpkin terrible names. He kicks Nutmeg and shot at Pepper. No doubt he pulled the trigger twice earlier tonight. Yes, I agree. Clay *is* that evil."

"Progress. Slap on that poultice, shortsweetin'." Stone slid his arms under her pillow.

"Shortsweetin'," Spicy repeated. "That's the Tug Valley word for sugar and the first real evidence that you grew up here," she teased him. "As for the poultice it's a *long shot* both your kidneys are still intact to be covered by it."

"That's right, we have two kidneys. Good girl."

Standing over him, Spicy spread the poultice medicament to his wound with infinite tenderness. Covering it with several layers of linen, she selected a couple of long strips to tie all the way around him in order to secure the poultice in place. When he lifted his washboard stomach off the mattress, she slid the linen strips under him. He collapsed, trapping her hands against his belly. He groaned and Spicy tingled as she worked her hands out from under him. She tied the strips in knots at his back and clipped the excess linen with her scissors.

"So what's in that poultice?" he asked looking up at her from the bed.

Stepping back, more than a bit warm from her efforts as well as Stone being in her bed, Spicy swiped at her brow and then grinned. "Snips and snails and puppy-dog tails."

"But I want your sugar and spice and," his brazen gaze roamed down her body and back up, "all things nice."

Far from being insulted, Spicy felt complimented. Maybe because she wanted him, too. Whatever that wanting might include. Maybe because he was a big-city, educated doctor. And if such a man thought her to be sugar and spice and all things nice then maybe she was more than a backward little hillbilly.

"Spicy, before you haul off and wallop me," Stone said with a yawn, "that doesn't mean I'll get what I want."

"Stone, I can't do," she took a step but when he grasped her skirt and tugged, she sat down on the side of the bed, "all things nice with you."

"A woman I know thinks it's naughty, but with you it would be so nice."

"Naughty? What woman thinks that?"

What was the Vanderveer woman's first name? Stone picked up her scissors off the bed and made a cutting motion. "It's like her name's been severed from my mind." Then handing the scissors to Spicy, he tilted his head and asked. "Why can't you do all things nice with me?"

"That woman isn't your wife, is she?"

"Hell no." He frowned in surprise. "I'll be faithful to my wife."

"You're welcome to sleep here tonight, but I can't do more because of Clay."

"After our conversation surely you're not going to honor the betrothal your folks made with McCoy. Are you?"

"Not exactly. In fact, I told Clay I would never marry him if he killed you." Spicy's shoulders sagged as the weight of the world descended. "But with the new deal—" Snipping the air with her scissors, she set them on the bedside table and started to stand up but Stone caught her forearm.

"What new deal?" Stone's voice sounded ominous. Spicy felt an itch and scratched her neck. "Answer me, Spicy."

"Clay said tonight he won't kill you, if I agree our getting hitched was back on track," she blurted out and rubbed her shoulder. "I didn't agree or disagree, but if I don't marry him, I can't realize my fondest dream."

"Slow down. Don't scratch. What's your fondest dream?"

"A family of my own. Even more than being a book-learned healer using real modern medicine, I want to be a mother. And for a baby I need," she shrugged, "you know."

"A man."

"A husband." Spicy pulled her arm free. "I'm stuck with Clay."

"My aunt would say malarkey. Get unstuck. If your parents were still here and knew what we do about McCoy, they wouldn't want you anywhere near him. Let's get out of these," he rolled to his side to get a better view of her and grimaced, "bloodthirsty mountains."

"What?"

"You're damn well not going to marry Clay McCoy because of me. Let me help you cut your ties to him. After the election, come with me to Philadelphia. You can enroll in the Women's Medical College there. Then in September, I'll be appointed the chief of surgery at the university's teaching hospital. If Jet and I escaped Tug Valley so can you."

"Chief of surgery," Spicy repeated in awe. "Oh, Stone." She folded her hands over her heart. "That's wonderful. You could do so much good for the people in Tug Valley."

"There's no hospital here and I don't plan to operate in the woods."

"No, of course not." Spicy's throat grew raw with emotion. "You have to go back." Standing, she walked to the window and opened the shutters to let in the night breeze. Peering in the direction of Peter Creek, she said, "It's too dangerous for me to leave Lumpkin to fend for himself. I have to stay and help people here the best I can."

From behind her, Stone urged, "You could help people in Philadelphia."

Turning to him she asked, "Exactly how long did it take you to become a doctor?"

"Six years."

"Six years," she breathed in awe. "I don't want to wait that long to start my family."

"Pennsylvania Hospital has a nursing school that only takes one year."

"Yes, a nurse," she whispered the words as if they were spun of pure gold. She gazed at the gorgeous, muscular man. Whereas she usually curled up on her side, he sprawled across her bed like a blanket. She was so utterly and completely wrapped up in him, she took a step closer before stopping. "No, Stone. I can't go with you."

"I'll give you the baby you want."

"I want at least two."

"So do I."

"But I couldn't accomplish becoming a nurse *and* a mother."

"Yes, you can. Have faith."

"Faith," Spicy echoed, the seed planted.

CHAPTER 18

STONE'S NEXT THOUGHT WAS THAT HE WASN'T free to give Spicy one baby, much less two. But he sure wasn't going to have any children with...what the hell was her name?

Spicy promised great lovemaking, two babies, and Tug Valley. His fiancée represented no sex, no babies, and Pennsylvania Hospital. He'd invested years pursuing his goal to become chief of surgery. He cared for Spicy more than he was ready to admit. If she cared for him, he could be the father of her babies. Like her, he wanted a family. A happy one.

Their hearts were so close together while their lives were mountains apart.

"Stone," Spicy smiled as she sat back down beside him, "things can never work out between us any more than they worked out for Roseanna and Johnse or Romeo and Juliet."

"Johnse said they just weren't right for each other," Stone told her. "I didn't push the subject but I don't understand why Devil Anse allowed Johnse to marry Nancy McCoy, but not her cousin, Roseanna."

Spicy brushed a lock of thick, black hair off his forehead. "My guess is Devil Anse hates Roseanna's father, Ol'Ranel, worse than he hated Nancy's father, Asa Harmon McCoy."

"All this hate is a pile of pig piffle," Stone groaned in mock agony.

Spicy laughed and the mood lightened. "It appears my sage, chamomile, and primrose poultice has somewhat restored your sense of humor."

Stone looked at the sexy siren, wanting her like he'd never wanted any woman, anywhere, at any time. He whispered, "I thought it was your sugar and spice making me feel so nice, little girl."

"It's the snips and snails and puppy-dog tails also in the poultice, little boy."

Stone growled playfully, "Little boy?"

Spicy giggled. "Big boy."

"Yeah." Stone caught a lock of her hair and twined it around his finger. "Have I told you how good you smell or how soft your hair is or how beautiful you are?" She shook her head. "I'm telling you now." She blushed. "The blue moon is tomorrow night, right?"

"Yes."

"Good. I'll wait for it right here in your cabin if you'll sleep with me. Otherwise, I'll have to pole across the river and probably tear out all of my new sutures."

"You can sleep in my bed and I can sleep in the other bedroom."

Around a grin, Stone said, "I might become delusional during the night, wander into the forest and drown in the creek."

Spicy laughed. "Talk about malarkey."

"Are you gonna take off that pretty red dress or sleep in it?"

"I can't do anything nice with you."

"For tonight." Without another word, Spicy placed her hand over his eyes and closed them. Stone heard movements, but kept his eyes shut. When she lay down in his arms, she wore only her nightgown. He molded her full breasts to his naked chest and felt her tremble. Reassuring her, he whispered, "This big boy is tuckered out, little girl."

WHEN STONE WOKE the next morning it was to the mouthwatering smell of bacon. No sooner did he wonder if the piglet was still alive than here it came. Right behind the piglet, Spicy sashayed into the bedroom wearing a snug, lemon-yellow dress that accentuated her every curve. She shooed the piglet back to the front room and twirled to Stone with a smile. It was nice not to wake up alone as he usually did in Philadelphia, but even better because it was Spicy with him. He could easily imagine her being the best part of his morning routine.

"And here I thought Pig Piffle might be breakfast," he said and stretched.

"Pig Piffle?" Spicy laughed. "I guess the piglet has a name." Stone crooked his finger and she glided to him. When he reached out a hand she took it. "How's your back?"

"You've been quite the medicinal remedy I needed," he said as she once had to him.

"Good. Come have some bacon and eggs. Then I'll change your bandage."

That sounded perfect. It was so perfect the sun flew across the morning sky. As they sat in the rockers on the porch, Pepper strutted back and forth and ate berries out of Stone's hand. When Stone asked about his shirt, Spicy pointed to the clothesline. A warm breeze waved his washed and mended shirt next to a nightgown and a couple of the simple homespun dresses he'd seen Spicy wear. He didn't realize it was past noon until his stomach growled. He retrieved the clothes and donned his shirt as Spicy began fixing a midday meal. He offered to help her but she motioned him to an overstuffed chair between the sofa and bookcase.

On a table with a lamp his medical book had been placed on top of Shakespeare's *Romeo and Juliet*. Shelved in the bookcase were books on the spice trade and herbal treatments which he figured she'd read a hundred times. He picked up the tragic love story and Spicy made no comment. The feud between Juliet's family, the Capulets, and Romeo's clan, the Montagues, stemmed from an old grudge he likened to the damn disputed hog. Romeo and Juliet's families fought because they'd always fought, similar to the Hatfields and the McCoys.

That brought back to mind the problem of Clay McCoy. Even though he'd claimed to be leaving for a few days, Stone didn't let down his guard. His gut said he and McCoy would meet sooner than later. But he refused to let concern over an inevitable confrontation intrude on his precious little time with Spicy.

No one bothered them as they ate, laughed, and shared stories throughout the day. While he and Spicy got to know each other better, Pepper investigated Pig Piffle. Seeing Nutmeg had accepted the piglet and with Stone stroking Pepper's neck, the rooster didn't peck Pig Piffle.

It seemed to Stone it was only minutes before the sun hovered low on the evening horizon. Still not allowing him to do anything but keep her company, Spicy fixed supper. This relaxing day had evaporated way too quickly for Stone, but he consoled himself knowing Spicy's once-in-a-blue-moon night of mountain magic was upon them.

"What do you think?" Stone asked when twilight found them back in the rocking chairs on the porch. The stars twinkling in the sky helped sprinkle enough light to let Stone see the one shining beside him. "Is it dark enough?"

"Yes," Spicy said.

"I'm ready." Out of respect for her opinion that things couldn't work out between them, Stone hadn't made a move toward her. But the more time he spent in her presence the more he wanted things to somehow work out. He stood and held out his hand. When she took it, he tugged her to him for their first kiss of the day. She responded, leaning in close. He kissed her a second time and with a wink said, "Let's go."

"Does your back hurt or can you carry your own candle?"

He chuckled. "I think I can manage a candle." Vanishing into the cabin she reappeared with a pail and two lit candles, each with a needle poked through it. "What're the needles for?"

"To keep us safe from evil spirits while we hunt for the magic."

"Now, Spicy, surely you don't—"

Raising an arched brow, she said, "Take your needle out if you dare."

"Speaking of evil, the back door is latched. Let's latch the front door," Stone said. Spicy nodded, handed both candles and the pail to him and hopped onto the bench under the window sill. She reached through the small window and Stone said, "You knew I couldn't tickle you while holding both candles."

"That's right," she giggled. "I almost fell on my head last time."

"I wasn't about to let that happen."

As Stone admired her wiggling fanny the latch fell into place across the door. After securing Pig Piffle to the post, Spicy took her candle and the pail. With Nutmeg scampering alongside them, they were off on their adventure. Stone wouldn't have missed this unique quest for the world. Spicy knew her way through this deep and dark primeval forest like the woodland nymph she was. Even though this was enemy territory, with Spicy, Stone felt at home.

No, Pennsylvania was home. Suddenly the thought of leaving Tug Valley was a shot almost as painful as a bullet. Ina few short weeks he needed to be in Philadelphia ready to take over the surgical department and marry...why couldn't he remember her name? He knew one thing—she would never venture through the woods day or night in search of mountain magic.

As Spicy held her candle in her right hand, the flickering light reflected in her blueberry eyes. Sugar-maple curls poured around her breasts, shoulders, and back like sweet syrup. Her supple body, bathed in lemon-yellow and as willowy as blades of grass, swept a golden glow through the purple fog of the moonlit meadow. Spicy possessed a wild, ethereal loveliness Stone had never before witnessed.

"Isn't it exquisite?"

"Exquisite." Stone's voice was husky. He swallowed and teased, "Hope I don't get lost."

Spicy slipped the pail over her left forearm and held the candle with her left hand. As Stone had intended she grabbed his hand. Nutmeg dashed ahead of them seeming to know where they were going.

"The magic is just ahead in the laurel thicket."

"The magic is wherever you are," Stone said. He squeezed her hand and gazed down at her. But she was thoroughly intent on finding the magic.

"Come on." Her silken voice caressed him in a whisper, "It's close."

Under the full moon and scattered stars lay a hidden glen. The night breeze wafted the scent of pine and wildflowers across the mist-shrouded, secluded valley. The gurgling of Blackberry Creek reached Stone's ears as Spicy dropped his hand. As graceful as a doe she skipped away from him. When darkness threatened to steal her, Stone sprinted after her like a protective buck. His eyes didn't miss a move as she knelt beside a fallen tree. Setting aside her pail, Spicy picked up a small branch and brushed away leaves.

"The magic hides inside old poplar logs," Spicy said softly as if she feared someone besides Stone would hear her.

Stepping over the log and facing Spicy, before his disbelieving eyes, a yellowish-green florescence illuminated the darkness. How could this be? Stone's logical mind sought an answer. As Spicy waved a leafy branch the mysterious sparkle took on different shapes.

"Must be some kind of fungus," Stone said.

"It's fire dropped from the stars." With the enchantment

of a child and conviction of an adult, Spicy said, "Tonight it's shimmering in this secret castle where the fairies are dancing to celebrate your presence."

Rubbing his temple, Stone muttered, "Yeast maybe or some kind of mold."

"Mountain magic found in the moonlit mist is called," Spicy dropped the leafy branch and finished, "fairy fire." On her knees, candle clutched over her heart Spicy glanced up at him. Embraced by the emerald-green forest with the yellow candlelight flickering against her lemon frock, Spicy magnified the mystifying radiance. "What do you think?"

"Fairy fire," Stone whispered to the angelic woman waltzing across his heart.

Spicy broke off the bark where the fairies glimmered and carefully placed each piece into her pail until it was full. Slipping one small piece into her pocket, she stood and motioned to Stone. Once again, Nutmeg stayed close as they made their way through the woods toward Blackberry Creek. At the edge of the water Spicy handed Stone her candle and slipped away.

"Stay where you are and watch, Stone Hatfield."

CHAPTER 19

As if I could take my eyes off you, Spicy McCoy, Stone thought.

She dashed a few yards upstream and vanished. Silence reigned and he was just about to call out to her when she sashayed back into view. Carrying her empty pail, she knelt near the water and motioned for Stone to do the same. Woven deeply into her mystical web, he sat beside her. Taking their candles she wedged them into the ground, smiled at him, and then looked upstream. He followed her gaze and watched fire dance on the water.

Transfixed, Stone stared as twinkling lights slowly floated past them on the surface of the lazy creek. In the stillness of the blue-moon night they watched until the very last of the fairy fire had melted away into the purple shadows.

"Have I repaid you for your advice about Abigail's tonsils?" Spicy asked.

"Yes."

"If it's all right, I'd love to study your medical book until you leave. Then after the election we can part ways, each with a clear conscience."

"Maybe my goal is to leave with a guilty conscience."

"The forest fairies would never inspire a guilty

conscience." There was a thoughtful pause before Spicy smiled. "Did I spark it?"

"Are you sparking with me, sugar'n spice?"

"Maybe so, long shot."

"Please don't stop."

As Stone pulled her to him the pain from his gunshot wound was a dull twinge. A much more urgent ache was his craving for the fairy fire in his embrace. He lowered his mouth to hers. When he parted his lips, she did the same and he traced her lips with his tongue. As her delicate fingers slipped through his hair, he shivered and slid his tongue past her teeth. After a quick intake of breath, she opened her mouth to his probing kiss. Stone tugged her across his lap. She tasted sweeter than the blackberries along the creek and was far more pliant than the brambles on which the berries grew. When he raised his head her arms wound like grapevines around his neck, holding him close.

"Am I hurting your back?" Spicy asked.

"No, and I don't want to hurt you." He brushed soft curls away from her face.

"What you mean?"

Under a cozy canopy of leafy trees in the light of their candles Stone gazed at Spicy. Her eyes glittered with a little girl's trust and her shapely body promised a woman's delight. Stone's yearning pumped the blood though his veins and sent it surging hard and fast into his loins.

"I mean I have to go back to Philadelphia."

"But you're here tonight."

Spicy cupped the back of his neck. That was all Stone needed. He closed his eyes and brushed her lips with his. She circled his mouth with her tongue as he'd taught her and he groaned. Like a pebble thrown into a pond, his craving for her rippled out from his loins washing over him from head to toe. Stone wanted more with Spicy than tonight. So much more.

Finding the buttons on her scooped bodice he unfastened the top one. He felt her tremble but she didn't stop him. Instead she threaded her fingers through his hair. Shivers swept up and down Stone's spine. He undid the remaining buttons and slipped his hand inside her dress. She gasped and shock waves assailed him. She wasn't wearing the customary camisole most women wore. He caressed the bare skin of her full breasts and the tips beaded against his palm. He lowered a kiss to her throat and she leaned her head back over his arm. Her hair fell in luxurious waves toward the ground and he imagined the silky tresses brushing his chest. Candlelight teased him with the pouting peaks of her breasts which resembled sugary drops of maple syrup. His mouth watered. Using a fingertip he circled one of her nipples. She closed her eyes and when her lips parted in a moan, he lowered his kiss to her left breast.

"Mmm, yes," she breathed.

Soul deep and beyond. Spicy's every whisper, her every touch, her every move radiated a seductive, hypnotizing loveliness incomparable to any other woman Stone had ever known. He tasted and circled the maple peak with his tongue and she responded by arching her back. She exuded such sensual femininity his blood pulsed harder and faster into his manhood.

"I want you, Spicy," he groaned against her satin flesh.

"More, Stone."

With pleasure. He planted a hungry kiss between her breasts and Spicy moaned his name. If just looking at her stirred his desire, holding her exposed and so vulnerable with his name escaping her lips enslaved him as her captive. Stone teased her right nipple with his tongue yearning to be one with her, to share the liquid fire that would ignite from their passion. His manhood had fully distended his fly. He showed Spicy the effect she was having on him by placing one of her hands to his rock-hard arousal. As her fingers and palm molded to him, Stone pictured taking her in a quick, carnal act of possession.

Gently squeezing him, she murmured, "You're a *mountain* of magic, Stone."

With her compliment, he eased her off his lap to a thick carpet of pine needles spread across wild grasses and leaned over her. Slipping his hand between their bodies, Stone put his fingers to his fly and undid the top button. He'd go back to Pennsylvania and tonight would become a distant memory. He could forget what he damn well wanted to. Was he losing the restraint he'd maintained for the last twenty-four hours? He'd not always gone slowly with women but he'd always retained that ability. No woman had ever stolen his control.

Until tonight? Until this woman? Until Spicy McCoy.

Could he leave her behind to deal with whatever consequences she'd face? Perhaps the baby they'd talked about? All alone? Probably ostracized? Definitely exploited and abused by Clay McCoy? Stone sat up bringing her with him and buttoned her bodice.

"I don't deserve your magic, Spicy."

CHAPTER 20

SPICY WAS CONFUSED. THIS WASN'T THE FIRST time Stone had pulled back from her. Was her inexperience with men so obvious and repulsive? Spicy flinched at that likely probability. She would never have guessed men kissed women's breasts. It was absolutely exhilarating and she wanted him to do it again. But she must have responded poorly or reacted incorrectly. For her, the very sight of this gorgeous man sent her heart hammering against her ribs. Her hands always grew damp, her knees weakened, and butterflies fluttered in her tummy. She could never think of the right things to say to him and always second guessed the words she did spout. Sometimes just a smile might do but she often resisted because of her childish dimples. Though she didn't fully understand where Stone's wild kisses and bold caresses would lead, she wanted him to take her there. Tonight her instincts screamed that if she didn't follow Stone all the way she would never know what it meant to enjoy the journey.

"Stone, I want—" she began just as Nutmeg raced past them.

"Shh," Stone ordered as a breeze blew out both candles.

"But I..." Spicy's impulse to admit she wanted to make love with him vanished as surely as the candlelight. Left in the dark, she figured such a confession wasn't proper anyhow.

"Did you hear that?" he asked.

"You mean Nutmeg scurrying past?" Spicy was deaf to everything but Stone.

"Get up." In one swift move he stood, hauling her up with him.

"What's wrong?" Spicy cried.

"Run!"

Grabbing her hand, Stone took off and Spicy hurtled after him. Striving to keep up, she heard a loud snort at her back. Clay McCoy always snorted when angry.

"Who's there?" Spicy wailed.

"A damn hog," Stone barked.

Relief. Sort of. "There *is* an unclaimed razorback loose in the woods."

"Now's a helluva time to tell me."

With no candles and the charging hog not far behind them, Spicy took the lead. Leaving the glen and creek she darted into the dense woods. Swiping at tree limbs and following familiar trails, Spicy moved through the forest at breakneck speed.

"Are you still with me?" she called over her shoulder.

"Yeah," Stone answered at her heels.

"I didn't mention the hog because I thought you knew they run wild in order to feed," Spicy explained over her shoulder. "After they're fat their owners round 'em up."

"You can't trust those ugly, long-legged, half-wild, dumb mongrels!"

"The hogs or their owners?" Spicy asked.

"Neither. Both. Keep running."

Spicy laughed. Stone was not only outrageously appealing, he was funny. She'd been so swept away by the wanton pleasure he'd awakened in her, she had all but forgotten the feud which destroyed lives and tore love asunder. Johnse and Roseanna had been called Romeo and Juliet more than once. Fortunately, their doomed love affair had not ended in the double suicide Shakespeare penned in his play. But Spicy sensed the Hatfield man behind her could break her heart as completely as Roseanna and Juliet's hearts had been broken.

Stone wasn't in her heart. Was he? Didn't the liberties she'd just allowed him tonight indicate that he was? Yes. But she shouldn't let that happen again. She had explained to Stone there was no future for them. She'd even said she couldn't do all things nice with him. So, what she ought to do next was encourage Stone to paddle across the river and stay there because she obviously lacked the willpower to tell him no. After the election he would leave Tug Valley. Thus, her heart would be safe from the same misfortunes of those gone before her. She'd keep telling herself all of this.

Along with these dawning notions, dim lights in the distance meant someone had lit not just one but several lanterns on her porch. Realizing the snorting of the hog had faded, Spicy slowed her pace as they neared her front yard. Stone must have figured out the same thing she had about the lantern light because he took the lead again.

"Spicy?" boomed Lumpkin's voice.

"Yes," Spicy called out, wondering what Lumpkin's reaction would be to the man whom Clay swore shot him. "Stone's with me," she said as they walked out of the forest.

"Got lost?" Lumpkin was holding the piglet at the bottom of the porch steps.

Realizing that's why he'd lit the lanterns, Spicy shook her head. "Took a walk."

"Hey there, pardner," Stone said to Lumpkin as they came to a stop near the porch.

"Hey there, Just Stone."

"His name is jus—" Spicy caught herself.

Stone chuckled. "I go by Stone." Lumpkin nodded. "I heard you were shot last night like I was, Big Lump."

"Yes, sir," Lumpkin replied, cuddling the piglet against his chest.

"Lumpkin, I brought you something." Spicy pulled the

piece of florescent bark out of her pocket and handed it to him.

"Fairy fire." Lumpkin slipped it into his pocket. "Thank you."

"After all the trouble, it's nice of you to come back and keep an eye on Spicy." Stone smiled and then slowly Lumpkin smiled.

"Stone, we've been lucky not to have had a visit." Spicy couldn't say Clay in front of Lumpkin so she improvised with, "From Pignut." To be sure Stone knew who she meant she inclined her head in the direction where the infamous gang up Peter Creek lived. "But should the trip be cut short for some reason there will be trouble if you're here."

"Ahh...Peter Pignut." Stone added a first name and clenched his jaw. "My shotgun's in the cabin and right now I'm going to use it to chase off that hog."

"Clay wants it," Lumpkin said.

As if on cue, the rampaging hog burst out of the forest toward them. Spicy screamed and Stone stepped in front of her. Pepper had started toward them but made a quick turn-about to the chicken coop. The piglet squealed and rooted out of Lumpkin's arms, falling at his feet. The razorback charged them like a mad bull. Lumpkin made a grab for the scared piglet and missed. But suddenly the stampeding hog faltered. Shaking its head it sputtered to a stop at the far edge of the yard. The hog stumbled and fell flat as Lumpkin recaptured the piglet and held it to his heart. Spicy glanced at Stone. He held a large rock. Looking back at the hog, there was a similar rock near its head. With a single blow Stone had knocked the hog out.

"I guess a man named Stone would be handy with a rock," Spicy teased in a shaky voice and glanced at Lumpkin to see if bad memories had been triggered.

"Lucky shot." Stone shrugged. "That razorback's gonna have one big bump on his noggin tomorrow."

"Big bump," Lumpkin agreed. Then an ear-to-ear grin appeared on his pie face and he chuckled, pointing at the fallen razorback hog. "Big Bump." Nuzzling the piglet, Lumpkin then indicated the unconscious razorback's unmarked ears and said, "Just Stone's hog."

"No." Stone laughed and held up a hand. "Thanks, Big Lump, but I won't be here much longer." He glanced at Spicy and she forced herself to smile. "You keep Big Bump."

Lumpkin's grin faded. "Not ta home."

Spicy knew Lumpkin was well aware Clay would take the hog away from him at home. For all of Clay's talk of the Hatfields being land greedy, Clay, by hook or by crook as her father used to say, was always scheming to add to his holdings. Almost as if she could hear Papa's voice in that precise moment, Spicy knew beyond a shadow of a doubt Clay only wanted her for her cabin and five acres surrounding it, not to mention the well.

"Lumpkin, you can keep Big Bump and the piglet here," Spicy offered as Stone grabbed a lantern from the porch, walked to the hog, and squatted. "In fact, Shadow hopes you'll help him build a pen for the piglet."

"A pen," Lumpkin agreed enthusiastically. "What's piglet called?"

"Pig Piffle," Spicy answered as Stone examined the hog.

Lumpkin thought for a moment and then laughed heartily. "Pig Piffle."

"Stone named him." Spicy couldn't remember the last time Lumpkin had laughed. Years. She smiled at Stone knowing he had no idea what a milestone it was for Lumpkin to chuckle, much less laugh. Spicy folded her hands under her chin and laughed, too. "I think Pig Piffle is a girl so if Big Bump is a boy maybe they'll have babies someday. A hog business could give you financial independence, Lumpkin."

"Forest fairies." Lumpkin patted the fairy fire in his pocket.

"Riches in countless varieties," Stone said.

"Yes." Spicy's heart melted. Both men remembered what she'd said about the fairies bestowing good fortune upon good people. With an appreciative glance at Stone, she said, "Gotta start somewhere, Lumpkin."

"Yup." Stone winked at her and Spicy saw acknowledgment in his eyes.

"Gotta start somewhere," Lumpkin repeated, lumbering to Stone and hunkering down beside him. He held the piglet's hind end close to the lantern light. "Pig Piffle's a girl."

"And the hog's a male," Stone said. "Big Bump was on the rampage because there's an infected thorn and the stub of a branch imbedded in his left hind flank."

"His butt, Just Stone," Lumpkin said helpfully, looking at the razorback.

"Like a thorn and branch from one of my rosebushes?" Spicy asked.

"Yeah. Close to his testicles," Stone said. "Ouch."

"His balls," Lumpkin clarified. "Ouch."

"Yeah," Stone agreed and clapped Lumpkin on the back. "What say we remove it while he's knocked out?"

"Yes, sir," Lumpkin agreed importantly with another big smile.

Spicy marveled at the easy camaraderie between the two men. Clay would never have asked Lumpkin's opinion and Lumpkin never smiled at Clay. Spicy saw hero-worship in Lumpkin's eyes and her heart swelled with love. For Lumpkin, of course. Yet, her eyes were on Stone's dark head and broad shoulders.

"We'll need some rope to tie his legs and snout so he doesn't bite our arms off when his rock-administered anesthesia wears off," Stone said.

"There's extra rope on the porch near the spot where I tie up Pig Piffle." Spicy retrieved the rope and handed it to Stone. He pulled a wicked knife out of his boot and sliced through the rope. She unlatched the cabin door and lit another lantern and a lamp. When she returned outside, Lumpkin had safely secured the shoat and was helping Stone hogtie the razorback.

"All right, let's haul this hog over to the porch where there's light," Stone said.

"Stop. You're both my patients and I forbid either one of you to aggravate your wounds by dragging Big Bump to the porch steps. I'll do it," Spicy told them. When both men erupted in laughter Spicy smacked her hands to her hips. "You don't think I can move Big Bump?"

"No," Stone and Lumpkin chuckled together.

As Spicy stomped to the unconscious hog, Stone nudged Lumpkin with an elbow. Lumpkin put a hand over his mouth and chuckled. Spicy grabbed the hog's front legs and yanked. Her head snapped back, her feet skidded out in front of her, and she landed with a plop on her fanny. The men struggled to hold back their amusement, but when Spicy laughed they hooted and howled because the hog hadn't budged an inch.

"As entertaining as this is, Spicy, and trust me it is, please stop," Stone said, still chuckling as he helped her up. "That hog's not even full-grown, but he already outweighs you."

Lumpkin easily picked up the hog and tossed it over his shoulder. As Spicy watched him cart the hog toward the porch, her own feet left the ground.

"Stone!" she gasped as he swept her up and tossed her over his shoulder. "Put me down. You'll hurt yourself."

"You can kiss it and make it better if I do."

Her heart pounding as he carried her across the yard, Spicy got up her nerve to say, "If that's the required treatment I will do so, Dr. Hatfield."

"Well then, it hurts like hell," Stone replied.

Before she could talk herself out of it, Spicy tugged Stone's shirttail out of his pants and kissed his bare skin just above the linen covering his stitches. Stone leaned forward and Spicy prayed her wobbly knees wouldn't buckle when her feet touched the ground. Standing before the mountain of muscular man, she looked into his smoldering silver eyes.

"I think that kiss was hot enough to cauterize my wound," Stone said.

Spicy grinned and bit her lower lip. "Happy I could help."

"Come on, you can assist me with the razorback." Stone grabbed her hand and they walked to Lumpkin and the hog. "We're gonna do this together."

"We?" Spicy gasped. "You mean you."

"We. I'll tell you what to do."

"My mountain medicine consists of herbs, spices, poultices and…well…"

"Well what?"

"I've never cut into anybody. That's why I'm so in awe of you being a surgeon." She wrung her hands. "But I've decided I don't want to learn about surgery. I can't do it."

"If you can suture, you can slice," he said firmly. "Boil a knife and then come here."

She shook her head. "No, Stone, I just can't."

Stone's deep voice was clipped, "Let's get this done while the hog's still out."

"Yes, sir," Lumpkin prompted Spicy as to the correct answer.

"Yes, sir," Spicy replied, well worth it to see Lumpkin's gap-toothed grin.

Stone inclined his head and as she left to boil the knife, he and Lumpkin began tying the hog's hind legs to a porch post. After securing his front legs and snout, they arranged the lanterns close to where the hog lay unconscious on the ground. Spicy returned carrying the knife to Stone on a cotton towel.

"Back in record time with our surgical instrument," Stone said with a tease.

"Yes, but Stone, I—" she began on a hopeful note.

"But Stone, nothin'," he said. "C'mere."

He sat down on the second step up from the ground. He grasped Spicy's arm, spread his legs and positioned her on the step below him. Tucked tightly against his crotch, the furthest thing from Spicy's mind was the hog's private parts. She really wanted to turn and wrap her arms around the muscular man holding her against his.

"Big Lump, hold the hog's upper body in an iron-tight grip," Stone said and Lumpkin did so. Then to Spicy he said, "The knife is called a scalpel."

"Stone, I—" Spicy was about to protest one last time as he handed her the knife.

"You pull this off and you'll be a legend on both sides of the river," Stone told her. She gazed over her shoulder and he gently kissed the spot she'd smacked on the raft. "Are you going to take this golden opportunity to get some surgical experience or not?"

"It is my rosebush thorn after all." This man had been shot because of her. Yet, he was willing to teach her and help Lumpkin with his hog. "Yes. Tell me what to do."

CHAPTER 21

"In nursing school they teach medical and surgical components of medicine. Graduate nurses are qualified to assist in the operating room." And with that, Stone said, "Break the skin."

At least when Stone leaves for Philadelphia he won't remember me as a coward, Spicy thought. She placed the knife to the hog's hind quarters. She trembled from head to toe and pushed but the skin didn't break. Her hand shook so badly she tried to steady it with her other hand, but to no avail. Stone's right hand closed over Spicy's and together they broke the skin. That began to penetrate the razorback's unconscious state.

Stone warned, "You've only got seconds to remove the thorn so Big Bump and Pig Piffle can mate next spring."

"Gotta mate," Lumpkin agreed.

Spicy quickly glanced at Lumpkin. She hadn't thought to check his reaction to her being wedged between Stone's legs until now. His encouraging grin told Spicy he saw nothing wrong with her being molded to Stone. Spicy took a deep breath and with Stone talking her through it, she surgically removed the thorn and attached branch stub.

"How'd I do?" she asked, her hands trembling from the ordeal.

"Damn fine," Stone praised. "I want you to assist me in surgery."

"How'd I do?" Lumpkin asked.

"Damn fine, pardner," Stone said.

"Where's my pail?" Spicy asked. "I can drop this thorn and branch into it."

"I guess we left your pail in the woods. Drop it on the towel," Stone said. She dropped it. "Close the incision."

"I didn't boil a needle and thread."

"I'm not getting close enough to this razorback to take out any sutures." Stone placed the knife over a lantern flame. "We'll cauterize it to stop the bleeding and prevent further infection." Addressing Lumpkin he said, "Hold him tight because this'll wake the dead."

Stone handed Spicy the red-hot knife. When she hesitated, he closed his hand over hers again and they cauterized the wound. That got the hog's full attention. He snorted and fought against his restraints but was no match for the ropes and Big Lump. Stone suggested they leave Big Bump tied and provide him with water and food for the night to aid his recovery.

"He's all yours, Lumpkin," Spicy said.

"Thanks, Spicy." As Lumpkin petted the hog's head the animal calmed at his touch.

"I truly could not have done it without Stone," she replied.

With heartfelt sincerity in his voice, Lumpkin said, "Thank you, Stone Hatfield."

"You're welcome," Stone replied with a smile. "Let Big Bump walk around in the morning, but keep him tied up until you mark his ear and get your pen built. That way no one can take him from you, pardner."

"Yes, sir, pardner," Lumpkin said, beaming for all he was worth.

Stone drew up a bucket of water from the well and poured it over his and Spicy's hands. "Ten points for courage," he said.

"Ten? I not only cauterized your wound with a kiss but Big Bump's with a knife."

"You're right. Twenty points."

"That's my thirty to your ten, Dr. Hatfield. Think you can catch up?"

"I'd better because first one to reach a hundred wins."

"What's the prize?"

"We'll think of something."

Stone lowered his head and kissed her. Then he took the bucket of water to Lumpkin and poured the rest of it over his hands. Spicy walked onto her porch longing for another kiss. Her heart was full at seeing Stone's unwavering kindness to her cousin. On the downside, Lumpkin would take it hard when Stone left the valley. Lumpkin wouldn't be the only one.

Under the blue moon she would have let Stone make love to her, if he hadn't pulled back. Maybe he didn't want to chance leaving her with a child since she'd refused to go to Philadelphia. He probably knew as she did having an illegitimate baby was almost as shameful as being a sharecropper in Tug Valley. She'd have her cabin, land, and mountain-medicine practice which meant she could raise a child alone. But Stone wouldn't have his son or daughter. And the child wouldn't have his or her father. Wanting Stone and everything he offered that she couldn't have, Spicy vowed to strengthen her willpower against temptation.

"Let me change your bandage and make sure you didn't pull out the sutures," she said when Stone joined her on the porch.

Stone yawned and sauntered into the cabin. It was late and Lumpkin was tired, too. So even though Clay was gone and Lumpkin would have their place to himself, he said he'd like to stay on Spicy's porch near Big Bump and Pig Piffle. Spicy gave him a hug and promised a hearty breakfast the next morning. She said goodnight and shut the cabin door. Noticing Stone's shirt over a chair next to the table, she picked up a lamp and made her way into the bedroom.

On his stomach, eyes closed, Stone lay sprawled in her bed. Two nights in a row had to be wrong. Why then did sleeping with this man feel so right? His sinewy arms had closed around a pillow, bunching it under his head. Spicy could almost feel his embrace. He'd removed his binding and kicked off his boots along with his britches. His woolen drawers fit snugly to his slightly rounded, very male buttocks. As for his muscular thighs, she'd felt their strength when they were clamped against her on the porch steps.

"Dr. Hatfield?" she asked teasingly. When a low groan escaped him, Spicy grew warm at the dizzying current of hot desire coursing along her nerves. "Am I to assume you're spending another night with me?"

"If you'll let me. I'm sleepy, sugar'n spice," he said around another yawn. "As you can see the sutures are intact. We can put new bindings on in the morning."

Holding the lamp a bit closer she confirmed he was correct. "All right."

"Besides, I gotta fever."

Placing her hand to his forehead, she said, "No, you don't."

"That's what you think."

"What if a McCoy, other than Lumpkin, finds you here?"

"You've never had to nurse a patient through the night?"

"You're my first man."

At that, Stone opened his eyes and seductive lightning struck Spicy with its quicksilver blaze. "Happy to be your first man, little girl." When his eyes closed again, his lips almost imperceptibly turned up at the corners. He moved over in the bed making room for her and asked, "Did you latch the front door?"

"Yes."

"Then crawl in bed with me."

THE NEXT MORNING, Stone woke to Pepper crowing and Spicy curled spoon-fashion in his arms. Knowing she could have spent the night in the other bedroom, Stone tightened his embrace around her as a breeze fluttered the curtains. When Pepper crowed again, Stone heard Lumpkin talking to his new pigs. Spicy stirred beside him. Stone was a world away from Pennsylvania and yet there was nowhere he'd rather be than in Spicy McCoy's Kentucky bed. Eyes shut and clad in a shorter nightgown she rolled to her back.

"Morning," Stone whispered in her ear.

"Good morning." She smiled and opened her big blueberry eyes.

Under the circumstances Stone knew he didn't deserve her and he'd admitted it. But he'd dreamed of her all night long. When he ran his hand across her flat tummy, she threaded her fingers through the hair on his chest. He cupped her hip and gave her a gentle tug. She rolled to him molding her skimpily clad body to his naked skin. When he kissed her, she flattened her hand over his heart and kissed him back. She moaned as his fingers trailed up her ribs. When she caressed the back of his neck, he filled his hand with her right breast. His thumb brushed her nipple, beading the tip as his manhood hardened against her softness.

He groaned. "Know what I want for breakfast?"

"Cinnamon sticks, bacon, scrambled eggs, and coffee?"

"No."

"Sure you do," she teased. "You rest and I'll be back with breakfast."

Stone grumbled but let her scoot out of bed. He watched every move she made in the gown she'd probably worn for a decade. She scolded him for looking as she removed a lavender dress out of a small wardrobe next to a tin tub. He closed his eyes but not before he noticed this dress was the last one in her armoire. He'd seen her in the forest-green dress the day they'd met and others the shades of oranges, plums, roses, and lemons. She deserved so much more.

Swaying out of the room she left the door slightly ajar. Closing his eyes, Stone listened to her humming the tune from the blueberry patch as she padded barefoot around the cabin. "When Johnny Comes Marching Home Again" had gone from being one of his favorite tunes to his most favorite. He remembered Ellison's remark about him marching back home as a doctor. Just coincidences. It wasn't long before he smelled coffee brewing and bacon frying. Through the window he could tell that Big Lump was feeding his pigs as he whistled the same tune.

"Mornin', Just Stone," came Big Lump's voice through the narrow window.

"Morning, Big Lump," Stone replied. Big Lump seemed to call him Just Stone when he was happy and Stone when he was serious. "How're Big Bump and Pig Piffle?"

"Damn fine, pardner," Big Lump said and went back to whistling.

Stone chuckled as he rolled out of bed. After pulling on his britches and boots he strode into the front room just as Spicy took a tin of cinnamon sticks from over the fire in her hearth. He guessed he'd surprised her because she twirled to him and cinnamon sticks flew.

"I told you to stay in bed and rest."

He laughed at her entertaining antics—the cinnamon on her nose, maple-sugar curls in wild disarray—and said, "Yeah, I don't always do as I'm told."

"So I've noticed."

Luckily, all but one of the cinnamon sticks had stayed on the tin or landed on the table. Nutmeg snatched up the one on the floor and darted out the open front door. Spicy set the tin down and sliding an arm around her waist, Stone kissed the cinnamon off her nose. The dimples he adored framed her smile and she pulled out a chair for him. He sat and she placed the stray cinnamon sticks on the tin. Watching her lick her fingers, Stone's mind wandered.

"Coffee?" she asked.

"Yes, thanks," he replied, trying to reign in his thoughts.

Spicy poured three cups. She fixed a plate for Lumpkin and called to him. He appeared at the front door and thanked her, taking his coffee and plate to the porch. As Big Lump talked to his pigs, between bites of breakfast, Spicy's eyes glistened.

"I haven't seen Lumpkin truly happy since he was hurt," she said. "I can't remember the last time he laughed, much less whistled. It's all because of you, Stone. You're the first man to treat Lumpkin as an equal. He worships you. Thank you."

Like when she'd told him being a surgeon was the closest thing to being God, Spicy had a way of humbling him to the point of rendering him speechless. Stone could only nod. She brought two plates to the table laden with bacon and scrambled eggs. Freshening their coffee, she then sat across from him, and they chatted between bites. When they finished breakfast, Spicy set their plates aside on a counter to be washed. Then she placed a bowl of water, proudly announcing it had been boiled and cooled, beside her scissors and fresh linens on the table.

"When's Clay back?" Big Lump asked with a note of concern as he returned with his plate which he set next to the others.

CHAPTER 22

"Maybe in a couple of days," Spicy said picking up a fresh washcloth.

Mention of Clay put a frown on Stone's face. After Big Lump left the room, Stone asked, "Why does McCoy sell his moonshine in Williamson, West Virginia, when there are three times the people in Pikeville, Kentucky?"

"Williamson is on the Tug Fork River. Clay's superstitious about staying near the river." Spicy shrugged. "He believes the mountain magic can't find his profits if he does business close to the river since the fairies live in the forest."

"At least McCoy knows he's bad," Stone said. "But I think the real reason he goes to Williamson is because Johnse sells his whiskey in Pikeville. McCoy doesn't want the competition." Rubbing his forehead, he added, "They sell their moonshine in opposite states from where they live because the revenuers can't track them as easily."

Spicy waved her hand indicating Stone should scoot back from the table and turn around on the chair. When he'd done so, she commented his sutures were intact though he'd slept without his bindings. Then she began washing away bits of poultice.

"I've heard making corn whiskey is illegal. Clay says

that's not true, no one cares, and revenuers are trespassers. If the authorities didn't want moonshine made they'd stop it."

Stone was incredulous. Whether it was more so over McCoy's lies or the fact Spicy believed him was a toss-up. "West Virginia and Kentucky both care. But revenuers know if they come into these hills and valleys they won't get out alive. Wake up to reality, Spicy."

"Clay says no one should tell our farmers they can't distill their corn into whiskey. They don't tell me that I can't bake corn into muffins."

"You don't sell your muffins." Stone twisted to one side to look at her. She scratched her neck and dug at her hip. "Selling untaxed whiskey eliminates the revenue due the government. We have to abide by federal and state laws. Not by Hatfield and McCoy law."

"McCoy and Hatfield law is the law of these hollers."

"Ouch!"

"Sorry!"

Stone felt his back. "Did you yank out a suture?"

"No, there was a piece of dried poultice stuck to your wound." Rubbing her collarbone with one hand, Spicy held out her other hand and patted the air as if that could stop him from turning and twisting. "All five stitches are intact."

"Sutures."

"I'm going to suture your mouth shut."

"You'd have to control your psychosomatic scratching first."

"Tarnation!" Spicy fumed. Stone raised his brows in an open challenge for her to stop scratching or sew his mouth shut. Instead of scratching, she made a twirling motion with her hands and he turned around. "Behave or I'll use unboiled water to finish cleaning your wound."

"Sheriffs and deputies, like the revenuers, are reluctant to come into this lawless land," Stone said, taking his chances with the water. "And when a crime occurs, authorities from one state usually don't cross the Tug Fork River to capture a person in the other state. So, if you're going to sell moonshine or shoot a man, don't do it in your own state."

"Are you referring to Clay tracking and shooting you in West Virginia?"

"And to the McCoy who crossed into West Virginia and shot my father," Stone said. "How old was Clay eleven years ago?" Spicy stepped to his side as she placed the wet cloth in the bowl and picked up a dry towel. When she didn't answer, Stone snared her arm. "How old?"

Spicy squared her shoulders. "Nineteen."

"Plenty old enough to kill a man and go to prison."

"For what motive?"

Stone growled, "Jealousy over not owning a big house and mountains?"

Bristling, Spicy shot back, "Hatfields have more land than McCoys."

Stone let go of her and smacked his hand on the table. "McCoys receive a fair percentage for sharecropping Hatfield land."

"Pig piffle!" she huffed, but Stone could tell her heart wasn't in it.

"Pig Piffle's ou'chere," Big Lump called helpfully.

Stone chuckled as the hint of dimples indicated Spicy was trying not to laugh. "We're acting like the feud was bred into us, too." He added less ferociously, "Let's stop."

"Yes, let's." Spicy gently dried his skin. When he stood, she carefully wrapped fresh linen strips around his torso. Placing her hands over her heart, she looked up at him. "I hoped by treating both Hatfields and McCoys I could heal the feud a little bit. But to cut out the hatred infecting Tug Valley will take a very sharp kni—scalpel. And time."

"Time," Stone repeated. With a sigh, he pulled her into his arms. "I know."

"Ol' Ranel's a'comin'," Big Lump said, poking his head in the doorway as Pepper squawked in the yard.

"Tarnation," Stone grumbled teasingly. "Thanks, Big Lump."

"Hide!" Spicy gulped and grabbed Stone's hand.

"I'm not going to hide, but I'll leave," he said as she tugged him into her bedroom. "I need to go check on Logan anyway." Spicy nodded and headed to the front door. Before Stone closed the bedroom door, he told her, "I'll see you later."

"Hello," came Spicy's greeting from the front porch.

Stone figured Randolph McCoy had to be around fifty-six or seven by now. Though that made him roughly fourteen years older than Devil Anse, he was reputed to be no less sharp and every bit as vindictive. Years ago, Stone's path had crossed Ol' Ranel's a time or two. His eyes were dark and his hair cropped short. A bushy mustache had trailed his turned-down lips, but he didn't wear the long beard like many mountain men. He had married his first cousin, Sarah McCoy, who was known as Aunt Sally. Ol' Ranel and Sally had sixteen children, most of whom worked on other people's farms. Devil Anse swore Ol'Ranel only worked at gossiping and complaining, which explained why he had so little to show for himself. Had Ol'Ranel heard about the shootings and come to ask questions? Or to make accusations?

"I see you brought Nancy and Mary with you," Spicy said somewhat loudly, surely warning Stone who and what he was up against.

Footsteps shuffled across the porch. Stone figured to stay in the bedroom and hope all three would come inside the cabin. Then he'd leave through the back door. But he had to be careful because the back door was located on the side of the cabin and his exit could be seen from the porch. It sounded like at least one visitor had entered the front room.

Ol'Ranel asked, "Whose store-bought lookin' white shirt's on the chair? Whose shotgun and moonshine's that? What man is here, Spicy McCoy?"

Too late, Stone remembered those items were in the front room and not the bedroom. *Tell him they belong to a patient, Spicy*, he thought.

"What makes you think the shotgun's not mine?" Spicy asked. "That shirt belongs to one of my patients and moonshine makes for good anesthesia."

Ol'Ranel said, "I don't see no patient."

"He was here," Big Lump said.

"Have you ever known Lumpkin to lie?" Spicy asked.

"What I knowed is thar ain't nobody ta home in Big Lump's head," Ol'Ranel replied.

"Damn," Stone breathed, knowing there was somebody very much to home.

"Lumpkin was smart enough to claim a hog nobody else around here has been able to catch," Spicy said.

"Didje catch that razorback what nobody owns?" Ol'Ranel demanded.

Big Lump continued with determination, "Marked his ear and buildin' a pen."

That was the longest sentence Stone had ever heard him speak. Owning something meant everything to Big Lump.

"What brings you here, Ranel?" Spicy asked.

"Trouble. We come to tell you about it," he replied.

From the sound of his voice it seemed Ol' Ranel had turned and spoken as if the others were still out on the porch.

"Please, come in. I'll pour some coffee," Spicy said.

"We's fine in these here rockin' chairs," one of the women replied.

Through the thin walls and open windows Stone could hear every word. More shuffling sounded as if Ol' Ranel had returned to the porch.

"Mary, if'n yer not too ashamed, tell Spicy what happened," Ol' Ranel said, but no one responded. "Nancy, since yer married to Johnse Hatfield, tell Spicy how Cap Hatfield done whipped yer sister, Mary, with a cow's tail," Ol' Ranel prodded. Like Johnse, Cap's father was Devil Anse. Two years younger than Johnse, Cap was considered the single most dangerous Hatfield. Whereas Johnse leaned toward a good-natured attitude like his Uncle Ellison, Cap was said to take offense somewhat easily. Much like Clay. When neither woman spoke, Ol' Ranel continued, "Cap said he done it on accounta the girls been carryin' Hatfield *tales* to me."

Stone vividly recalled Devil Anse complaining that Johnse's wife, Nancy, was *one tale-tellin' McCoy girl what needs to have her flappin' trap shut*. But surely Devil Anse didn't approve of Cap, trying to silence his brother's wife by taking it out on her sister, Mary. Spicy was going to be mad about this. Damn, he was mad about it. How dare any man strike a woman. With or without a cow's tail. Stone shook his head and sighed. Only in Tug Valley.

"Clay don't have no store-bought shirts, white or not," a woman said.

"Heard mention of a shotgun, too," the other woman commented.

"Thinkin' on it, Clay totes a rifle not a shotgun," Ol' Ranel added.

Of all people to come here, why'd it have to be ones known to thrive on gossip?

"Have you been sparkin' with two men at the same time, Spicy?" the first woman asked.

CHAPTER 23

"THIS IS MY HOME AND MY LIFE AND I'LL THANK
you all to mind your own business," Spicy said. "If Mary
needs treated, I will see to it. Otherwise I've heard enough
gossip for one day."

Stone's sentiments exactly. It sounded as though all
three visitors were entering the cabin for the treatment—his
opportunity to get out of Spicy's way. Wishing he didn't
have to leave his shotgun and shirt behind, Stone neverthe-
less quietly unlatched the back door and slipped outside.

"Howdy!" said a youngster, popping around the corner of
the cabin. "Who're you?"

That brought Ol' Ranel and the women scurrying right
back to the front porch before Stone could get out of sight.
He'd never run from a fight and wasn't going to run from
this one.

"Who're you?" Ol' Ranel echoed the blond boy's
question.

"Shadow McCoy," Spicy and Big Lump said at the same
time.

"I ain't talkin' 'bout Shadow. Confess the corn, Spicy,"
Ol'Ranel griped. "Who's the half-nekked man in yer yard?"

"He's my business," Spicy said with cool conviction.

One of the women giggled. "He's mighty big business."

"He's as handsome as he is big," the other woman gushed.

"That I do confess," Spicy said, gazing directly at Stone.

Women had told him he was handsome all through school—during his residency and on hospital rounds. But it had never meant much until hearing Spicy thought so.

"Good morning," Stone said to the visitors on the porch.

"Mornin'," said the woman without scratches on her arms. She came down the porch steps and stopped a few feet away. "I'm Nancy McCoy Hatfield, Johnse's wife."

"I'm Stone Hatfield," Stone said more to Shadow than Nancy. Then addressing Johnse's wife, he added, "I'm Johnse's friend."

"Hatfield?" Ol' Ranel blared and tromped down the steps, stopping next to Nancy. "I told Clay t'other day I heared a Hatfield was livin' right across the Tug Fork. That's you."

"Welcome, Shadow," Spicy said and waved at the boy as if the biting tension didn't exist. "Are you here to work on the pigpen?"

"Yes, ma'am."

As Ol' Ranel glowered at him, Stone's admiration soared for Spicy. She unfailingly played fair no matter the risk to herself—putting neighbors in their place while championing a giant, welcoming an innocent boy, and standing her ground for himself. What he wouldn't give to always have Spicy in his corner. Exactly what would he give? He knew the answer lay more in what he would have to give up.

"Lumpkin, please feel free to cut those trees in back of Stone," Spicy suggested and pointed. "You and Shadow can use them for your pen and make my front yard a little bigger at the same time. There's an ax and a saw over by the chicken coop."

"I brung a hammer and nails, Big Lump," Shadow said excitedly, motioning to the burlap bag slung over his shoulder. "I like yer razorback. What's his name?"

"Big Bump," Lumpkin replied, showing Shadow how he'd marked the hog's ear.

"A right-perfect name," Shadow said. "Ain't our pigpen gonna be some pumpkins?"

"Some pumpkins," Big Lump agreed as they strode toward Stone and the nearby trees.

"Mary, I'll get you some honey to help heal your scratches and welts and then you can be on your way," Spicy suggested, the crispness back in her voice. "As you can see, by the bindings around my patient's mid-section, he was injured and needs to be on his way before he pulls out his sutures."

"His what?" Mary tittered.

"Sutures! Stitches!"

"Why're you gettin' in such a pucker, Spicy?" Nancy asked.

"I'm not angry," Spicy replied. "But I am frustrated about the gossiping and whipping."

"You sidin' again' us McCoys and stickin' up fer them greedy Hatfields?" Ol'Ranel glowered from Stone to Spicy and back to Stone.

"I wouldn't side with any Hatfield or any McCoy who struck a woman," Spicy replied calmly. "The feuding needs to stop."

"But," Mary chimed in, "The Hatfields is rich, the McCoys is poor and what else is there to talk 'bout 'cept the feud?"

"Talking about the feud perpetuates it," Spicy reasoned.

"Yer talkin' like a goldurn book," Ol'Ranel grumbled. "What's perpet...perpet...what's that highfalutin word mean?"

"Perpetuates means you're fueling the feud," Spicy explained, hands on her hips. "Proof of that is what it just cost Mary." Looking from Ol' Ranel to Mary and then to Nancy, she said, "Nancy, think of the peace you could build between the clans by saying Johnse is a good husband instead of claiming you've henpecked him into obedience."

Ol'Ranel cackled. "I's right fond of the henpeckin' story."

Spicy's sigh was clearly one of disgust. When she disappeared inside, Mary joined Ol' Ranel and Nancy in the front yard. Stone turned his back on the glare and stares as Big Lump and Shadow selected the first tree to chop down for the pig pen. Stone didn't expect the good advice Spicy had given would be heeded. But he hadn't missed a syllable and was proud of her talk of peace when faced with the feud. Spicy emerged from the cabin with the honey, descended the steps, and walked to Stone. Ol' Ranel was ready for more.

"Ever'body knows Cap Hatfield's always lookin' fer trouble," Ol' Ranel said.

"Our version of Cap is your son, Tolbert," Spicy lowered her voice to add, "and Clay."

"I argie it's Devil Anse and Cap what perpets the feud."

"No more than you and Tolbert," Spicy insisted. "Tolbert got himself appointed as a deputy and then he and your son, Bud, arrested Johnse Hatfield for carrying a concealed weapon in the fall of 1880." Spicy shook her head, saying, "And that was ridiculous because most every man in Tug Valley carries a gun for hunting."

Getting more and more riled, Ol' Ranel glowered. "Devil Anse and his Hatfield posse took Johnse back afore Tolbert and Bud could get him to the sheriff in Pike County."

"And no physical harm was done to Tolbert or Bud by Devil Anse and his clan. Stop filling your McCoy clan with jealousy of the Hatfields."

Damn, Stone thought, *she's not pulling any punches.*

Ol' Ranel raised a fist and railed, "Devil Anse thinks he's better'n me on accounta he's got all that timberland."

Spicy handed the honey to Mary and said, "I wish honey could sweeten dispositions and heal all the wounds from the feud. Believe me, the McCoys aren't the only victims."

"But Devil Anse got an extry five thousand acres on accounta he done cheated good ol' Perry Cline," Ol' Ranel protested.

Stone prayed Spicy knew the true account.

"Good ol' Perry Cline was caught cutting timber on Devil Anse's land," Spicy clarified. "That's why the courts awarded Cline's land to Devil Anse." Looking from Ol' Ranel, to Nancy and then Mary, she said, "I hope as Mary's injuries fade the three of you will consider helping the feud fade."

Ol'Ranel hollered, "Laws! How can the feud fade when Devil Anse lords his wealth over us by makin' McCoys work his dad-blamed timberin' business?"

"Let's get the facts straight here as we did concerning Perry Cline," Spicy shot back. "Devil Anse has kept a lot of McCoys from starving to death by offering them a fair wage for a fair day's work. Now, isn't that right, Randolph?"

Stone knew he and Spicy were once again of like mind.

"It ain't right we's poor and they's rich. God blast all them Hatfields ta hell!" Ol'Ranel was screaming now. "Jist who's side is you on, Spicy McCoy?"

"Stop!" Stone strode within a few feet of Ol' Ranel. Towering over the older man, he warned, "I've stayed out of this fight until now. But you yell at Spicy one more time and I'll cut your damn fool tongue out of your head."

Both visiting women's mouths fell open. Ol'Ranel shut his. *What the hell,* Stone thought, *they would have somebody and something new to gossip about when they got home.* Following Stone, Spicy took an extra step placing herself between him and the McCoys.

"Stone, for your sake," Spicy pleaded over her shoulder, "take a deep breath."

Stone glared over her head at Ol'Ranel and growled, "Get lost and don't come back."

"I's gettin'," Ol' Ranel muttered and ambled away toward the woods.

Nancy gave Stone a nod and followed her uncle. Mary stared open-mouthed at Stone.

"He's mine," Spicy snapped. "Blackberry Fork," she

ordered and pointed due west as to where Ol' Ranel lived. "Go!"

Mary skirted around them and caught up with the others. Hands on his hips, Stone watched the women disappear into the woods. But Ol' Ranel turned and faced them.

Pointing at Big Lump who had paused in chopping a tree, Ol' Ranel shouted, "Sure hope Clay don't whoop him fer keepin' a secret 'bout yer sparkin'!"

"Get outa here, McCoy!" Stone yelled. Damn, these feuding hills and valleys mixed confusion and contradictions into a man's ordered soul.

"Stone, please," Spicy turned to him, placed her delicate hands to his jaw and lowered his head until his gaze connected with hers, "don't get caught up in the feud."

Stone ran a hand through his hair. "It's hard not to."

"Trust me. I know," Spicy whispered and wrapped her arms around him.

Toting an ax, Big Lump and Shadow, cuddling the piglet, walked toward them. All things considered, both had taken the dispute in their stride.

CHAPTER 24

"BALDERDASH?" LUMPKIN ASKED SPICY.

"Yes," Spicy replied to the word she had taught him about gossiping. The heated clash of clans that had just erupted, in which she had assumed a leading role, would intensify Clay's hatred and jealousy. But she wasn't sure how to break it to Lumpkin or advise him on how to deal with it.

"Big Lump," Stone began, "I don't want you to walk into a hornet's nest at home, so you should know that Ol' Ranel, his nieces, or someone else may carry *tales* to Clay that'll make him mad at you, Spicy, and me. Take no crap from Clay, pardner."

"Take no crap." Big Lump smiled nonplussed.

Take no crap, Spicy thought. Man-to-man and well said.

"Shadow's my lil' pardner." With that introduction, Lumpkin patted the boy's shoulder.

"Pleased to meet you, Shadow." Stone extended his hand.

Shifting the piglet to the crook of his left arm, Shadow took Stone's hand and repeated, "Pleased to meet you. Big Lump says you're a doctor. Did you know Spicy doctors folks, too? Did you know you ain't got no shirt on?"

"I haven't had a chance to put my shirt on this morning." Stone chuckled, then gazing at Spicy he said, "I'm learning more about Spicy every day. Did you know she operated on Big Bump last night?"

"Big Lump done told me," Shadow said. "Talking 'bout a hornet's nest," the boy began naively as he cuddled the piglet again, "there's one hanging from a limb of a tree we's thinking of cutting. Want us to knock the nest down, Spicy?"

"Actually, it's one of my beehives. If you look closely I have three." Spicy pointed in different directions. "They're my honeybees. I keep roses and wildflowers growing around the yard for them and each fall they give me the honey I need for my teas, tonics, and treatments."

"Don't they sting ya?" Shadow asked in awe.

"No. They can be controlled with smoke and won't sting you if you don't bother them."

Stone appeared amazed. Big Lump and Shadow glanced around, there were plenty of other trees to chop. Then the giant and boy turned in perfect harmony and went back to their work. Stone walked Spicy inside and caught her hand in the middle of the front room.

"You didn't have to defend the Hatfields to those McCoys."

"I told the truth. Like you do."

"Like when you told them I'm yours?"

"You are mine. My patient."

Stone cocked a brow and grinned. "Just your patient?"

"To tell the whole truth," Spicy hesitated, then squared her shoulders, "I'm proud to have the smartest, bravest, and most handsome man I've ever known in my life as my patient."

"Aww, Spicy." Stone pulled her into his arms. With his hand buried in the curls at the back of her head, he whispered, "You are the smartest, bravest, and most beautiful woman I've ever known in my life. Please don't make me leave Tug Valley without you."

"Right now, the important thing is for you to leave

Raccoon Hollow." With her ear to his bare chest, Spicy listened to his heartbeat. "Clay may get back early and show up."

"I've met just about everybody else. McCoy's next."

"No." Spicy leaned back and looked up at him. "I hope you never meet him."

"McCoy knows where I live." Stone lifted his chin in the direction of the woods. "Those three McCoys who just left will have every detail of my presence sorted out and spread by the day's end. Anything they can't sort out, Nancy'll try to pry out of Johnse."

"Exactly. What happened will escalate Clay's vendetta against you." Spicy eased out of his arms. "Maybe you'd better not go home."

"Right," Stone agreed. "Like I said, I'll check on Logan and be back."

"No, I mean you'd better go to Ellison's place or Devil Anse's house. There's safety in numbers."

"Like hell I will," Stone said. "I'm not afraid of McCoy."

"I know you're not." She clasped her hands to her heart and said, "But it will be easier for me to hold Clay to the new deal not to kill you if he doesn't find you here."

"I'm not letting you fight my battles by reminding McCoy you're going to," Stone clenched his jaw and gritted through his teeth, "marry him."

"Clay is my battle, not yours. And whether or not I marry him is my decision and not yours," Spicy said as firmly as she possible could. "If you go now, maybe there won't be any trouble. If you confront Clay, I feel certain only one of you will live to talk about it."

"I'll be the one."

"Stone, listen to yourself." Spicy had to get through to him. Placing both hands to his muscular upper arms, she squeezed. "You're considering a fight to the death when saving lives is why you walk this earth. You're not a killer. And you can't be chief of surgery if you are the one who's killed."

"I won't be killed and I don't want McCoy to hurt you."

"So, it's safer for you," when he frowned, she inclined her head and corrected with, "for both of us and Lumpkin if I'm alone in my cabin when Clay returns." Spicy's eyes stung and her throat ached as she did her best to release not only her physical hold, but her emotional attachment to Stone. "You can remove your own sutures on Friday." Her hands fell to her sides.

"That sounds ominous," he said. A single tear spilled down her cheek and he gently thumbed the tear away. "When will I see you again?"

"I don't know."

"Please come home with me."

"I can control things only if I'm on the Kentucky side of the river."

"You can't control McCoy from either side of the river." He paused and sighed. "Whatever you do, don't let your guard down, Spicy. He's not stupid and that's in part what makes him so dangerous."

"I will be fine."

"You are the most defiant woman I've ever met." Stone ran a hand through his hair, stalked to the door and called, "Big Lump!" Big Lump immediately stopped what he was doing and lumbered toward him. Stone said, "I'm going home to check on my horse, see about my aunt, and take care of some business. Promise me you won't leave Spicy alone day or night."

Big Lump thumped his heart and smiled broadly. "Day'r night, Just Stone."

Spicy watched Lumpkin return to his work with Shadow. Then she took in Stone's every move as he put on his shirt and buttoned it before tucking the tails into his pants. A frown and a couple days' stubble darkened his handsome face with worry. His chest, with the light furring of black hair showed in the opening of his shirt. In the crotch of his snug pants was the sexy male bulge capable of becoming as hard as his gun. Tingles popped out on

Spicy's skin remembering how his body had been pressed to hers in bed the past two nights. Noticeable through his white shirt, the bindings caught her attention. Along with brains and brawn, he had a reckless, dangerous air. In truth, her liaison with Stone was nothing but reckless and dangerous.

But most of all, Stone Hatfield was a good man.

"I detest this feud," he grumbled.

"Then leave Tug Valley now." Spicy was torn between falling on her knees and begging him to stay forever and shoving him out of the door for his well-being and future. "Don't wait for election day."

"I promised my aunt I'd take her to the Magnolia Precinct. She says it's an all-day festival. The social event of the year."

"At least stick to your Magnolia Precinct and don't come into Raccoon Hollow."

"I need to head back to Philadelphia a couple of weeks or so after the election in order to prepare for taking over the surgical department." Stone frowned. "One last time, will you come with me and enroll in Pennsylvania Hospital's School of Nursing?"

Becoming a nurse and having a baby with Stone. Spicy had never wanted anything more in her entire life. Taking a deep breath and letting it out she said, "Clay used to regularly beat Lumpkin. When I found out I threw such a fit Clay hasn't hit him for a while. But now, Clay has shot Lumpkin maybe with the intention to kill his brother." When Stone opened his mouth, she held up a hand. "Before you suggest it, we can't take Lumpkin away from Abigail and the only life he's ever known." Shaking her head, Spicy said, "I can't go with you."

"You mean you won't."

"I mean I can't."

In the middle of the front room it was a silent but raging standoff as they stood toe-to-toe. When Stone clenched his jaw, Spicy pictured touching the cleft in his strong chin. But she didn't. Cocking his head to one side and then the other, he muttered a couple of choice curses.

"On Friday, Aunt Hilda and are I are fixing supper at my house. She wants to meet you. It will be an early meal so she can get home before dark. You and Big Lump are both invited." He let out a frustrated sigh. "I won't leave Tug Valley without saying goodbye to you."

"I believe we're star-crossed. Just say goodbye now."

"We're not Romeo and Juliet." His tone had been aggravated but then a charming grin touched his lips. "But as the story goes, *'Love is a smoke raised with the fume of sighs. Being purged, a fire sparkling in lovers' eyes'*. That's what I believe, Spicy."

Spicy's body heated. Oh how she wished she and Stone could have made love. At least once. His quicksilver eyes smoldered as the quote hung in the air. "The next line in the play is, *'Being vex'd, a sea nourish'd with lovers' tears.'* And that's what I believe, Stone."

"You'd better come for supper, Spicy McCoy. Five o'clock. Or else."

"Or else what, Stone Hatfield?"

"I promise I'll be back to get you."

Stone swept her into his arms and when his mouth came down on hers, Spicy didn't want the kiss to ever stop. To never hold this man in her arms again, to never see him again, to never make love to him seemed a punishment worse than death. She clung to him, pouring herself into the kiss. Stone hugged her tightly and then released her. Picking up his shotgun and the moonshine jug, without another word he headed out the front door. She followed him as far as the porch. He crossed the yard to Lumpkin and Shadow and she heard them telling him how they were going to build the pen. Stone left them smiling and waving at his back.

As Stone passed the porch, he smiled at her. Spicy's heart cried out to go with this once-in-a-blue-moon man to his mountain and never look back. But she didn't. She stood rooted by feuds as Stone vanished into the woods. Gazing toward West Virginia, she swiped at the tears streaming down her cheeks.

"Is your big pardner coming back?" Shadow asked Lumpkin with the same hero-worship on his face that Spicy saw on Lumpkin's when he interacted with Stone.

"I hope so," Lumpkin said, as he and Shadow stood in Stone's wake.

"Go home, Stone," Spicy murmured as fervently as a prayer. "To Pennsylvania."

CHAPTER 25

STONE GLARED ACROSS THE RIVER FROM WHERE HE stood on his porch. He'd stopped winding the mantel clock since Spicy had said she'd fix it. During the long days and night she'd been without her, his heart didn't seem to be ticking right, either. He'd removed his own sutures and now twenty-four hours later, he rotated his shoulders with no pain. A half hour ago, he had urged his Aunt Hilda to eat her supper, but she wouldn't touch a bite without Spicy and Big Lump. She had followed him outside and was sitting in a rocker keeping him company.

"Stony, did she actually say she'd be here?"

"No."

"Maybe she's too frightened to come to West Virginia."

"Nah, she doesn't scare easily." Stone clenched his jaw. "Maybe it's my stupid 'or else' keeping her away. It was said in jest, but that McCoy pride is fierce."

"The same for us," Aunt Hilda pointed out. "The Hatfields are the most hospitable folks you'd ever want to meet until you cross one of them. They protect family to a fault. Ask Cap."

"Yeah, I saw the cow's tail marks on Ol'Ranel's niece," Stone replied.

"Perhaps Spicy is understandably upset about that."

"Yes, but she defended the Hatfields to Randolph McCoy." Stone looked over his shoulder at his aunt. "He's a cantankerous old coot."

"Most McCoys would describe Devil Anse as a blood-thirsty old coot." Aunt Hilda's face was devoid of opinion or prejudice. "I wonder which is worse."

With a nod at his aunt, who like his mother wore pretty store-bought dresses and her hair pulled back in a bun, Stone complimented her, "If there were more people like you, Aunt Hilda, there would be no feud."

"Thank you," she replied. "There seems to be someone very much like me who lives in a cabin across the river."

"You should have seen her the other day." Stone stared toward Kentucky again, but it was Spicy he saw in his mind's eye. "Talking to Ol'Ranel, she was so calm and collected. She's so smart and so kind. And so beautiful."

"And you're so in love with her."

Stone jerked his spine ramrod straight and faced his aunt. "No, I'm not."

"Malarkey." His aunt held up her hand to silence any protest he might have. "If she doesn't come for supper tonight, are you going to paddle the Tug Fork? If you do, will you tell her about your business in Logan two days ago?"

"I don't know." Stone thought back to his decision requiring the trip to Logan. He'd known what he wanted and the only honorable way to achieve it. "Maybe."

"Stone, are you at least going to go see Spicy before you leave?" Aunt Hilda prodded.

"Yeah." Crossing the porch and stepping inside his house, he picked up his Colt .45 off the foyer table. He checked to make sure it was fully loaded. "Right now."

His aunt stood and said, "Don't go with a gun."

"I'm sure not going over there without one."

"I'll wait right here until you return. Please be careful."

Stone stuck the pistol in the back of his pants. After untethering Logan from the hitching post, he took the road across the clearing. Down through the woods, his stomach tied itself in a knot. Something told him he'd picked a bad time to go to Logan. When he came out by the river and blueberry patch he was met with two well-armed men on horseback.

"Stone," Ellison called with a wave. "We heard you got shot."

Johnse asked, "Do you know who did it?"

"Devil Anse sent us to make sure you were alive," Ellison added.

"Tell Devil Anse I'm fine. I know who shot me but I can't prove it," Stone said, straining to see into the woods across the river. Ellison and Johnse both followed his gaze toward Kentucky. "Thanks for riding out my way, but I have to go check on a friend."

"Spicy McCoy," Johnse said. "We heard that, too."

"Hey!" Stone shouted as Big Lump charged out of Raccoon Hollow toward the river's edge. Spicy was sure to appear any second. But there was no sign of her.

Big Lump's single motion of waving him across the river shot terror through Stone. For a split second, his eyes met Ellison's and then Johnse's. They knew well what they could be up against. Stone bailed off Logan and raced to pull his canoe out of the bushes. The other two men were on the ground right behind him and tethered the horses. Stone jumped into the canoe and grabbed the paddles as Ellison and Johnse gave the canoe a running push into the river.

"Where is she, Big Lump?" Stone asked, leaping out of the canoe in Kentucky.

"Clay's got her."

CURLED UP IN A FETAL POSITION, Spicy rasped, "Hot."

Praying that being taken from her cabin was just another one of her nightmares, she slowly opened her eyes. Sadly not. The thin mattress was filthy. Cracks in the log ceiling explained the smell of mold while spat tobacco and moon-shine jugs littered the plank floor. Across the square room dirty tin plates covered a rickety-looking table. Down a narrow hallway, called a dogtrot, skunk carcasses hung on hooks. She'd not been here since her bedside vigil when Lumpkin had lain unconscious in the leaky lean-to at the other end of that dogtrot.

Clay McCoy's cabin. Spicy wanted to cry.

The stench of something boiling in a pot over the hearth made her stomach roll and smothering heat enveloped her flesh like the flames of hell.

"Lumpkin?" She was too ill to speak above a whisper.

Clomping footsteps came to a stop near the end of the bed. Spicy slowly tucked her chin to her chest and cringed. Eyes as flat as mud. Orange hair and mustache. Face red with rage.

"Water," Spicy begged.

"You don't need no water." Clay scowled with a nod toward the hearth. "I's gonna fix what ails you with skunk tongue'n blood soup."

Spicy retched over the side of the bed, but nothing came up. Her stomach was empty, her mouth dry, and throat scratchy. Her bones and joints ached with pain she was so sick.

"Why am I here?"

"I heared Stone Hatfield was in yer cabin. He cain't never get to you now." Clay grabbed up her pail, his features contorting with fanatical jealousy. "Was you sparkin' with Philadelphy at the crick?" Spicy didn't answer. "I found two candles next to this here pail, so don't tell me he wasn't with you." Extending his arm, Clay shook the pail at her. "What didje put in this pail fer him? Yer drawers?"

"Fairy fire," Spicy said. Clay flung the pail across the room as if it had burned him. "Where's Lumpkin?"

"That ignoramus don't care 'bout you." Clay spat tobacco, his thin lips turned down at the corners. "He's busy sparkin' with some plug-ugly Hatfield whore."

"Abigail Hatfield is nothing of the sort. Abby is lovely and kind and adores Lumpkin."

"When I got to yer cabin he was buildin' a pigpen with some stupid kid what run off the second he seen me. I's takin' the piglet that kid had hold of an' rebranding the razorback's ear."

"No." Spicy closed her eyes to shut out the awful man, his cruel words, and grimy hovel.

"Wake up!" Clay roared. "We's gonna talk 'bout Hatfield. Was he in yer bed?"

Hearing Clay's movement and heeding Stone's warning not to let her guard down, Spicy lifted her heavy eyelids. Clay rounded the end of the bed, hatred clenching his fists. Down the middle of his forehead a blue vein throbbed as he loomed over her like a death sentence.

"I sutured the bullet wound you put in Stone's back."

"Yeah, I shot him awright," Clay admitted. "He's from Philadelphy so he's a Yankee."

"The Civil War was over years ago." Spicy wasn't surprised by Clay's admission since she and Stone had already figured Clay was the one guilty of shooting him and Lumpkin. But his confirmation made her even sicker.

"It'll always be war with them Hatfields."

"No. Especially not with Stone who's as kind as Abigail. He's a doc—"

An animal-like howl erupted from Clay, stopping her defense which Spicy realized too late she should never have started. Grabbing handfuls of Spicy's clothing, Clay jerked her upper body off the bed. His nose touched hers and his chewing-tobacco breath gagged her.

"I been real *kind* fer over a year!" Clay hollered in her face. "But we ain't doin' things yer way no more. We's doin' 'em my way." The vein in his forehead pulsed. "One more word 'bout Stone Hatfield an' our deal's off. I's kill him today. You understand me, woman?"

"I understand," she managed. "I need water. I'm so hot."

"Yeah?" Clay's snarl was ice cold. "I's gettin' fevered seein' you in yer purdy white nightgown."

As he dropped her back on the thin mattress, Spicy recalled starting out the day in her own bed. Accustomed to Pepper's crowing, she'd paid little attention when he woke her from a dream about Stone. Her first conscious thought was the decision to accept Stone's supper invitation so she and Lumpkin could say a proper goodbye. With her next breath a painful pinch had jarred her fully awake. Staring into the darkness, except for the unexpected pinch, the only thing amiss was the back door. She'd forgotten to latch it again and it stood slightly ajar. Wouldn't be the first time Nutmeg had managed to open an unlatched door.

Spicy remembered rising and latching the door. Lying down again, dizziness and nausea had soon ensued, preventing her from going back to sleep. The next time Pepper had crowed, Spicy had a fever. Too sick to get out of bed, she'd rested. A couple of hours later, in the distance, she'd heard Lumpkin and Shadow working on the pigpen. She had managed to call to them from her window, urging them to come inside and fix whatever they wanted for a midday meal. She'd had no appetite. Her symptoms had steadily worsened throughout the day. Spicy eventually admitted to herself she was too sick to go to supper. But before she could send Lumpkin on without her, Clay had arrived. She'd been too weak to prevail against him when he picked her up and carried her out of the cabin.

"Spicy?" Lumpkin had called from the direction of the new pigpen. "Yer better?"

Clay had sneered, "Shut the hell up, imbecile."

Spicy heard Lumpkin say, "Take no crap."

Though Clay ignored Lumpkin, Spicy wanted to scream for him to get Stone. But protecting a surgeon, a skilled doctor who could save countless lives, was far more important than saving her own skin. Thus, Spicy remained silent as Clay carted her across the front yard. Nutmeg had bared his teeth and growled ferociously at Clay. The honeybees seemed to sense something was amiss and buzzed frantically as Clay passed a nest. Squawking all the way, Pepper had flapped himself clear off the ground trying to dig his sharp spurs into Clay.

"Wring that pecker-head rooster's neck an' bring him to me, you stupid hog-stealer," Clay had ordered Lumpkin over his shoulder. "I's gonna fry him up for supper."

The woods swallowed them and her cabin had vanished. Josiah and Uriah Cline, always up to no good, had met them alongside Peter Creek. Never mind them now because Clay had just unfastened a strap of his overalls. Leering at her, he was starting on the other strap.

"What are you doing, Clay?"

"I's gonna get that Hatfield Yankee outa yer blood. McCoys is Confederates. Yer gonna act like my Confederate pet from now on."

Clay let his overalls fall around mud-caked brogans. Looming over her in dirty underwear, he yanked his right foot out of his overalls and then his left.

Suddenly Spicy was much more afraid than ill.

CHAPTER 26

"THAT'S WHERE YOU LIVE?" STONE ASKED BIG Lump at the edge of a cornfield.

"Yes, sir."

Through the cornstalks Stone stared at a small cabin with a dogtrot and lean-to. The roof sagged, warped shutters hung on single hinges, and foul-smelling smoke poured out of a crumbling chimney. Obviously McCoy hadn't used his moonshine profits to improve his standard of living.

"What's Clay do with his money, Big Lump?"

"Hides up high."

"Up high?" Stone hadn't expected that. "Like on a shelf?"

"By the river."

Stone thought a moment. "In a treetop?"

"Yup."

No doubt to keep it from the fairies or the revenuers, whoever should catch up with him first. Stone looked back at Clay's shack. He certainly understood the many reasons why Spicy felt she couldn't leave Big Lump to fend for himself. But inconceivable to Stone, was the idea of spirited Spicy married to Clay McCoy and living out her life in this dead-end dump.

Hunkering down, Stone sprinted toward the second

largest moonshine still he'd seen in Tug Valley. There was the traditional boiler pot over a rock firepit for heating the corn mash, copper coil for distilling it into an alcoholic liquid, and more copper tubing sloped down into a wooden collection barrel. Stone crouched behind piles of gunnysacks filled with corn. Big Lump squatted between extra barrels and shucked husks.

Straight ahead, about twenty feet, two men sprawled across a roofless porch. Clad in slouch hats, overalls, and brogans, one man sat propped against the cabin's front wall while the other lay on his back. Both men were asleep and neither man was Clay.

No wonder Big Lump slept on Spicy's porch. There, he had a roof, a lantern, rocking chairs, and the bench with his pillow and blanket.

The seated man's mouth gaped open and a brownish substance streaked his long beard. The man lying down was snoring loudly enough to cover footsteps. Stone eased a few paces closer before the man sitting up, roused. Only one eye opened all the way as he lifted a jug to his mouth and chugged. Ducking behind the stacks of corn, Stone motioned for Big Lump to do the same. The supine man sneezed into his palm, wiped his hand across his chest, and resumed snoring. The other man choked and spat a stream of what appeared to be tobacco juice. Throat cleared, his mouth went slack. One eye closed and brown drool dripped onto his beard.

Stone wanted to vomit. "Who the hell are they?"

Big Lump whispered, "Josiah and Uriah Cline."

"Go back to Spicy's house, Big Lump. You were never here. Got it, pardner?"

"Got it, pardner."

～

So THIS IS HELL, Spicy thought.

She was burning up while a demon weighed her down.

Spicy ached so badly, taking a breath was painful. The pinched place radiated stinging jabs throughout her body.

"You're hurting me, Clay. Get off."

Instead Clay's head lowered and his mouth ground punishingly against hers. Holding her wrists above her head, he wedged himself between her legs. His other hand tightened on her jaw so she couldn't turn away from his mouth. She clamped her teeth to his bottom lip. "Damn you, bitch!" Clay yelped and reared his head. "You bit me last time I kissed you. Don't ya know how to kiss a man?"

"I know when I want to."

"When's that gonna be?"

"When she's with me."

Stone! Spicy's heart thumped wildly. Infinitely relieved for herself, she was desperately afraid for Stone. He hauled Clay off her, releasing him with a shove that sent Clay stumbling backward. Shock flickered across Clay's face, but Stone's expression was one of murderous rage. Regaining his balance, Clay squared off with Stone. Clad in filthy underwear, Clay looked ridiculous while Stone, dressed in a blue shirt, snug black pants, and black boots was resplendent. The glaring contrast of good and evil between these two men was a trumpeted message powerfully delivered. As long as she lived, Spicy would never forget this moment. Hoping to mediate between an archangel and a devil, Spicy tried valiantly to sit up. But unable to even raise her head, she lay terrified and shivering.

"So we finally meet, McCoy," Stone growled, taking charge.

"How'd ya know where I live?" Clay shrank back and hollered, "Big Lump!"

Stone's eyes never leaving Clay, he asked, "Are you all right, Spicy?"

"She's fine, Hatfield," Clay answered for her. "Get outa here."

"I'm sick, Stone," Spicy replied.

"Step aside, McCoy. I'm taking her."

"My Winchester says she ain't goin' nowhere."

Clay reached toward his rifle, propped near the head of the bed. His hand stopped in midair as Stone aimed his pistol squarely between Clay's crossing eyes.

Jaw clenched, Stone gritted, "This Colt says I'm taking her outa here. Now, move."

Clay laughed. "Josiah!" he yelled. "Uriah!"

"Bad negotiators," Stone said nonchalantly.

"Big Lump!" Clay hollered a second time, again receiving no reply. "Damn useless, soft-brain anyhow." Clay's eyes darted frantically searching for help that wasn't coming. "Shoulda made sure the sorry sack o'shit was dead in that blueberry patch."

"You're a monster, Clay McCoy," Spicy cried.

"Shut up, snatch!" Clay blared.

Stone grabbed Clay by the throat and nailed his back to the nearest wall. Slamming the revolver against the blue vein between Clay's eyes with enough force to break the skin, Stone cocked his gun.

"Don't talk about her, to her, or ever touch her again. You got that, McCoy?"

"Take her," Clay said, blood streaming down his nose and face. "All's you'll get is my leavin's. I done had her. An' when yer gone, I'll have her ever night 'til death do us part."

In the narrowing of Stone's eyes and the working of his jaw muscle, Spicy could see Stone wrestling with the urge to blow a hole through Clay's head. Stone's nostrils flared as he breathed deeply. Letting his anger rush through his teeth, Stone grinned.

"Hell no, you won't, McCoy because I'll surgically remove your testicles in the most painful way possible and feed 'em to Big Lump's hog." With that Stone released Clay and yelled, "Ellison! Johnse!"

Johnse Hatfield swaggered inside like he owned the place. Reputed to be friendly, Johnse looked anything but at the moment. In addition to Roseanna and Nancy, Johnse's sandy hair and blue eyes had sent many a mountain belle's heart aflutter. Stone, however, was the only man who'd ever succeeded in making Spicy's heart skip beats. Though both Stone and Johnse could be called lady-killers, Spicy knew Clay feared they were man-killers, too.

"Clay, here, is not only my competition, but he was with Tolbert and Bud McCoy when they arrested me for having a gun," Johnse said. "What say we shoot him with his Winchester?"

"No. Pl-please, Johnse," Clay sputtered. Johnse laughed as Clay nervously reminded Stone, "I said you could have Spicy. Take her and leave me be."

"I don't need your sniveling permission, McCoy," Stone growled.

"Come on, Stony," Ellison Hatfield said as he filled the doorway with calm and strength. "It's sundown. Let's get the hell outa Kentucky while the gettin's still good."

Stone swiped Clay's blood off the barrel of his Colt across the mattress and shoved the gun in the back of his britches. He grabbed the Winchester and handed it to Johnse.

"Clay crushes like a cockroach under a man's heel," Johnse said with a big grin. "Takes dynamite to break stone."

"Johnse, you sound like my brother, Jet." Stone chuckled. "He said something similar to me after I became a surgeon." Stone glanced at Clay as if reminding him he could easily make good on his threat. Then he smiled down at Spicy. "Ready to go?"

"Yes," Spicy whispered.

Clay snorted. "I hope you knowed there ain't a McCoy in this valley gonna let you treat 'em after today, whore."

"McCoy!" Stone barked, making a half-turn to glare at him. "Shut those bloody lips Spicy gave you, or they'll join your balls in the hog trough."

Clay swiped at the blood on his lips as if picturing Stone slicing them off. Then Stone scooped Spicy off the dirty bed. As she rested her head on his broad shoulder, he let fly a string of foul curses. She held onto him the best she could as he sprinted across the room.

"Stony!" Ellison called from the porch through the open door. "What's wrong?"

"Her temperature's sky high. Let's go!"

In Stone's arms, Spicy gave herself up to blissful blackness until blessed coolness washed over her entire body. Strong arms supported her, yet she was sure she was floating. Slowly coming to, she saw a million twinkling stars and two quicksilver eyes.

"Stone? Where are we?"

CHAPTER 27

"IN THE TUG FORK ON THE WEST VIRGINIA SIDE," Stone replied.

"We're in the river?"

"Yes."

"West Virginia water feels like heaven," Spicy said.

"You were hotter'n hell in Kentucky," he told her. "By the time I got you to the river you were going into convulsions. Wonder what McCoy would have done about that."

"Let me die like Polly and the baby."

"Spicy," Stone sighed, as he kept her floating in the river. "When you were late for supper I came down to the river where I met up with Ellison and Johnse. Then here came Big Lump barreling out of the woods, telling me Clay had you. What happened?"

With her head on Stone's shoulder, Spicy asked, "Are you keeping your stitches dry?"

"Took 'em out yesterday. We're talking about you."

"Despite your 'or else'," Spicy began, "I was planning to come for supper."

Stone chuckled. "I'm sorry about the 'or else'. I was just teasing you."

"Thank you for keeping your promise to come get me," Spicy whispered looking up at her rescuer with stars as his backdrop. "I woke up dizzy and sick with a fever. I decided to send Lumpkin without me just before Clay showed up."

"Wait. Slow down. Did you eat something McCoy gave you?"

"No." Spicy heard someone ask how she was.

"Better, Ellison." Slowly swishing her through the cool water, Stone turned toward the bank and said, "This river siren will live to sing another day."

Spicy's heart danced. Did Stone really think she was a siren?

"I wish she'd sing to me," Johnse joked.

"You're married, Johnse. Besides, Spicy's mine."

Johnse laughed and agreed, "I know she is."

Ellison asked Johnse, "Did you hear Stony tell McCoy if he didn't leave Spicy alone he'd surgically remove his balls?"

"Yeah. And feed them and his bloody lips to Big Lump's hog," Johnse added and howled with laughter.

Spicy couldn't stifle a giggle. "Shame on you, Stone." Then the thrill of him referring to her as his was cut short at realizing only two men stood on the shore. "Where's Lumpkin?"

"He led us to Clay's cabin. But I sent him back to your place and he understands not to say he had anything to do with us finding you," Stone replied.

"He has no way to protect himself from Clay without me."

"Johnse dropped Clay's Winchester off to Big Lump on the way past your cabin," Stone said. "I told him to sleep inside in your folks' bedroom with the doors latched."

"Thank you." Spicy felt some relief.

Holding her close, Stone carried her out of the river. "Tired?"

"Yes," Spicy murmured, eyelids drooping.

"Spicy, I heard you defended the Hatfields to the McCoys. Like you, I wish the feud would die instead of people," Ellison said from the riverbank. "Thank you."

"You're welcome, Ellison," she whispered.

〜

SPICY'S next awareness was a pain so fiery she shivered with icy goose bumps. She tried to focus on her surroundings, but it was pitch-black. Struggling to distinguish her recurring nightmares from her fondest daydreams, she feared the worst— Clay's cabin. Hadn't Stone come for her? Had she imagined that? Had Clay hurt him? Where was Stone? Where was she?

"Stone?"

A muscular presence stirred at her back and a strong, but gentle arm circled her waist.

"Right here."

Spicy recalled floating under the midnight sky. "Are we at your house?"

"Yeah. In my bed."

Spicy vaguely thought she shouldn't be in his bed. But this was the most comfortable bed she ever lain in and she was exhausted. When Stone's intimate embrace tightened, she let him pull her closer. "I don't feel sick anymore."

"The river broke your fever," he said.

"Still a little dizzy." She rested peacefully until the pinched spot stabbed her again. Reaching between their bodies, she slipped her hand into the back of a pair of drawers. "Something feels swollen, hot, and throbbing."

"Swollen and hot anyway," he said. "Don't scratch."

"I wasn't scratching." Spicy had brushed the male part of Stone. Tonight, like it had been at the creek on the night of the blue moon, it was as hard and long as a plump ear of sweet corn. Thrills instantly swept through her. She was wide awake as Stone pulled her hand out of the drawers. Wrapping their arms around her waist again he molded her body to his.

"Oww, stop."

"Stop what?"

She had given this big, powerful man an order in his bed and felt totally safe doing so. That certainly hadn't been the case with Clay. What was happening to her? She didn't care. Having Stone hold her in his bed felt languid and delicious. She wished this night could go on forever. And then her skin throbbed again.

"Oooh," she cried. "I have a pinched spot that feels like the thorn we cut out of Big Bump must have felt."

"Before you go on a razorback rampage, I'll take a look."

Stone rolled out of bed. Spicy stayed on her left side in an effort to manage the pain on her right side. Stone padded away from the bed and a moment later soft, yellow light filled the cozy, clean bedroom. Over large, open windows sheer curtains fluttered, letting in a refreshing night breeze. Carrying a lamp and his medical bag toward her, Stone wore only a pair of low riding drawers. Spicy remembered threading her fingers through the masculine black hair on his muscular chest, after the fairy fire had floated down the creek. She wanted to touch Stone there again. And have him touch her.

As he pulled up a chair and sat down at her bedside, Spicy's attention shifted back to his snug drawers. His legs had spread and Spicy didn't resist looking. What had been pressed to her moments ago was a sexy male bulge now at eye level. Stone set a bag on the edge of the bed and her line of vision was cut off. Placing the lamp on a bedside table, Stone opened the bag. He tilted it toward Spicy but teased her with only a fleeting glimpse.

She gazed up at him. "I wasn't nearly done looking, Dr. Hatfield."

"Me neither," he replied with a cocky grin that spiraled Spicy's pulse. "But in case you're wondering," he began as he took a jar out of the bag, "my Aunt Hilda removed your wet nightgown and gave you a sponge bath here in my bedroom."

"Yes," Spicy said, realizing she was clad in a man's shirt and drawers. "I vaguely remember her helping me. Is your Aunt Hilda still here?"

"Sound asleep." Stone smiled. "She made me stay downstairs until she was done getting you into my clothes. I told her that was ridiculous since I often see naked women and men in my line of work."

"Your aunt was sweet and caring. I like her."

"She likes you, too, and thinks you're beautiful. It was so late by the time we put you to bed, I wouldn't let her go home in the dark. We both agreed I couldn't leave you to take her, but knowing Aunt Hilda she will be gone first thing in the morning."

"I'm glad she's here safe and sound."

"Where's your pinched spot? I'll use the salve I told you about to ease the pain."

Spicy grimaced. "It's on my...my...you know."

"Breast?"

"No!" Even though he'd seen and kissed her breasts, a blush crawled up her neck.

"Tell me where it hurts and I'll make it better."

This man's bedside manner was irresistible. She was torn between feeling totally wanton and completely morti-fied. But Stone was a physician. A surgeon. At the moment, she was his patient. No need to be embarrassed. But surely she didn't have the right to feel the daring desire he was eliciting in her. Conflicted by a touch of shyness and oodles of yearning, Spicy playfully buried her head under a pillow before answering.

"It's where?" Stone tried to lift the pillow off her head. She held tight and mumbled the location again. "The right cheek of your bottom?" She confirmed that from under-neath the pillow. "Since I'm a doctor I guess I can't refuse to treat you even though your wound is in a most distressing location."

"Sorry." Spicy had heard the chuckle in his deep voice and a laugh escaped her. But the pinched spot zinged her again and she whimpered. She took the pillow off her head, so that she could speak and be heard clearly. "Pull down my drawers and make it better."

"Dear God, give me strength." Stone glanced toward the

ceiling and his voice suddenly sounded husky. "Roll onto your tummy and don't tell me how to do my job."

Spicy rolled onto her stomach and clutched the pillow. She held her breath as Stone lowered the sheet. She squeezed her eyes shut when he flipped up the shirttail.

"Have you seen many naked women, Stone?"

Grasping the waist of the drawers, he replied, "I don't keep track of how many naked patients I've seen." He tugged the underwear down just a couple of inches and paused. "Now I'm going to ask you a question as a doctor and I want you to answer me honestly."

Spicy slid a hand down her hip and grasped the drawers. "You've seen and kissed so many naked ladies you lost track?"

"Who said anything about kissing?" Stone laughed. "I can tell you there's one woman in particular who said there would never be any kissing—naked or otherwise. Why do you care?"

"Don't you want me to answer your question, whatever it is?"

"Yes. Did Clay hurt you before I got there?"

She threw his question back at him, "Why do you care?"

"You might require medical treatment." Stone met her gaze. When she didn't reply, Stone drew out her name warningly, "Spicy..."

"Stone..." she drawled his name in the same fashion. "Answer me and I'll answer you."

"Did McCoy bed you?"

"Nope."

"Nope, McCoy didn't bed you or nope, you won't answer me?"

CHAPTER 28

"THANKS TO YOU, CLAY HAS NEVER HAD ME IN OR out of bed."

Stone bowed his head in relief and when he looked at her again, he whispered, "Good."

"I'm not trying to pry into your life where it's not my business," Spicy said earnestly. Yet when he pulled on her drawers again she held them firmly in place. "But—"

"Are you going to let me see your pinched spot or not?"

Ignoring his question, she continued, "But what I'm really asking or maybe saying is I think you hold yourself back with me because among the women you've known there is one very lucky lady in your life."

As he admired the set of dimples above her saucily rounded, partially exposed derrière, Stone shook his head and gave voice to his fondest dream, "You'd be my lucky lady number seven and the luck would be all mine." Gasping at the information, the implication, or maybe both, Spicy's eyes widened before she buried her face in the pillow. Stone chuckled, thoroughly enjoying every moment until he lowered the drawers to the tops of her thighs. "What the hell?"

"What?" she asked, looking over her shoulder.

"When did you get this so-called pinched spot?" he asked.

"Right after Pepper crowed yesterday morning." She went on to explain finding the back door ajar and thinking Nutmeg had scurried into the cabin.

"Your initial pain, dizziness, and the onset of nausea were caused by a bite. Have you ever had trouble with spiders in your cabin?"

"Not since I scooped an almost drowned baby Nutmeg out of Blackberry Creek. Raccoons eat spiders."

"Raccoons eat anything," Stone said. "There's a welt on your bottom the size of a silver dollar. In the center is a dark-red dot." Taking a magnifying glass from his doctor's bag, he peered closely. "I see a set of fang marks. I'm guessing a brown recluse. I've seen bites where the skin reacts much worse to the poison. Twice now you've been lucky."

"Lucky? How?"

As seriously as possible, he said, "I didn't have to drill a hole in your pretty head after your concussion and I don't think your sexy fanny will fall off from the spider bite."

Spicy laughed. "That's not funny."

"Sure it is," he chuckled.

Rolling her eyes she asked, "Why did I get so sick and run a fever?"

"On top of being poisoned you probably had an allergic reaction to the spider's venom."

"I've never heard of anyone on my side of the river being bitten by a brown recluse."

"This salve will help it heal." Stone uncapped a jar he'd taken out of his medical bag. He dipped a finger into the salve. "Did McCoy even bother to ask what made you sick?"

"No, come to think of it, he didn't. He just said he was going to cure me with skunk tongue and blood soup."

"Or kill you," Stone grumbled. As he touched the salve to her soft skin, he had to concentrate to keep his lower body from hardening again. He told himself Spicy was just another patient as he'd never had this reaction to any other female patient, no matter how attractive. "Done," he said out loud before he did more than a doctor would do. "Next we'll elevate your fanny above your heart to help lessen the pain and swelling."

"Thank you, it already feels better." She grasped the shirttail to tug it down.

"The shirt will soak up the salve. Let's slide a pillow under your hips."

Her expression was dubious. "Sleep next to you with my naked fanny up in the air?"

"Sounds good to me." Stone replied sincerely then grinned. "It's a big bed. I'll try to stay on my side."

"More importantly, stay calm when I tell you something." Still on her tummy, Spicy reached out and placed her hand on his knee. "Clay admitted he shot you."

"No surprise there," Stone replied, unruffled. "We know he was the gunnysacker who tried to kill Big Lump in the blueberry patch, too. You were right, McCoy is a monster and I'm the reason he tried to rape you."

"I'm the reason Clay shot you. Let's call it even."

"Hell no." Finished with the salve, Stone smacked the cap back on the jar. "McCoy should be held responsible for what he attempted to do to you. If you ever have to defend yourself against a man, you kick him between his legs as hard as you can. Understand?"

"Yes." After letting that information settle she told him, "Clay said you're a Yankee like me and it will always be war with the Hatfields."

"The right side won that war," Stone said. "But McCoy doesn't care about right and wrong. He's vicious and vindictive. He fights to further his own best interests. From what you've told me even your rooster and raccoon know he's a threat."

"Clay ordered Lumpkin to kill Pepper so he could fry him for supper."

"Big Lump won't do that," Stone assured her. "But McCoy's damn well losing control which makes him even more dangerous."

"Yes." Spicy shivered and continued, "Next time I see him, I'll tell him a spider bite won't stop me from crossing the river to see you."

"Don't get close enough to tell him anything." Stone felt far from calm as he gripped her hand atop his knee. "You stay away from him."

"Not until I accuse him of trying to kill me." Spicy shook off his hand and grasped the drawers. "With skunk tongue and blood soup." She tried to pull the underwear over her fanny, but Stone stopped her.

"No. For the love of God, don't antagonize him." Stone tugged her drawers off, kicked them under the bed and repeated, "No."

"Stone, I can't go around half naked."

"I'll keep you that way if you don't promise to stay on this side of the river," he warned her with a frown. When she smiled at his scowling threat the dimples on her face and those on her fanny melted his heart. "I mean it, Spicy."

"I know you do and I appreciate your concern," she whispered. "I'll bet Josiah Cline was the gunnysacker holding me back in your blueberry patch. When he was a teenager, his right eye was almost gouged out during a fight alongside Clay. He lost sight in that eye and the torn lid healed half-closed. I can't be sure it was him. But Josiah's the bigger bully of the two and he also calls Lumpkin names."

"Big Lump doesn't deserve any of that. He deserves a good life." The idea of either one of the Clines he'd seen on that porch, holding Spicy as Clay cracked open Big Lump's skull raised Stone's loathing of Clay McCoy to yet another level. As Spicy lay on her tummy so beautiful and vulnerable, Stone said as coolly as he could, "It's in McCoy's best interest to eliminate people who stand between him and you."

"And my cabin, five acres, and a well."

"Right. So let's be careful."

"You get thirty points for rescuing me," Spicy said, with a smile changing the tone of their conversation. "That's my thirty to your forty, long shot."

"Whatever will you do to catch up, sugar'n spice?"

"I'll think of something."

$$\approx$$

WHEN THE MORNING sun warmed his eyelids, Stone rolled over and reached for Spicy. Her side of the bed was cold. He shot to a sitting position and was instantly awake. Throwing back the sheet, he feared where she had gone and why. He rolled out of bed and pulled on his pants. Shirtless, he jogged barefoot across the landing. Sure enough the bedroom his aunt had slept in was empty. She was probably back home by now. Stone hurried down the stairs and yanked open the front door.

The position of the morning sun told him it was about eight. How long had Spicy been gone? Had she left with his aunt? To the right, he glared toward the river as though it had stolen her from him. Swinging his head to the left, he saw her in the blueberry patch near a long-forgotten garden where vegetables and herbs once thrived.

A vision of perfection. The essence of femininity. A fairy dance of fire.

Her slender back was to him and her sugar-maple curls tumbled nearly to her waist. Stone swung a leg over the porch railing and watched her. Barefoot, she wore his shirt which she'd slept in, but he saw no sign of his drawers underneath it. She'd rolled the sleeves up, but still his shirt was miles too big for her delicate frame. As she turned slightly reaching for berries he saw her drop them into a bowl from his kitchen. When she rubbed the right cheek of her fanny, fierce protectiveness surged within him.

Stone glowered back across the river, despising Clay

McCoy and all he'd put Spicy through. His gut said they didn't know the half of it. Despite threatening Clay to keep his hands off Spicy, Stone didn't believe he would. Clenching his fists atop his thighs, Stone silently swore Spicy would never marry the bastard.

"You look mad enough to swallow a porcupine backwards."

At the sound of Spicy's lilting voice, Stone snapped out of his anger over Clay McCoy. The picture in the berry patch shoved all thoughts but those of Spicy out of his head. The morning sun kissed the gorgeous woman holding the bowl of berries and Stone hopped off the railing to do the same. He landed on the soft grass and joined her just as she popped a berry into her mouth. He would forever associate blueberries with Spicy McCoy.

"What are you doing out here without your doctor's permission?"

"Good morning." Before answering him, she put a blueberry to his lips. He chewed it while she said, "I'm gathering berries to make extra special pancakes for you. By the way, I saw your Aunt Hilda and thanked her before she left."

Stone nodded. "How's the spider bite?"

"Much better." Spicy's angelic smile was radiant. "Thanks to you."

"Well, damn, I thought I might have to kiss it to make it better." He placed both hands to her cheeks and kissed her lips. Raising his head, he asked, "Spicy, are there any other men who give you trouble besides McCoy?"

"You mean other men who want to kiss me?"

Uncomfortable with that image Stone grumbled, "Yeah."

"Two or three in the past. But Clay threatened them. You're the first man to stand up to him." Spicy tilted her head and said, "I think your real question is whether or not there are other men I'd like to kiss."

"Are there?"

"Just the one," she said, bringing a smile to his lips. She

started to say something else, hesitated, and closed her mouth. She shrugged and looked away.

"What?" Placing his fingers to her chin, Stone turned her head and clearly saw naiveté in her expression. "You can tell me anything."

CHAPTER 29

"When Clay pinned me down...it...umm—" She choked, blushed, and cleared her throat. "It was—"

"It was what?"

Holding the bowl against her tummy with the heels of her hands, she lifted her fingers several inches apart. Cutting the distance in half and then half of that, her eyes grew large as she said, "So small compared to yours."

Stone grinned, despite his rage at McCoy. "Taking my measure again?" He cocked a brow and his male pride soared. Knowing the answer Stone asked anyway, "How would you know how big mine is?"

Perhaps emboldened by his grin, Spicy's dimples dotted her cheeks and she said with a saucy tone, "Well, *long* shot, I've seen your big, plump ear of sweet corn outlined in the front of your pants. I've had my hand on top of you and felt you pressed against me in and out of bed."

Stone pulled her to him and kissed her forehead. "Spicy," he began, wrapping her and the bowl of blueberries in his embrace. "I—" Had he been about to say he loved her? He just met her a few weeks ago. "I want you so damn bad. I can hardly think of anything but you."

"I told myself to fight temptation, but I can't because I

—" her voice broke. She looked up at him and said, "I don't want to share the journey with any man but you."

Yeah. He loved Spicy McCoy.

"You're gonna take me places I've never been before, sugar'n spice."

"Only if there is no special woman you kiss in Philadelphia."

Spicy had opened this door twice now. She'd gone through it first by telling him of the betrothal pact her folks had made with Clay McCoy. She'd even told him of the recent deal to keep him safe by agreeing to marry McCoy. Spicy was a woman of principle and deserved to know if he were free to kiss her and take her on that journey. What would she say if he told her about agreeing to marry—what the hell was the Vanderveer woman's first name?

"Come on." Stone took her hand and sensed her trepidation as he walked her to the porch. He figured the spider bite was situated just high enough on her fanny to allow her to sit without pain. She took a seat in one of the rockers as he sat in the other one. "Comfortable?"

"Yes. Fine." Clutching the bowl of berries, Spicy asked, "But why do I feel like I'm about to get some very bad news?"

"I went to Logan the other day and sent a telegram to Pennsylvania Hospital's current chief or surgery, Dr. Victor Vanderveer. You remember we talked about him?"

"Yes, he was the mentor who took you under his wing."

"Right. I told him I could not honor my betrothal to his daughter. I said it wasn't fair for her to marry a man who never loved her and never will."

"So, you're engaged to your friend's daughter." Spicy's lips quivered and her eyes glistened. "I was right about you holding back. You were honoring your commitment."

"No, I never honored it and she never expected I would," he admitted.

"Then I expect her heart is breaking at this very moment."

"No. What I mean is she doesn't love me, either. She's the one who said there would be no intimacy. It was nothing more than an arranged marriage. Vanderveer wants me to be the next chief of surgery and he wants his daughter to be married to that surgeon."

Spicy's arched brows furrowed. "What do *you* want, Stone?"

"I want to take over the surgical department, but I don't want to marry his daughter. I already told you I want children, so the marriage would have been a disaster on many levels. Since Vanderveer engineered this *deal*, I felt he should be the one to receive my telegram breaking it." Stone held out his hand to Spicy but she didn't take it, instead gripping the bowl in her lap. "Trust me, she is as relieved as I am right now."

"What's her name?"

"I knew you were going to ask me that," he said, scratching his head.

Spicy asked incredulously, "You can't remember her name?"

"Not when you're with me."

"I'd say that is a psychosomatic reaction, Dr. Hatfield."

"Touché." Stone chuckled. Touching two fingers above his right brow he gave her a salute. "I'd say that's an accurate diagnosis, Dr. McCoy."

"Thank you for being honest, but the circumstances you just described don't explain why you hold back when you're with me."

"When I return to Pennsylvania Hospital, I don't want to leave you ostracized from the McCoys or resented by the Hatfields."

"I see." She nodded. "Like Roseanna after the affair with Johnse."

"Yes." Stone ran a hand though his hair and added, "Or leave you to raise a child alone."

"You're trying to save me from myself."

"I invited you to supper, hoping you wouldn't cross the

Tug Fork back to Raccoon Hollow. If you won't go with me to Philadelphia, you could live here." He splayed a hand. "I realize being on this side of the river isn't a magic answer to keeping McCoy away from you. But at least it would give you some space and you'd be in another state here in West Virginia."

"Now whose heart is on his sleeve? That is if you were wearing a shirt and had a sleeve," she teased with a soft smile. When he smiled back she said seriously, "I was trying to save you, too, by urging you to stay here on your mountain and out of Kentucky. Stone, I don't feel I belong on this side of the Tug Fork River. Certainly not alone."

"But—"

"But thank you anyway," she said cutting him off and continued, "in the meantime, it seems our hearts are free to explore all manner of mountain magic."

Stone wondered what he'd done to deserve time with this once-in-a-blue-moon woman. Standing, he pulled her and the bowl of berries into his arms. Hugging her, he said, "Let's go inside. I want to examine your spider bite."

"I'll think about it."

"What do you mean you'll think about it?"

She admitted being bashful as to letting him examine her fanny in broad daylight. However, once they reached his kitchen, with coaxing, he was allowed to lift the shirttails. He reported the spot was much smaller and faded to pale pink. In turn, she inspected his bullet wound which was healing nicely but would leave a thin scar. Together they made the blueberry pancakes. Once again, Stone imagined his morning routine including Spicy.

"By the way, your Aunt Hilda invited us to supper tomorrow," Spicy said, stacking three pancakes on a plate for Stone and two on her plate. "But I don't think it occurred to her I have only my nightgown here."

"Or maybe she knows I bought you something in Logan," Stone said, setting a jar of Aunt Hilda's maple syrup on the table.

"You did?" Spicy asked, placing the plates of pancakes on the table.

"Yes," he said, as they sat down across the kitchen table from each other. "A dress to replace the one that got stained when I found you in my blueberry patch the day we met."

"A dress? From a store?" Spicy's eyes flew open. She clasped her hands under her chin and a smile lit up her face. "Are you telling me you purchased a real store-bought dress for me?"

Her happiness danced across his heart. "That's what I'm telling you."

"A store-bought dress," she whispered in awe. "Everything I've ever owned came from cloth my mother spun on our old loom. I never enjoyed spinning and making clothes so I don't do it." Shaking her head in apparent disbelief, she said, "I can't wait to see my store-bought dress. I'll repay you, I promise."

"Repay me by promising to stay out of McCoy's reach."

"I promise," she replied sincerely. "At least until you're safely out of Tug Valley."

When he didn't reply, Spicy's smile faltered and she focused on pouring maple syrup over her pancakes. Stone knew when he was gone Spicy would be back in her cabin and facing things on her own. He replayed the conversation in his head about letting the chips fall where they may where she was concerned. He was letting the chips scatter with his appointment as chief of surgery. If Vanderveer canceled the job offer due to the canceled betrothal, Stone decided he didn't deserve the promotion. No matter what happened in Pennsylvania, he needed to figure out this situation in Tug Valley.

"Since neither of us is going anywhere just now," Stone began as he reached across the table and placed his hand on hers, "I'd be honored to have you stay with me. You're welcome to sleep in the bedroom of your choice."

With a shy smile she said, "I don't know if it's right or wrong for me to be here. But letting people keep them apart didn't end well for Romeo and Juliet. I'll follow my heart."

Sweet Jesus, Stone prayed, *if that means she's sleeping with me give me strength.* At least for tonight, he'd keep his hands to himself due to how sick she'd been. But after that? Rarely had he spent the whole night with a woman. Never without having bedded her. As he and Spicy ate their breakfast, each lost in their own thoughts, Stone realized he had followed his heart in making that trip to Logan. He had been following it every time he simply held Spicy in his arms without making love to her.

Because he was in love with Spicy.

"Stone Hatfield!" came a grating shriek from the front yard.

His thoughts rudely jarred, Stone scooted back from the table. "What now?"

He sauntered down the hallway and Spicy padded after him. Before he opened the door he grabbed his Colt .45 from the foyer table and looked through a window. A figure, wearing a black cape over a black dress, stood a few feet away from the bottom porch step.

"Vorticia Hatfield," Stone said, shoving the gun in the back of his pants.

"I've never seen her before. She doesn't cross the river into Kentucky."

"I'll find out what she wants."

"She claims she can see everything, including the future," Spicy said.

"Balderdash," Stone said and winked at Spicy.

"I'm not afraid of her."

"Wait here just the same." Stone opened the door and strode across the porch, leaving Spicy standing in the doorway.

In sharp contrast to the Hatfield witch's black clothing, long white hair straggled around her shoulders. A thousand lines creased her face while a crooked smile displayed nary a tooth. Perhaps the most notable thing about her was the fat, black rat perched on her left shoulder. She put something near the rat's mouth and, revealing jagged teeth, it crawled among strands of her twisted hair to eat it. The crone, to whom atrocious powers were credited by both Hatfields and McCoys, perused a bare-chested Stone and a half-naked Spicy with a black-eyed glare.

"Barren!" Vorticia shrilled and pointed at Spicy. "If'n you want a baby, she cain't never give you one, Stony."

"State your business, Vorticia," Stone said gruffly.

CHAPTER 30

SPICY STOOD FROZEN, BUT HER VERY SOUL REELED.

She and Stone had talked about babies twice. At her cabin he'd said he wanted two. If she couldn't have children, Stone's alliance with her would be as devastating for him as the one with the Vanderveer woman. Or would it? She and Stone weren't betrothed, and he'd just said he didn't want to leave her with a baby to raise alone. Though she'd told Stone she needed a husband for a baby, if she couldn't conceive she didn't need any man. Yet, she still wanted to make love with Stone. She felt confused and conflicted because Stone wasn't just any man.

Stone Hatfield was the man she loved.

Suddenly, Spicy's heart leaped to the top of his mountain. She had fallen in love with Stone! With her next breath, Spicy's heart plummeted and shattered. Her destiny was not to have the man she loved or the babies she wanted only Stone to give her. He was leaving and she was barren. Her fondest dreams would never come true. Life could be so cruel and unfair.

"What are you doing out of Coffin Cave, Vorticia?" Stone asked, evidently recalling that's how locals referred to the infamous cavern.

"My den," Vorticia informed him with a wave of a bony hand.

"Yeah, of doom. I own the mountain where you're squatting."

"But we's cousins."

"A hundred times removed," Stone growled.

Vorticia's eyes flicked to Spicy to say, "In a vision I done seen somebody at yer house was poorly and I came to make her well. Got the cure—richeer'n my gunnysack."

"Whatever's in the gunnysack, we don't want it," Stone said. "I've treated my patient and she's fine."

"I guess my cures ain't good enough fer the high'n mighty city doctor and his," Vorticia spat, "McCoy whore."

Stone's voice was low and fierce, "Do not call her that."

"Sorry if'n I heared-tell wrong about her." Vorticia wheezed pitifully.

"I'd like to know who's telling it," Spicy spoke up.

Vorticia cackled. "I's sure you would."

"Get off my mountain, Vorticia," Stone growled. "And don't come back."

"Ain't no hard feelin's on my part, so I's leave the copperhead innards." Vorticia pulled a revolting glob halfway out of the gunnysack. The rat ran out from under her hair and down her arm, but she quickly shooed it back to her shoulder. "Put 'em on her spider bite."

"The hell I will," Stone said. Vorticia shoved what she claimed were snake entrails back into the sack and with a shrug, took a step. "Stop," Stone ordered. The Hatfield witch stared at them oozing malevolence from every pore. "Who told you she had a spider bite?"

"I ssseee," Vorticia hissed like a snake, tapping a long fingernail near her right eye.

Stone raised his chin, squared his shoulders and stood his ground. Despite her scanty attire, Spicy crossed the porch to his side. With a parting hiss at Spicy, Vorticia slithered through the grass and vanished into the woods.

Hands on his hips and glaring after Vorticia, Stone said, "She's working with McCoy."

Spicy shook her head. "All of the McCoys are terrified of Vorticia."

"McCoy might be afraid of the fairies," Stone clenched his jaw, "but he's overcome his fear of the witch."

～

"HELLO YOU TWO," the lovely woman, in her mid-sixties, said. On either side of the sunny yellow door of her white frame house were yellow window boxes full of yellow daisies. "I'm so relieved you could make it."

"Hello, Aunt Hilda," Stone said. "Spicy and I appreciate your invitation," he added as they stood on her porch.

"Please come in." She ushered them into her home and closing the front door said, "Since Spicy missed our meal together I told her yesterday morning I hoped she would be well enough to have supper here this evening."

How different Stone's aunt was compared to the Hatfield witch. From her neatly coiffed chignon to her white blouse and dark skirt, from gray eyes the color of Stone's to her welcoming smile, everything about this refined lady said she was a friend and not a foe. Not quite forty-eight hours since her rescue, in Stone's care, Spicy had thrived and thus, here they were indeed.

"Thank you again for helping me when I was too ill to help myself, Mrs. Hatfield," Spicy said with a grateful catch in her voice.

"No thanks necessary at all. But, just the same you're welcome." Taking Spicy's hand, Stone's aunt patted it. "Please call me Aunt Hilda, like Stone and Jet do."

In the front room of her house, Aunt Hilda admired Spicy's new dress. Fitting Spicy perfectly, the frock had a V-neck, elbow length sleeves, and slim skirt for summertime. The soft fabric was pale blue and dotted with a tiny blueberry pattern. Stone said the moment he saw it he knew it was meant for her. Spicy beamed up at him.

"She cried, so I wasn't sure if she liked it." Stone winked at Spicy.

Aunt Hilda wiped a tear from her own eye and led the way toward mouthwatering smells. She seated them at a table covered with a lace cloth in a homey kitchen near a tidy hearth. A bowl of red and yellow apples, she said were from her apple trees, served as a centerpiece. She poured chamomile tea into delicate cups with matching saucers and pointed to an apple spice cake she'd baked for dessert. Spicy felt at home. Stone inquired as to his aunt's comment of being relieved they could make it for supper.

"Besides being happy Spicy felt up to the trek," she began with a warm smile at Spicy, "I'm making an unexpected trip into northern West Virginia and I didn't want to miss this chance for the three of us to visit. I'm leaving after supper to get an early start tomorrow morning. A friend of mine, Connie Staton, has been wheezing for more than a year. I've insisted a trip to Wheeling Hospital is long overdue and Connie finally agreed."

"Is there anything I can do?" Stone asked.

"No." Aunt Hilda shook her head. "It's not a surgical problem. I think it's consumption. Yet tried-and-true cures such as horseback riding, a meat-only diet, and opium haven't improved Connie's condition. Neither has bleeding or purging helped."

"Aunt Hilda, none of that will help."

"Connie doesn't smoke or chew tobacco." Aunt Hilda rubbed her forehead. "So where the consumption came from is beyond me."

"Tobacco doesn't cause it," Stone said quietly and ran a hand through his hair. "Dear God, we need a hospital in Tug Valley."

"Yes, we do," Spicy agreed firmly as his aunt echoed the sentiment. "What does cause consumption, Stone?"

"In March of this year, German microbiologist Dr. Robert Koch reported his discovery of the tubercle bacillus."

"What's that?" Spicy wanted to know.

"It's the cause of consumption or what's now being called tuberculosis. Dr. Koch's research reveals that tuberculosis is not genetic as we once thought. It's a microorganism transmitted by infected people to others," Stone answered.

"As in a hug or a handshake?" Aunt Hilda asked.

"No. It's in the sputum. When an infected person coughs, sneezes, sings, or even talks, the microorganism can become airborne and is transmitted when inhaled by another person."

Astonished by Stone's explanation, Spicy sat silently taking it all in as did his aunt.

"I hope Connie can receive the cure when we are in Wheeling," Aunt Hilda finally said.

"Aunt Hilda," Stone began, his brow furrowed, "there *is* no cure. Unfortunately, tuberculosis is a death sentence."

"Oh, no," she sighed. "How long does a person have?"

"Prognoses vary depending on the patient. Usually one to five years."

Spicy took it upon herself to pour more tea. Chamomile, known for its calming effects, had been a good choice. She caught Stone's eye just as something occurred to her.

"Vorticia was wheezing this morning," Spicy said, wondering if it was fakery.

Stone shook his head and confirmed her suspicion, "That was a snake oil wheeze to make us feel sorry for her."

"Vorticia?" Aunt Hilda asked.

"Yes. She paid us a visit. Remember when you said Vorticia lived with bats, rats, and snakes?" Stone asked. When his aunt nodded, he said, "I think she's got spiders for hire."

"I wouldn't doubt it," Aunt Hilda replied. "But what makes you think so?" Together, they told her the whole story ending with Vorticia's pet rat and snake entrails. Aunt Hilda gazed across the table at Spicy and said, "I don't hold with the feud and I don't make judgments based on a person's last name." Including Stone with a smile, she asked, "Would you like to stay here? My place is so secluded, the only visitors I've had are the two of you and occasionally, Connie. You're welcome to stay for as long as you'd like."

"Actually, that was a favor I was about to ask," Stone replied. "We were all set to stay at my house until Vorticia darkened the doorstep. No one will know to look for Spicy here."

"Since I'm heading to Wheeling, you'd be doing me a favor. I can leave Daisy for Spicy to ride." Aunt Hilda looked at Spicy to say, "Daisy is a large draft horse strong enough to pull a plow through rock, but she's as gentle as a kitten." Then to both of them she said, "Connie has a brother, Ronny Staton, who could look after Daisy. But Ronny lives alone and with no one to help him, he will have enough to do at his place and Connie's without taking care of another horse along with my cow and chickens. I've been canning all summer, so there's plenty to eat along with a big helping of peace and quiet."

Spicy smiled and Stone said, "Thanks, Aunt Hilda."

At that point, Aunt Hilda turned her attention back to the supper she was preparing and Spicy pitched in wherever she could. With each passing minute, she came to like Stone's gracious aunt more and more. Ham and fried potatoes were on the menu, including collard greens sprinkled with bacon.

"I made an apple spice cake for dessert," Aunt Hilda said and handed a tin to Spicy.

Spicy set the tin on the table and took her chair beside Stone. She still found herself a bit self-conscious when eating in front of Stone but their midday meal had been shared hours ago and she managed to clean her plate. Stone was hungry, too, and ate heartily. They all enjoyed chatting and no one had room for cake when it came time for dessert. Spicy offered to help wash and put away dishes, but Stone said she should rest and he helped his aunt.

Spicy moseyed outside and gave Logan, who had brought them here, slices of a big red apple. Taking a seat on a porch swing padded with a thick quilt, and alone with her thoughts, she realized her nerves had been scraped raw from the ordeal with Clay. She trembled knowing what would have happened without Stone. Being at Clay's mercy not only meant he would have forced himself on her—it was a death sentence. Her life would essentially be over if she had to face it fending off Clay, especially after falling in love with Stone. Spicy scratched her head as she prayed for Lumpkin's well-being and rubbed her throat hoping Abigail's tonsillitis hadn't returned. Touching her left ear she fretted about Shadow's hearing. Lastly, she wrapped her arms over her tummy and her shoulders sagged as Vorticia's words of being barren echoed in her heart.

"Spicy, are you feeling ill?" Stone asked, opening the front door.

CHAPTER 31

"No," Spicy replied, quickly glancing up from her lap. "I'm fine." She forced a smile as Stone let his aunt step through the door ahead of him. "I love your porch swings, Aunt Hilda."

Aunt Hilda took a seat in a swing opposite of Spicy. Stone placed a carpetbag beside her then pulled the front door shut and sat down next to Spicy.

"Stone and Jet used to each commandeer a swing to see how high they could make the swings go before bailing out," Aunt Hilda said with a shake of her head. "How those boys managed not to kill themselves I'll never know."

"It was Jet's idea," Stone joked as his aunt and Spicy both laughed.

"It was Stone's," Aunt Hilda said. "He's still Jet's hero."

Stone's arm came around Spicy and she felt better. Scooting her closer on the bench seat he molded her to him and she forced her worries aside. Before long the clip-clop of horse hooves and clattering of wagon wheels sounded.

"Is this your ride?" Stone asked as a buggy appeared on the path to the house.

"Yes." Aunt Hilda stood and when she spoke love and concern laced her voice. "You have enemies as deadly as tuberculosis, Stone. If you need help, ask for it. There are plenty of Hatfields who care about you and know how to use a gun. Ronny Staton lives in Warm Hollow, a few miles east of here. He's a kind man always willing to lend a hand as well."

"Good to know." Stone stood up by his aunt. "It's almost three hundred miles to Wheeling, so you won't be back in time for the election."

"Women can't vote anyway." Aunt Hilda shrugged. "I just go to the elections to trade recipes, sample baked goods, and hear the latest news. Magnolia Precinct is where I bought Daisy from Abe and Flora Weddington a couple years back." Looking at Stone while inclining her head toward Spicy, she said, "At least your trip home hasn't been in vain. Go and enjoy yourselves."

Spicy couldn't remember ever missing an election. She and Mama had always baked berry pies and, along with Papa and the rest of Raccoon Hollow, celebrated elections with all-day picnics. Their precinct site was Jerry Hatfield's house on Blackberry Creek. Spicy stood to say goodbye and Aunt Hilda gave her a hug as the buggy rolled to a stop.

"Conrad Staton." Aunt Hilda said, with a twinkle in her eye. So Connie was a man.

"Hello, folks," Connie called from the buggy and tipped his hat.

"Connie, this is my nephew, Stone, and his friend, Spicy McCoy," Aunt Hilda said.

"Pleased to meet you both," Connie said, then coughed.

"No kissing," Stone ordered his aunt in a hushed whisper as he hugged her goodbye.

Aunt Hilda laughed softly. "We're just good friends."

Perhaps due to not feeling well, shyness, or because Spicy was a McCoy, Connie kept his distance. Hilda plucked her bag off the swing and, signaling they should stay on the porch, walked to the buggy alone. Connie alighted and helped Aunt Hilda into the buggy. Stone draped his arm around Spicy and they waved goodbye as the buggy clattered away.

A warm breeze feathered through the daisies in the yellow window boxes. At the far end of a wide yard of green grass, the setting sun glimmered between the trees along Mate Creek. Except for Spicy's concerns across the Tug Fork, the late afternoon atmosphere was quiet, sultry, and perfect. Stone sighed as he gazed in the direction of his mountain.

"Aunt Hilda and my mother wanted to stay close, which is why this house and mine were built with only the valley we crossed coming here, between our mountains," Stone said. "Not too far from here on my side of the valley is my favorite place on the Stony Mountains. On a rise, are ten acres of flat land with trees and water and a nice view. If you're up to a hike, maybe you'd like to be my first guest there and have some apple spice cake washed down with Johnse's finest white lightning."

"Yes, I'm up to it." Spicy wanted all of this and so much more only with Stone. He had appeared in her life so suddenly, immediately playing a role in her every waking thought. Whatever would she do when this man was gone? "I'd love to visit your favorite place."

"Great. We can see if the two magnolia trees I planted years ago are still thriving. If you'll toss the cake tin into a basket, I'll put Logan in the barn with Daisy."

Heart dancing in anticipation, Spicy entered the house and searched the kitchen for a basket. Loving Stone with all her heart, she yearned to show him just how much. If he left these hills and valleys after tonight, then she was merely number seven and not so lucky.

Let me be more, Spicy prayed, leaving the kitchen with a basket of cake.

"Ready?" Stone asked on the porch, taking the quilts off the swings.

"Yes."

Stone tossed the quilts over his left shoulder. Looping his finger in the stoneware, he slung the moonshine atop the blankets and held out his other hand to Spicy. Barely feeling the ground under her feet, Spicy slipped her hand in his. The sky glowed pink and orange as a welcome breeze brushed aside the heat.

Leaving the house, they walked a grassy path to Mate Creek. As the path faded the only sounds were chirping crickets, an occasional croak of a frog, and the bubbling stream. At Stone's side, Spicy padded across the ground softened by leaves, grasses, and pine needles. Crossing the lush valley, a gentle incline took them further into the woods and higher up the side of Stone's mountain. About the time Spicy wondered if they were lost, the two most beautiful magnolia trees in all of Tug Valley came into view. They flourished on either side of a crystal clear waterfall. A warm wind wafted the sweet scent of the huge white blossoms all around Spicy as the falling water soothed her nerves with its sprinkling song.

"I never knew this waterfall existed." Spicy stared in wonder as Stone winked and tugged on her hand. "Like finding a hidden treasure."

Stone led them out of the seclusion of the woodlands along Mate Creek to the edge of an overlook. Pine trees gracefully parted as if purposely surprising them with the view he had mentioned. Spicy gave Stone an awestruck glance that said *nice* was an understatement. Puffy clouds fleetingly framed the moon in a near perfect heart shape. Emerald green colored the rolling hills as the narrow valleys lay deep, dark, and mysterious. At the foot of the double mountains the Tug Fork River, which could ravage and rage, flowed serenely. It was as if the panoramic landscape had been strategically painted on an endless canvas just for them.

"My version of mountain magic," Stone said.

"Like fairy fire, it's too breathtaking to be real," Spicy whispered. "I've only seen your mountain from my valley. Viewing it from this ledge with you is seeing a whole new world."

Smiling at her, he said, "Never more beautiful."

They spread out the quilts, one on top of the other. Spicy sat down on the left half while Stone took up most of the right half and placed the jug between them. Along with magnolia trees, pine-scented evergreens provided a cozy nook of seclusion with the waterfall and creek in the background. Stone uncorked the moonshine and tipped the jug to his lips as Spicy set two plates of apple spice cake on the quilt. Realizing she'd forgotten forks, she broke off a piece of the apple dessert and offered him a bite. He grabbed her hand and ate it from her fingers. Spicy broke off another piece and nibbled. Stone drank from the jug again and then held it out to her.

"I've never had moonshine."

"Try it," he said and when she hesitated he added, "Spicy, you're shivering and it's not because it's cold. A little moonshine'll make it easier on both of us."

"You mean I'll be able to eat in front of you more easily?"

Stone cocked a brow. "I mean making love will be easier."

"Are we going to make love?"

"Aren't we?"

Spicy nodded shyly. "At least we know I can't conceive."

"I've been waiting for that." Stone shook his head and took her hand. "Don't believe that old crone. Vorticia's got more bats in her belfry than Coffin Cave."

Spicy nodded but without much conviction and said, "Hand over the anesthesia."

Stone's smile was both sexy and compassionate. "Good girl."

When he held out the jug again she took it and tipped it to her lips. She swallowed twice before the moonshine indeed struck like lightning. Her eyes teared, her throat burned, her hands shook, and she gasped for air. Stone took the jug before she dropped it. His lips quivered and he laughed. "That could cure a person or kill them!" Spicy cuffed him in the ribs.

"Oww!" Stone grabbed his side.

"Oh no! Did I come too close to your wound? I didn't mean to."

"C'mere and make it better," he challenged and moved the plates aside.

Spicy would gladly accept his challenge. She licked her fingertips and Stone's eyes smoldered. Placing her hands to his upper arms she eased him back on the soft quilts. She leaned over him and felt his right hand cup the back of her head. Closing her eyes, she touched her lips to his. Stone's left arm came around her and he tugged her on top of him. Excitement coursed through Spicy. Never had she lain atop a man. Did this mean the kissing was up to her? That was a nerve-racking responsibility. What if she made the kisses too short or too long? What if he got bored? She touched her tongue to Stone's lips as he'd taught her and his arms tightened around her. His right hand slipped under her hair to the nape of her neck and his left hand tenderly splayed over the exact spot of her spider bite. The tips of her breasts beaded against his hard, muscular chest. As for hard, he was long and rigid against her soft belly.

Spicy lifted her head and not wanting to scare him by saying she loved him, she masked it with, "Do you realize I want you so badly I've left my home for you, Stone?"

CHAPTER 32

"I WANT YOU SO BADLY I'VE OFFERED YOU MINE,"
Stone said. The revelation Spicy had left her home for him,
even temporarily, had not completely taken hold. But it
thrilled him to know this beautiful woman desired him as
much as he did her. Lying on top of him, a sugar-maple curl
slipped down her cheek and he brushed it back behind her
ear. In a whisper he said, "You belong with me on my side of
the river, Spicy, you just don't feel it, yet."

"Make me feel it, Stone."

Stone's blood had pounded hot and hard into his loins.
He rolled Spicy off him to the soft quilts. As he rested on his
side, her eyes sparkled up at him and her arms laced his
neck. Heaven and Earth—she made them both move. *I love
you, Spicy*, Stone thought.

"If you don't feel it, tell me and we'll stop," Stone heard
himself say. Why had he made such an offer? Maybe because
he'd never been in love with any of the women with whom
he'd had sex. But he was in love with Spicy and he wanted
her to love him, too. Only then might she feel she belonged
on his side of the Tug Fork.

Crazy? Unreasonable? Damn, he'd better be good.

Leaning over her with a smile, he closed his eyes and
touched his lips to hers. His heart hammered, cravings raced

through him, and his kiss deepened. Opening his mouth opened Spicy's. Stone slid his tongue inside and explored.

"Mmm," she moaned into him.

Stone knew she was naked underneath her new dress. Go slowly for her sake, he cautioned himself. Wanting her breasts pressed to his bare chest he began by undoing the buttons on his shirt. Surprising him, she unfastened the front of her dress and he groaned his approval. Tugging his shirt out of his britches, he then folded back the sides of her bodice. She was gorgeous and he yearned to see all of her. Sitting up, Stone looked to his left—evergreens, woods, dusk, and privacy. To his right—magnolia trees, waterfall, mountain, and seclusion.

"Stone, what's wrong?"

"I'm deciding if it's safe to strip you," he said. Her skin popped out in gooseflesh, beading her nipples into delicious maple syrup drops. His mouth watered. He'd paid close attention on the way to this rise and had seen no signs of trespassers. Plus, he owned so much land he knew there were no hogs running wild on his mountain. "We're alone."

Bringing her to a sitting position beside him, he gently eased her arms out of the sleeves and nudged the dress to her waist. She bowed her head with a shake spilling her long locks around her face, shoulders, and breasts. Putting a finger under her chin, Stone tipped her head up. His eyes holding hers, he swept the curls over her shoulders. His passion for her had elevated him to an aching state of arousal. This breathtaking woman was a carnal awakening. After ho-hum sex and semi-celibacy she was sorely testing every ounce of his restraint. As though she'd read his mind, Spicy lay back down and raised her hips. Stone took the invitation to lower the dress from her waist to her thighs.

Boldly admiring her sensual female body he said, "I bought you a camisole and panties in Logan. But something told me not to give them to you, yet."

She giggled nervously. "A real store-bought camisole and panties?"

"Yeah. But I thought that might appear too forward."

"And now?"

For an answer Stone tugged her dress down her legs and tossed it behind him. She lay completely naked before his hungry soul. Possessing a full bosom, tiny waist, and shapely hips, the belly button on her flat tummy resembled the dimples in her cheeks. At the juncture of her thighs a sugar-maple vee could be his.

"*You* are too breathtaking to be real, Spicy."

"It's this ledge. It's as magical as fairy fire."

"Nah, it's you."

Stone unbuttoned his fly. His manhood straining against his drawers, he leaned forward and molded his naked chest to her bare skin. He kissed her pink lips, her dainty ears, down her neck, and across her throat. Raw lust. Spicy had brought his once-healthy appetite for sex back with a vengeance. And he was free to act on it. Trailing kisses to her right breast, he took a peak in his mouth and placed his hand on her tummy. Nibbling her left breast, he trailed his hand south and with gentle fingers caressed the satin folds between her legs.

Misty dew on petal-soft skin.

Spicy moaned his name and Stone shoved his pants below his knees. When he rolled on top of her, a gulp escaped her lips. But with her next breath, she spread her legs letting him nestle his hips between her thighs. Always before he just wanted to grab his pleasure and run. But not with Spicy. He was a seasoned guide and he would take his time with this virgin territory. She'd never said she was a virgin, only that McCoy hadn't had her. Would he love Spicy any less if she had lain with another man? No, he'd lost his heart to her and there was no getting it back. But male pride said he wanted to be her first lover. Her only lover. Wrapping her arms around his shoulders, her fingers threaded through his hair and she pressed on the back of his head. Closing her eyes, she parted her lips. Stone lowered his mouth to hers and touched his arousal to her warm velvet.

"Yes?" he whispered, wanting her to sense she belonged here.

"Yes. Love me, Stone."

Spicy met his thrust, gasped, and tightened her arms around him. Sensing he'd entered unexplored terrain, he gently plunged all the way in before pulling back. The rhythm of a dance as old as the mountain was brand-new for the two hearts joining two bodies in becoming one. Faster and harder they made love in the shadows of the sweet magnolias. Mate Creek, its water falling, crooned a song of surrender. Stone's heart pounded against her breasts as her body gripped him internally. Buried to the hilt, his tongue played with hers. Spicy's ecstasy triggered his and he throbbed into her warm cocoon where her rapture squeezed him repeatedly. Moving within her and never leaving her, the pleasure was as unique as the blue moon. When their heartbeats finally slowed, the mountain shrouded them with a blanket of solitude in their starry-sky retreat. Stone eased up to his elbows and smiled down at the woman he loved.

Lust and ecstasy. Unforgettable and explosive. Satisfaction and contentment.

"Spicy, with Mate Creek at our feet and me embedded in you like coal in the mountain, tell me where you belong."

"With my heart on your mountain," Spicy whispered. "You're the long shot I said you were in every way."

"From now on, only with you, sugar'n spice."

When he rolled off her to his back, he tugged her to him and saw a spot of blood behind her on the quilt. When they made love a second time it was a little faster and a little harder. Just as magical and fiery. Afterwards, when they were dressed, Stone noted a flash of surprise on Spicy's face as she spied the smear of red. She silently scooped up the quilt and took a step toward the creek, no doubt to rinse away her blood.

Stone caught her, swept her into his arms, and molded her to his heart. "Spicy, you were a little virgin."

"Yes," she whispered tentatively. "Is that good or bad?"

"Like finding a hidden treasure."

Spicy's sensual smile was radiant and she hugged him fiercely. Stone kissed her, hoping the ledge of this mountain would forever be where he broke the chains binding this beauty to a miserable existence. So, too, the chains pulling him back to Philadelphia?

CHAPTER 33

"I SUPPOSE THE SITUATION WITH CLAY MAKES IT too dangerous to cross the river to check on Lumpkin," Spicy said in Aunt Hilda's kitchen the next morning.

"Especially on Election Day when emotions run high and anything can and does happen," Stone replied, climbing out of a big tin tub.

Earlier, he had filled the tub, in an alcove off the kitchen, as Spicy gathered eggs. While she had bathed, he fed the horses. As she'd cooked breakfast, he took a turn in the tub. With a towel slung low around his waist, and combing his hair back with his fingers, he sauntered into the kitchen. In Philadelphia, he usually skipped this meal. But in Tug Valley he wouldn't miss it, especially when the sexy woman with him was wearing only his shirt.

The previous night they had slept in a room with two beds. Spicy had ever so generously offered to sleep in the other bed so as not to crowd him. But he'd crooked his finger and with a sassy dance, she'd crawled naked into his arms. Now she was scooping ham and eggs onto plates alongside cracklin' biscuits topped with apple jam.

"Folks'll come and go back and forth across the river while visiting various precincts all day," Spicy said as Stone sat down at the kitchen table. "Some will pass right by my cabin on their way to Jerry Hatfield's house." She gave Stone twice the helping size of her breakfast before taking a seat across from him. "Surely Clay wouldn't cause trouble with so many witnesses."

"Witnesses never stopped any of the feuding," Stone reminded her after a sip of steaming black coffee. "Let's stick with West Virginia's Magnolia Precinct. We'll see Ellison and Johnse or someone else who typically visits precincts across the river. They can bring us word from Kentucky about Big Lump."

"I know that's the smart thing to do," Spicy agreed but then ate in silence.

After several bites of ham and eggs, Stone asked, "What's wrong?"

"Nothing," she said lifting one hand to scratch her neck and the other her head.

In the last twelve hours those hands had brought him pleasure sweeter than the jam on his biscuit. They had guided him to a secret waltz where no other man had ever been invited.

"Please answer me."

She hesitated and then let it spill in rapid fire, "I can't hide from Clay McCoy forever. Your aunt will come home and even though I admitted I belong on your side of the river, you have to return to Philadelphia. I have to go home. I may as well just get it over with today."

"Slow down." Stone figured now was a good a time to tell her. "I'm not going back."

"Balderdash," she said with a tsk and a scratch. "Of course you are."

"I decided not to when we were out on that *ledge* last night," Stone said meaningfully as he stared her in the eyes. "I told myself to sleep on my decision and I did."

"I don't understand." Spicy tilted her head in obvious confusion and rubbed both temples. "What would cause such a change of heart?"

"You."

"No, not me." She shook her head, reared back in her chair, and dug at her shoulder.

"Don't scratch." Stone gestured with both hands for her to relax. "Yes, you."

"No, Stone." She plopped her elbows on the table and put her forehead in her hands.

"Yes, Spicy."

Raising her head, she looked across the table at him. "If you were going to stay, do so because of your ability to help people in Tug Valley." The emotions crossing her face spoke of sincerity and respect, of admiration and compassion. "Stay for Abigail Hatfield who may need a tonsillectomy. Stay to deliver the next baby who can only survive by cesarean section. Stay to save the lives of mothers like Polly." Both sadness and hope crossed Spicy's face. "Stay and figure out what to do about Shadow McCoy's ear so he doesn't lose his hearing. Stay because of people who suffer traumatic fractures like Lumpkin's and to diagnose patients like Aunt Hilda's friend, Connie Staton."

Stone stared hard at her. "There are illnesses, expectant mothers, broken bones, and diseases everywhere." With a tight smile he added, "Not to mention spider bites."

"And gunshot wounds."

"I can treat those wherever I am."

"But you can't operate in the woods." Spicy's expression and voice were empathic as she'd repeated what he had once said. He suspected she was scratching her arms under the table.

"If it takes selling my mountain, a hospital needs to be built in Tug Valley." He reached across the table and she brought both hands from her lap to hold his. She squeezed as if grasping at his words. "Like it or not, I'm staying because of you."

"What about Pennsylvania Hospital?"

"I need to tell Dr. Vanderveer, not to mention my brother, Jet, of my decision in person. I practically lived at the hospital the past few years. Other than the books I mentioned and some clothes, Jet can have whatever I leave behind."

"This would be a huge sacrifice on your part."

"It comes with huge benefits." He smiled as tears glistened in her eyes. "In Philadelphia, there are other physicians who can run the surgical department of the hospital. But in Tug Valley, folks have to travel a long way to receive such medical treatment because here, there are no hospitals or local physicians trained like I am."

"There is no one," Spicy's voice broke, "like you. Anywhere." Tears, more than when he'd given her the dress, trickled down her cheeks. She swallowed hard. "I knew out on that *ledge* last night if you left me I was just number seven and not so lucky. But I promised myself I'd let you go with a smile."

"I'm the lucky one, Spicy. I can't leave because I've fallen in love with you."

Without hesitation, she said, "I'm in love with you, too."

"C'mere." Stone tugged on her hands and then let go. He scooted his chair back as she rounded the table to him. Wearing only his shirt made it easy for her to straddle his thighs. His towel slipped away and bare bottom met bare lap as she wrapped her arms around his neck. Stone molded her body to his and said, "I can set up a small practice while we work on bigger plans. Gotta start somewhere."

Clutching him tightly, Spicy promised, "I will help you every single step of the way, every single day."

"Will you help me with this?" he teased and pressed himself against her.

She raised both brows. "I believe I have just the treatment."

"I believe you have the *only* treatment." Stone lifted her and sliding his hot, hard inches into Spicy's velvety, soft grip was the exclusive cure he needed.

～

ENTERING the Magnolia Precinct in her pretty, new dress, Spicy's heart danced on a mountaintop of joy. She loved Stone Hatfield and he loved her! They would figure out the future together. They'd celebrated by spending half the day in bed. Even their midday meal had been enjoyed in bed. Her happiness had never known such heights. She wished her folks could have lived to see this magnificent day. She smiled thinking how happy not only Lumpkin would be with his new friend staying but Aunt Hilda would be thrilled to have at least one of her nephews back.

Yes, on Election Day anything could happen.

Spicy had ridden Daisy to the precinct alongside Stone who rode Logan. It was a festival atmosphere at Abe and Flora Weddington's place. Their property was a mainstay of the precinct and the voting process was in full swing. Long tables were laden with food, thus no one would leave hungry. Seated in comfortable chairs on summer grasses, folks sipped tea, lemonade, or moonshine. Some took the opportunity to buy or trade horses, cows, or goats, while others mingled with laughter rising here and there. The clank of horseshoes and squeals from happy children filled the air.

"I don't know if you remember me from years ago, but I'm Stone Hatfield," Stone said after he and Spicy sought out the Weddingtons to introduce themselves.

"Of course we remember you, Stone," Abe said standing beside two checker players he introduced as his grandsons, Henry and Tommy. Abe was big and balding in contrast to his petite wife, Flora, who wore oodles of gray hair piled on top of her head. "Your aunt and mother, God rest her soul, always talked about you and Jet. We're sorry for your loss."

"Thank you both. This is Spicy McCoy," Stone said, smiling at her.

"Spicy, you've set a new standard for the ladies," Flora said, holding the hand of a little girl. "I just took a splinter out of my granddaughter's finger, but never a thorn out of a hog."

As they laughed and chatted Ellison joined them. He had already voted and was just leaving the election site. He voiced being glad Spicy was up and around again. His next stop was across the river to visit the Blackberry Precinct at Jerry Hatfield's house. Yes, he'd be happy to check on Lumpkin on his way past Spicy's cabin and send news back across the river. Spicy so wished more people on both sides of the Tug Fork were like Stone and Ellison. With a wave, Ellison was gone. Folks always made the most out of Election Day and following the same party mood of previous years, this late afternoon was no exception.

Dr. Stone Hatfield's presence certainly did not go unnoticed. People practically lined up to speak to him and quite often to ask his medical advice. With love and admiration, Spicy listened as Stone unfailingly responded with patience and grace. Conversations mixed with good food kept them longer than they'd intended.

"Hello, Stony." The man walking up to them was Devil Anse's older brother, Valentine 'Wall' Hatfield, who served as a justice of the peace in the Magnolia Precinct. "I heard you were back. It's been awhile."

"Hello, Valentine, yes it has. Nice to see you again," Stone replied and shook hands before turning to Spicy. "This is Spicy McCoy from the Blackberry Creek Precinct."

"Is this the one and only Spicy McCoy who removed a thorn from a razorback's butt?"

"Told you that would make you a legend," Stone said and chuckled.

"Yes, sir." Spicy nodded with a smile at Valentine.

Valentine chuckled. "This particular hog story is a happy one. I've been hearing the tale told and retold by both Hatfields and McCoys today."

"So have we," Stone agreed with a grin.

"She's as brave as she is beautiful, Stone."

"That she is."

Smiling first at Stone, Spicy looked at Valentine. "Thank you, Justice Hatfield. I couldn't have done it without Dr.

Hatfield's assistance." Then returning a compliment she said, "Before my father, Calvert McCoy, passed, he always spoke of how fair Valentine 'Wall' Hatfield was. He said you were the wall between opposing forces and rendered impartial decisions, such as acquitting Squirrel Huntin' Sam and Paris McCoy in the death of Bill Staton, even though Staton was a friend of the Hatfields."

"Thank you, Miss McCoy, I appreciate that for certain," Valentine said. "My district is the smallest of the four here in Tug Valley and all's been fairly calm today. Since the votes are spoken aloud there's the occasional boo or hooray, but folks know I frown on that."

"Not so calm on Blackberry Creek, Valentine," called a gray haired, bespeckled gentleman, toting a Colt .45 much like the gun shoved in the back of Stone's belt.

CHAPTER 34

"Hello." Valentine waved to the man approaching them. "Always a pleasure, sir."

Spicy glanced up at Stone who acknowledged her concern with a squeeze to her hand. Justice Hatfield introduced the man as Ronny Staton, Conrad Staton's brother. Before Valentine could in turn introduce Stone and Spicy or inquire as to what was happening across the river, he was called away to handle Magnolia Precinct business. Stone made their connections between his Aunt Hilda and Ronny's brother, Connie. Ronny said he'd ridden his horse, Gus, here earlier, crossed the river, and was on his way back home.

"Hilda has mentioned you and your brother, Jet," Ronny replied. "Nice to meet you."

"It's nice to meet you as well," Stone said to Ronny and introduced Spicy.

Ronny nodded politely at Spicy and said, "You're the folks Ellison asked me to give a message to before things got rowdy at the Blackberry Precinct. He said to tell Stone Hatfield and his friend, Spicy, Big Lump McCoy is fine. He said Big Lump is at Spicy's cabin working on a pigpen with Shadow McCoy. Abigail Hatfield is making sure they eat and rest."

"That's wonderful." Spicy beamed up at Stone and then to Ronny said, "Thank you."

"What's the problem at the Blackberry Precinct?" Stone asked.

"It was just after I was visiting with Ellison when Tolbert, Pharmer, and Bud McCoy arrived. You know them?" Ronny asked.

"I do," Spicy said, "mostly through Clay McCoy."

"Clay," Ronny said the name as if it put a bad taste in his mouth. "He was there drinking and booing votes with the Cline brothers, who I swear ain't never put soap and water together." With a disapproving shake of his head, he continued, "Anyhow, the trouble started when a Pike County Hatfield by the name of Elias, who is Preacher Anderson C. Hatfield's younger brother, showed up. He goes by Bad Lias mostly to distinguish himself from his cousins—Devil Anse and Ellison's brother, Elias, known as Good Lias."

"I thought the Pike County Hatfields and McCoys got along," Spicy said.

"So did I," Ronny said. "But Tolbert seemed to be spoiling for trouble and started hounding Bad Lias saying he owed him a dollar seventy-five for a fiddle. Bad Lias said he done paid Tolbert for the fiddle a good three years ago."

Spicy sighed. "I just spoke to Ol' Ranel about Tolbert the other day."

"Tolbert was making all kinds of disparaging remarks to Bad Lias and he was ready for a fight but Constable Matthew Hatfield restrained him. Even Ellison was getting enough of it."

"That's saying a lot because Ellison's known as a peacemaker," Stone said with a glance to the west. "How was the situation when you left?"

"Well, sir, not good." Ronny adjusted his spectacles and said, "I figured it was time to leave when Tolbert called Bad Lias a filthy Hatfield and Bad Lias called Tolbert a lying McCoy. I heard more yelling but by then I was to the creek and couldn't make out the words."

"I'm going over there," Stone grumbled.

"No," Spicy gasped and clutched his hand with both of hers. "It will be dark soon. Please don't go."

"Dr. Hatfield?" a man yelled, running onto the scene from the direction of the river. Obviously frantic and not knowing who he was looking for he shouted again, "Dr. Hatfield?"

"I'm Dr. Hatfield." Stone raised a hand in the air and asked Spicy, "Who's that?"

"Zeke McCoy, Sunshine and Shadow's father."

"Over here, Zeke!" Ronny yelled and gave him a wave.

"Dr. Hatfield?" Zeke asked. Slowing to a stop he politely nodded at Spicy and Ronny.

"Yes," Stone offered his hand and Zeke grasped it. "I've met your son, Shadow, Mr. McCoy. He's a fine boy."

"Thank you, sir. Shadow likes you, too." Zeke paused and gulped a breath. "All hell's done broke loose at the Blackberry Precinct. Otis Hatfield and I were asked to find you and Spicy, Dr. Hatfield." Looking to Spicy, he added, "Otis headed to your cabin, Spicy." To all of them he said, "A couple of folks took off to find Dr. Rutherford."

Spicy tensed, expecting the worst, terrified at how dire the worst could be. Other people had heard or seen Zeke and began moving closer, gathering in whispering groups to listen.

"Please call me Stone," he said. "What happened?"

"I'm Zeke," he replied, a mixture of anger and shock. "I don't know where to start." Rubbing his forehead, Zeke looked at Stone. "I'd just voted at the Blackberry Precinct when I saw Tolbert McCoy push Bad Lias Hatfield."

"It was getting bad when I left," Ronny confirmed with a frown.

"Zeke?" Stone prodded.

"It went from bad to worse, Ronny." Zeke looked from Ronny to Spicy and back to Stone. "Ellison Hatfield stepped between Tolbert and Bad Lias." Frowning, Zeke said, "Ellison yelled, 'I'm the best damn man on Earth!' Tolbert hollered back saying, 'I'm hell on Earth! I could whoop any man here.' Ellison yelled, 'You're a damn dog. Fight me.' I couldn't believe my eyes at what happened next."

"They came to blows?" Stone asked.

"Yes. Ellison is so big and strong, even when Bud and Pharmer McCoy jumped into the fight he was holding his own. Until..." Zeke stopped, closed his eyes and shook his head.

Spicy placed a hand on Zeke's arm and asked, "Until what, Zeke?"

Zeke took a breath and opened his eyes. "Until Bud started stabbing Ellison."

Stone barked, "What the hell?"

"Bud must have stabbed Ellison two dozen times or more," Zeke said, eyes watering. "When Ellison managed to pick up a rock, Pharmer grabbed a gun from somebody's holster and shot Ellison in the back."

At the Magnolia Precinct, everything suddenly blurred for Spicy—the crowd, angry shouts, people scrambling, wailing cries. Even the clouds above her head appeared ominous as if ready to storm and spiral the tempest shaking the very ground beneath her feet. Nothing seemed remotely real and every second was petrifyingly painful.

"Since you and Otis were asked to find us, then Ellison is still alive," Stone said, strangely calm as if the doctor in him had kicked in.

"I don't know how, but yes, he was alive when I left," Zeke confirmed.

"Where are the McCoy brothers?" Ronny asked, checking the bullets in his pistol.

"Being tracked down by Hatfields," Zeke replied.

"I don't have my medical bag with me. I'll have to make do with whatever Jerry Hatfield has at his precinct," Stone said, glaring in the direction of Kentucky.

Knowing there was no stopping Stone from going to Ellison's aid, Spicy said, "I'll get your medical bag and meet you there."

"No, with the McCoys on the run and Clay in the mix, you stay in West Virginia."

"How about I go with Spicy to get your bag?" Ronny offered. "I can bring it to you."

"No, I don't want to leave Spicy alone."

"I'll go with them, get your bad, and bring it to you across the river," Zeke offered.

"Yes," Stone agreed to that plan. "Thanks, Zeke."

"No!" Spicy argued. "I need, I want to help save Ellison."

"Spicy, you know exactly where my medical bag is at the house. Go with Ronny and Zeke to get it. Then go straight to Aunt Hilda's or Ronny's place and wait for me there. Please."

When she hesitated Stone gave her a look that signaled she was wasting her breath and Ellison's time by arguing. Spicy nodded sharply, Stone pulled her into his arms and kissed her. She prayed it wouldn't be the last time just as he released her. One never knew in this valley.

"I'll borrow a horse and have it and yours rounded up at the riverbank," Zeke said.

"Whatever you do, don't let Clay McCoy or Vorticia Hatfield anywhere near Spicy," Stone said to Ronny and Zeke as he swung himself onto Logan.

"Will do." Ronny then called to Abe Weddington and motioned to Zeke.

"Don't let your guard down, Stone," Spicy said, feeling helpless.

Stone gave Spicy a tense smile and turned his horse toward Kentucky. The sky darkened on Stone as he galloped out of the Magnolia Precinct and disappeared over a rise. Spicy knew the best way she could help was to get his medical bag. Abe's grandson, Henry, rode a horse out of a barn leading a saddled mare for Zeke. Henry would ride with Zeke to the Tug Fork. At the river, he'd retrieve Logan and deliver him along with the mare, named Ethel, to Stone's place. Furthermore his grandfather, Abe, had said to leave Ethel, for a day or two, just in case she was needed.

Spicy, Ronny, Zeke, and Henry mounted their horses and headed to Stone's house.

∿

"CLAY SAYS we's gonna fix yer flint, Hatfield," said Josiah, the Cline with a sightless eye and its lid permanently at half-mast. A single lantern lit the interior of a godforsaken shack. "Yer gonna wish you's colder'n a wagon wheel by the time we's done skinnin' you alive."

Stone had a sliver-sized view through a hole in the burlap meant to blind him. Uriah swiped a hand across his runny nose as Josiah chewed and spat tobacco in a cabin even worse than Clay McCoy's. This dirt floor, ten-by-ten hovel was empty except for a couple of filthy cots shoved in one corner and some moonshine jugs in another.

Assuming Clay McCoy and the Clines might be lying in wait in Raccoon Hollow, Stone had not let his guard down. But he hadn't figured on McCoy dropping on top of him from a tree and the Clines bolting forward with rifles and rope. McCoy had lucked into the ambush after witnessing Zeke take off to find him. As furiously as Stone had fought, he was no more of a match for three-on-one than Ellison against Tolbert, Bud, and Pharmer McCoy. Pulling a gunnysack over his head, the Clines had tied his hands and marched him through the backwoods at the end of their rifles as Stone had said Clay would have done had he refused to help Polly.

McCoy hadn't accompanied them to this dump. Instead he'd sneered in Stone's face how he had kept silent at the Blackberry Precinct, knowing whoever searched Spicy's cabin was wasting their time. He had already hunted for them there. Stone had been right to hide Spicy at his Aunt Hilda's place. Malevolence dripped like blood as McCoy swore to find Spicy and destroy any innocence she had left before he shared her with the Clines. Of course Stone refused to give him any information on her whereabouts, resulting in McCoy smashing the butt of his rifle above Stone's left brow. Shouting over his shoulder as he ran to the river, McCoy reminded the Clines he was starting at Stone's house and if Spicy wasn't there, someone at the Magnolia Precinct would know something. Stone cursed himself for not pulling the trigger the day he'd had his Colt .45 pressed between McCoy's eyes.

Stone sized up his current situation. Josiah, rifle at this side, sitting in the dirt across the foul one-room hut, emptied the last drop from a jug of moonshine into his mouth. Posted near the only door in or out Uriah, rifle on his right side, clutched a moonshine jug on the left. Josiah had taken Stone's Colt .45 and shoved it into in the pocket of his overalls. It was still there because he could see the handle. Stone's knife, however, was securely hidden in his boot. If they drank themselves into the same stupor of oblivion they'd been in the first time he had seen them, he might be able to get his knife and cut through the ropes binding his wrists and ankles.

"He don't talk much, do he?" Uriah sniffled and spat blood. "Think he's 'fraid?"

"I think he broke my cussed nose." Josiah coughed, his nose trickling blood.

Stone watched a hog lumber into the Clines' cabin as if it lived inside and apparently it did. Moseying across the room, it rooted itself against a back wall. Two more razor-backs reached the door at the same time. Grunting and snorting, the bigger one pushed its way in first. A fourth hog waddled in and together the pigs took up more than half the cabin. That shed light not only on the lack of furnishings but the Clines' infamous stench.

"I's suspicion Clay ain't sharin' no piece o' Spicy," Uriah whined to his brother.

"If'n he don't we's toss the piss-proud prick into that snake pit." Josiah spat tobacco, turning dirt into sludge and taunted Stone, "Ain't you got nothin' to say 'bout Spicy?"

"Done had her," Stone said dismissively with a strategic shrug.

"That'll fry Clay's vittles!" Josiah whooped.

"I's drink to that!" Uriah hollered only to find his jug was empty.

"Got an extra jug of moonshine?" Stone asked.

Uriah sneezed into his hand and wiped it on the front of his overalls. "Yeah." He got off the ground and stumbled around a pig on his way to the corner full of grimy jugs.

"We ain't givin' no moonshine to no Hatfield, you flap-mouthed fool. Didje forget he come near to whippin' us'n Clay?" Josiah swiped at his blood nose. "Our moonshine's only for McCoys." Pointing with his rifle barrel, he said, "Fetch me 'nother jug over here, pig brain."

Uriah followed Josiah's order, also taking another jug for himself. They reacted just as Stone had hoped by making a show of chugging their moonshine since he had none. Then snickering over Clay's anticipated reaction when they told him Stone had already had Spicy, the brothers literally clapped their filthy hands in ghoulish delight. They proceeded to sneeze and cough while burping and slurping the white lightening. Stone counted the minutes, praying the rumor of McCoy's moonshine being stronger—though not as palatable— as Johnse's was true.

Where in God's name was Spicy right now? Had McCoy gotten his hooks into her? Please let her be safe at Aunt Hilda's house or at Ronny Staton's place. What about Ellison? Was he hanging onto life or had he succumbed to his wounds? Did Devil Anse know about his brother by now? How many deaths would result from this disaster?

Stone wanted to jump out of his skin, but focused on blending into the wall.

CHAPTER 35

SPICY AND RONNY HAD WAVED TO ZEKE McCOY and Henry Weddington as the two galloped away from the front of Stone's house with the medical bag in tow.

"I'm going to take Stone's mantel clock with us," Spicy said on the porch. "It's not running right and I offered to clean it. Maybe that will keep me occupied while I wait for him."

Spicy hurried into the house. Removing the weight which made the beautiful clock tick, she placed it safely inside the black case with the ivory face and gold hands. She carried the clock to the porch and handed it to Ronny. After she mounted Daisy, he returned the clock to her. They had ridden Daisy and Gus hard, so they trotted them into the barn for water and oats.

"I should have gone with Zeke," Spicy fretted to Ronny as he lit a couple of lanterns to illuminate the barn's interior. With great care, she set the clock on a sturdy shelf. "I need to do more than just work on a clock. I want to help Stone save Ellison."

"I understand how you feel. I've been friends with Ellison all my life," Ronny replied, kindness and concern etching his weathered face. "But your job is to keep yourself safe and my job is to get you to Hilda's house or to mine to wait for Stone."

"Let's ride to Hilda's house. It's closer and Stone doesn't know where you live," Spicy had suggested, her nerves frayed.

Henry Weddington met them in the barn with Logan and the mare named Ethel in tow. Henry reported Zeke had made it safely across the river with Stone's medical bag. Henry was going home to the Magnolia Precinct, but as planned would leave Ethel with them. Spicy and Ronny thanked him and saw to it that Logan and Ethel had their share of water and oats.

"While the horses rest and eat, let's go back to the house. I'll leave Stone a note telling him we decided to head to his Aunt Hilda's," Spicy said.

"Then we best skedaddle because it's getting dark and those are rainclouds in the sky," Ronny replied.

She and Ronny retraced their steps to the house. Ronny stayed guard on the porch with one of the lanterns. Lighting her way with the other lantern, Spicy returned to the library and found a piece of paper along with a pen and inkwell on the desk. She was relieved there was still ink in the jar and dipped the pen into it. Clay couldn't read, but still she was careful to give her location in a one word code.

Where was Stone? Had he found Ellison at Jerry Hatfield's house? Did he get there in time to save his friend? What would Ol' Ranel McCoy say about the stabbing and shooting? There would be horrendous consequences to the terrible crimes committed by his sons.

Spicy jumped as a blast shattered the quiet. Grabbing the lantern, she ran to the foyer. Yanking the front door open, she was confronted by the crone whose face bore a thousand wrinkles and on whose shoulder perched a rat.

"Clay!" Vorticia shrilled. "She's here!"

Spicy screamed so loudly, the witch backed up hissing. Clay climbed over the porch railing near the spot where Stone had sat while watching her pick blueberries. Though that tender morning seemed forever ago, Spicy vividly recalled Stone saying Clay and Vorticia were working together. Both of Clay's eyes were swollen and turning purple and his other front tooth was gone. Tearing her shocked gaze off Clay, Spicy saw Ronny. Slumped in a rocking chair, the flickering lantern light showed he had taken a bullet to the head.

"You killed Ronny Staton?" Spicy gasped.

"With his own pistol." Clay's grin, oozing blood, was scarier than usual.

"Why? Why would you do that?"

"He was in my way." Clay scowled, coming toward her. "Just like Philadelphy."

"What do you mean?" Spicy asked, holding the lantern with one hand and crushing the note to Stone with the other. "Have you seen Stone?"

"You askin' me if'n Dr. High and Mighty is dead?" Clay sneered. Closing in on her, he grabbed her lantern and note. "What's this here say?"

Spicy didn't reply, so he handed her note to Vorticia who uncrumpled it.

"Swings," the witch said, squinting. "I got a swing fer ya."

Ignoring her, Spicy asked Clay, "Do you know something about Stone?"

"He's over yonder with the Clines. They's to wait fer two hours after they smelt the smoke afore followin' us. I don't want Philadelphy catchin' up and tryin' to steal you again."

"They's gonna meet up with us in my den," Vorticia stated proudly. "Where Stony's dead body cain't be found."

"Where we's killin' Philadelphy real slow whilst you watch," Clay said. "It's the only reason that Yankee's still alive."

"I don't believe you. You lied about shooting Stone once before."

"So, then I shot him fer real."

As truth dawned, Spicy said, "Stone kicked your tail like you've done to my raccoon more than once."

Clay squinted his puffy, blackening eyes and swiped the back of his arm across his bloody mouth. "Philadelphy jumped me fer no good reason and knocked out my best tooth."

"That's another lie." Spicy lifted her chin and squared her shoulders. "But if you do have Stone, I'll marry you today if you release him alive and well."

"Yer gonna marry me awright," Clay assured her. "Then I'll skin that pesterful raccoon you pulled outa the creek fer our weddin' supper."

"Wolfsbane!" Vorticia criticized, shaking her head. "Poison's easier'n drownin'."

Waving Vorticia off, Clay told Spicy, "We cain't get hitched today on accounta Ellison Hatfield finally got what was comin' to him and the justices o' the peace're busy."

"Ellison is a good man," Spicy said.

"Look what it got him." Clay struck a match. He tossed it under the rocking chair which held Ronny's body.

"Burn!" Vorticia screeched, throwing Spicy's note into the fire.

"Stop!" Spicy shouted at both of them and moved to stamp the fire out but Clay blocked her. "What's wrong with you, Clay? Why do you hate everyone and everything?"

"Because." He cursed the match as it flickered out and struck another one. He tossed it near the first one and the flames caught.

"Because why?" Spicy demanded.

"Ever'body startin' with Big Lump keeps gettin' in my way with you."

"Didje know Clay and Josiah done tried to kill Big Lump twice?" Vorticia informed Spicy. "Once in the blueberry patch and once in Raccoon Holler? Josiah done the distractin' and Clay done the shootin'"

Clay glowered at Vorticia, then smirked at Spicy and

defended himself as though she'd understand, "You shoulda been pickin' berries with me insteada him."

"Lumpkin and I were ten years old," Spicy cried. Hearing the reason behind the truth she already knew still landed like a blow. "You were nineteen and busy chasing girls your age."

"You's mine even back then."

"I was never yours," she said as Clay struck another match and tossed it into the fire burning the porch and the rocker. "Haven't you burned enough Hatfield property?"

"Philadephy ain't gonna live to need it."

A rain-scented breeze blew across the porch, but instead of dousing the fire it fanned the flames. Fire caught hold of Ronny's pant leg and Spicy took a step toward him. Vorticia snatched her arm and the rat ran down to the witch's hand. Spicy jerked out of Vorticia's grasp before the rat could touch her.

"Put the fire out," Spicy pleaded. "I'll do whatever you want."

"Burn!" Vorticia shrilled again and kicked over the lantern setting beside Ronny.

"You bat-dung ol' hag!" Clay shouted as the glass shattered and the flames spread underneath the rocking chair. "We coulda used both lanterns to get to yer cave."

"I don't need no lantern, you chinless carrot top!" Vorticia shot back, turning Clay's battered face even redder. "Stony's house'll be ashes, he'll soon be dead and I ain't aworrin' 'bout him forcin' me outa my den where coal gives me powers."

"Dear God," Spicy whispered in terror. They were both insane.

"God didn't help yer folks," Clay said nonchalantly.

Vorticia said, "Thanks to me soaking their pork in 'nough wolfsbane to kill ten wolves."

"The two of you poisoned my mother and father?"

"They was in my way!" Clay blared as if she wasn't getting the message.

"No, they weren't. You had them fooled."

"Foolin' 'em was too much work."

"My father asked you to marry me and my mother approved, Clay."

"Not 'til I put 'em on their deathbeds." His face was the mask of a maniac. "I told 'em if'n they didn't convince you of yer betrothal to me I'd kill you in front of 'em."

Spicy realized, "Which is why you stayed there holding my hand until they passed."

"Got the useless cripple and spin-wheeler outa my way." Clay snorted and spat blood as he moved to the other side of the porch all the while striking and tossing lit matches.

"You hate me like you hate everyone. You know I don't want to marry you so why would you want to marry me?"

"On accounta you'll come 'round to likin' me when there's nobody left to rescue ya.

Besides, I hafta marry you to get yer property, you stupid Hatfield-lovin' whore."

"I'm not a whore and I'm not stupid. I just wanted to hear you admit all of it."

Clay glared at Spicy, madness burning in his flat-brown eyes as he shrugged. "If'n you don't come 'round you'll get real poorly and die."

"Wolfsbane!" Vorticia cackled, descending the steps away from the burning porch.

"Clay you're going to catch the whole mountain on fire."

"His mountain," Clay spat in contempt. "That'll settle some hash for the Hatfields."

"Ain't gettin' to the backside, though," Vorticia mumbled.

"No and it cain't jump the river to get to the McCoys." Clay grabbed Spicy as the fire raged and yanking her off the porch, said to Vorticia, "Let's get the horses."

"Horses is hell-hated beasts of death and I ain't gettin' near none!" Vorticia shrieked.

"Fly yer broom, witch," Clay said, heading to the barn.

"Find my cave, madman. The Clines done been here, but you ain't."

"Shit!" Clay hollered, "Philadelphy's horses can burn."

Spicy stopped in her tracks. "I won't take another step until the horses are free."

"You move or I's shoot you and the horses." Taking hold of a rope tied to his belt, Clay held her at gunpoint as Vorticia tied one end of the rope around Spicy's waist. "Won't be no escapin' durin' the night."

Not doubting for a second Clay would shoot her as he had Stone, Lumpkin, and Ronny, Spicy refrained from fighting back as Vorticia knotted the rope. The barn door was ajar which gave her hope the horses could free themselves if the fire spread. Clay jerked hard on the rope and she stumbled forward. Remembering where Stone told her to kick a man, if she could get close enough again without being shot, she'd do her damndest. At the edge of the clearing she stole a final glance at the house over her shoulder. Her heart broke as flames shot smoke and ash spiraling into the twilight sky.

Stone would never forgive her. Spicy would never forgive herself.

CHAPTER 36

STONE HAD SMELLED THE SMOKE THE PREVIOUS evening when it drifted into the Clines' hut and penetrated the gunnysack over his head. However, the Clines couldn't smell themselves or the hogs, much less the smoke. When he brought it to their attention they sniffed the air, fired their rifles barely missing him, and accused him of trying to trick them so he could escape. By the time the Clines might have come around to realizing something was burning, it had begun to rain. Water dripped through the sagging roof snuffing out the smoldering scent of smoke and turning dirt into mud. In such close quarters, rope securing his hands and feet and with both Clines guarding him, Stone had remained trapped. Making a horrible situation even worse, his captors had evidently built up a tolerance to the moonshine because they had remained conscious. The pigs rooted, the Clines guzzled, and the night had seemed endless.

Dawn had come and gone hours ago. Twice when Stone had moved enough to keep his circulation from being cut off Josiah and Uriah had fired their rifles, warning him to stay put. Daylight streamed into the rancid pigsty showing him the fingers of his guards bent around the triggers of the weapons pointed directly at him. On the plus side, since the

Clines had been too ignorant to take turns staying awake and sleeping, Uriah had just passed out. His snoring had lulled Josiah into shutting his eyes, at least the one he could see with was closed. His mouth gaped open as he drooled a combination of tobacco spit and moonshine onto his beard.

Finally. Stone struggled against the ropes securing his ankles as he worked to pull up his pant leg. That accomplished, he reached into his boot, his fingers seeking the handle of his knife pressed against his inside calf. Gaining a tenuous grip on it, he inched the knife upwards, got a better hold, and pulled it free. Turning the knife upside down with the blade to the rope around his wrists was no easy task. But succeeding, he cut. Up and down he sawed at the rope.

Uriah snorted in his sleep. Stone didn't move a muscle. Josiah stirred, took a swig of moonshine and hacked up some putrid brown spittle. Stone was a statue until Josiah's mouth fell open again. Stone cut until his wrists broke free of the rope. Only then did he soundlessly remove the gunnysack from his head and carefully slide his booted feet under him.

Josiah belched. Stone paused. Uriah sneezed. Stone stood.

Stone needed his Colt .45 and there was only one way to get it. Four silent steps took him across the mud and hogs to Josiah Cline's side. Taking a quick glance at a snoring Uriah, Stone leaned down and grasped the barrel of Josiah's rifle. Sure enough, Josiah woke and pulled the trigger. The bullet slammed into the wall exactly where Stone had been sitting moments prior. Stone buried his Bowie knife in the center of Josiah's heart. His eye stared in disbelief as Stone yanked his Colt free. With a final belch, Josiah slumped over his moonshine jug. Dead.

Flat on his back, eyes closed, Uriah mumbled, "That yer rifle? Smelt smoke?"

Quickly, Stone pulled his knife from Josiah's chest and wiped the blade on his overalls. Sliding the knife back into his boot Stone grabbed Josiah's rifle and stood. Uriah, managing to sit up, gaped at seeing Stone standing in the middle of the shack. Uriah pulled the trigger of his rifle also striking the spot where Stone had been tied up. Before Uriah could readjust his aim, a Colt .45 bullet exploded his heart. Uriah slapped the mud. Dead.

The pigs snorted as Stone grabbed Uriah's rifle and stepped around the bodies. Slinging both rifles over his shoulder he didn't look back. First and foremost in his mind was finding Spicy. She was in jeopardy all because of him. She would surely blame him for being captured by Clay and rightly so. Stone prayed he wouldn't lose her.

Outside, the sky was once again growing as stormy and furious as Stone felt. He paused to get his bearings. Twenty-four hours prior, he'd arrived with the gunnysack over his head and he didn't recognize this part of Peter Creek. He was up a creek, all right. In any event, when he'd rescued Spicy from Clay after the spider bite, they'd not passed the Clines' pigsty. Not sure how far he was from McCoy's hell-hole, he knew Spicy's cabin lay northeast.

Stone took off along a worn path he figured would either lead him to McCoy's place or Blackberry Creek. Either way, he could find his way to Spicy's from there. Sure enough, he probably hadn't gone a quarter of a mile when Clay McCoy's cornfield and moonshine still came into view. Stone didn't take any chances and made his approach as if fully expecting to find McCoy holding Spicy hostage. Remembering how he'd walked in on McCoy with Spicy underneath him, Stone's stomach clenched. Whether Spicy forgave him or not, Stone would never forgive himself if McCoy succeeded in raping her. The place looked deserted and he eased closer using cornstalks and sacks of corn to shield himself like he and Big Lump had done the last time. All was silent. He peered into a window. Empty. Stone knew his way now and sliced through the woods. Dusk hovered over Blackberry Creek as he splashed across it.

"Hey!" somebody yelled from the other side. "Who goes there?"

"Stone Hatfield."

"Otis Hatfield here," he said, lowering his rifle and coming out from behind a tree. "Stone, have you heard what happened during the election?"

"Yes." Stone stepped onto dry ground. Catching his breath, he extended his hand to Otis and they shook. "I know Ellison was stabbed and shot by three McCoy brothers."

"A savagerous act." Otis was clearly upset. "Ellison's brother, Elias, who we know as Good Lias was at the Blackberry Precinct and took charge of Ellison."

"Do you know how Ellison is or where Good Lias has him?"

"I don't know. I'm sorry," Otis replied sadly. "The McCoys didn't get far and done been caught. Bad Lias's brother, Preacher Anderson C. Hatfield who's a justice of the peace in Pike County, ordered two Pike County constables to arrest 'em and take 'em to the Pikeville Jail. But they wasn't in much of a hurry and stopped at Floyd McCoy's home for supper."

Stone shook his head at the ways of Tug Valley. "Have you seen Spicy today?"

"With all the trouble and smelling smoke coming from somewhere, I went to her cabin to check on Abigail, but Spicy wasn't there," Otis said. "Big Lump was working on a pigpen with Shadow McCoy. Big Lump ain't gonna let nobody hurt my Abby or Shadow, neither."

"Was Clay McCoy there?"

"No." Otis grimaced in distaste. "My daughter and me have a deal. If Abby sees Clay anywhere she's to high-tail it home."

"I'm working on a similar deal with Spicy. Thanks, Otis. I've gotta go."

Stone sprinted alongside Blackberry Creek. Swiping at tree branches and ducking low limbs, the area soon became familiar. A bit further and he realized he had reached the spot where fairy fire had magically danced its way down this stream. *Please, God,* Stone silently prayed, *let me see fairy fire with Spicy again. Please God, let Ellison live.*

Hovering rainclouds threatened to burst any moment as more smoke wafted his way. Spicy's cabin lay in the distance and this time the smoke was curling from her chimney. Could she be home and cooking? As he reached the front yard, Zeke McCoy emerged from the cabin with the medical bag in hand. Shadow, Abigail, and Big Lump followed him onto the porch.

"Just Stone!" Big Lump bounded down the steps and caught him up in such a bear hug, Stone's feet momentarily left the ground. Letting go, he said, "Happy seeing you."

Despite everything, Stone couldn't help but smile. "I'm happy to see you, too, pardner."

"Howdy, Stone," Shadow said, hurrying to him. "We finished the pigpen yesterday. Pig Piffle and Big Bump's in it. See?"

"Howdy, Shadow." Stone patted the boy's shoulder and glanced toward the pen where the pigs were rooting in the mud outside, not inside a cabin. "That is a mighty fine pen. Good job." With a smile at Shadow and Big Lump he acknowledged Abigail. Then looking back to Big Lump, he asked, "Is Spicy here?"

"No," Big Lump said, his shoulders slumping.

"Stone, we've been worried about you. Yesterday, I went to Jerry Hatfield's house expecting you to already be there," Zeke McCoy said and handed him the medical bag. "I waited at the Blackberry Precinct for hours and finally came here last night."

"How was Ellison?" Stone was concerned about him and anxious to find Spicy.

"He was holding on. I don't know how or where Ellison is today," Zeke replied. "I heard two Pikeville constables were in charge of the McCoy brothers and spent last night at John Hatfield's house."

Stone absorbed the news, deciding what to do next. Not knowing the whereabouts or conditions of Spicy and Ellison was sheer torture. "I think it's probable Ellison is in West Virginia by now. Devil Anse won't leave him in Kentucky," Stone surmised.

"Agreed," Zeke said. "Devil Anse and Valentine will want the McCoy brothers kept in Tug Valley despite their cousin, Preacher Anderson, ordering them to be jailed in Pikeville."

"Yes, I imagine so," Stone agreed. "Any chance you've seen Clay McCoy?"

"No." Zeke's grimace was similar to Otis Hatfield's reaction at the mention of Clay McCoy. The others shook their heads. "Clay and the Clines were long gone by the time I got back to the Blackberry Precinct with your medical bag."

Stone figured he'd crossed the river and run into Clay and the Clines shortly before Spicy, Ronny, Zeke, and Henry had arrived at his house to get his medical bag. Immediately after the ambush, McCoy had crossed the Tug Fork, then hearing Zeke and Henry making their way down to the river, he'd hidden in the woods. Once Zeke was gone and Henry had ridden back up the hill, McCoy had snuck up to Stone's house planning to capture Spicy as he'd threatened. Apparently, neither McCoy nor Spicy had been seen since.

"You look like you've been in a fight, Stone," Zeke said. "What happened?"

"I was ambushed." With scraped knuckles, Stone swiped away dried blood near his left brow. He'd have another scar thanks to McCoy. He told them what he'd pieced together, adding he'd been held prisoner for nearly twenty-four hours. Big Lump shook his head in disgust and Zeke said he wasn't surprised. Abigail looked horrified and Shadow was ready to fight Clay and the Clines. Pepper strutted to Stone's side. "I got here as fast as I could."

"I's real sorry," Big Lump said, anger in his eyes.

"Not your fault, Big Lump," Stone said. "Do you know where the smoke came from?"

"No," Zeke answered simply. "Was dark when we smelled it."

Stone suddenly recalled Uriah asking Josiah if he had

smelt smoke. In that moment, he knew what had happened. "My gut says Clay set my house on fire and has Spicy," he said with fierce control of his emotions. "I'm going over there to find her."

"Goin' with you," Big Lump said as Nutmeg scampered onto the porch.

"Big Lump, you stay here," Stone urged, not wanting to put him in danger. "You're needed to look after Spicy's cabin, your pigs, Nutmeg, Pepper, and the chickens."

"I'll go with you, Stone," Zeke offered. "That is if Big Lump and Abigail wouldn't mind letting Shadow bunk here tonight."

"I's goin'," Big Lump said with finality.

"Me, too," Shadow said as his father shook his head no.

"Abby?" Big Lump asked, turning to her.

"I would be happy to look after things here at Spicy's cabin if Shadow will stay and keep me safe," Abigail said with a subtle glance at Zeke. "It will be our way of helping Spicy and Ellison. Right, Shadow?"

"Right, Abby," Shadow said importantly, puffing out his chest.

"You still have Clay's rifle with you, Big Lump?" Stone asked and when Big Lump nodded, Stone said, "Get it." Noticing Zeke had his own rifle and extra bullets, he handed Uriah's rifle to Shadow. "Don't be afraid to use it."

"We just finished eating and have food left." Abigail turned and going into the cabin said over her shoulder, "I'll pack some for you."

"Thank you." Stone kept Josiah's rifle over his shoulder as Zeke handed bullets to Shadow who expertly loaded the gun. When Big Lump returned with Clay's rifle and Abigail with burlap bags of food, Stone looked at Abigail and Shadow. "Go inside and latch the doors."

Abigail hugged Big Lump who closed his eyes and smiled broadly as he wrapped arms like tree trunks around her. Zeke McCoy embraced his son and then Shadow and Abigail hurried into the cabin and shut the door. Pepper strutted toward the henhouse and Nutmeg took off for a night of hunting. When Stone heard the front door latch fall into place, he motioned to Zeke and Big Lump. The skies opened up again with a vengeance. This squall was as torrential as the day Spicy had suffered the concussion while crossing the raging river. He silently vowed to cross the Tug Fork at any cost.

On a dead run, Stone led the way out of Raccoon Hollow.

CHAPTER 37

Traipsing through marshland-like woods to the backside of the Stony Mountains, Spicy couldn't see two feet in front of her. The rain was that heavy. Dragged behind a madman and a witch to Coffin Cave was a far cry from hiking with the physician who'd stolen her heart, astonished her with a glorious view, and made magical love to her.

Had Clay and the Clines really captured Stone? Or was that another lie? Did Stone know his house had been set on fire? Had the barn burned? Was Lumpkin safe? If the Clines didn't have Stone, had he saved Ellison? Had Tolbert, Pharmer, and Bud McCoy been caught?

Her swirling thoughts were as relentless as the current storm. During the previous night, the rain had stopped only to pour buckets again. Spicy desperately hoped the drenching had prevented the fire from spreading to Stone's barn and across the mountains. Seeing the beautiful home in flames had scorched her soul. His parents were gone and now the house they'd shared was surely gone. But his brother and the job he deserved at Pennsylvania Hospital awaited him. With every breath she prayed to see Stone alive but every step put distance between them.

"Move!" Clay shouted, jerking hard on the rope tied around her waist.

"Stop doing that!" Spicy yanked the rope back in her direction.

"Bitch," Clay sneered and jerked the rope even harder.

Spicy stumbled, but didn't fall. Despite the fabric of her new dress between her and the rope, her skin was rubbed raw. In the thundering downpour and starless gloom they'd trudged on mile after mile, the witch leading the way. After an endless night and morning of walking, it was late afternoon when Vorticia's sudden shrill stabbed every nerve in Spicy's body.

"My den!"

"Damn time," Clay mumbled.

"Welcome," Vorticia cackled like the demented.

"I ain't goin' in no cussed cave in the dark," Clay said.

Despite Vorticia stating she didn't need a lantern to find her cave, Clay had carried the one he'd had until it was rained out, then he'd tossed it. Vorticia dug behind some bushes where a lantern set hidden under a slab of rock. She held the lantern for Clay who, after several attempts, was able to light it. Vorticia held her lantern aloft and Spicy saw the black eyes and fang-like teeth of the rat riding on the witch's shoulder among wet strands of twisted, white hair. As Vorticia hurried inside, Spicy could not imagine having to follow her. But Clay gave Spicy a hard shove from behind and brought up the rear. A tunneling decline into the cave was not only immediate but slippery as mud alternately slid under or sucked at her feet.

Eerie shadows, cast by the lantern, danced like demons along the inside walls of the cave. A reverse draft brought with it a hideous odor of things long dead. Cobwebs brushed the sides of Spicy's face and when she batted at them she scraped her arms along rough rock. Something crawled past her on the cave wall but was gone before she could see what it was. A second skittering caused Spicy to stifle a scream as a red and brown centipede with its long antennas and dozens of legs brushed her shoulder. Another centipede followed right behind it until the witch snatched it off the wall and fed it to the rat. Spicy thought she might be ill with terror. The tunnel took a turn, leveled off, and the dank smell of wet dirt and stale air along with that awful stench of decay assailed her.

"Home sweet home," Vorticia said, walking into an open area nearly as big as Spicy's cabin with a slightly higher ceiling.

Clay pushed Spicy again and she managed to elbow him hard in the gut. He shoved past her and jerked the rope, forcing her into the somewhat round interior. Vorticia veered right and picking up a candle lit it from the lantern flame. She lit a torch imbedded in the cave wall and then another torch and another. With each additional torch, new horrors slithered into view.

From hooks embedded in the walls hung carcasses of rabbits, skunks, muskrats, squirrels, and opossums. Makeshift shelves housed dozens of jars holding dead toads, frogs, salamanders, and lizards while other glass containers imprisoned live earwigs, cockroaches, beetles, and crickets.

"For my spells and incantations," Vorticia boasted without being asked.

Another torch displayed the spiders. Spicy had suspected they were coming and cringed. Two huge, see-through glass jugs lay on their sides. In the first container venomous black widows, too many to count, spun their webs. In the second jug dozens of brown recluses gathered in poisonous clusters.

"Is them bats hangin' from the ceiling?" Clay asked Vorticia.

"My precious cauldron's roost." She raised her candle in recognition of the bats.

"I hate bats," he said.

Clay jerked a torch out of the wall and flung fire toward the ceiling blackened with bats. Hundreds of bats dropped and spiraled. Clay cursed and swung at them with the torch. As they swooped and dove erratically, Spicy shielded herself as best she could. Stepping on something that moved, she jumped back and focused on the ground. Rats. Black, gray, and brown, the rodents scurried through the muck and disappeared into a pile of bones. Human bones. Skeletons with bits of fabric clinging to them and tufts of hair stuck to severed skulls lay discarded like wormy vittles. Spicy had never fully believed the grisly stories, told on both sides of the Tug Fork, until this moment.

Vorticia shrieked at the top of her lungs, "Stop vexin' my bats'n rats, Clay!"

"Get 'em outa here, witch!" Clay hollered.

"My bats don't feed 'til night!"

"I's gonna torch 'em all."

While Vorticia screamed unintelligibly, Clay swept the ceiling with flames and the bats swarmed out of the cave. When Spicy looked up only a handful of bats remained. Her attention riveted on a hook from which the swing, Vorticia had mentioned, dangled over an ominous pit.

"I's done cast a wicked death spell on you fer that, Clay!" Vorticia warned.

"Shut up! Where we keepin' the whore 'til the Clines get here with Philadelphy?"

"Over the hole o'course," Vorticia spat sourly and pointed.

"Is that yer snake pit the Clines done told me 'bout?" Clay asked.

"Yeesss," Vorticia hissed. "Where my copperheads conjure up killin' venom."

"What's ta keep 'em from crawlin' outa that hole?"

"Usually the walls is too slick from mud slidin' into the cave."

Usually? Spicy said nothing and hoped her face showed no fear. But her stomach rolled, her legs nearly buckled, and she prayed to wake up from this nightmare. How had she fallen from a mountaintop of heaven with Stone into this pit of hell with Clay? Why had the beautiful house adorned with its pretty porch and rocking chairs burned, yet this rat-infested witch's cave crawling with deadly snakes and spiders thrived?

One thing Spicy believed with her heart and soul was if Stone survived, and he had to, this den of doom on Stony Mountain would not.

"Lower the swing." Clay's expression oozed malice. "I'll tie her in it whilst we wait fer the Clines. They cain't be more'n a couple hours behind."

~

THE TUG FORK was dangerously high and swift when Stone, Big Lump, and Zeke made it to the riverbank. It was dark as they piled into the canoe which Stone had hidden in the brush before the ambush. With their weight and strong paddling they kept the boat from drifting and crossed the turbulent river in record time.

At the top of the rise, Stone raced out of the woods. Though he'd tried to prepare himself, what met his eyes brought him to a physical halt and mentally dropped him to his knees. Amid the smoldering ruins of the house only the chimney had survived. Memories with his family flashed painfully across his heart. Stone thanked God for the rain that had prevented the fire from spreading across the Stony Mountains and beyond taking lives along with other homes. But as he surveyed the devastation before him, what tore Stone's very soul to shreds was not having Spicy safe and sound in his arms.

Stone looked to the east. The barn was intact. He sprinted forward where his porch had been and instantly saw a body under charred embers. He'd seen burned bodies at the hospital but for a split second fearing it could be Spicy, his heart almost stopped. Looking closer, the spectacles and size of the corpse told him who it was. There was nothing he could do for him now. But he would personally see to it Ronny Staton received a proper burial.

Zeke and Big Lump came up behind him but gave him

space. Without a word, Stone turned and led the way to the barn. He was surprised to see Logan, Daisy, and Gus— figuring Clay would have stolen them. Zeke said the fourth horse, Ethel, was on loan from the Weddingtons. Zeke also told them Vorticia was said to have once flung a copperhead at a horse and nearly been trampled along with the snake. Claiming all horses were beasts of death she'd never ridden since. In any case, the animals seemed rested and unfazed. They'd take Gus for Spicy when they found her. Daisy being such a large horse could best manage Big Lump.

"I'm powerful sorry about your house," Zeke had said to Stone.

"We build new." On Big Lump's round face was a smile of hope and affection.

With a nod at Zeke, Stone said to Big Lump, "I know you and Shadow sure could."

"Not the first time Hatfield property has mysteriously caught fire," Zeke grumbled.

Hanging his head, Big Lump said, "Clay and Clines."

Stone placed a firm hand on Big Lump's shoulder and gave him a squeeze. That was all Big Lump needed to lift his chin and square his broad shoulders again. As Stone turned to grab the reins to Logan, he noticed the mantel clock on a shelf. Emotions flooded him, knowing Spicy had somehow saved the one thing he cared about in the house from going up in flames. He told himself the clock meant he had time to save her. It had to mean that.

"It'd be a miracle if Spicy somehow escaped all of this and made it to my aunt's house," Stone said far more calmly than he felt. "But let's check."

"If she's not there?" Zeke asked.

"The only clue I have is Josiah Cline mentioning a snake pit. That must mean Clay was headed to Coffin Cave. But I haven't been on the backside of the mountain since I was a kid."

"I hunted near the witch's cave a couple of years ago," Zeke said. "I think I can find it. We'll know it's the right place if there's a rock next to the opening that looks like a coffin lid."

"Right," Stone replied, vaguely recalling having seen it.

"Ready, pardner?" Big Lump asked Stone, rifle over his shoulder.

"Ready, pardner."

They grabbed some oats, packed them onto Gus and saddled up. Stone, holding the reins to Gus, galloped toward his aunt's homestead. Leaping off Logan even before the horse could stop, Stone ran, calling for Spicy. Big Lump gathered some apples while Zeke noted the cow and chickens were asleep. Spicy wasn't there, though the house was safe and untouched. But this confirmed Spicy was in McCoy's clutches and anything but safe and untouched.

"They have a whole day's head start." Stone mounted Logan again and with a glance at Zeke and Big Lump, said, "Let's find that hellhole as fast as we can."

They rode into the night through dense, soggy terrain, up hills and down valleys splashing headlong across countless rocky creeks. Before dawn the next morning the rain lessened, letting the moon and stars help guide their way around the backside of the mountain. With every mile, Stone had prayed for Spicy's life to be spared.

McCoy wasn't depraved enough to kill her. Was he?

At sunrise, the rain stopped and they let the horses drink from a stream rushing high and fast. Morning light dappling through the treetops seemed harsh and jeering without Spicy. They fed the horses the oats and apples Big Lump had picked at Aunt Hilda's house. As the horses rested, Stone lowered his gaze to the forest floor his heart bleeding with love and terror. If Spicy blamed this horror on him and hated him for this very personal feud, he'd spend the rest of his life trying to win her back.

"Stone, though they must have traveled on foot they most likely reached this backside of your mountain even before we left your aunt's house. I'm sorry we didn't catch up with them like we hoped," Zeke said, placing a hand on

Stone's shoulder. "No doubt I made a wrong turn or two along the way."

"Zeke, it is a miracle you got us here through the dark and rain by daybreak. You did a great job," Stone assured him, meeting his gaze. "Vorticia probably has shortcuts nobody else knows to take."

"Lotta bats fer daylight." Big Lump pointed to the treetops.

"Good observation, Big Lump," Stone agreed. "Something or someone scared them from their roost into the forest."

Zeke nodded. "We're close enough now we should walk."

The men silently led the horses through the trees. The ground being wet under feet and hooves dampened any noise. They hadn't gone far when Stone spotted a casket-sized entrance in the mountain. Next to it set the rock lid.

"Coffin Cave," Stone whispered and pointed with the barrel of his Colt .45.

CHAPTER 38

"HOW MUCH LONGER YOU 'SPECT WE GOTTA WAIT on them corn liquored Clines?" Vorticia whined.

"I 'spect 'til they get here," Clay grumbled.

Clay had dragged himself into a chair to the right side of the snake pit and remained there. Rubbing her head, Vorticia sat in a rickety chair left of the hole. Suspended in the swing between them, Spicy's toes dangled level with the opening above the pit of vipers. The so-called swing was a frayed rope with a hangman's noose for a seat. The rope looped through the crude hook in the cave ceiling which Vorticia had credited the Clines with installing in exchange for the brown recluse. Spicy's entire body ached and to prevent her legs from going numb, she kept adjusting herself back and forth as much as she dared without causing the rope to further unravel.

Prior to being imprisoned in the swing Spicy had fought furiously. The moment Clay had set Ronny's pistol on the chair she'd kicked him between the legs. As Clay doubled over and fell to the ground, Vorticia grabbed her. Spicy had yanked a handful of hair out of Vorticia's head and thrown it, along with the rat tangled in it, into the hole. Hissing like the witch, the copperheads had emitted a rancid, cucumber-like musk odor. Vorticia's shrieks over her rat had sent any remaining bats swarming out of the cave.

Before Spicy could follow the bats, Clay—curled in a ball —had grabbed the gun and fired a shot. Spicy had halted in her tracks as he cocked the gun a second time. For feeding her rat to the snakes, Vorticia demanded Clay put the noose around Spicy's neck. Clay had considered it but instead forced Spicy to slide her legs through the noose. Vorticia had tied Spicy's hands to the rope as Clay held the gun on her and vomited. It had taken Clay at least two hours to physically recover to the point he could assist the witch in hoisting her over the snake pit. Spicy figured those two hours had extended the life of the fraying rope and therefore her own.

Clay had remained in the chair clutching the end of the rope which Vorticia had looped around a large boulder. Starting out six feet above the snake pit every so often Clay had loosened the rope, dropping Spicy ever closer to the opening of the hole. Each time, Vorticia had cackled, urging Clay on. Having felt the rope give on its own, Spicy had stopped shifting her weight. Swaying eye to eye with Clay, she covertly glanced at the ceiling. Several more strands of the rope had unraveled over the hook. She sat as still as possible.

"Hey, pet." Clay jerked on the swing. "I said I wanna hear how yer gonna spend yer days earnin' my forgiveness fer sparkin' with Philadelphy."

To help lessen her movements, Spicy was making no eye contact with them and remained silent. But hanging between a brutal madman on one side and a vile witch on the other, there was no way out. If she couldn't have Stone, death by copperheads in the snake pit, which couldn't be more than five minutes away, was preferable to life with Clay McCoy.

"I's make her talk." Vorticia hurried to pull a burning torch from the wall. With a toothless sneer slashed across her wrinkled face and white hair matted in blood to a bald spot, she raised the torch toward the fraying ends of the rope over the hook. "Beg him fer yer life, whore or I's set the rope afire."

"Talk, snatch," Clay said, giving Spicy a hard sideways shove toward Vorticia.

"Ripe! She's ripe, Clay!" Vorticia screeched as Spicy swung so close to the witch she could feel the heat of the torch. "Can ya still get her with child?"

Clay boasted across Spicy, "Soon as them Clines get here with Hatfield."

"I'm here," came Stone's deep voice.

Stone walked into the pit of hell alone. Spicy's heart almost stopped as muscles, bruises, blood, and fury blocked the filtered daylight from Coffin Cave's entrance. Torch light flickered across Stone's face. His scowl and clenched jaw said he was here to end this particular feud. Signaling he was ready to do battle, his broad shoulders squared as he planted his booted feet slightly apart. A Colt .45 in his right hand and a rifle slung over his left shoulder indicated Stone Hatfield planned to win this war. He made eye contact with Spicy just long enough to encourage her with a wink. Only Stone would have the confidence to wink at her in what he had labeled the den of doom. Her hopes soaring, Spicy smiled at him.

"Where's them Clines?" Clay demanded, managing to stand by holding onto the rope.

"Peter Creek," Stone replied, striding further into the cave. "Let's do this the easy way, McCoy. Release Spicy and we'll be on our way."

"Stony, Clay made me help him. I's jist a poor ol' lady." Vorticia's torch wavered close to the rope as she suddenly began her snake oil wheezing. "You an' me, we's Hatfields."

"What happened to Josiah and Uriah?" Clay asked, eyes darting here and there.

"Already told you they were bad negotiators," Stone said.

Spicy rolled her eyes toward the ceiling to show him the condition of the rope.

"Here's *my* negotiatin', don't come no closer," Clay warned as he purposely let the rope slide through the hook. Spicy dropped about a foot below ground level into the pit. "I swear I's gonna feed Spicy to them copperheads."

"No!" Lumpkin roared.

Managing to shove his way out of the narrow entrance, Lumpkin—toting a rifle—stomped to Stone and stood imposingly on his right side. Zeke McCoy followed Lumpkin's entrance into the torchlit cave and took up an armed position on Stone's left.

"Two McCoys turnin' again' a McCoy and sidin' with a Hatfield?" Clay asked.

"But us Hatfields stick together," Vorticia said taking a step toward Stone.

Clay made a frantic grab for Vorticia or her torch it was hard to say which. Maybe both. Clay came away with the torch as the witch slipped on the edge of the muddy pit. She slid halfway into the hole before catching hold of Spicy's left leg. Stone raced forward as did Lumpkin and Zeke. But when Clay swung the fire toward Vorticia and thus Spicy, Stone stopped and held his hands aloft halting Lumpkin and Zeke. With a bloodcurdling scream, the witch tried to avoid the flames by turning loose of Spicy and digging talon-like fingernails into the edge of the slimy hole. Clay's eyes glazed over as he spiraled into such depths of insanity any hope of reaching him was lost.

"So much fer yer wicked death spell ya cast on me," Clay said.

"Help me, Clay!" Vorticia shrilled.

Holding the torch close to Spicy, Clay worked his way around the back of the hole and stomped on Vorticia's fingers. The witch disappeared, her screams following her to the bottom of her snake pit. After a sickening thump, the hissing grew frenzied. Vorticia wailed and Clay snorted. When the snakes had silenced Vorticia, Clay smirked.

"I kilt yer old man, Philadelphy, on accounta he seen me and Josiah gunnysack Spicy and Big Lump," Clay said in the monotone voice of madness. "Shot him in the back richeer'n West Virginny."

"No!" Spicy had held herself in check as long as she could. Glaring at Clay, she said, "You wanted me to tell you how I'm going to spend my days? If he'll let me, I'll spend the rest of my life making up to Stone for the death and destruction you've caused him."

Clay bellowed his outrage, raising the torch toward the hook on the ceiling. As he glanced up to make sure the flames caught the rope on fire, Stone leaped forward and grabbed Spicy. As the remaining strands broke, Stone and Spicy hit the dirt. He rolled them away from the snake pit as Lumpkin moved to block Clay from getting to them. Clay viciously swung the torch in his brother's face causing Lumpkin to stumble and fall halfway across the hole. Only Lumpkin's size kept him from plummeting to the same death as the witch. As Clay tried to kick Lumpkin into the pit, Zeke wrenched the torch from him. Stone jumped to his feet as Lumpkin stood. Spicy, her hands still tied to the rope, scooted out of the noose.

A Colt .45 and two rifles pointed at Clay. With no rope to jerk and no torch to swing, Clay's expression appeared as feral as any trapped animal.

Still on the ground, Spicy warned, "Clay has Ronny Staton's pistol."

Clay glared at her. Then slowly, he held up his left hand and bowed his head in defeat as if Spicy's latest betrayal was his final undoing. Reaching around his back with his right hand, he cautiously brought Ronny Staton's gun into view as though he planned on surrendering it. Though her hands were still tied to the noose, limiting her ability to defend herself and with her legs half-numb, Spicy managed to rise to her feet next to Stone. In that split second Clay aimed the pistol directly at her.

Three bullets struck Clay McCoy at close range. If Spicy

had to guess, the one from the Colt split the vein and skull between Clay's eyes and the rifles blew holes in his chest. Knocked backward, staring, and mouth agape, Clay stumbled into the pit with the snakes, the witch, and her rat. Snakes struck until peace reined.

"Dumbass got hisself shot," Lumpkin said matter-of-factly and looked at Spicy.

"He can never hurt you again, Lumpkin," Spicy replied.

"Burn the place?" Zeke asked Stone, slinging his rifle over his shoulder.

"Hell yes," Stone said.

Stone turned to Spicy and hugged her tightly. With a kiss to her forehead he gently released her, pulled his knife out of his boot, and sliced through the rope around her wrists.

"I love you, sugar'n spice."

"I love you, too, long shot."

"Yeah." Stone chuckled and glanced around the cave. "This was kind of a long shot."

"You missed the bats flying in the belfry," Spicy said, teetering between hysterical giggles and unstoppable tears. "When Clay complained you knocked out his *best* tooth I almost laughed." She took a small, but calming breath as did Stone. "You get thirty points for bravery."

"You get forty," Stone said. "Seventy to seventy. We're tied."

Zeke tossed the torch he'd taken from Clay into the pit of vipers. "Good riddance."

Lumpkin scowled at the hole and echoed, "Good riddance."

Stone tipped his head to Lumpkin in agreement as Spicy hurried to hug her lifelong friend. Stone grabbed a torch out of the wall and dropped it onto the chair where Clay had sat holding the raveling rope. Spicy tossed a torch onto the witch's chair. Lumpkin took a torch to the carcasses of woodland creatures needlessly killed to be used by the wicked. Any stray rats remained buried under the bones of victims, for whom nothing could be done. The bats had demonstrated the good sense not to return. Spicy held tight to Stone's hand as he led the way out of the cave. With Daisy's help, the four of them sealed the coffin lid over the entrance.

The Stony Mountains would forever entomb the evil and the innocent.

CHAPTER 39

"THANK YOU AGAIN, ZEKE, BIG LUMP," STONE SAID
as they arrived at the Magnolia Precinct.

They'd reached the Weddington family home before Ellison's place or Aunt Hilda's house to get information and to
return the horse they'd borrowed.

"Yes, thank you all." Spicy added, "I'd be dead if not for
the three of you." When she'd said *you* she smiled at Stone,
acknowledging there would have been no rescue if not
for him.

Stone hadn't been shocked when Spicy confided McCoy
had admitted poisoning her folks. Thinking it best to be
forthcoming about it they told Big Lump. As innocent as his
brother was guilty, Big Lump had cried upon hearing that
news. Big Lump deeply regretted the murders of Stone's
father and Ronny Staton as well as despising his brother's
indirect killing of Polly and her baby. Spicy had gently
remarked they were all safer with Clay gone and Big Lump
didn't hesitate to agree. Stone and Zeke had wholeheartedly
supported Big Lump's decision to shoot Clay before he
could shoot Spicy.

"We did what had to be done," Zeke said to Spicy.

"Had to be done," Big Lump agreed.

Zeke then voiced intending to pay Abe for the use of the

horse he was riding. Stone waved the offer away and dismounted Logan. If there was any charge, he would pay it. He'd only taken a couple of steps toward the house where they'd last spoken with Justice Valentine 'Wall' Hatfield when Abe Weddington emerged.

"I see you're back with Ethel," Abe called with a wave.

"Thank you, Abe," Zeke returned with a wave and also dismounted.

"I'd like to pay you for the use of your horse, Abe," Stone said.

Abe insisted there was no charge for Ethel. "Helping out, especially during a crisis, is the right thing to do," Abe said. Knowing Tug Valley as he no doubt did, Abe didn't ask where they'd been or why it took so long to return.

"Thank you, Abe," Stone replied. "You remember Spicy, of course, and with us is Big Lump McCoy."

"I never heard one bad thing 'bout Big Lump McCoy," Abe complimented with a smile. "It's nice to meet you."

Big Lump nodded. "Nice meeting you."

"As for Spicy McCoy, I could never forget the courageous lady who tackled a razorback and lived to tell about it."

"You don't know the half of her courage," Stone said proudly as Spicy gave Abe a nod and a wave. "In addition to returning your horse, I'm hoping you can tell us the latest news about Ellison."

"Still alive a couple hours ago," Abe replied as a worried frown replaced his smile. "Good," Stone said. "Abe, if you know of an undertaker, Ronny Staton's body is in the ruins of my house on the other side of Mate Creek. If his brother, Connie, makes it back to Tug Valley I wouldn't want him to find Ronny in his current state."

"Already done, Stone," Abe assured him. "Been friends with the Staton brothers for decades. The spectacles on the body we found on your porch told us it was Ronny. Everybody's sorry your house burned down." Splaying his hand, Abe said, "Y'all look tuckered out, please come in. Flora is just dishing up supper. We'll tell you what we know. My grandsons'll feed and water the horses while we eat."

It had been nearly twelve hours since they'd shared what Abigail had packed. If alone, Stone wouldn't spare the time to eat. But in truth they and the horses needed nourishment and to rest for an hour. Big Lump was already dismounting.

"Much obliged, Abe," Stone said and walked to Spicy who slid off Gus into his arms.

Abe snapped his fingers bringing Henry and Tommy hurrying to each take the reins of two horses. Telling his grandsons their suppers would be waiting for them after seeing to the horses, Abe ushered his guests inside the house. Large, tidy, and filled with appetizing aromas, the home was a welcome oasis. In the rectangular dining room Abe gestured to a long table, he said was once taken up by their four sons. They lived nearby and Abe expressed being blessed to have them, their spouses, and the grandchildren in their daily lives. Flora Weddington joined them bringing extra plates. Smiling and talkative, she said she was accustomed to feeding a big tribe. With everything going on the last two days she'd cooked enough chicken, ham, succotash, buckwheat cakes, and sweet potato pies to feed the whole precinct.

"Please sit down everyone," Flora said motioning to the table and chairs. "I just placed supper on the table so it's good and hot."

"It looks delicious," Spicy said and tugged Stone into the chair beside her. Zeke and Big Lump sat down across from them. "We've been traveling all day. This meal is heaven-sent."

Despite Stone's darkest fears about Ellison and escalation of the feud, he agreed with Spicy about the meal. Plates were filled and as they emptied, the Weddingtons encouraged seconds along with black coffee to get them back on their feet. Famished, Stone and the others had mostly listened adding an occasional comment here and there to the polite conversation.

260 | LYNN ELDRIDGE

"That was a fine supper. I don't think any of us could have gone much longer without it," Stone admitted after his last bite of pie. He thanked them as did the others. Since supper was over Stone felt it was acceptable to ask, "Can you tell us more about Ellison?"

"Yes, but the situation is not good," Abe replied.

Flora, seated at the opposite end of the table from Abe, said, "The whole community's been in a state of shock for the past two days."

At that point, Abe and his wife took turns bringing them up-to-date. As Otis Hatfield had told Stone shortly after he'd escaped the Clines, Ellison's brother, Good Lias, had taken charge at the Blackberry Precinct. Good Lias had also been the one to notify Devil Anse of the assault, but by that time it was quite late in the evening.

"Devil Anse and Justice Valentine 'Wall' Hatfield didn't get over to Kentucky until the next morning," Abe told them. "That's when Devil Anse arranged for Ellison to be brought home to West Virginia."

"We didn't figure he'd leave Ellison in Kentucky," Stone replied.

"Who's got custody of Tolbert, Bud, and Pharmer?" Zeke asked.

"THAT'S ANOTHER KETTLE O'WORMS. OL' Ranel McCoy argued with Devil Anse's cousin, Preacher Anderson C. Hatfield, a Kentucky justice of the peace, demanding he not send his sons to Pikeville with the constables," Abe told them.

"Preacher Anderson tried to convince Ol' Ranel they'd be safer in jail than in the woods where Devil Anse could get a hold of them," Flora explained.

"The two constables in charge were only a mile down the road to Pikeville with the McCoy boys when Justice Valentine caught up with them," Abe said.

The Weddingtons said Justice Valentine also appealed to the constables to return the McCoys to the Blackberry District where the crimes occurred, instead of taking them out of district to Pikeville. The constables explained Preacher Anderson had given the order to take the prisoners to the Pikeville jail. But on the other hand, Justice Valentine was every bit as well respected and commanded equal authority.

"Deciding between those two Hatfield justices would be difficult," Spicy said.

"Yes, indeed. That's exactly what I thought," Flora agreed.

"Justice Valentine said he needed to be near his brother, Ellison, during the trial which he wants held south of Blackberry Creek," Abe added. "The constables agreed this made sense and backtracked with Justice Valentine to Preacher Anderson's house."

Stone asked, "Where was Devil Anse when these negotiations took place?"

"Kentucky. Waiting for them at Preacher Anderson's place along with a posse of twenty family members and friends," Abe replied. "Some of the posse had helped capture the brothers the evening before."

"That was about this time yesterday so Preacher Anderson invited Justice Valentine, Devil Anse, and some of the posse to have supper," Flora added.

"I can imagine the debate at that table." Stone shook his head.

"Me, too." Abe nodded. "Devil Anse got himself all riled up during the dispute between Justice Valentine and Preacher Anderson as to where the McCoys should be tried. In the end, Devil Anse got up from the table and stormed outside where he called on his posse to fall into line in order to make sure the Hatfields kept custody of the McCoys."

"So, Devil Anse maintained custody?" Stone asked.

"Yes, he and his posse loaded the McCoy boys into a

corn sled and hauled 'em down Blackberry Creek to the Tug Fork River," Abe said.

"Where's they at?" Big Lump asked.

"In West Virginia," Abe replied with a kind smile at Big Lump. Then looking back to Stone he said, "In the old abandoned schoolhouse at the mouth of Mate Creek."

"All through last night Sally McCoy, the boys' mama, and Tolbert's wife, Mary, begged Devil Anse for the boys' lives," Flora said. "All day today, Justice Valentine's been questioning witnesses."

"What have the witnesses said?" Spicy asked.

As kindly and succinctly as possible since three people at the table were McCoys, Abe reported, "We heard the witnesses swore to Justice Valentine that Tolbert and Bud stabbed Ellison and Pharmer shot him in the back."

"Where's Ol' Ranel?" Zeke asked.

"He's done gone or fixin' to go to Pikeville to get help for his boys. Maybe regretting the constables didn't get 'em there as instructed in the first place," Abe said with a helpless shrug. "That was a couple hours ago, when we last heard Ellison was still alive."

"What did Devil Anse say to Sally and Mary?" Spicy asked.

Flora dabbed her eyes and replied, "Devil Anse said if Ellison survives, the boys would be taken to the authorities in Pike County."

"If Ellison dies?" Zeke asked.

"The McCoys will die," Stone answered.

"That's right," Abe confirmed.

CHAPTER 40

"I'm going to Ellison's place on Mate Creek," Stone said.

Vividly remembering Ellison saying he wanted Stone to take care of him if he ever got sick, Stone scooted back his chair from the supper table and stood. Never would he question his decision to rescue Spicy, but it had always been his intention to help Ellison as well.

"I figure Doc Rutherford's with Ellison," Abe assured Stone.

"Two heads are better than one and I have my medical bag with me," Stone said.

"I'll go with you, Stone," Spicy said.

"I'll come, too, if you need me, Stone," Zeke said.

"Me, too," Big Lump said.

"Thanks, Zeke, Big Lump," Stone said, shaking his head. "You two go see about Shadow and Abigail. Spicy and I will stay in West Virginia and check on Ellison."

Abe said he'd send his grandsons with Big Lump and Zeke to the Tug Fork and they could bring the horses back to his place. Everyone thanked the Weddingtons again for their generous hospitality then followed Abe outside. Stone and Spicy mounted Logan and Gus, leaving Daisy and Ethel for Big Lump and Zeke. Having first gained Abe's permission, Stone flipped a half dollar to each of the grandsons who had put their suppers on hold to feed and water the horses and now to ride them back home. The boys caught the silver coins and stared at the seated Liberty on one side and heraldic eagle on the other. Bursting with gratitude and excitement, they ran to shake Stone's hand and then raced to show their grandfather. Big Lump and Zeke mounted their horses and each tugged an overjoyed grandson up behind them. Waving goodbye to the men and boys who were heading southwest, Stone and Spicy headed southeast.

"What should I do?" Spicy asked Stone as they reached the road to Ellison's place. He'd told her Ellison and his wife, Sarah Ann, had ten children. Spicy knew as Hatfield farmers they had a good amount of land and crops. She wondered what in the world would happen to everyone and everything if Ellison didn't survive his wounds. "I want to help Ellison the best way I can. If you think it would cause trouble for me to go inside, I will gladly wait right here for you for as long as it takes, Stone."

"Ellison likes you Spicy. After you were bitten by the spider, he went with me to rescue you from Clay," Stone reminded her. As the home came into view people could be seen mingling on the porch and in the yard. Some were going in or coming out of the house. "He also checked on Big Lump and sent word to us about him so you wouldn't worry."

Besides Hatfields, Spicy recognized folks with the last names of Vance, Mounts, Rutherford, Mayhorn, Chafin, Murphy, Varney, Carpenter, and Whitt. Every person there wore desperate expressions and none bore the last name McCoy.

"If you're sure," Spicy said.

"Yes, I'm sure Ellison would want you to come with me," Stone said at the hitching post. "But it's up to you."

"I'd be honored."

They dismounted and Stone grabbed his medical bag with one hand and Spicy's hand with the other. He nodded to folks here and there, but didn't stop to talk. Crossing the porch, Spicy prayed silently. She'd received a miracle when Stone found her in that cave and saved her life. She prayed for another miracle this evening. *Please God, spare Ellison's life. Please.*

They stepped inside the house and Spicy could feel the hopelessness hanging heavy in the air. Though she didn't personally know Ellison's wife or children, it was easy to figure out who Sarah Ann was as she graciously greeted Stone. He introduced Spicy and Sarah Ann nodded. She led the way to a bedroom and entered before them. The doctor reported in addition to being shot, Ellison had been stabbed twenty-six times and gave them a sad shake of his head.

"Ellison, Stony and his friend, Spicy, are here to see you," Sarah Ann said softly.

In bed, Ellison opened his eyes. The despair and pain on his face stung Spicy's eyes with tears. Stone sat down on the side of the bed next to Ellison and placed his medical bag on the floor. Spicy instinctively knew that was a bad sign. With one look, Stone's unspoken prognosis said Ellison was too far gone to save. Stone carefully took Ellison's abraded left hand, subtly placed two fingers to his inner wrist and smiled with compassion as he assessed Ellison's pulse.

"Ellison, I know you've been well cared for," Stone began with a nod to the doctor who no doubt had done everything he could, "but I would have been here sooner had I not run into some trouble."

Ellison slowly took in the fresh cut near Stone's eye, a bruise on his cheekbone, and the scraped knuckles he'd received in his battle with Clay and the Clines. Spicy had kissed all of Stone's wounds, never mentioning the tender skin around her waist which they had yet to see. Stone had refused to use any of his limited medical supplies on himself. In turn, Spicy insisted the rope burns around her wrists from being tied to the noose didn't need salve.

In the faintest of whispers, Ellison managed, "Your house burned."

"I needed a new house anyway," Stone said with an easy grin and shrug.

Spicy's heart swelled with love for Stone as he simply let Ellison think the trouble was the loss of his beautiful big home rather than divulging a single detail of what else they'd survived. Spicy swiped tears off her cheeks and Ellison noticed the rope burns on her wrists. His eyes closed and when they opened, they glistened.

"Clay?" Ellison rasped.

"Gone," Stone said reassuringly as Spicy nodded. "I brought Logan home for you."

Ellison made the smallest of motions to Stone who leaned over to hear what he had to say. Spicy stepped back to give them privacy. It took several seconds and she couldn't hear a word nor did she try.

When Stone sat up, he said, "Thank you, Ellison. I promise."

Ellison smiled and closed his eyes. Stone bowed his head and gave Ellison's hand a gentle pat. He stood then leaving the doctor with his patient.

Spicy took Stone's hand and squeezed her love, understanding, and support. Her heart bled and her soul cried over the horrific injustices meted out because of the feud. Stone squeezed her hand back and led the way through the house. They met up with Sarah Ann and some of the children who thanked them for coming to say goodbye. Stone pulled a wad of money out of his pocket and without even counting, pressed it into Sarah Ann's hand. Stone urged Sarah Ann to please let them know if there was anything they could do to help. Bereft, Sarah Ann hugged Stone and then turned to Spicy.

Spicy instantly wrapped her arms around Sarah Ann, clasping her new friend, suffering such tragedy, to her heart. Meeting Stone's eyes over Sarah Ann's shoulder, Spicy felt she had known him and these Hatfields forever. How had she lived before this man entered her life? Sarah Ann let go and another lady wrapped an arm around her, walking her back to Ellison.

Spicy followed Stone outside to the hitching post and realized she'd never thought about money until today. His clothes, the boots, the house, the medical supplies—not to mention being absent from his job since July—and the job itself, indicated wealth. In addition, he owned a mountain of coal. But all Spicy cared about was the sorrow etched on his handsome face—cut and bruised because of her. On their return trip around the mountain, Stone had quietly told her of the ambush by Clay and what had transpired at the Clines' cabin.

"Stone, please tell me how I can best help *you* now," Spicy choked out.

"When Ellison dies within the hour, and he certainly will, the McCoy brothers' death warrants are signed," Stone said quietly. "I'm going to the schoolhouse to see if Devil Anse can be persuaded into turning the McCoys over to the Pikeville authorities."

"Maybe I can comfort Aunt Sally and Mary."

"Maybe you're not going anywhere near the place." Stone frowned with concern. This beautiful and unique woman was always so willing to help, even if it meant putting herself in danger. "I sympathize with you wanting to comfort those who are hurting, but not where McCoys are being held prisoner by Hatfields."

"I understand the mood at the school will be nothing like here at the house. But—"

"It sure as hell won't." Before Spicy could argue further Stone added, "You just asked me how you could help me." When she nodded, he pulled her into his arms and hugged her tightly. "Please go to Aunt Hilda's and wait for me there. I'll join you as soon as I can."

"I hate what Clay and the Clines put you and others through because of me," Spicy said. "But Aunt Hilda and Connie certainly deserve to know Clay murdered Ronny."

"You've been through just as much hell because of me, Spicy." Stone stood her back and said, "With Clay and the Clines it was kill or be killed. Trust me, McCoy would have shot you over my dead body. As for my aunt and Connie, I doubt they're home, yet. We can tell them about Ronny together. For now let me try to stop three executions."

Spicy's voice took on a note of wonder. "Even though the McCoys attacked a Hatfield and will be as guilty of murder as Clay McCoy, you'd try to stop their deaths?"

"Yes," Stone said with conviction. "Tolbert, Bud, and Pharmer are outnumbered, unarmed, and innocent until proven guilty."

"You are the fairest man I've ever met."

"Let me leave remembering the dimples I love, framing your smile," he said.

"Be careful," she whispered, standing on tiptoes she gave him one last kiss and hug.

"I'll be fine. You be careful, too, or else," he said with a chuckle.

"Or else what?" she asked, leaning back to look up at him.

"Or else I'll deduct points from your score and you'll be behind."

"That's not how the game works."

"Sure it is."

"Tarnation!" Spicy laughed.

Spicy would never again resist smiling at Stone because of her dimples. Back on their horses they were both smiling. Quite an accomplishment considering they were dealing with some of the worst circumstances of their lives. The horses trotted to the end of the road. There they parted ways, Spicy riding north toward a Hatfield house as Stone galloped west in hopes of saving McCoy brothers. With Clay, Vorticia, and the Clines gone, surely any threat of losing Stone was gone. Spicy glanced left to blow him a kiss but he had vanished over a hill.

CHAPTER 41

STONE THOUGHT ABOUT WHAT HE'D PROMISED Ellison.

Maybe his house burning down was confirmation to begin again, think bigger, build stronger, and commit without fail to improving everyday life here in Tug Valley. He had Spicy to thank for his change of heart. Had he never met her, he'd have left the area when his aunt went to Wheeling Hospital instead of deciding to make a difference.

Certainly ridding two states of Clay McCoy—a murdering maniac who would have continued to kill, harm, and maim the innocent was an unexpected start. Vorticia Hatfield, a dangerous conspirator to murder, in addition to the people she'd killed on her own, was no loss. Nor would the Clines, willing accomplices to evil, be mourned by anyone in Tug Valley.

Stone's thoughts went back to Ellison. When he had whispered to him, Stone knew it would be the last words he'd ever hear him speak. It wasn't surprising the man known to want peace had spoken volumes of generosity, love, and compassion with only seven words.

Seven words from Ellison's heart which Stone would forever hold in his.

Stone rode through Warm Hollow in deep thought. He

steadied himself when the schoolhouse, at the mouth of Mate Creek, came into view. The old log building had a forlorn and forgotten look to it, but was certainly anything but abandoned now. Stone saw guns on every shoulder and in every hand or holster. Upon spotting his arrival, a man he didn't recognize walked to the door of the school and called inside to Devil Anse. Dismounting Logan, Stone tethered him to a low hanging tree branch and held up both hands to show he was there in peace. Striding forward, Stone held out a hand to Justice Valentine Hatfield who greeted him.

"I told Anse the last time I saw you was when you headed over to Kentucky to Jerry Hatfield's house," Valentine said.

"I ran into some trouble," Stone replied.

"Yes. Too bad about your house," Valentine said. "Everybody will pitch in down the road and help you rebuild it. We were sorry you weren't with Ellison, but we understood. Hated to hear about Ronny Staton. Do you know who put a bullet in his skull?"

"I heard it was Clay McCoy."

"No wonder McCoy's done run off. I hope he never comes back."

"That's the consensus," Stone said evenly as Johnse and Cap, possibly Ellison's two favorite nephews, emerged from the schoolhouse and headed toward them. "I just came from seeing Ellison."

"After being stabbed twenty-six times and shot in the back, I don't know how Ellison didn't die on the spot," Valentine said.

"They didn't hit a major artery or he would have passed within an hour," Stone said.

"Was he still alive when you saw him?" Johnse asked as he and Cap reached them.

"Yes," Stone replied.

"The stab wounds quit bleedin' so why ain't he gettin' better?" Cap demanded.

Johnse put a hand on his younger brother's arm. "He

was shot, too, Cap." With hope in his eyes, Johnse asked, "Is he gonna make it, Stony?"

People began walking forward and crowding in close to hear the latest on Ellison.

"Ellison had to have lost a lot of blood at the scene and is surely hemorrhaging internally," Stone said. At the confusion on faces, he explained, "Even though his external wounds have stopped bleeding he is bleeding inside his body. Because of that his heart isn't getting enough blood. His labored breathing leads me to suspect either the knives or the bullet resulted in a pneumothorax which means a lung was punctured and collapsed."

"If we had a hospital, could you have helped him?" Valentine asked.

"Very possibly although it may have taken several surgeries," Stone said. "We are making strides and discoveries in medicine every day. Depending on the severity of damage, sometimes lungs can heal on their own in a couple of months."

"So our uncle ain't gonna live?" Cap growled.

"I'm here to talk to your father," Stone replied.

"Come on, Stony," Johnse said and pointed toward the schoolhouse.

Valentine parted the crowd and led the way. Johnse walked alongside Stone and Cap fell into step with them. Entering the schoolhouse, Devil Anse and several members of the posse Stone had heard about from the Weddingtons were guarding Tolbert, Pharmer, and Bud. If the hopeless despair at Ellison's house was tangible, the righteous anger in the schoolhouse rivaled a physical blow.

"Anse, can we speak outside?" Stone asked, not wanting to talk in front of the McCoys.

"I'm sorry 'bout yer house." Devil Anse stood and shook Stone's hand.

A man, who had been part of the crowd listening to Stone, entered the room and stated bluntly, "Ellison ain't gonna make it 'cause we ain't got no hospital."

Several members of the posse shouted and shook their guns at the McCoy brothers.

"Is that right, Stony?" Devil Anse asked.

Stone took hold of Devil Anse's arm and led him out of the schoolhouse. Valentine, Johnse, and Cap followed and kept others at bay. Stone repeated what he had just said about Ellison's condition and prognosis. He urged in the worst case scenario, which was Ellison's imminent death, to allow the McCoys to be taken to Pikeville. Devil Anse in turn explained there was a social justice on the mountain and he'd fought long and hard to establish himself as a leader. The McCoys had pushed him too far when they attacked his brother and he would not let it go unpunished.

"Anse, the McCoys can't defend themselves," Stone said. "If you execute unarmed men in cold blood, you'd basically be doing to them what they did to Ellison."

Two wrongs didn't make it right was challenged with an eye for an eye.

Valentine said, "Good Lias and I already argued for a lesser sentence if Ellison dies. Our younger brothers, Smith and Patterson, have washed their hands of this completely."

Stone nodded to Valentine and said to Devil Anse, "There hasn't even been a trial. You could worsen the feud if you execute men who are innocent until proven guilty."

"It'll end the feud," Devil Anse replied.

Stone searched for the right words. "There will be warrants issued on every man who pulls a trigger. There will be indictments for murder and you could all land in prison unable to care for your families."

"Don't worry, I got that done figured out," Devil Anse told him. "Charlie Carpenter, a schoolteacher, can read and write. He's gonna write up a pact which we's all gonna sign agreein' to remain silent and protect each other from the law. Them McCoy boys'll be given the chance to say their last words."

No matter what angle Stone presented there was a counter argument. The concerns of two wrongs not making a right, no trial being held, the enormity of the illegal act of execution, serving life in prison, internal family conflict, and escalating the feud fell on deaf ears.

An eye for an eye would prevail.

Stone was informed when, rather than if, Ellison passed the McCoys would be taken from West Virginia directly across the Tug Fork River where they would be tied to pawpaw bushes on the Kentucky riverbank and shot by every member of the posse. It was forty-eight hours after the attack at the Blackberry Precinct when one of the men, whom Stone had seen while at Ellison's home, arrived with news.

Ellison Hatfield was dead.

Devil Anse rounded up his posse. Stone watched, understanding the rage of Anse and the others as he cared about Ellison, too. Coincidently, Pharmer, the one who shot Ellison in the back, was nineteen—the same age Clay McCoy had been when he shot Stone's father in the back. Stone's pain and fury over finding out Clay indeed had murdered his father tore at his soul. He wasn't sorry Clay McCoy was dead. Though the circumstances of McCoy's demise were vastly different, as Clay would have shot Spicy had he not been shot first, there was something to be said in defense of an eye for an eye.

"You comin' Dr. Hatfield?" one of the posse called.

"Will anyone be left alive for me to treat?" Stone asked. When several men shook their heads, he replied mostly to himself, "Then no."

Standing near the school, he faintly smelled smoke floating across the Tug Fork River. What was burning now? As to the river, he'd heard someone in the crowd say the long-awaited bridge had been completed. He sighed in defeat as Devil Anse and the others herded the McCoy brothers toward the river. He'd seen enough. Taking the reins to Logan, Stone turned his back on the feud. Even though his brain told him there was nothing he could do to stop the executions, his heart was heavy. He was somewhat surprised the horrors of the last two days had strengthened his resolve to remain in Tug Valley instead of leaving for Pennsylvania.

Nudging Logan into a gallop, Stone headed for the valley between his mountain and Jet's. Picturing a beautiful woman whose blueberry eyes enchanted him even more than fairy fire and whose sensual dimples never failed to wipe any frown off his face, he allowed the pain to momentarily fade as he imagined kissing her raspberry lips.

Amid this hell, Spicy McCoy was a heart full of heaven.

CHAPTER 42

WHEN SPICY REACHED AUNT HILDA'S HOUSE, AS Stone had predicted, no one was at home. There were however, three telegrams which had been delivered. She couldn't help but wonder what was next. Surely these messages didn't hold bad news. It seemed they'd had their share. The wires were all addressed to Stone, so of course she didn't open them. Letting herself into the house, she placed the telegrams on a shelf in the kitchen.

Never had she yearned for a bath more than she did at this moment. Walking through the house to the bedroom she and Stone had slept in, she grabbed the carpetbag they'd brought with them from his house. After retrieving what she needed, she hurried back outside.

"Gus, with any luck we'll meet up with Stone right where we need to," Spicy said as she gave the horse an apple. "If not, we'll wait."

Back in the saddle, she crossed the north half of the Stony Mountains. Picturing a gorgeous man with coal-black hair, she could almost feel his muscles rippling under her hands. Whenever he cocked a brow or crooked his finger, tingles erupted from her scalp to her toes. At the edge of the green valley between the two peaks, a man on horseback galloped toward her.

Riding out of hell, Stone Hatfield was paradise on a mountain.

Across the valley the horses raced, slowed, and met up side-by-side. Without a word Stone pulled Spicy off her horse and across his lap. Arms twined bringing soft breasts to a hard chest. Supple lips met and warm tongues played. Spicy buried her hands in his hair and Stone flattened his palms and fingers to her back.

Gunshots blasted the silence. Stone's lips never left hers and Spicy clung to him. Within the next few seconds at least fifty rounds were fired. Spicy trembled and felt Stone absorb her shivers as their hearts beat and bled in sync. Kissing through the executions cemented a bond never to be broken. Across the Stony Mountains the echoes of death slowly faded into the distance. Only then did they loosen their holds on each other. Spicy knew there were tears on her cheeks and saw them in Stone's eyes. Even in his absence, he'd been closer to Ellison than she ever was to Tolbert, Pharmer, or Bud. Still, they were all connected in Tug Valley and four more neighbors had died this day because of the feud.

Whereas the poisoning of her folks had nothing to do with Stone, the same could not be said of his father's death, since it had involved the attack on her and Lumpkin in the blueberry patch. Spicy knew in her heart of hearts, Stone would never throw that up to her and hoped in time his anguish would fade. Even so, here was an opportunity to rescue this strong, good man from torment and sorrow as surely as he'd rescued her from a madman and a witch.

Not saying a word, Spicy winked at Stone as he often did at her. She slipped out of his arms and back onto her horse. Nudging Gus into a gallop, she flew across the valley and up the hillside. Stone caught up and she knew he had guessed where she wanted to go. She let him take the lead as she wasn't sure she could locate their private ledge. Nearing it, they dismounted and walked the rest of the way to the Mate

Creek waterfall. There they let the horses mosey away to drink, rest, and graze.

Spicy kissed Stone as she unbuttoned his shirt. She pulled his shirttails out of his pants and ran her fingers through the black hair on his muscular chest. Peeling off his shirt, she dropped it to the ground. Unfastening the top button of his pants revealed his indented navel and below it, his hardness brushed her fingers.

"I think you're due for some of my mountain medicine, Dr. Hatfield."

"Please treat me."

"I'll need to take your measure in order to properly treat you."

With that said, Spicy boldly looked him up and down. Oh what a sexy, virile man he was from that cut on his brow to the cocky grin on his lips. She touched the cleft in his strong chin and trailed her index finger down his neck. Fanning out the fingers of both hands across his broad chest she molded her palms to his flat stomach. Circling his navel with her thumbs, his quicksilver eyes narrowed invitingly. Pushing his britches down his legs, she tugged his feet out of his black boots. He stepped out of his pants and stood before her in low riding, snug drawers. Daringly she tugged down his drawers and cupped her hands to his firm male buttocks, pressing him against her tummy.

"Mmm," Stone groaned, "my turn."

Spicy stepped back and he unfastened the buttons on the dress he'd given her. When they were undone, she reached into her pockets and then Stone eased the dress to her waist. She pulled her arms free of the sleeves and he let the dress flutter to the ground around her feet. Naked, she tingled in her most secret place.

"Dammit," Stone growled seeing the rope burn around her waist, but she placed a fingertip to his lips.

"I'll give you ten points if you bathe with me in the waterfall, long shot."

Stone swallowed his anger and when he spoke his voice

was deep and coaxing, "I'll give you twenty points if you let me wash you, sugar'n spice."

"My ninety to your eighty and I take the lead again."

That accounting stated, Spicy arched a brow and handed him the bar of soap and wash cloth she'd taken from her pockets. Turning, she crooked her finger over her shoulder and wearing slipper-like shoes sashayed to the creek. When he caught her on the bank she grasped his hand and walked into the stream, which was higher than usual due to the recent rain. Warm from the scorching August sun, the water temperature was perfect. With every touch to his bare flesh she hoped to banish the pain and replace it with pleasure.

Spicy stepped underneath the waterfall first and squealed with delight. Giving Stone a tug, she pulled him under the refreshing, spraying shower with her. Wrapping her arms around his neck, she pressed her wet body to his. Kissing her, Stone lifted her off her feet and she hugged him tightly praying he felt her love sizzling through her skin into his. When her feet touched the creek bed again, she stepped forward into the falling water. Stone smiled and rubbed the soap between his hands. Playfully, he swept one soapy hand over her face and one over his own. She giggled as they rinsed their faces in the spray. Then kissing her fingers she tenderly touched them to the healing cut near his eye.

Pulling her toward him, Stone soaped his hands and washed her neck and shoulders. He gave her the soap and as he caressed her breasts she leaned her head back and lathered her hair. Placing his hands at her back he supported her while she rinsed her hair in the waterfall. When she stood straight again, with a wicked smile he faced her away from him. She soaked up his attention as he washed her back and bottom ending with a surprise kiss she'd longed to feel on her faded spider bite.

"My turn," Spicy said, holding out her hand for the soap.

Stone narrowed his eyes appraisingly as he looked her up and down. A tight grin tugged at his lips as he clenched his strong jaw. Giving her the soap, he placed his hands on his hips. Spicy rubbed soap in his hair and down his neck. She slid the soap from one broad shoulder to the other and down the chest she loved feeling molded to her breasts. She turned him around and soaped his back. When she came to the wound she'd stitched closed above his kidney, she pressed her body to his before washing his firm buttocks. He turned to her and cocked a rakish brow. She took the challenge and tenderly soaped every inch that made him male. He groaned and spreading his arms wide stood directly under the waterfall letting it shower away the soap from his head to the bubbles running down his legs to his feet.

"My turn again," Stone said, his voice husky.

With the lazy confidence of a mountain lion, he plowed a hand through his thick mane. Taking the soap from her, he scrubbed it between his hands and tossed it over his shoulder. When he slipped a soapy hand between her legs, Spicy nearly swooned with hot, craving delight. He took his time and then catching the clear water in his hands, rinsed her just as gently. Taking her hand he gave her a playful unexpected yank. She fell into him with a laugh as he ducked through the spray to the backside of the waterfall. Only a mist sprinkled them as he leaned her against age-old rocks smoothed by eons of cascading water.

Velvety. Ravishing. Hungry.

The man who'd stolen her heart nudged her legs apart and she twined one arm around his neck as he lifted her up. Wrapping her legs around him, she guided his rigid hardness to her warm center. Aching to have him inside her, in sheer ecstasy she pushed downward, enjoying the slide of his manhood as two became one. She moaned his name as they moved faster and harder. Never in Spicy's wildest dreams could she have imagined being so happy, so satisfied, and so head over heels in love. How lucky she'd been the day he'd caught her swiping his blueberries. She would always be grateful to Stone for that new memory replacing the old one of the gunnysackers.

Letting pleasure reign over pain, within moments, Spicy spiraled to the edge of ecstasy. Stone plunged hard and fast and when he groaned her name, she vibrated around the length of him, absorbing his hot pulsing throbs deep within her.

"I love you so much, Stone Hatfield."

"Awww, Spicy. I love you, too," he whispered. "Will you marry me?" She squeezed him internally as her arms tightened around his shoulders. "Is that yes?"

"Yes, yes, yes," she whispered ecstatically. "I will marry you."

Stone kissed her lips and Spicy tasted her own happy tears. She was going to marry the only man she would ever love. They hugged, then one became two and he touched her feet to the creek bed. Sunset had come and gone as they walked hand-in-hand out of the waterfall. Her mind spinning with dreams come true, Spicy danced on a cloud to her horse and opened the saddlebag. Her heart pounding with joy she turned with a clean pair of britches for Stone and for her, the new camisole and panties he'd bought. She pulled on her silky, soft underwear as Stone stepped into his pants and boots. They plucked up their discarded clothes and placed them in their saddlebags. Then Spicy glanced up and down Mate Creek.

"Lose something?" Stone asked.

"When you proposed, my shoes fell off in the creek."

Stone laughed. "Forget 'em. I'm gonna buy you a whole new wardrobe."

Spicy grinned. "From a store?"

"From a store."

When Stone crooked his finger, she could barely feel the ground under her bare feet as she hurried to him. He helped her into the saddle and asked if she intended to ride through the descending darkness wearing only her underwear. For an answer she smiled and nudging Gus, charged down the mountain. In the valley, the once-in-a-blue-moon man passed her by and then let her catch up. Her hair dried in the breeze as she sailed ahead and when he caught up again she blew him a kiss. This time they vanished over the hill together.

It was a wild and wonderful chase across the Stony Mountains.

CHAPTER 43

"Tarnation!" Spicy exclaimed as they finished breakfast the next morning. "With everything that's happened, I forgot to give you your telegrams." Sitting at Aunt Hilda's table across from Stone, she hopped up and walked to the shelf where she'd left them. "You're very popular."

When they had gotten back from their waterfall showers and chase across the mountains, Spicy had washed their clothes while Stone settled the horses in the barn. Just as she finished pinning her dress to the clothesline her feet left the ground as she was swept into strong arms. Stone carried her into the house and straight to bed. He'd peeled off her sheer underwear and shocked her by teaching her something new. Her velvety petals still smoldered from his blazing hot kisses. Eagerly, she had reciprocated along Stone's hard length until he'd groaned and rolled on top of her. Hearts racing, bodies joined, and when breathing had returned to normal they fell into long overdue exhausted sleep. Being in a comfortable bed, they'd snoozed well past sunrise. Upon waking, they'd lingered in each other's arms speaking in the soft tones of lovers. While she'd cooked breakfast, he'd tended the horses. At the kitchen table, they'd agreed not to dwell on the horrors they'd survived on the back side of the mountain.

"I have a message for you," Stone said as Spicy handed him the telegrams. After she'd refilled their coffee cups, Stone snared her hand. He set the wires aside and tugged her across his lap. Lifting her hair he whispered in her ear, "I love the way you toot my flute."

"Music to my ears," Spicy flirted, arms circling his neck.

With a low growl, Stone's eyes shut and his mouth closed over hers. After the kiss, Spicy returned to her chair. As he picked up the first telegram, she licked her lips provocatively. Stone cocked a brow and she innocently pointed, directing his attention back to the message in his hand. He chuckled and Spicy sipped her coffee as he opened the telegram. After reading it, he handed it to her and opened the second one. The first telegram stated Connie had been admitted to Wheeling Hospital and Aunt Hilda would be staying in Wheeling indefinitely. The doctors had agreed with Stone as to the diagnosis of tuberculosis and would do what they could for Connie whose case was advanced.

"Should we send a telegram letting them know about Ronny Staton's murder?" Spicy asked staring at the telegram and knowing the sad news about his brother would certainly not help Connie's poor health. When Stone didn't answer, she glanced up. "Stone?"

"We'll tell them in person," he said, raising his head to look at her.

"What do you mean?"

"This second wire is from Jet," Stone said. "He received the telegram from Aunt Hilda about our mother. He's heading to a conference in Pittsburgh and wants me to meet up with him there to talk and," he chuckled, "make sure I'm still alive."

"I knew you were the wild one when your Aunt Hilda told that story about the porch swings," Spicy said with a smile, then frowned. "Jet knows you are in feud territory and is worried about you. You don't take things lying down."

"I've taken you lying down." Stone's grin was cocky. "And on my lap and standing under a waterfall."

"Stone!" Spicy gasped her cheeks heating to ten shades of red.

"Jet's just as wild. Even though he's only twenty-four he's already a respected prosecuting attorney in Philadelphia," Stone said with pride in his brother, then glanced back at the message. "According to the dates he's given in the telegram, it will be easy to meet up with him in Pittsburgh at Monongahela House on the Monongahela River. I'll wire him to confirm and suggest he travel with us to see Aunt Hilda and Connie in Wheeling."

"You go. I'll wait for you at my cabin."

"Oh hell no, you won't," Stone said, shaking his head. "If you think I'm leaving you here and traveling three hundred miles away, you have another think coming."

Splaying a hand, Spicy said, "There's no danger now. I can check on Lumpkin and find out about the final arrangements for Ellison and for Ronny Staton."

"We will do all of that together this afternoon. Four McCoys, two Hatfields, two Clines, and a Staton just died violently within days of each other. Don't tell me there's no danger."

"Clay McCoy, Ol' Ranel's sons, and the Clines are dead. Vorticia Hatfield is dead," Spicy reasoned. "Ellison and Ronny were certainly never threats to us. I think it's safe to say I'll be just fine while you're away." She punctuated that with a sharp nod of her head.

Outside, a morning breeze drew attention to the clothesline where Stone's shirt and britches, along with her blueberry dress, fluttered in the warm wind.

Stone gazed across the table at her. "You don't have anything to wear to a fancy hotel in a big city like Pittsburgh."

"That's exactly right." Lifting her chin and folding her

arms under her breasts, Spicy said, "I'm not going to embarrass you or myself."

"I think it's safe to say you will have plenty of new dresses to hang in the wardrobe of that hotel."

Spicy's mouth dropped open. "No, I was teasing you about the store-bought—"

"And new shoes." Stone held up a hand and asked, "Now what's your argument?"

"Stone," she huffed with a mixture of angst and love. "I am not spending your money."

"It's my money so I guess we'll buy underwear, too. Although I prefer you naked."

Spicy placed both elbows on the table, plopped her chin into her hands, and sighed. "I prefer you naked, too." Stone handed her the telegram from Jet as he tore open the third one. When Spicy glanced up at him this time, a scowl creased his handsome face. "What's wrong?"

"Victor Vanderveer received my telegram breaking the betrothal. He's heading west with his daughter and wants to know if I can meet them in of all places," he lifted his eyes to hers, "at Wheeling Hospital."

Spicy rolled her eyes. "Now I'm definitely not going."

"Since when are you a chicken?"

"Since…I don't know."

"Since never," Stone said and went back to reading the message. "Vanderveer wants me to meet up with someone and says that's why it has to be in person."

"His daughter," Spicy said, only half joking. "So, you'd best remember her name."

Stone bowed his head in thought. "Starts with an *E*." When he met her eyes again, he had a boyish grin on his face. "Her name is Eunice."

"He wants you to meet up with him and Eunice."

"Then I will tell them I'm going to marry you." Serious again, Stone sat forward in the chair, reached across the table and grabbed her hand. "Know what?"

"What?"

"You haven't scratched and I remembered her name. We can do this."

"I don't know…" Spicy looked away and her voice trailed off.

"Would you like to know what Ellison's last words were to me?"

Meeting his gaze she nodded. "Yes, of course, if you'd like to tell me."

"Keep Logan. Marry Spicy. Build a hospital."

"Oh, Stone," Spicy whispered with a choke in her voice. She remembered Stone stuffing a pile of money into Sarah Ann's hand and knew it was mostly to help the family but also to pay for the horse. She rose from her chair and found her way back onto Stone's lap. "The first day I laid eyes on you in the blueberry patch I knew you were a man to match a mountain."

"I knew you were the proverbial needle in a haystack and I'm not going to lose you." His mind made up, his expression was determined. "So we're going to Pittsburgh and Wheeling, we're going to get married, and we'll work on building that hospital. Yes?"

"Yes," Spicy said, her heart singing with hope and happiness.

"The Vanderveers' timing actually coincides well with Jet's trip. Aunt Hilda and Connie aren't going anywhere anytime soon. So let's take care of business here first. Then we'll travel to Pittsburgh, get Jet and go take care of business in Wheeling."

Stone suggested they leave Gus in the barn so they could pick up Daisy at the Weddingtons' place. Spicy cleared away the dishes and plucked their clothes off the line as Stone saddled the horses. When they were ready to go, Stone stepped into Logan's saddle first and then Spicy mounted in back of him. She teased him by pressing her breasts against his broad back and spreading her fingers over his button fly. When he threatened to pull her around in front and make love to her in the saddle, she hugged him all the tighter.

The Weddingtons' homestead seemed to be the center not only for voting, but general visiting and catching up on the latest news. Greeting them, Abe reported the pastor of the church which Ronny had attended would conduct a funeral and gave them the time and location of the service. There was a Staton family cemetery, so Ronny had a final resting place.

Their next stop was Ellison's house. The mood was somber and the house filled with grief-stricken people. Devil Anse initially frowned seeing her with Stone and then nodded. Cap was there and understandably agitated. Johnse, his typical pleasant self, spoke to them briefly. They paid their respects to Sarah Ann and promised to attend Ellison's funeral. Leaving the house and not being in a hurry for once, rather than pole or paddle across the Tug Fork River, they found their way to the brand-new northern bridge.

"In addition to the hospital, we need a southern bridge on my mountain for better access to Raccoon Hollow," Stone said.

Spicy asked hesitantly, "To take the place of our blueberry patch?"

"Never."

They left West Virginia as the horses trotted over the bridge. In Kentucky, riding Logan and Daisy south, Spicy spoke of Lumpkin. He'd be on his own when they traveled to Pittsburgh and Wheeling, but she didn't fear leaving him now. Spicy said Lumpkin had disliked working Clay's moonshine still, had avoided living with him since their father died and had never trusted the Clines. Instead, he enjoyed hunting, fishing, being with friends like Shadow and Abby and building things. In addition to the pigpen, he'd built her henhouse and chicken coop.

"Spicy! Just Stone!" Lumpkin shouted, sitting on the riverbank with Shadow. Getting to his feet he lumbered toward them with Shadow at this side. "Yer back!"

CHAPTER 44

"LUMPKIN! SHADOW!" SPICY CALLED AND WAVED, reining in Daisy.

Stone dismounted Logan, went to Spicy and let her slide into his arms. He smiled as Spicy ran to her cousins and hugged them. Stone was the recipient of one of Big Lump's famous bear hugs and received a smaller version from Shadow. Big Lump and Shadow said they had been sent by Abby and Sunshine to catch some fish to add to their supper. So far they had each caught several large, flathead catfish and smallmouth bass.

"Big Lump, I smelled smoke coming from this area yesterday," Stone said as they paused under some sweetgum trees. "Do you know what burned?"

"Clay's cabin," Big Lump replied.

"We done heard he ain't comin' back so we burned it," Shadow said proudly. "Had lots and lots of buckets of water ready from Peter Creek so the fire didn't get away from us."

"Abby and Sunshine helped," Big Lump said.

"We picked all the corn and brung it to Spicy's cabin," Shadow added. "We's havin' a picnic in the front yard today."

"Good thing Clay didn't keep his money in the cabin,"

Stone said, looking at Big Lump. "You need to get it and keep it safe, Big Lump. Do you know where it is?"

Big Lump nodded and motioned to them. Stone caught Spicy's eye and could tell she had no idea about the hidden money. She smiled her gratitude at Stone's concern. Big Lump only had to walk a few paces before pointing to the top of a towering sugar maple tree. About two-thirds of the way up, there was a clump in the branches resembling a bird's nest.

"There." Big Lump pointed. "Cain't reach it."

"I can," Shadow said, sizing up the situation.

"But the limb with the nest is hanging out over the river," Spicy noted.

"If it can hold a man, it can hold a boy," Stone replied looking up through the branches.

"True. Sugar maples are," with a raised brow and a dimpled smile, missed by Big Lump and Shadow, Spicy nudged Stone, "strong and hard." He thoroughly enjoyed it when this sexy siren flirted with him and grinned at her. "Of all these trees, maples are the easiest to climb because the limbs are like stair steps. I've climbed a few to hide."

Big Lump chuckled. "Clay never knowed."

"I like to climb. Here I go," Shadow said.

"Wait." Stone pulled his knife and its sheath out of his boot and gave it to Shadow. "It'll be tied down."

Shadow stuck the sheathed knife in his back pocket and scaled up the center of the tree like he lived there. Spicy stayed where she was as Stone and Big Lump shifted here and there to stay underneath Shadow just in case. They called out directions to help Shadow find the nest among the branches. Edging out on the limb, Shadow shouted he'd found a metal box.

"Be careful, Shadow!" Spicy cautioned as the boy and a breeze off the river both shook the leaves overhead.

"It's tied down like you said, Stone," Shadow called. "I have to cut the rope."

"Let the box fall if you need to, Shadow," Stone replied.

Shadow cut, the branch fluttered, and the box fell. It hit several branches on the way down through the limbs. It dropped into the river and Big Lump was right there to scoop it up.

"You've got a talent for fishing valuables out of the Tug Fork," Stone congratulated Big Lump with a wink at Spicy.

Spicy clapped for Big Lump as Shadow shimmied down the tree. Big Lump walked toward them, holding the box. With urging from Spicy and Shadow, he glanced at Stone who nodded. Big Lump unlatched the box which was packed with greenbacks, gold, and silver. Spicy blinked back happy tears and Stone shook his hand. Big Lump plucked out a silver half dollar and flipped it to Shadow as he'd seen Stone do with Henry and Tommy Weddington.

"Thank you, Big Lump!" Shadow said, obviously surprised and overjoyed.

"What now?" Big Lump asked.

"You can have your pig farm and I can help," Shadow suggested excitedly. "We's already added four new hogs to the pen with Big Bump and Pig Piffle."

"That's great." Stone suspected where the hogs had come from and wondered what had happened to the bodies of their dead owners. "You can open a bank account, Big Lump."

"Lumpkin, since I'm staying with Stone you're welcome to live in my cabin," Spicy began, "and marry Abby?"

Big Lump glanced at Shadow. "And marry Abby?"

"And marry Abby!" Shadow beamed.

Metal box under his arm, Big Lump and Shadow grabbed their fish and poles. Stone and Spicy mounted Logan leaving Daisy for Big Lump and Shadow. In the saddle of the huge draft horse Big Lump leaned down, his left arm bent at the elbow. Shadow took hold and the giant tossed the boy behind him as if he weighed nothing. Stone swept his hand forward purposely letting Big Lump take the lead. Spicy slipped her arms around Stone's waist and kissed his back from his left shoulder to his right. Medicine and surgery were definitely paths to easing the pain and suffering of folks and Stone had dedicated his life to the pursuit. But being a physician was not the only way to help people—he'd learned that from Spicy—the definition of empathy and compassion at its finest. Stone patted her thigh and sighed with happiness.

The weather was just right for a picnic and though there was sadness in these hills and valleys, Stone envisioned a brighter future. Here in the present, he was as thrilled as the others for Big Lump's good fortune. It was a victorious gallop through the deep Kentucky woods.

"Hello!" Spicy called to Abby and Sunshine, rocking in the chairs on her porch.

Lumpkin and Shadow had just ridden into view ahead of them. Abby and Sunshine rushed to greet them with Abby stating the last time she'd spoken to Stone no one knew where Spicy was. The young ladies shared they'd been taking a break from cooking and baking while waiting for Lumpkin and Shadow to return from the river. The parents were joining them for supper soon and the girls immediately begged Spicy and Stone to stay. Lumpkin and Shadow whooped with joy when she and Stone accepted the invitation.

Inside, Spicy showed Lumpkin and Stone a secure and dry hiding place underneath the floorboards in her folks' former bedroom, where the metal box could be securely concealed. Stone promised to take Lumpkin to a bank later on where his money could earn interest. Next, Spicy gathered up her few clothes, personal items, and favorite spices as Stone packed up her books. This time gunnysacks served a good purpose. Lumpkin whistled her favorite tune as he and Shadow cleaned the fish before turning them over to Abby and Sunshine to fry.

Back outside, Stone remarked that Big Bump had recovered well and Pig Piffle had grown. Using smoke, Spicy demonstrated how to get honey from her beehives without being stung. Pepper strutted around the grassy front yard as the chickens fluttered and pecked in their pen. Nutmeg scampered up for a taste of the honey and Spicy's attention. Stone and Lumpkin carried the kitchen table outside as Shadow followed them with plates and utensils.

Zeke and Goldie McCoy arrived with sweet potatoes, mashed potatoes, and quilts. Otis and Martha Hatfield were right behind them with two pumpkin and two apple pies and more quilts. Placing the food on the table and spreading out quilts, they all pitched in to set up the picnic in the sunlight-dappled yard where they could enjoy the flower-scented breeze. Plates were piled high and everyone enjoyed helpings of fried fish, endless ears of corn on the cob, the delicious potatoes, and loaves of fresh bread lovingly baked by Abby and Sunshine. Honey drizzled atop the warm bread was an extra treat and the pies were devoured.

There were stories to be shared and some better left buried. Though nothing would outshine the magical night of fairy fire with the man of her dreams, this picnic with Stone and their friends was a special event. No sooner had that thought crossed Spicy's mind than Stone wrapped an arm around her. Her heart was full and she kissed his cheek.

"After the funerals of Ellison and Ronny, we're traveling to Pittsburgh for a few days," Spicy told them toward the end of the evening so no one would worry about their absence.

"Going by train?" Zeke asked.

"Yes. We'll hitch Daisy to my Aunt Hilda's buggy for the trip to the depot," Stone said. "Conrad Staton's horse and buggy are boarded there so Spicy and I will drive two buggies home and pick up my aunt later."

"Too bad the train depot's so far away," Otis said.

"Yes, we need a train through these hills as much as we need a hospital," Stone replied.

"That's right, we need both," Zeke said as the others

agreed. "Stone, we've got room in our barn for Daisy and the buggy. Let me take you to the train depot. When you return, you won't have to drive two buggies home."

"I can keep Logan and Gus in our barn until you return," Otis offered.

"That would be much appreciated," Stone said to the McCoy and Hatfield families so willing to lend a hand and to heal wounds old and new. Stone pulled money out of his pocket, but Zeke and Otis shook their heads no.

Zeke quietly said what they were all thinking, "Thanks to you, we're all safer now."

"Stone has a brother." Abby nudged Sunshine with an elbow. "His name is Jet."

Sunshine blushed before bashfully nodding her blond head. "I've heard."

When the food was gone and the picnic put away, Stone and Spicy stowed the gunnysacks on the horses. Hugs and handshakes were exchanged and for this group of folks, life had become far more enjoyable in Raccoon Hollow. Lumpkin walked with them to the edge of the property where Logan and Daisy were grazing.

"Thank you, Spicy." With a gap-toothed grin, Lumpkin had tears in his eyes, letting his simple words cover so much.

"You're welcome," Spicy choked out in a whisper as she hugged him.

Lumpkin looked to Stone and stuck out his hand. "Thank you, Stone."

"You're welcome, pardner." Stone shook Lumpkin's hand and then asked, "Big Lump, before or after you burned Clay's cabin, did you happen to go to the Clines' place?"

"Yup," Lumpkin said matter-of-factly. He inclined his head to the pigpen indicating where the four new pigs had come from.

"Did anybody bury the Clines?" Stone asked.

"Hogs ate 'em, pardner."

Yes, life was a whole lot better in Raccoon Hollow.

CHAPTER 45

"PITTSBURGH IS REALLY SOMETHING," SPICY whispered.

Enjoying her wonder, Stone replied, "It reminds me of Philadelphia."

The sun had risen through the window of their private compartment on the train. Never had Stone enjoyed daybreak and cozy quarters more than when he was with Spicy. They had ventured to the dining car for a hearty brunch and soon the outskirts of Pittsburgh had captured their attention. After the train had chugged into Union Depot, he'd hired a buggy to take them to Monongahela House. Consisting of a comfortable tufted seat for two and a driver's bench, their ride was harnessed to a regal chestnut. The driver, a talkative chap perhaps in his mid-fifties, proudly proclaimed he'd been born and raised in Pittsburgh.

"Monongahela comes from the Unami language spoken by the Lenape people," he called over his shoulder as the horse, which he'd said was a Morgan, clip-clopped toward a bridge. "Monongahela means falling banks and this area is the ancient homeland of the Lenape, also known as the Delaware Indians. Pittsburgh is the city of three rivers. The Monongahela River, which we're about to cross, is one of the few rivers that flows from south to north."

Before traversing the bridge over the Monongahela River, their driver paused so they could read a large sign. The Monongahela Bridge, made of wood, had opened in 1818, and was Pittsburgh's first bridge. Though strong enough to sustain the daily pedestrian, livestock, and wagon passage, it had succumbed to the Great Fire of Pittsburgh on April 10, 1845. This second bridge, a wire rope suspension type, had proven inadequate to handle both bridge and river traffic. Hence a third, more dependable, larger, and taller, bridge, the Smithfield Street Bridge—perhaps halfway finished and being constructed out of steel and masonry piers—would eventually accommodate the daily travel. Not only that, the versatile new bridge would allow for the Pittsburgh Railways and the streetcar system. The sign concluded its history by stating the Smithfield Street Bridge was scheduled to open in March of 1883.

"Makes our new bridge back home seem trivial," Spicy said.

"I know what trivial means and our bridge back home is not pig piffle." Stone chuckled, recalling their first conversation in the blueberry patch. "Both bridges are significant." When Spicy nodded and smiled he said, "We'll visit again when the Smithfield Street Bridge is finished. In the meantime we've got other bridges to cross."

Spicy agreed as they headed over the bridge in front of them spanning the busy river. Steamboats puffed out black smoke as their paddlewheels churned up the water. The impressive vessels chugged past each other along with barges and the towboats propelling them. Stone pointed and explained when veering east the water traffic would float onto the Allegheny River. If one navigated west they'd find themselves on the Ohio River. In any case, there were no rafts and poles or small canoes with oars on the mighty Monongahela.

"Welcome to what some folks are calling the Golden Triangle," the driver said with an expansive wave of his hand as they reached the other side of the suspension bridge.

Smithfield Street paved their way into the heart of Pittsburgh bustling with people, buggies, wagons, and horses. As a streetcar passed them the driver stated there were a thousand factories in the area. The horse-drawn trolleys rolling by on steel railways helped transport people to and from work and home. Hence, the critical need for the up-and-coming Smithfield Street Bridge specifically designed to manage the steadily growing city.

"Coal is burned to provide energy for all of the factories," Stone said. "If Pittsburgh continues to meet the country's need for iron it will become the steel capitol of the world."

Clattering along the busy streets to their hotel, Spicy said, "My father told me that during the Civil War, Pittsburgh was the arsenal of the Union Army. He said the Union Navy's *USS Monitor*, was cast here. Had Papa not broken his leg and been discharged from the Navy, he would have been assigned to serve on the *Monitor*." She sighed. "He said his broken leg was a blessing in disguise because the *Monitor* capsized and sank on New Year's Eve in 1862, during a terrible storm off Cape Hatteras."

Remembering Spicy mentioning the *USS Monitor* when telling him about her folks and moving to Kentucky when she was a baby, he wondered if she was already a little homesick. Stone said, "Luckily, your father got to meet your mother in the hospital and hence I have you." When a smile touched her lips he said, "Pittsburgh is famous not only for its bridges but for locomotives, tunnels, and rail cars."

"Yes, indeed," their jovial driver joined in. "Nobody can sell steel rails better than Andrew Carnegie. Pittsburgh is a hotbed for steel and rail companies and their tycoons. Some of our other local tycoons include Henry Clay Frick and A.W. Mellon. I suppose our odd man out is tycoon Henry J. Heinz because instead of steel and rails he bottles horseradish, sauerkraut, celery sauce, vinegar, and pickled cucumbers." Holding up his index finger the driver said, "But it's his ketchup that's my number one favorite."

"You're my number one favorite," Stone said, wrapping an arm around Spicy.

"You might be mine, too, depending on what ketchup is."

Stone laughed, enjoying her sassy tease. "It's a thick sauce made from tomatoes that's good on bratwurst and potatoes."

"Be sure to sample our nectar of the gods known simply as Monongahela," the driver said. "It's our locally made whiskey distilled on the river."

With a grin, Stone told Spicy, "Big-city moonshine."

Stone heard her take a deep breath. Maybe she wasn't as comfortable as she appeared. He recalled his early days in Philadelphia and its big-city way of life being a lot to absorb. But the afternoon sun was shining and a summer breeze wafting off the Monongahela River made for a pleasant drive. Yet, he noticed Spicy clasp her hands tightly in her lap while gazing at the folks crowding the sidewalks. Women in stylish dresses strolled along with their arms linked through those of men in dark suits. Mothers pushed baby buggies or held the hand of a child as they hurried into colorful markets or browsed open-air bazaars. Men, some wearing derbies and some not, came and went from tall buildings, banks, shops, or other places of business.

Their driver motioned to all the activity and said, "Pittsburgh is home to at least a hundred and sixty thousand people making it the twelfth largest city in the United States."

"Tarnation," Spicy whispered.

"What?" Stone asked. "What thoughts are running through your pretty head?"

"I'm thinking Pittsburgh is a world away from the one where I grew up," Spicy said and smiled at him. "I told myself the same thing about you once."

"You'd have been too young to remember the Tidewater area of Virginia where you were born, but it's a world away from where you grew up, too. There's a lot more to life than Tug Valley. Right?"

"Right. I'm sure this feels like home to you since it reminds you of Philadelphia."

"True, now. But it took some getting used to when I first moved there."

"Monongahela House," the driver announced and reined in the horse at the curb on the corner of Smithfield and Water Streets. "The original house burned down in the same fire that took the Monongahela Bridge. Two years later they had built three hundred of the finest rooms west of New York City under the roof of this new house."

"House? I don't see a house," Spicy said.

"That's what they often call a well-appointed establishment like this one," Stone said.

Tilting her head back, Spicy shaded her eyes and stared into the sky. "Overwhelming."

The American flag atop the hotel flew so high it waved among the clouds. The massive, six-story hotel took up an entire block of the picturesque city along the trafficked riverfront. Spicy seemed barely aware of Stone exiting the buggy or the driver handing over the single carpetbag. Thanking him for the guided tour, Stone assisted Spicy out of the buggy. She stood gaping at the building until Stone snared her hand and led the way across the wide sidewalk.

Spicy had chosen to wear the blueberry dress Stone had bought for her. Even a little worse for wear, he knew it was her best frock. Underneath it were the camisole and panties he'd also bought for her. None of the ladies they'd seen thus far were so casually attired and most wore hats. Clad in a beige shirt, suspenders, and brown pants, Stone had purposely dressed casually so as not to make her feel uncomfortable. Spicy held her bare head high as he escorted her to the imposing brass and glass double doors of the hotel.

A uniformed doorman swept open a door for them and Spicy entered ahead of Stone. Inside the hotel, carved pillars stood just inside the double doors and were duplicated straight ahead at the bottom of a tall, winding, black walnut staircase. A towering domed ceiling and crystal chandeliers flickered high above white marble floors. Art in gilded frames decorated paneled fresco walls. Plush leather upholstered furniture and matching wing-backed chairs set on thick oriental carpets.

Stone placed Spicy's arm through his as they walked toward a long desk also made of black walnut. With a sign that read *Registration*, the desk boasted a gleaming shine, lines of sophisticated appearing guests, and three clerks clad in suits. They stopped behind a couple obviously attired for an important occasion. As the gentleman arranged for accommodations the blonde with him gave Stone a coy smile. He ignored her. Turning her attention to Spicy then, the blonde noted her simple dress with a look of pity and turned her back.

"Philadelphia is also a river town like Pittsburgh," Stone told Spicy with an easy smile. "The Schuylkill River flows into the Delaware River."

"If I remember correctly, Philadelphia is home to the Liberty Bell in Independence Hall," Spicy said, ignoring the blonde's actions. When Stone agreed she added, "As you may have noticed when you packed my books, my father had two on America history. Philadelphia is also where the Declaration of Independence was adopted and the Constitution of the United States drafted and signed."

"Philadelphia's City Hall also housed the Supreme Court from 1790 to1800. George Washington took the oath of office in New York City, but for ten years the nation's capital and Supreme Court were in Philadelphia where Washington and then John Adams served as president."

"Philadelphia is also home to Pennsylvania Hospital and my *favorite* doctor," Spicy added and sighed. "I don't know how you can leave such a big, fine city for Tug Valley."

Before Stone could reply a hotel clerk addressed them. Stone gave his name, signed a register, and the mannerly fellow presented him with a key. Saying their room was next to Mr. Jet Hatfield's, he handed Stone a note. Then tapping a bell, the clerk called out to a young man he aptly referred to as the bellboy. The uniformed bellboy hurried forward and took their carpetbag. Escorting them to their room on the third floor, he enthusiastically recounted the hotel's history of previous guests.

"President Abraham Lincoln is just one of many presidents to have stayed with us. John Adams, Andrew Jackson, Andrew Johnson, Ulysses S. Grant, Rutherford B. Hayes, and James Garfield stayed here before, during or after their presidency."

"That's an impressive roster," Stone said.

"Yes, sir, it sure is," the pleasant young man agreed. Encouraged he rattled off, "Other famous folks who have signed Monongahela House's register are Mark Twain, Jenny Lind, Charles Dickens, Carrie Nation, P.T. Barnum, General and Mrs. Tom Thumb, Horace Greeley, and Prince Louis Napoleon of France."

"Did you get to meet any of them?" Spicy asked politely.

"Yes, ma'am," he replied earnestly. "Mr. Barnum treated me to two free tickets to his circus and Mr. Twain gave me his book, *The Adventures of Tom Sawyer*, and autographed it for me. His book is why I learned to read."

Reaching the third floor, the young man opened their door and set their carpetbag down on an ottoman. Stone dropped several coins into the bellboy's hand who thanked him and left.

"The note is from Jet," Stone said, in their lofty room boasting a brocade sofa, high-backed chairs, and two large beds covered in the same fabric as the drapes. Striding across the room he pushed the velvet drapes further apart, revealing a grand view of the waterfront. With a glance at the note, he told Spicy, "Jet wants to meet us at Feu sur la Riviere."

"What is that?"

"A French restaurant."

"What's it mean?" Spicy asked.

"No idea." Stone shrugged. "We'll ask when we get there."

"I think I may have gotten into some nettles, Stone."

Though she no longer scratched, the expression on her beautiful face said overwhelming had become an understatement. Stone placed her arm through his again and swept her right back out of the room they'd just entered. Down the carpeted hall, the staircase, and across the lobby, Spicy held on tightly. The doorman acknowledged their approach with a courteous bow and opened the front door for them. With the same look of trepidation she'd had that long ago day when she'd whirled to face him in the blueberry patch, Spicy stopped short.

"Come on," Stone said and gave her a gentle tug onto the sidewalk.

"Where are we going?"

CHAPTER 46

"To shop before we meet up with Jet for supper."

Spicy was prepared once again to protest spending his money. But when Stone tilted his head and cocked a rakish brow, she laughed and said, "I'd love to."

Shopping for ready-made dresses was a spectacular event. The pretty stores along the riverfront were as splendid as the magnificent hotel. Whether it was for the sales or because Stone was so charming, the female shop-keepers could not have been friendlier. Spicy was fairly certain it was Stone. Whereas she would have selected one dress, two at the most, Stone bought two dozen. Reticules— a small bag to carry a lady's money, calling card, and hand-kerchief— none of which Spicy had, along with shoes and boots were added to the wardrobe haul. In a boutique called Unwhisperables Spicy selected petticoats, camisoles, and nightgowns. When she showed Stone a pair of loose and frilly, below-the-knee drawers called pantalets, he frowned saying he preferred her short-drawer panties. Spicy shushed him and added both to the pile. Since they could carry no more, it was handy or perhaps shrewd of the shop owners to have a business selling trunks for women and men smack-dab in the middle of the clothing stores.

Saratoga & Steamer Trunks buzzed with activity as the Monongahela River was a hub of river travel for people and cargo alike. Stone bought two trunks and the first one overflowed with Spicy's new wardrobe into the second trunk. He asked the store manager to hold onto both trunks until the second trunk was filled and paid him to have the trunks delivered to Monongahela House.

Stone grabbed Spicy's hand and they headed into the next shop where a sign on the window read *Haberdashery*. It turned out to be a large store where men's suits, shirts, ties, suspenders, pants, shoes, and boots were sold. Asking her advice, which Spicy knew he didn't need, Stone chose some clothes and shoes though not nearly as many as he'd bought for her. After paying the shopkeeper, who happened to be the owner, the gentleman assured Stone he would personally see to it that his items were packed into the half empty trunk next door.

Leaving the shop, Stone hailed a buggy and said, "It's fitting the most beautiful lady wearing one of the finest dresses in the city should have supper in a first-class restaurant."

Stone was clad in a black derby hat, black suit, white shirt, and shiny black shoes. Spicy had chosen a silver dress with thin black stripes. It was one of her favorites because the colors reminded her of Stone's metallic eyes and coal-black hair. She carried a black satin reticule with tassels and wore snug black boots which laced above her ankles. In a hat boutique a shopkeeper had expertly twirled Spicy's hair into an elegant chignon at the nape of her neck. She placed a dainty capote just above it assuring Spicy city ladies weren't fully dressed without such a stylish hat. Her silver capote was trimmed in black and tied with a black satin bow under her left ear.

"Hungry?" Stone asked her as a buggy driver reined in a horse at the curb.

"Starved," Spicy said, stepping into the buggy.

"Feu sur la Riviere." Stone had apparently pronounced it

correctly as the driver nodded and tapped the reins to his horse.

"How big is Philadelphia?" she asked as they curved around another busy corner.

"Probably eight hundred and fifty thousand."

As much as Spicy had dreamed of Stone remaining in Tug Valley and treating the people there, she was second-guessing herself at every curb, curve, and corner. If Pittsburgh was even a trifle taste of the life Stone had been living, how *could* he leave a progressive city like Philadelphia? The hills and valleys of West Virginia seemed embarrassingly backward with this stark comparison. Thinking to repay Stone for saving her life by pulling him into a waterfall with her, suddenly felt completely inadequate. What she should do to repay him was to push him toward a bright future at Pennsylvania Hospital. It was selfish to drag him into the past where he'd been shot, ambushed, and forced to kill or be killed.

The buggy slowed but her thoughts swirled. Was Stone supposed to marry Eunice? Maybe that's why this trip had worked out the way it had so he could meet up with her in Wheeling and rekindle whatever they'd had. Perhaps she needed to think of other people instead of herself and those in Tug Valley. The driver reined in the horse in front of the French restaurant with its name in gold letters on the door. They'd no sooner stepped out of the buggy onto the sidewalk than a version of Stone burst out of the building.

"Stony!" the man similar to Stone in height and weight called and, smiling from ear-to-ear, sprinted toward them. With his black hair and gray eyes, he was almost as handsome as his older brother. Almost. "Good to see you."

"Jet, it's good to see you, too." Stone swung an arm around him.

"Our mother," Jet said and sighed, "I can't believe she's gone."

"I'll fill you in." Stone squeezed his shoulder. "I'd like you to meet Spicy McCoy."

Spicy extended her hand and Jet took it with both of his. "What a pleasure, Spicy."

"It's nice to meet you, Jet. I've heard nothing but great things about you."

"Maybe from Aunt Hilda," he teased his brother and shrugged.

"From Stone, too," Spicy assured him and smiled.

"Thanks." Jet glanced from Spicy to Stone. "She's beautiful. Does she have a sister?"

"No," Stone chuckled and took Spicy's hand. "But she has a cousin, named Sunshine."

"Does she now? Sunshine." Jet cocked a brow and grinned. "Come on. I made a reservation." He led the way across the sidewalk to the restaurant.

Seeing the gold letters again reminded Spicy to ask the name of the restaurant and she hoped to pronounce it like Stone had, "What does Feu sur la Riviere mean?"

"Fire on the River," Jet replied.

Spicy glanced at Stone who also looked surprised as she whispered, "Fairy fire on Blackberry Creek."

"No moon tonight. Meant to be," Stone said and winked. "By the time supper is over gas streetlamps will light up the city."

"What do you mean?"

At Spicy's curiosity over gas streetlamps, he wrapped an arm around her and said she'd just have to wait and see the magic for herself. As they entered the restaurant light flickered from chandeliers and wall sconces. The only candles Spicy noted were in a silver candelabra atop a grand piano. A gentleman Jet referred to as a maître'd escorted them to a table set for three covered with a snowy white cloth, fine China, and sterling silver. The man pulled out an upholstered chair for Spicy and when she was seated, the men sat as well. The maître'd said he would return with complimentary tumblers of Monongahela, along with a wine list and menus. This was a far cry from a fish fry picnic on quilts in the yard of a lantern-lit log cabin with glassless windows.

Spicy felt completely out of her element but here she was. She'd listen and learn and commit to memory every second with Stone whether it was meant to be or not.

"You've been gone for weeks," Jet said. "We have catching up to do."

"Little brother," Stone began, "you have no idea."

STONE DISEMBARKED the Baltimore and Ohio Railroad's first-class passenger car. The trip from Pittsburgh to Wheeling was sixty miles and had taken only two hours from start to finish. He assisted Spicy down the train steps and Jet followed her onto the depot's boardwalk. As Stone and Spicy received their trunks, Jet hailed a large buggy to transport them and their luggage to their next hotel—McLure House. From there they would go to Wheeling Hospital to see Aunt Hilda and check on Connie. Stone would also meet up with the Vanderveers.

If he was concerned about what the Vanderveers had to say or with whom Victor wanted him to meet, Stone was much more concerned about Spicy. During their stay in Pittsburgh, he had sensed the sexy and feisty, once-in-a-blue-moon woman inching away from him. She had grown quieter, didn't smile as much and stopped reaching for his hand. Stone thought back to the night of their showers along Mate Creek. When Spicy had galloped away from him, during their chase across the mountains, for a fleeting moment a cold image had plagued him—Eunice—gaunt face, skeletal hands, shapeless dark clothes. He had quickly thrown off the icy chill and raced after the sexy river siren who had seared his flesh with her naked body in the waterfall.

He'd been so sure nothing and no one could separate him from Spicy.

Their last full day in Pittsburgh, she'd denied anything was wrong at breakfast as they ate in the Monongahela

House's outdoor courtyard. But she'd made a cryptic comment saying the surrounding walls of rosebushes, with their impenetrable thorns, prevented those who did not belong from entering the premises. Picturing the rosebushes below her cabin's windows, he agreed. That afternoon, he had taken her on a trolley ride to an ice cream parlor and they both laughed at her delight over her first taste of the frozen treat. During a relaxing stroll she assured him anyone accustomed to parks as lovely as Allegheny Commons would be crazy to accept less. Stone had pointed out he preferred the waterfall and scenery from their private overlook on his mountain. Later during a romantic supper cruise on her first steamboat, she had suggested there were many river sirens to be caught. Stone guaranteed her he had caught the only river siren he wanted. She promised to make their night in bed as dreamy as their trip. And had she ever. The tunes she played were second to none. They'd dodged death and fatal feuds. He couldn't lose her now. Whatever mountain was coming between them had to be crushed.

Reaching McLure House on the corner of Market and Monroe Streets, they found this landmark hotel unique as it was built in a circular shape. The establishment had opened its doors thirty years prior in 1852, and become a mainstay. A doorman, posted between hitching posts and watering troughs, snapped his fingers and bellboys saw to their trunks. In the lobby, Victorian sofas and chairs perched on parquet floors. On the walls were framed photographs of President Grant and General Sherman, who had stayed in the grand hotel during the Civil War.

"We're in good company again," Stone said, wrapping his arm around Spicy.

"I've been in excellent company," Spicy replied with a smile at him and then at Jet.

"It's noon, let's eat before we leave for Wheeling Hospital," Jet suggested.

"Jet's always hungry," Stone said and chuckled.

"I just know how Stone is when he hits the door of a hospital." Jet glanced at Spicy. "We won't see him again for days."

"Not true in this case," Stone said. "I won't be operating on anyone."

CHAPTER 47

Spicy wished Stone could surgically remove her heart. Perhaps it was significant she had worn a red dress speckled with small black dots because it matched her soul which was already hemorrhaging from pain and descending darkness. She had picked out most of her frocks, but Stone had chosen this outfit because he liked the scooped neckline of the dress. He'd said the red fringe on the matching hat danced around her face like fairy fire.

No matter how she looked on the outside, inside her stomach twisted like a wrung out dishrag leaving her with no appetite. But neither was she about to dampen the spirits of two hungry men. The hotel concierge pointed them toward The Vagabond, a colorful dining room offering a midday special of roast beef, red potatoes, and baby carrots. Since it was served family style, she hoped the small portions she took were not noticeable.

Fancy hotels, expensive meals, train travel, steamboat jaunts, and trunks full of store-bought clothes represented the affluence Stone and Jet had attained through education and hard work. They were accustomed to living this way and deserved it all. But as each day had passed, the more she silently berated herself for trying to prevent this surgeon from heading up his own department at Pennsylvania Hospital. Spicy reckoned The Vagabond accurately described her drifting in and soon out of Stone's life.

They left the dining room and crossing the lobby to the foyer, Stone said to her, "You didn't eat much." So he had noticed. "Did you not like it?"

"It was delicious," Spicy said. Holding the drawstring of a red satin reticule, dotted with black beads, Stone had stuffed so much money in it she barely had room for her hanky.

"Do you need to rest here while we go to the hospital?" Jet asked.

"No." Stone gave his brother a look as a hotel doorman opened the door for them. Glancing back at Spicy, Stone said, "Aunt Hilda will want to see you."

"If I go with you now to see Aunt Hilda, maybe I could return to our room while you meet with the Vanderveers," Spicy said.

"Where to, sir?" the doorman asked Stone, ready to hail a buggy.

"Wheeling Hospital," Stone replied.

"I can hail a buggy at the hospital and make sure she is safely on her way back here to the hotel later," Jet offered as the doorman walked to the curb along the street.

"Jet." Stone shook his head. "No."

"Why?" Jet asked, confusion clearly written on his handsome face. "What's wrong?"

"I'll tell you both what's wrong," Stone said, sweeping back his jacket and resting his hands on his hips. "Spicy has run from me before or pushed me away when she thought it was in my best interest."

"Is that right?" Jet framed it as a question, but Spicy knew he believed his brother.

"Yes, because I think—" Spicy began and was cut off.

"I think you look ready to run again." Stone frowned at her. Then addressing Jet, he said, "She didn't need to run in the past and she doesn't need to run from the present."

"I disagree," Spicy said and continued, "I think you need

to accept Dr. Vanderveer's offer to be the chief of surgery in Philadelphia and I need to return home."

"I'm not having this conversation on the street," Stone said as a shiny, gray buggy pulled by a big, gray horse stopped for them. "Let's go."

"I don't want you to bury yourself and your talents in Tug Valley." Spicy backed away toward the door of the hotel. "Philadelphia is where you belong."

"Stop." Stone reached out, caught her arm and looked at Jet. "Get in the buggy, Jet, and I'll put her between us so she doesn't jump out the other side."

"She wouldn't try to escape us like that," Jet said, half-amused and half-alarmed.

"She sure as hell would," Stone replied.

"I do like a woman with spunk," Jet said.

"Just get in the damn buggy, Jet," Stone said. "Please."

Jet climbed into the buggy and held out his hand for Spicy. "Come on."

"Tarnation," Spicy seethed under her breath.

Jet grabbed her hand as Stone gripped her waist. Lifted and tugged into the buggy, Spicy found herself blocked on both sides by Hatfield muscle. In trapping her, Spicy was convinced Stone was unfairly trapping himself. The driver lightly snapped the reins to the horse and the buggy clipped away from McLure House. On the way to Wheeling Hospital, Stone filled Jet in on how she had run after their first meeting in the blueberry patch.

"She hopped onto a raft and poled herself across the Tug Fork," Stone told Jet. "The second time she crossed the river it was against my advice and she nearly drowned."

"I recovered just fine from that little spill," Spicy said.

"That little spill gave her a concussion," Stone across her to Jet. Stone raised a scolding brow at Spicy and continued, "I wanted her to stay with me, but she went home where Clay McCoy got his hands on her."

Spicy said, "It was none of your concern or business where I was."

"I was concerned and made you my business," Stone reminded her sharply.

"By taking me at gunpoint," Spicy told Jet.

"Yeah," Stone growled and looked back at Jet. "The barrel of a Colt between McCoy's eyes convinced him to let her go after Ellison, Johnse, and I negotiated our way past the Clines." His eyes on her again, he asked, "Would you rather I had left you with them, Spicy?"

"No, of course not!"

"Then I found a spider bite from a brown recluse on her cute little butt."

"Stone!" Spicy's cheeks burned as red as her dress. "You said although it was in a most distressing location, as a doctor you couldn't refuse to treat me."

With a huge grin, Jet said, "I'm so glad I didn't miss any of this."

"What?" Stone and Spicy asked simultaneously.

"The two of you. At Pennsylvania Hospital when Stone barks orders it's, 'Yes sir! Right away, sir! At your service, sir!' from the entire hospital staff." Jet saluted after giving the examples, then blew out a sigh and shook his head. "No one, and I mean absolutely no one, talks back to Dr. Stone Hatfield."

"Not only does she talk back, she kicked my shin before she ran the first time, so watch out for that," Stone said.

In her own defense Spicy said, "Jet, I also sutured his wound after he was shot."

"The rifle wound you told me about in Pittsburgh. I'm so thankful we didn't lose you, Stone. Or you, Spicy." Jet sobered. "Aunt Hilda will be just as sorry as I was to hear about Ellison's death. But I appreciate being up-to-date."

When they reached Wheeling Hospital the driver reined in the horse. Jet paid the man who thanked him as Stone helped Spicy alight. Unlike their first driver in Pittsburgh, this one seemed happy to be rid of them as he quickly took off without a backward glance.

"There's one more thing," Stone said as the three of

them paused on the walk in front of Wheeling Hospital. "I proposed to Spicy."

"That's great." Jet hugged him. All smiles again he said, "No offense meant toward Eunice, but I have to admit this is a relief, brother." Then Jet asked Spicy, "You said yes?"

Spicy longed for the intimate moment when she'd accepted Stone's proposal. Besides saying yes by squeezing him internally, she had tightened her arms around his broad shoulders hoping never to let him go. When she didn't answer Jet's question, Stone answered for her.

"She said yes three times, Jet."

"It's a woman's prerogative to change her mind," Spicy said.

"When hell freezes over."

"Brrr." Spicy pretended to shiver.

"Feels like hell, all right," Stone said. "This is another conversation I'm not having on the street. Except to say you're the most defiant woman I've ever known."

"You're the most pigheaded man I've ever known."

It was Jet who put his hands to his hips this time as he looked from Stone to Spicy, back to his brother and chuckled. "I've never seen anybody do this to you before, Stony."

"Only Spicy," Stone agreed.

Spicy explained, "Some bridges are not meant to be crossed together, Stone."

"We'll see." Stone grasped her hand and stormed toward the hospital entrance with Jet on their heels. "Let's get this over with."

Jet raced ahead, opened the hospital door and swung his hand in the air. "After you."

Spicy could tell Stone was in his element the moment they entered the hospital. With a nod at Jet to stay with her, he released her hand and stalked across the lobby. Just beyond a front desk and to the left was a hallway. Above the door at the end of the hall a sign stated it was the operating room. To the right a sign pointed to doctors' offices. Straight ahead appeared to be a corridor to the main area of the hospital where patient rooms were located.

Tapping a foot to the floor, as she stood beside a plaque on the wall, Spicy read that the hospital had been founded in 1850, by the Visitation Nuns and later became affiliated with the Sisters of St. Joseph. During the Civil War, the hospital had been used by the military. Spicy glanced around and indeed there were nuns clad in black tunics and veils with white coifs across foreheads and around necks. Nurses' uniforms consisted of round, white caps and full, white aprons over long, white dresses. Both nurses and nuns were busy pushing patients in wicker wheelchairs, assisting their family members, or directing visitors to rooms or doctors' offices.

Stone was given Conrad Staton's location and motioned to them. It occurred to Spicy the next conversation wasn't going to be any easier than the ones they'd just had on the street and in the buggy. Spotting Aunt Hilda halfway down a hall talking to a gentleman in a white frock coat, they quietly approached.

"Jet," Aunt Hilda said and waved. Not having seen him in years, her eyes teared as they embraced. She hugged both Stone and Spicy and introduced them to Connie's physician. "Dr. Clark, these are my nephews, Stone and Jet Hatfield." Grasping Spicy's hand, making her feel wanted, she said, "And my good friend, Spicy McCoy."

"Pleased to meet you," Dr. Clark said. "Dr. Stone Hatfield?" he asked as he shook Stone's hand.

"Yes," Stone replied.

"Your reputation precedes you, sir. Dr. Vanderveer who is here visiting before returning to Philadelphia has sung your praises," Dr. Clark said, still shaking his hand. "It's an honor to meet the surgeon about to take over at Pennsylvania Hospital, Dr. Hatfield."

"Thank you," Stone said, not denying or agreeing and withdrew his hand. "Do you know if Dr. Vanderveer happens to be here?"

"A few days ago he ran into a friend here in Wheeling, an Erskine Hazard, who he knows from upstate New York. He and Mr. Hazard went for a midday meal but Dr. Vanderveer should be back any time."

Stone inclined his head as to the information. "What's Mr. Staton's prognosis?"

"I don't expect him to leave the hospital."

"I figured as much."

"Dr. Clark," another doctor in a white coat called at the end of the corridor. "You're needed for an emergency consult."

"The flu has hit the city and hospital staff hard, so we are short-staffed. But if there's anything I can do for you folks, please let me know. I'll be here the rest of tonight and all day tomorrow," Dr. Clark said. "Again, an honor to meet you, Dr. Hatfield." He nodded at the others and excused himself.

"Connie's sleeping," Aunt Hilda said. "Would you like to visit in the family waiting room?" She gestured down another hall toward an area arranged with sofas and chairs, tables with reading materials and big windows open to a breeze.

"Yes." Stone proffered his arm to his aunt which she took. "Coming?" he asked Spicy.

CHAPTER 48

"Yes," Spicy replied and smiled at Aunt Hilda.

In the family waiting room of Wheeling Hospital, the conversation was undeniably difficult as Stone and Spicy shared in telling what had happened to Ronny Staton. Spicy, sitting on a sofa beside Aunt Hilda, was glad she had decided to come. After all, it was her responsibility, not Stone's, to be held accountable for the role she had played leading up to Clay shooting Ronny. Stone said he was the one at fault for triggering Clay's jealousy. Looking in from the outside, Jet and Aunt Hilda both adamantly stated Clay McCoy was the only one to blame for the tragedies starting with Lumpkin's head injury. Jet offered to get coffee and by the time he returned, Aunt Hilda knew Ellison was dead, too. When Aunt Hilda broke down, Spicy instantly scooted closer and wrapped her arms around her. As the nephews looked on, somewhat helplessly, Spicy gently rocked her, tucking Aunt Hilda's head against her neck.

"Dr. Hatfield, I'm so glad you're still here!" Dr. Clark called out, raising a hand as he jogged toward them. "Could you lend us your expertise in the operating room?"

"I'm not licensed to practice in West Virginia," Stone said as he stood.

"Please, we need you, sir," Dr. Clark pleaded.

Stone frowned. "Surely you have another surgeon you can consult."

"Both surgeons who could have operated are out sick with the flu," Dr. Clark said. "From what I can see, the worst injuries are in the area of the patient's throat and abdomen. He's struggling to breathe, bleeding profusely, and without a surgeon we'll lose him."

"Let's go," Stone said with a look of apology directed at Spicy.

Spicy would not vanish under these circumstances. "I'll wait right here."

From the waiting area, Spicy, Jet, and Aunt Hilda watched Stone go. Dr. Clark talked and gestured to him as Stone listened, removing his suit jacket as they made their way down the hospital corridor. Another doctor in a white frock coat approached his fellow physicians and whatever he said caused Stone to sprint to the end of the hall and disappear around the corner to the operating room.

Jet said, "I like being an attorney. But my brother saves lives."

"It's who he is," Spicy said knowing she would always be in awe of Stone. Jet agreed and Aunt Hilda patted her hand. "I practice mountain medicine with spices and herbs, but I've never saved anyone's life." She recalled only too well the tragic loss of Polly and her baby. Never did she want to lose another mother and baby or any patient if she could help it. Spicy glanced around at the nurses and nuns in admiration of the education and dedication it took to qualify them to work alongside the physicians and other staff in caring for patients and their families. "Stone wants me to enroll in the one-year nursing program at Pennsylvania Hospital."

"Would you want to do that?" Aunt Hilda asked.

"I told Stone I couldn't abandon a lifelong friend," Spicy replied. But now Lumpkin would be loved by Abby, helped by Shadow with his pig business, and living without fear in the cozy Raccoon Hollow cabin. In regard to how overwhelming the big-city life felt, she admitted, "I moved to Tug Valley as a baby and the back side of the Stony Mountains is the farthest I've ever been from home until this trip."

Sitting across from them, Jet said, "I didn't want Stone to leave Tug Valley at first."

"Neither did I," Aunt Hilda said, shaking her head.

"But I adjusted to Philadelphia and I've seen how much being a doctor means to my brother," Jet said, staring down the hall. "It's why he practically lives at the hospital."

"This is my first time being in a hospital," Spicy admitted.

Jet looked back at Spicy and his aunt. "Today is just one example of the difference Stone makes with his skills as a surgeon."

Aunt Hilda said to Spicy, "The nursing program could add to your skills."

Spicy found herself nodding. "Stone has tried to tell me that more than once."

"Sometimes a picture is worth a thousand words," Jet said with a shrug and a smile. "Come with us to Philadelphia for a year. Then you can return to Tug Valley, with all the knowledge of a trained nurse who graduated from Pennsylvania Hospital."

"I agree with Jet and Stone," Aunt Hilda said. "What do you have to lose?"

"Nothing," Spicy realized. "Stone says the training at Pennsylvania Hospital includes both medical and surgical components." Maybe she could have saved Polly and her baby with such training. Maybe in the span of twelve months she had everything to gain, including a life with Stone. "Stone says I could even assist him in surgery."

"Like this afternoon when they are short-staffed and desperately need help," Jet said.

"Speaking of needing help, I'd better check on Connie," Aunt Hilda said.

Aunt Hilda excused herself. It was Spicy's first chance to visit with Jet alone and she treasured getting to know more about Stone through Jet's eyes. He regaled her with stories from their boyhood on the mountains. There was love in his voice as he spoke of Stone getting him a room at the boardinghouse so he could attend the University of Pennsylvania Law School. They laughed as Spicy told him about the piglet Stone had named Pig Piffle and how her first surgery of sorts was when he had helped her remove the thorn from Big Bump. Jet wasn't surprised saying Stone had been dedicated to working in a hospital where he could teach less experienced physicians and assist doctors training to become surgeons. Operating on a patient in an emergency against state licensure protocol and certainly no payment was Stone. If possible, Spicy fell even further in love with her mountain-born man turned big-city surgeon.

As AUNT HILDA returned to the waiting area a wailing nun entered the hospital lobby at the opposite end of the corridor. The nun was obviously ill or distraught and a nurse hurried across the reception area to her. The nun fainted against the nurse and they both crumpled to the floor. Jet and Spicy sprang to their feet. Jet was only slightly ahead of Spicy as they rushed down the long hallway to help. Reaching the two women, Jet lifted the unconscious nun off the floor and Spicy helped the nurse to her feet. Aunt Hilda had spied a wheelchair and hastened to bring it to them. Jet placed the slumped-over nun in the wheelchair. The nurse thanked them and tried to push the wheelchair, but couldn't bear full weight on her left foot.

"Are you all right?" Spicy asked the nurse.

"I think I've sprained my ankle," she said.

"May I help you get somewhere to sit down?" Jet asked, taking hold of her arm.

"There is a resting room for nurses," the nurse said and then inclined her head to the nun. "But I need to see to the sister first."

"Does she have the flu?" Spicy asked. "Where may I take her for help?"

"I don't believe she's ill." The nurse pointed to another waiting room and said, "That's where families of patients in surgery wait. Her father's in surgery."

"I will get her there and stay by her side," Spicy said, taking charge of the wheelchair.

"Thank you so much, dear," the nurse said.

"I'll meet you there," Jet called over his shoulder as he walked the nurse in the opposite direction.

Aunt Hilda assured them, "I'll see what I can find out about the sister's father."

Spicy located a lever on the left side of the wicker chair which had two large wheels in front and a single smaller one in the rear. She lowered the back of the chair just enough to make the nun more comfortable and secure. Then she carefully pushed the cataleptic woman toward the waiting room. Once there, she found it empty. That made sense as Stone was the only surgeon in the hospital at least for the time being. Spicy sat down on the sofa next to the wheelchair, took the nun's right hand with both of hers and gently rubbed it. The nun's eyes fluttered open and she glanced around in confusion.

"You fainted," Spicy said, holding her hand. "Some friends of mine helped get you into a wheelchair. A nurse said to bring you here to the waiting room for families of surgical patients. Are you feeling any better?"

"Yes. Thank you," the nun said as Spicy released her hand. "Is the nurse who was coming to help me all right?"

"She may have a sprained ankle, but other than that she's fine."

"I didn't mean to cause a stir." The nun sat up straighter

in the wheelchair and Spicy helped by readjusting it for her. "But I heard my father was in a terrible buggy accident."

"Yes, that same nurse said your father was in surgery. My name is Spicy McCoy. I was visiting with friends when we saw you fall."

"It's nice to meet you, Miss McCoy. I'm Sister Eunice."

CHAPTER 49

"Sister Eunice," Spicy said. Could this possibly be Stone's Eunice? With pale-brown, eyes, a sallow complexion, and thin lips pulled into a tight line, she looked to be in her mid-thirties as Spicy knew Eunice Vanderveer to be. Though cloaked in the black and white nun's habit, it was obvious she was thin to the point of withered. "It's a pleasure to meet you."

"I don't have the strongest of constitutions," Eunice said as to fainting. She tried to work her way out of the wheelchair, but failed and placed a hand to the white coif across her forehead. "I need to find out about my father. I doubt he could be in surgery because there are no surgeons available. His name is Victor Vanderveer."

So this was Eunice and it explained so much. "I can verify your father is being operated on as we speak and Stone Hatfield is his surgeon."

"Stone is here?" Eunice asked. "I knew he was on his way." When Spicy nodded, the nun gazed skyward. "Thank you." Eunice crossed herself, grasped the rosary beads clipped to her belt, and held tight to the cross. "My father hopes to meet with Stone. Do you know him?"

"Yes, we met in Tug Valley," Spicy replied and folded her

hands over the reticule in her lap. "So you know your father is receiving the best of care."

"Yes, Stone has a God-given talent to heal. How is Stone?"

"He lost his mother and a good friend recently. But he's well. His brother, Jet, and their Aunt Hilda are here with him."

"I am so sorry to hear of their losses," Eunice said, then studied Spicy from the red hat and dress, to her beaded bag, to the black boots she'd chosen to wear with her new ensemble. When Eunice met her eyes again the torment on her long face had eased a little. She reached out and grasped Spicy's hand. "Are you a special friend of Stone's?"

Spicy didn't know how to answer with compassion and still maintain the truth. But there was almost a pleading in Eunice's eyes. "We've become close."

Eunice gently squeezed Spicy's hand and momentarily bowed her head. "Thank you, dear Lord, for a prayer answered." Slowly raising her gaze to meet Spicy's again, she said, "That's wonderful, Miss McCoy."

"Please call me Spicy," she said. "Jet should be here soon. Their Aunt Hilda went in search of information on your father's surgery."

Holding onto Spicy's hand, Eunice said, "You are lovely and the way you have helped me today speaks of your heart."

"You're welcome and thank you," Spicy said as Eunice released her hand.

"Stone may have told you my father sought to make a match between us." When Spicy inclined her head, Eunice shared, "I wasn't strong enough to admit to my father or to anyone that a secular life was not meant for me. Stone encouraged me to figure out my life's dream before I wasted away and," she swallowed hard, "be defiant enough to pursue it."

"That sounds like Stone," Spicy said. "He has encouraged me to become a nurse."

"The Lord put you and Stone in each other's path," Eunice said, her kind eyes shining with unshed tears. "Didn't He?" When Spicy nodded again she smiled. "Where?"

"Our paths crossed along the Tug Fork River, in a blueberry patch at the bottom of the hill where Stone once lived."

"Blueberries. The fruit of the spirit is love." Eunice sighed. "I secretly applied to the order of St. Joseph in hopes they could help me along my path. The day after Stone left for Tug Valley, I was accepted into the order. My heart is right for the first time in my life."

"I'm so happy for you, Sister Eunice."

Sister Eunice whispered, "I've even put on a pound or two."

Spicy smiled. "Good for you."

"Spicy, our heavenly Father is blessing all of us. I pray He will grant one more blessing and let my earthly father live."

"Eunice?" Jet asked, surprise in his voice as he stopped short near the entrance to the waiting area. "I apologize, but I didn't," he motioned to the habit, "recognize you earlier."

"Hello, Jet," Eunice replied. "I'm sure Stone will be just as surprised. Or maybe not."

"Sister Eunice?" another gentleman asked coming up beside Jet. The man removed his derby hat and with a polite bow of his head, said, "I don't mean to interrupt but have you heard how Victor is?"

"No, not yet," Eunice said. "Erskine Hazard, these are my friends, Spicy McCoy and Jet Hatfield. Jet's brother, Stone, is operating on my father as we speak. Please join us."

"Thank you." Mr. Hazard took a seat in a cushioned chair on the other side of Eunice. "I was with Victor when the accident happened. I've just come from the crash site." Looking from Eunice to Jet, he said, "I've heard great things about your brother from Victor."

"Thank you," Jet replied as he sat down near Spicy. "I

didn't realize Dr. Vanderveer was the patient until just now but I know Stone is glad he could be here to operate." Similarly to Spicy, he said, "Dr. Vanderveer is in the best possible hands."

"Victor would agree with you," Mr. Hazard replied. "He said Stone Hatfield had already far surpassed him the first year your brother was a practicing surgeon." Mr. Hazard turned to Eunice and patted her arm. "I'm not sure if you've heard but the accident was due to a broken wheel of the buggy your father and I were in. The driver of the buggy did an excellent job of keeping the horse under control, despite being injured himself. I was thrown clear, but Victor landed underneath the buggy. I summoned help for your father and the driver and then stayed with the frightened horse still strapped to the wreckage until the police arrived."

"Thank you, Mr. Hazard." Eunice grew a tad paler than she already was.

"I wasn't able to find out any specifics about the surgery except that it's over," Aunt Hilda said as she joined them. Introductions were made by Jet and his aunt nodded at Eunice then resumed her seat on the sofa next to Spicy. "I'm sure Stone will be here when he can."

"Thank you, Mrs. Hatfield," Eunice said and looked at Erskine Hazard. "While we wait, perhaps you can share how you happened to be here in West Virginia, Mr. Hazard."

"Certainly." Mr. Hazard made eye contact with each of them as he said, "I come from Matteawan in upstate New York, where Victor was born and raised. "While Victor studied to be a doctor I became interested in engineering. Victor went to work at Pennsylvania Hospital and I was hired as a civil engineer by the Norfolk and Western Railway at their headquarters in Roanoke, Virginia. No matter the distance he and I always kept in touch."

"I experienced a bit of train travel for the first time just recently," Spicy said. "It was not only fast and exciting, but comfortable."

"Too bad the trains don't reach the isolated mountains of Tug Valley," Jet said as Spicy and Aunt Hilda agreed.

"If I am correct, that is the area where the Tug Fork River is a tributary of the Big Sandy River. I'm familiar with such terrain. Matteawan is located on the shore of the Hudson River with Mount Beacon as the backdrop," Mr. Hazard said as everyone listened intently. "I'm headed to that part of your state on behalf of the railway to look for expansion in the area."

"That's why my father wanted you to meet Stone Hatfield," Eunice said, still ashen. "He and Jet were born and raised in that area of West Virginia."

"We need a hospital as well as the railroad," Spicy added.

"I'm looking to lay out a town in the area for a train station," Mr. Hazard replied. "Between Victor and myself, I certainly think we could assemble the right connections to get a depot *and* a much-needed hospital built."

"My firm may be able to offer help with the legal end," Jet said. Turning to Spicy he added, "And Spicy is interested in becoming a nurse."

"Did I hear right?" Stone rounded the corner and looked at Spicy as he stepped into the view. A long sleeved, white frock coat reached his knees.

"Stone!" Spicy was the first to greet him. But out of respect for Eunice she stayed in her seat rather than rushing into his arms as she longed to do.

"Are you considering enrolling in Pennsylvania Hospital's nursing school, Spicy?"

"Yes. I crossed a bridge while you were in surgery," she replied. His nod said he understood. "Stone, I still want a family but I will enroll."

"Music to my ears." Stone grinned and winked at her.

"This is how our Lord works." Eunice smiled at Stone and then at Spicy to say meaningfully, "Divine intervention."

"Hello, Sister Eunice," Stone said

"Hello, Dr. Hatfield," Eunice replied from her wheelchair. Gesturing to her father's friend she said, "Mr. Hazard was with my father when the accident occurred."

"Stone, this is Erskine Hazard from upstate New York," Jet said in introduction. "Mr. Hazard, my brother, Stone Hatfield."

"A pleasure to meet you, Dr. Hatfield," Mr. Hazard said.

"Same here," Stone replied and turned to Eunice. "Your father suffered two major areas of trauma."

Eunice's eyes fluttered and her voice wavered, "He's dead, isn't he?"

Before Stone could answer, Eunice fainted.

CHAPTER 50

STONE HAD IMMEDIATELY SENSED A COMPLETELY different attitude in Spicy's lilting voice, the shimmer in her blue eyes, and the smile he had been longing to see. He would ask all about her nursing decision later, but first he needed to complete his update on Victor Vanderveer.

As for Eunice, he'd heard from staff in the operating room she was serving at Wheeling Hospital as a nun from the order of St. Joseph. It fit completely with her character. So he wasn't as shocked to see her in a nun's habit as he figured Spicy, Jet, and Aunt Hilda must have been. The rosary in Eunice's lap and her collection of antique crucifixes made total sense now. He'd also heard she collapsed in the lobby. As a physician and as a man, he'd always thought of her as frail in body and spirit. Compared to Spicy's vibrant personality and energetic tenacity, the dissimilarity between the women was razor sharp. When told halfway to the operating room the patient was Victor Vanderveer, he had taken off running as he shared Eunice's concern about her father and his former mentor. But that's all they shared. Never had he been happier than at this moment not to have married her. He could relax, assured she was just as relieved.

As gorgeous Spicy gently patted Eunice's pale cheek and

softly called her name to rouse her, Stone pictured Spicy boldly galloping to him on horseback and kissing him through the gunfire explosions during the executions. Eunice was right, Spicy was heaven-sent.

"Victor was bleeding and gasping for air when they took him away from the scene of the crash," Mr. Hazard said just as Eunice came to.

"Your father is alive, Eunice," Stone told her. "I performed a tracheotomy because his hyoid bone, which holds up the tongue and helps open the jaw, was fractured in the accident. He was strangling from being unable to breathe properly."

"Oh my," Eunice gulped as if she might have trouble catching her own breath. Ghostly white, she asked, "What does tracheotomy mean?"

"It means I had to open a hole in the front of his neck directly into his windpipe," Stone replied. As Eunice nervously fingered her rosary beads, Stone saw Spicy poling across a raging river, falling, and vanishing under the water. "The tracheotomy has been around since ancient Greek physicians," he said. "In medical school, we studied George Washington's untimely death, most likely due to epiglottitis."

"Is epiglottitis anything like tonsillitis?" Spicy asked.

"They both cause a sore throat, but epiglottitis is often life-threatening because of the extreme breathing difficulty." Stone remained near the doorway and addressed them as a group, "Epiglottitis is a swelling of the epiglottis which is the flap that prevents food from entering the trachea, often called the windpipe."

"You did tracheotomies routinely in Philadelphia, right?" Jet said.

"Right. If President Washington had received a tracheotomy instead of having forty percent of his blood drained, he likely would not have died from a blocked airway at the age of sixty-seven." Stone let Eunice absorb the encouragement. Ever the advocate for medical advancement, he didn't add that the youngest of the three doctors attending Washington objected to the bleeding and argued for a tracheotomy. Unfortunately, he had been overruled by a senior physician and the "Father of Our Country" was bled a fourth and final time. "When Victor's hyoid bone heals in a month or two, at most, the tracheotomy can be reversed."

Eunice swayed against Spicy's side of the wheelchair and Spicy steadied her. With Eunice cloaked in layers of black clothing and slumped in the wicker chair, Stone's memory replayed Spicy wearing snippets of white lace and satin as she galloped ahead of him after they'd bathed naked in the waterfall. Stone's heart swelled with love for Spicy as she had surely figured everything out about Eunice while he was in surgery.

"I believe you said there were two major traumas," Spicy said.

Reaching for Spicy's hand, Eunice asked, "What's the other trauma?"

Stone thought of how Spicy had endured the deaths of both her parents all the while continuing to stand up to Clay McCoy, fight for Big Lump, and care for the sick and injured in Raccoon Hollow. Hopefully Eunice's work at the Wheeling Hospital would strengthen her.

"The other trauma was sustained in your father's lower right abdomen," Stone said, addressing Eunice. "I performed a relatively new surgery in this case, which is called an appendectomy. It means I removed his appendix."

Spicy held tight to her hand as Eunice sank into the wheelchair as though being swallowed by it. Stone's memory flashed an image of Spicy hanging over a snake pit as a witch taunted a madman to rape her. When freed, Spicy had stood up beside Stone and faced down a villain whose last aim was to shoot her. He hadn't needed this stark side-by-side comparison of the two women, but it was a visual he would take to his grave.

At that moment, Aunt Hilda caught Stone's eye and

tilted her head slightly toward Spicy and Eunice. When his aunt nodded approvingly, Stone knew she was remembering their conversation about Eunice and cutting himself free.

"It seems you have made excellent decisions," Aunt Hilda said as if referring just to the medical ones.

"I didn't know a person could live without an appendix," Eunice said to Stone.

"Barring any complications, Victor should recover from both surgeries."

"Thank you." Eunice let go of Spicy and crossed herself. "We'll always be grateful."

"I'm glad I was here," Stone replied.

"That's very good news," Mr. Hazard said to Eunice and looked at Stone. "Dr. Hatfield, before the accident, Victor and I were discussing the probability of the Norfolk and Western Railroad seeking to open up the southern coalfields for business."

"We've got some coal for sale," Jet said matter-of-factly with a glance at Stone who nodded in agreement.

"Excellent," Mr. Hazard replied.

Dr. Clark and a middle-aged nurse stopped at the entrance to the waiting room then and the physician said, "Thank you, again, Dr. Hatfield." Acknowledging Eunice, the doctor inclined his head toward Stone. "The best thing your father did was train this man. We could not have saved Dr. Vanderveer without a surgeon as skilled as Dr. Hatfield."

"We are in Dr. Hatfield's debt," Eunice managed, beginning to perk up.

When Dr. Clark bowed out, the nurse addressed everyone in the waiting room, saying with admiration, "Dr. Vanderveer is doing so well, we will be moving him to a private room within the hour." With a nod at the others, she said to Stone, "Since you won't be going back into surgery, Dr. Hatfield, may I take your coat for you, sir?"

"Yes, thank you." Stone removed the frock coat and exchanged it for his suit jacket which the nurse handed to him.

"Thank you, Dr. Hatfield, from all of us here at Wheeling Hospital," the nurse said, and went on about her duties.

"Dr. Hatfield, if Victor Vanderveer and I gather the resources to build a hospital in Tug Valley, would you run it?" Mr. Hazard asked.

"I would," Stone said without hesitation. He offered his hand to Mr. Hazard and they shook on it. Looking to Spicy, he asked, "And I'll have a trained nurse by my side."

"Yes, you will." Spicy stood and crossed the room to him.

"Praise the Lord," Eunice said and with help from Jet and Mr. Hazard stood up.

Jet, Aunt Hilda, and Mr. Hazard wholeheartedly agreed with Eunice. Aunt Hilda and Jet steadied Eunice as they talked with Mr. Hazard of the countless good things to come.

"You get ten points for going out on a ledge and that makes a hundred," Stone said to Spicy and pulled her into his arms. He kissed her and tasted the salty tears on her lips much like the ones burning the backs of his own eyes. "You win, sugar'n spice."

"You get ten points for taking such a long shot by exposing me to a whole new world and another ten for saving Dr. Vanderveer's life. That makes us even." Spicy swiped away the tears of joy on her cheeks. "It's a tie. What's the prize?"

Stone cupped a hand to the back of her head, pressed her to him, and whispered in her ear, "How about our prize being a wedding and the baby I promised you?"

"Yes, please. I can't wait to marry you," Spicy choked out and looked up at him. "I promise to give you the two babies we both want."

"Not only will I run the hospital, Mr. Hazard," Stone began, his arm around Spicy, "We might even sell you the land where you can build it."

EPILOGUE

Tug Valley, West Virginia
Summer 1887

STANDING AT HIS HOSPITAL OFFICE WINDOW, Stone gazed up the mountain toward Hatfield House as they called it. Built on their sentimental overlook the home never failed to catch his eye. Early afternoon sunlight spilled across the sprawling six-bedroom, white house boasting a front door the shade of blueberries with shutters and window boxes to match. The grassy front yard with its circular drive offered the panoramic view of rolling hills and lush valleys. To the right, a carriage house had plenty of room for two buggies and a wagon. On the left a big red barn sheltered Logan, Daisy, Gus, and a pony named Sage. Behind the house a blueberry patch, gardens, and meadow were surrounded by a white picket fence. Beyond that Mate Creek flowed and magnolia trees flourished.

All in all, life was grand on their mountain of heart and home.

Momentarily, Stone's mind went back to 1882 when times were not so great. After Ellison died and the McCoy brothers were executed, as Stone had predicted, Kentucky issued indictments for Devil Anse and twenty posse members. However, when no bloody revenge erupted from Ol' Ranel and the McCoys, no action was taken to extradite the Hatfields.

Hearts cooled and mountain justice prevailed.

Before leaving Wheeling Hospital, he and Spicy had been married in the chapel so Jet, Aunt Hilda, Connie Staton, and the Vanderveers could be present. The newlyweds had sent word of their wedding and plans back home. With their trunks of clothing, they had returned with Jet to Philadelphia. Connie had passed away a month later with Aunt Hilda at his side. For the next year, Stone and Spicy had shared his quarters in the boarding house.

Stone had immediately taken over as chief of surgery at Pennsylvania Hospital. Spicy had enrolled and completed twelve months of training at Pennsylvania's School of Nursing for Women. In 1883, the hospital graduated five nurses and Spicy was number one in her class. Before leaving Philadelphia, Stone had found and hired an excellent surgeon to assume his role at the hospital. Spicy had bid a tearful farewell to her fellow nurses with whom she had become good friends. Saying goodbye to Jet was the hardest. Though it was bittersweet, Stone and Spicy left Pennsylvania as they had much work to do in West Virginia.

Dr. Vanderveer had recovered well from his tracheotomy and appendectomy. Sister Eunice had continued her work at Wheeling Hospital until transferring to an order near her father in Philadelphia. By that time Victor Vanderveer was knee-deep in a brand-new project. Claiming he owed his life to Stone, Vanderveer had called upon numerous wealthy investors and construction of a much-needed medical facility was completed during the year Stone and Spicy were in Philadelphia.

Thus, here in the valley, sprawled Stony Mountains Hospital. The impressive hundred-bed hospital, with operating rooms following Stone's strict regimen of carbolic spray disinfection, ranked second to none. Several skilled surgeons and progressive physicians had followed Stone from Pennsylvania to care for the injured and sick packing the new hospital. For the first year after the hospital opened its doors, Spicy had assisted Stone in the majority of his surgeries as well as overseeing the hiring and mentoring of graduate nurses. She had also trained a dozen midwives.

Erskine Hazard had come through with his plans for the Norfolk and Western Railway. The train depot, built in a town plotted and called Matewan after his hometown in upstate New York, was connecting the outside world to the southern coalfields.

Big Lump had married Abigail Hatfield and Spicy had given them her cabin and land as a wedding gift. Stone added to the gift by having all of the windows enlarged and fitted with glass. Big Lump had steadily increased his bank account with a thriving hog business. Abby taught students in a new schoolhouse funded by a school tax. There was a Little Lump McCoy who had just turned four years old and was cute as a button.

Shadow McCoy at seventeen was a strapping, smart, and handsome young man who wanted to become a doctor like Stone. Stone had helped him apply for a scholarship at the University of Pennsylvania's School of Medicine and had no doubt Shadow would be accepted. Sunshine McCoy was twenty-three and had graduated from the midwife training at Stony Mountains Hospital. With such similar interests, Spicy and her cousin had grown even closer. Sunshine had a tenacious personality much like Spicy and was as sunny as her name.

Still practicing law in Philadelphia, Jet had recently admitted he had begun to miss home. In fact, Jet was due back today on the Norfolk and Western Railway. Zeke McCoy had offered to pick him up and drop him off at the hospital.

Stone and Spicy had stayed with Aunt Hilda while Hatfield House was being built. They had been in their new home about six months when Spicy reduced her hospital hours during the summer of 1884. Aunt Hilda had moved in to help out and lived with them now. This past week, at his insistence, Spicy had rested at home.

With Spicy on his mind, Stone left his office. Striding down a wide corridor, but not stopping to talk, he nodded at doctors, nurses, families, patients, and other staff. He smiled thinking back to that morning when he'd found Spicy and their three-year-old son, Cole, picking blueberries. Cole, named for the coal in the Stony Mountains, had been born the summer of '84, with hair as black as Stone's. The little boy's eyes were a silvery blue and he had a tiny cleft in his chin. Cole loved to glide with them in the swings that faced each other in the grassy backyard. Other times Cole would play with his toy trains or listen to Spicy read to him in the library. There, on the fireplace mantel between floor-to-ceiling bookshelves, set a clock with its black case, ivory face, and gold hands keeping perfect time thanks to Spicy. Stone was giving Cole riding lessons on Sage, which he loved. Sometimes Pepper strutted alongside them. When Nutmeg washed his food in the creek, as raccoons were known to do, Cole laughed and clapped his chubby hands.

Stone and Spicy suspected they'd conceived one if not both babies on moonlit nights under the Mate Creek waterfall. She'd stayed home this past week because they were about to add to their family. Spicy often told him she had the best of both worlds—being his wife and a mother, as well as enjoying one day a week working with him and other staff.

Her prize in the game they had won was his prize as well.

Back to this morning, Cole had run out of the blueberry patch to him and Stone had scooped Cole up. Tossing him high in the air, the little boy and his mother laughed. As Spicy had walked toward Stone with a bowl of berries her water broke. Aunt Hilda had been mixing pancake batter in the kitchen and had just come to the back door to collect the blueberries. They had left Cole with Aunt Hilda and though it was still far from the norm in many places, Stone whisked Spicy to the hospital to deliver this baby, just as he had Cole.

He always insisted the private rooms for deliveries were also disinfected with antiseptic. With women suffering a one-in-eight mortality rate, during or following childbirth, he wasn't taking any chances. Due to the brain damage and deaths he'd heard about when physicians used forceps, he'd never used them. When a baby needed turned, he'd succeeded in doing so or performed a cesarean section keeping mother and child alive and well.

"Excuse me, Dr. Hatfield," Sunshine said politely meeting up with him halfway to Spicy's room. Outside of the hospital she called him Stone. But here in doctors' offices, hallways, patients' rooms, operating or delivery rooms, waiting rooms, or nurses' desks, it was always Dr. Hatfield. Falling into step beside him, she said, "Mrs. Hatfield says you may join her for the birth of your baby."

"I sensed it was getting close. I'm on my way to her now." Stone chuckled and shook his head. "She is still the most defiant woman I know." He was so crazy about Spicy he sometimes still thought he might have lost not only his heart but his mind to her. What a lucky man he was. "My wife made me promise to go about my usual hospital business until she was ready to push the baby into my hands."

"Yes." Sunshine smiled. "She told me to go about my normal routine, too. But since the other three ladies in labor are being well attended by their doctors and midwives, I said my skills were meant for her. So, she let me stay with her and time the contractions."

Together, they were about to turn a corner into the hallway toward the women's ward, when a familiar voice called to them.

"Stone!" The man hurried toward them. "Did I arrive before the new baby?"

"Yes, just in time, Jet." Stone paused to greet his brother. "Jet, this is a very good friend of mine and Spicy's cousin, Sunshine McCoy. Sunshine, my younger brother, Jet."

"Hello, Sunshine." Jet was all smiles as he took in Sunshine's blond hair and green eyes. "Your father brought me here from the train depot."

"I knew Papa was heading to the depot to pick you up," Sunshine said with a blush Stone hadn't seen before today. "It's nice to finally meet you, Jet."

With a twinkle in his eye, Jet replied, "The pleasure is all mine."

"Sunshine, would you show Jet where he can wait?" Stone asked. "And maybe keep him company so he doesn't try to help Spicy escape before she's had the baby."

Jet laughed. "I'll never live down unknowingly trying to help Spicy escape when we were heading to Wheeling Hospital."

"I've heard a lot about you, Jet," Sunshine said. "But never that story."

"It's a really good one." Jet laughed. "I'll tell you while we wait."

Stone chuckled. "I'll send word when the baby arrives."

"Oh, you won't have to. The whole hospital is buzzing about your new baby," Sunshine said happily. "I had to keep shooing folks away from Spicy's room."

"No doubt," Stone chuckled. "Everybody loves her."

"Cup of coffee while we wait?" Jet asked Sunshine as Stone headed to Spicy's room.

"HELLO, DR. HATFIELD," Spicy said from her bed. When Sunshine had left, per Stone, she'd posted a midwife-in-training at Spicy's closed door to keep visitors out and infections down. Thus, Spicy was alone in her private room. Her heart never failed to flip-flop at the sight of the handsome man she had fallen in love with five years ago.

"Well, well, Mrs. Hatfield, I hear you're ready to deliver that second baby you promised me." Stone grinned and washed his hands in the bowl of sterilized water he had ordered. Taking a stethoscope out of his pocket, he leaned down and kissed her before listening to her heart.

"Kissing increases my heartbeat, Doctor," she said.

Stone whispered in her ear, "Mine, too, Nurse." He stood, swept a stray lock of sugar-maple curls away from her temple and said, "Your brother-in-law just arrived and Sunshine is keeping him company."

"Was I right about the sparks?"

"Yeah."

"Ooww!" Spicy moaned with a grimace.

Flattening a hand to her rounded belly, Stone said, "That was a hard contraction, Spicy. If you're sure you don't want me to administer the chloroform, you scream when you have to."

They'd discussed chloroform before Cole was born. Stone had told her that in 1853, Queen Victoria of England was chloroformed for the birth of her eighth child, Prince Leopold and again four years later with her ninth child, Princess Beatrice. However, Spicy decided she would only resort to chloroform in the case of a cesarean section. Stone had the medication standing by and prepared to use the open drop method introduced by Dr. John Snow. Another danger with any delivery was hemorrhaging as there was no sure way to stop it. But Spicy was confident nothing would go wrong as Stone took a sitting position between her knees.

"Tarnation!" Spicy gasped even louder and gripped the sheets on the bed.

Stone examined her and said, "Time to push, Spicy." Mere minutes ticked by before he told her, "The baby is crowning." He looked at her and smiled. "Push again." Spicy pushed and then closed her eyes between contractions. "Try not to drift off," he teased.

"Drift off?" Spicy didn't know whether to laugh or cry, so did a little of both. Melting at the love and compassion on Stone's face, she teased back, "I'm going to smack you with my pillow when this is all over."

"Deal. But for now, push again." She did so as Stone encouraged her with progress reports of the emerging head and then the shoulders. Next, there was blessed relief accompanied by a newborn cry. Spicy watched Stone cradle their infant in his arms. Their eyes met and she saw her tears of joy reflected in his. "Ten fingers, ten toes, and a dimple in both cheeks."

"I'm so happy," she whispered. Stone wrapped their baby in a freshly washed blanket and placed the infant in her arms. "Am I holding our son or daughter?"

"Thank you for our perfect little girl, sugar'n spice."

"Thank you for giving me the babies you said you would. I thought being a mother and a nurse was such a long shot at the time." Cuddling their precious newborn, Spicy looked at the dashing father and said, "If only we had a name."

"I remember telling you back then to have faith." Stone sat down on the side of the bed and suggested, "How about Faith for her name?"

"Yes, Faith," Spicy whispered. "It took once-in-blue-moon faith to get here."

"We moved hearts and mountains."

A LOOK AT: DESIRE IN DEADWOOD

Aces and eights, the dead man's hand. That thought shoots through Bolton River just before Wild Bill Hickok falls dead in the Number 10 Saloon. Then a bullet slams into Bolton.

In 1876 Dakota Territory, Deadwood is the most devilish and delightful, wildest and wickedest town on the frontier. Tansy Wiley, with a cloudy past, is hiding behind the name Jigger Crown, and fears Bolton is tracking her. Jigger rescues the handsome stranger from the saloon next door as chaos erupts. There to capture her or not, Bolton wants this sexy adventuress.

Afraid to run and afraid not to, Tansy decides to escape. A battle of wills ignites between the beloved barkeep and this mystery man in an isolated and violent Black Hills gulch. Longing and lust, tension and mistrust run rampant amidst a serial killer on the loose and a Texas rancher vowing to settle a score. The deck is stacked against Bolt and Tansy who fight to survive this town soaked in blood, whiskey and corruption.

AVAILABLE NOW

ABOUT THE AUTHOR

Lynn Eldridge is a former president of the West Virginia Chapter of Romance Writers of America and earned an honorable mention in their Golden Heart Contest. Lynn is the author of several historical and contemporary romance novels including, Desire in Deadwood, Remember the Passion, and Tame the Wild. Her next book, soon to be released, is Skyrocket to Surrender, and she is currently working on another historical romance titled Hearts and Mountains. In addition to her writing career, Lynn is a licensed clinical therapist and dedicates one day a week in an outpatient behavioral health facility in Charleston, West Virginia.

Made in the USA
Middletown, DE
22 July 2022